TOUCH & GO

Touch and Go

Copyright Peter O'Sullivan, 2014

Published by Peter O'Sullivan

posullivan@internode.on.net

Published in Queensland

Typesetting by Book Whispers www.bookwhispers.net

National Library of Australia Cataloguing-in-Publication entry

Author: O'Sullivan, Peter, author.

Title: Touch and go / Peter O'Sullivan.

ISBN: 9780992482206 (paperback)

Subjects: Detective and mystery stories. Suspense fiction.

Dewey Number: A823.4

TOUCH & GO

A novel by

PETER O'SULLIVAN

Acknowledgments

I need to acknowledge and thank many people who helped me bring this story to life. Particularly I would like to thank Mark Treloar; Paula Tobin; Greg Milles; and Barbara Hannell who gave me much needed feedback on my wacky first draft.

Special mention must be made of my brother Robert who not only provided feedback on the first draft but has always been there for me for consultations and advice.

Last but not least I would like to thank and acknowledge my beautiful daughter Kathleen, for the fearless and extremely valuable feedback she has given on this book from the very beginning to the end. Thanks Kathleen you were always going to be my harshest critic but also my most valuable source of feedback.

I also would like to acknowledge Rochelle and Andrew Manners for their publishing advice and editing assistance with this project.

Dedication

Firstly and foremost this book is dedicated to my wife Vivienne. She is such an amazing woman she does not even realize how great she is. Her journey to beat off and continue to deal with the threat of lymphoma is inspirational. She continues to touch many lives with her strength, genuineness and grace. Also her advice and edits on the many drafts of this manuscript have been greatly appreciated.

I can't end the dedication section without mentioning my God. From the very beginning, this story has been about touching people's lives. In many ways he is the real author of this book and I have just been the facilitator.

He who calls upon the name of the Lord will be saved. Romans 10:13

PROLOGUE

He was on his knees.

He was tired and he was hungry.

He was desperate.

How had it come to this?

It had started with a kiss. No, it started with a lie, only a small one at first.

It was just a little white lie, just an insignificant white lie.

But then he got carried away with telling little white lies here and there. The more he lied, the more he had to continue lying to cover his previous lies.

He found he was good at lying. Fancy a lawyer discovering he was good at lying.

But to what end?

To the bitter end.

He was to blame! He had caused this cyclone of destruction and despair, and now he was powerless to stop it.

"Oh, God! Oh, God!" he cried out.

"It's all my fault."

His knees hurt as they cut into the timber floor, his back ached, his head was pounding, but he was not getting up, he was not giving up. There was too much at stake.

How had he come to this?

It had all started just four months ago.

CHAPTER ONE

It was a cool, overcast morning with a westerly wind howling down the street. As Dan Grover closed his car door he sensed rain was coming, which was unusual for Brisbane in winter. Rain usually came in spring with late afternoon thunder storms, and then in summer it sheeted down from hovering rain depressions.

Dan bought a tall black coffee with a dash of milk and a slice of heavily buttered raisin toast from his favourite coffee shop, the Coff-inn and walked the short distance to his office. He lingered outside his office for a few seconds to sip his coffee and take it all in. It was a small, pokey office, in an outdated and run-down office block. It was in a depressed and grey part of town notable only for its litter and graffiti, but it was his office and he was proud of it.

He marvelled at how quickly it had all happened for him. What a ride it had been.

After obtaining his law degree, Dan scored a job with a mid-level city law firm. He realized quite early on in his career, that his calling in life was not to cross the t's and dot the i's on multi-million dollar slurry pipeline contracts.

No, there had to be more to practicing the law, than staring at a computer screen reviewing 100 page contracts all day and most nights.

After eighteen months of torturous contract work, Dan answered an advertisement for lawyers at Legal Aid Queensland, and worked there for four years in its criminal law section. He enjoyed helping people less fortunate than himself but the low pay and the bureaucracy eventually got to him.

So he went to work in a suburban law firm – *Bill Chadwick and Associates*.

He wondered what he had got himself into with old Bill never around most of the time and his files in a complete mess. But he liked old Bill despite him being grumpy, messy and forgetful. There was something in the way the old man always treated his clients with respect, no matter who they were or what they were accused of, that appealed to the young lawyer.

Dan sighed as he remembered the sad day Bill died in a single vehicle car accident. The police said that Bill was heavily medicated at the time and they were unsure whether he just passed out at the wheel, or whether he deliberately ran his car into a tree.

Dan shook his head. He still had trouble believing that old Bill had left his legal practice to him.

Bill was suffering from the early onset of Alzheimer's disease. Unbeknown to Dan, he had been hiring and firing associates at regular intervals over the past few years, in an effort to find someone he felt comfortable leaving his life's work to.

Besides Dan, Bill had only one other employee, a receptionist, cum-conveyancing-clerk, cum-paralegal, cum-bookkeeper, cum-typist, cum-you–name-it-she-did-it. Gloria had worked for old Bill for more than two decades.

After some initial friction about who told who what to do in the office, which was duly resolved by Dan submitting to Gloria on all things non-legal, they got on extremely well. Gloria even started to add a *y* to Dan's name and called him Danny. He discovered later that Gloria only added a *y* to your name, if she really liked you and trusted you.

Gloria had short, wavy, dyed brown hair, was overweight but not obese. She had single handedly raised her two teenage daughters, after her husband had died several years ago. Gloria was generally a happy person and she had an infectious laugh which morphed into snorts. Gloria's snorts sounded like a moose's mating call and it just cracked Dan up.

He paused and took a deep breath as he read the small sign at the entrance to his very own legal firm, *Chadwick and Grover*. The sign said it all. The legal practice was now his but he could not help but honour the old man who had handed the firm to him on a platter. Sure there would be obstacles but he was confident that he and Gloria (he couldn't let Gloria go), would overcome them. Perhaps one day, he would leave this legal practice to a young enthusiastic lawyer like himself, or perhaps to a son or daughter who might follow in his footsteps.

Life was indeed good for Dan Grover but as always with life, it changes.

*

Dan smiled and waved a greeting to Gloria who was seated behind the receptionist's desk and on a phone call. Gloria shot Dan a look of exasperation as she moved the handset away from her ear, before returning to her conversation.

Dan sat down in his small musky office, which had been old Bill's. The tiny office was surrounded by large filing cabinets and legal text books. The walls were wood panelled and adorned with several large legal caricatures of courtroom scenes that were as old as old Bill himself. The small desk was dominated by two large computer monitors and a printer which didn't fit anywhere else.

The physical conditions to interview clients and conduct other legal work such as research and drawing documents/letters/emails were cramped, but the office was also confidential, cosy and quiet. Dan loved it, especially as it was now his own.

He turned on his computer and began to read the emails that had already arrived for him that morning. As he read his emails, sipped his coffee and savoured his raisin toast this winter's morning, he was content.

"Danny, can I have a word with you?" Gloria asked as she waltzed into Dan's office as if she owned the place.

Looking up from gulping his raisin toast and reading an email that particularly interested him, Dan replied, "Sure, Gloria. What's up?"

"I have been going over a few things this morning and it's not looking good for us."

"What do you mean, can you be more specific? I know the Sharks are not playing well at the moment but I am sure they will come good, eventually."

"I don't mean stupid football. Dan this is serious!"

Gloria had raised her voice and used his real name; this meant that she was concerned about something and jokes about his football team would not be tolerated.

Dan recovered with as much interest as he could muster at the beginning of the day, "I am sorry Gloria. What's the problem?"

"Well, I have been going through the books and we have been losing money at a fairly rapid rate since Bill passed away."

"How bad is it?"

"It's bad. Many of Bill's old clients who had been with us for donkey's years have left. They only stuck with us because of Bill and now he is gone, they have gone."

"Donkey's years?" enquired Dan with a trace of a smile.

"You know donkey's years, that means, *like forever*, in young people's language."

"Ok, but I have been bringing in new clients since I started working here."

"Yes, you have done a great job in attracting new clients but most of those new clients are legally aided. You know Legal Aid doesn't pay us much to represent them. We have lost full fee paying clients and replaced them with legally aided clients."

Dan's smile vanished as he pondered the news.

"I have been thinking that you really don't need me to work five days a week. I mean unlike Bill you can type, scan, email and text; in fact unlike Bill you can actually use a computer and access the internet. We could cut costs if I scale back to two or three days a week. You would have a better chance of keeping the practice afloat."

"Wow." He hadn't realized the situation had become so grave, so quickly. He had been so intoxicated with actually owning his own show, that he had not really thought too much about the books.

"But we made a profit last year, didn't we?"

"We did actually make a small profit. But since then many of Bill's old clients have left us and the new clients you have brought in, just aren't paying the bills like the old ones used to. I am really worried, Dan. If it keeps going like this, you and I may not last another six months."

He knew Gloria was serious and she was not someone to over exaggerate things. He also knew that Gloria's whole adult life had been a financial struggle and she would find it really difficult to survive on a part-time wage.

"Gloria, I don't want you to cut back your hours. As the owner I will take a pay cut, until I can get the business up to full speed with more clients. I need you Gloria. How can I operate this legal practice without you? Besides who will get my Chicken Karaage, if not you?"

"Yeah, smoke will be blowing out of both my ears before the day comes when I will be getting lunch for you. You've got two feet; you get your own lunch, Danny boy."

Gloria smiled and chuckled. He was relieved to hear her call him Danny again. To continue the levity, Dan faked coughing; making stifled snorting noises which he knew would set Gloria off. Right on cue after his third stifled snort, Gloria laughed and involuntarily launched into several loud moose mating calls.

Dan sat back and laughed out loud until Gloria had regained her composure.

"Who's on first today, Gloria?"

"You have Alyssa Paschetelle at 9:00am and then you have Fay Castle's guilty plea in the Magistrates Court at 10:00am. Alyssa Paschetelle is a new family law client."

At that Gloria went back to her desk and Dan went back to studying his emails and finishing his breakfast. He would worry about his pay cut later.

After a short time Dan stopped what he was doing and raised his head. He heard raised voices coming from Gloria's reception area.

Dan walked out to the tiny reception area to see Gloria standing next to her desk with a small old woman raising her voice and throwing her arms around.

"Can I help?" Dan asked, eager to play the white knight and resolve the situation.

Gloria replied, "Danny this is Francesca Botticelli, Alyssa Paschetelle's mother. It's hard to understand her as she doesn't speak English that well, but it appears she is concerned that Alyssa's husband is waiting for her down the street. She is worried that Alyssa's husband may do something stupid. He is very angry at the marriage breakup and he has hit Alyssa before."

"Ms Botticelli can you call Alyssa and find out where she is. If she is not too far away I will go out and walk her to the office, so she is safe." Dan accompanied his words with actions such as using his hands pretending to call on a phone and then walking along the street arm-in-arm.

Ms Botticelli's upset demeanor calmed somewhat and she repeatedly nodded and said, "Grazie, thank you."

"Danny look!" Gloria screamed as she pointed out through the glass sliding door.

Dan moved quickly to the doorway and down the street saw a man involved in an altercation with a young woman holding a baby. Both of them were throwing their hands around and pushing each other. The man grabbed the baby out of the young woman's arms. With both hands free, the young woman began to punch and slap the man.

"No! Bambino!" yelled Francesca Botticelli.

The man then shoved the young woman to the ground with his free hand and kicked her while she was on the ground.

Dan had seen enough. "Gloria, call the police!"

With that he rushed out of the office towards the Paschetelles. Alyssa's husband saw him coming and immediately ran off in the other direction clutching a now howling baby.

Dan reached Alyssa Paschetelle in seconds and he bent over and asked her if she was alright.

She didn't answer his question but responded with, "He took my baby girl!"

"We have called the police."

"My baby, my baby girl!" she yelled with the pained helpless expression that only a distressed mother could muster.

"I'm Dan Grover, you were on your way to see me. Don't worry. I'll get your baby back."

He motioned for Gloria to come and comfort the distressed Alyssa Paschetelle.

Dan then ran to the end of the street but he could no longer see Alyssa's husband. But he could hear the baby, she was still crying. Dan turned right down a tight alleyway between a row of second hand clothing shops and pawnbrokers. The alleyway was dirty with food wrappers and other assorted litter items. He came to the end of the alleyway and heard the baby crying to his left, so he ran up the next street to his left. About half way up the street he could no longer hear the baby crying.

He was concerned he could no longer hear the baby but was also glad that he could stop running. He was more out of shape than he had realised. A few minutes of sprinting and he was really feeling it. His lungs were busting.

Dan rushed into a nearby bakery, panting and breathing heavily.

"Has anyone just seen a guy who was running and carrying a baby?"

No one answered. Everyone turned around to look at him but no one seemed to want to get involved.

"He has just hit the child's mother and taken her baby. Has anyone seen them?" Dan demanded.

Again there was silence, until an elderly woman turned to him, she must have been in her nineties. "He just ran past here, I am pretty sure he turned right into Gratwick Lane, heading towards the shopping centre."

"Thanks", Dan said. Before he left Dan looked at the rest of the people in the shop and shook his head in disappointment at their reluctance to get involved.

He ran towards the shopping centre and was fortunate to cross several busy roads without incident. Weaving around parked cars, while all the time scouting the people that were moving ahead of him, Dan almost fell over Alyssa's husband and the baby. To his surprise they were resting quietly on a bench outside the shopping centre.

Alyssa's husband saw Dan and bolted into the shopping centre. Dan sprinted after him. He had his second wind and was no longer feeling tired. Endorphins had kicked in and he was up for another physical exertion.

He chased Alyssa's husband down the stairs from the food court to the basement car park. Dan was gaining on the guy as he was struggling to keep up the pace holding onto the baby. Eventually Alyssa's husband exhausted, stopped at the end of the basement car park and faced Dan.

"Who are you and why are you chasing me?" he demanded.

Dan was sucking it in now, that last sprint through the shopping centre had taken all his reserves of energy. He was bent over with his hands on his hips, gasping in all the air that he could.

"I'm Dan Grover," he stopped to take in another intoxicating breath of fresh air. "I am a lawyer. I am acting for your wife, Alyssa". Dan stopped again to take in much needed air.

"Look mate, the baby needs to go back to its mother," Dan exclaimed.

"She is my baby too. Why should she have her?"

"Listen, Mr Paschetelle, I am sure we can resolve your family law issues later but right now the baby needs to go back to her mother."

Right on cue the baby started to cry again. Alyssa's husband tried to calm her but he was having little success.

"Come on, give the baby to me. Or if you want, you can come back with me to my office and hand the baby back to her mother there."

"Like hell I am going to give my baby back to her mother, she's a whore!"

At that Alyssa's husband began to march straight past Dan. Unsure what to do as he didn't want to tackle a guy holding a baby, Dan stepped in front of Alyssa's approaching husband.

"Please, Mr Paschetelle," he pleaded. "It will be better for you in the long run if we can sort this out now. You don't want us going to court and get an apprehension order, where the police will step in and take the baby off you."

Alyssa's husband apparently was not in a state of mind to accept Dan's quite logical advice and with his free hand he forcefully shoved Dan out of his way.

The force of the shove surprised Dan. He lost his balance and fell onto the bitumen car park grazing his hand and wrist, both of which started to bleed.

By the time Dan had jumped back to his feet, he noticed two figures had emerged from the shadows of the car park. They had in fact boxed Alyssa's husband in and were not letting him go any further. The baby was still crying.

Dan recognized them instantly from court. They were bikies from the

Vandals gang. One appeared much older than the other one. The older one was tall and skinny with a long grey pony tail and what appeared to be a rat sitting on his shoulder. He had a snake tattoo that was clearly visible slithering down the side of his neck.

The other bikie was shorter and stockier with a variety of tattoos which seemed to accentuate his bulging biceps. This guy was bald except for what appeared to be a long strand of hair like a rat's tail, hanging off the back of his head.

The older biker spoke first. "What's going on here? And shut that kid up!"

Alyssa's husband did not respond. Dan did.

"I am a lawyer. This guy has just beaten up the baby's mother and snatched her baby. I am trying to get the baby back to her mother."

Perhaps Dan had laid it on a bit thick for the bikies but it was largely the truth and he needed their help. He was aware that any self respecting bikie, for all their violence and criminal activity, would be appalled at a man striking a defenseless woman and taking her baby out of her arms.

The bikies moved slowly towards Alyssa's husband and started to flex and twitch. Alyssa's husband could no longer contain himself.

"Get out of my way you idiots. Who do you think you are? I have had enough of this bullshit!"

Dan winced; he imagined the bikies would not appreciate being spoken to like that. He was right.

The younger bikie moved so quickly that Alyssa's husband did not see him, or if he did, he was unable to react in time. He hit Alyssa's husband with one punch to the side of his head with such force and power that the sound it made on crashing into his jaw was sickening. With equal dexterity the older bikie moved in and swept the baby away from Alyssa's husband. The younger bikie then ferociously punched Alyssa's husband in the stomach causing him to buckle over.

The older bikie handed the baby to Dan.

"Thanks," Dan mumbled.

"Don't mention it. I am sure you can do us a favour some day." At that the two bikies disappeared as quickly as they had appeared.

Dan was none too pleased to be beholden to a bikie gang, certainly not one as dangerous as the *Vandals* but on the positive side, he had retrieved the baby unharmed.

He walked slowly back to his office with the baby uncomfortably tucked in his arms.

"Danny you've got the baby back. Good job. You can hand her to me," Gloria said with outstretched arms as her maternal instincts kicked in. The baby instantly began to settle in Gloria's arms.

"Where is Alyssa?"

"Well the police came and she and her mother went with them to find the baby," Gloria answered. "I will give them a call. How did you get the baby off her father? From what they told me, he is a pretty unpredictable and dangerous character."

He glanced at the clock. The baby rescue had taken longer than he realised. "It's a long story. I don't think I have time to tell it now, but as you know I am a pretty dangerous character myself." Dan then launched into a series of kung fu moves and made loud guttural noises like they do in martial arts movies.

"Yeah right," Gloria said while shaking her head and raising her eyebrows.

"Well actually, I had help from some bikies."

Gloria looked bemused and then she followed Dan's glance and looked at the clock. "You're right, tell me later, I want all the details, don't leave anything out. You had better go now or you will be late for court."

Dan gathered his car keys, mobile phone and Fay Castle's file and was almost out the door when Gloria said, "You know, Danny, you are a hero."

"Well, I wouldn't say hero exactly."

"I would. When are you going to tell that gorgeous wife of yours?"

Good question, when was he going to tell Elise he was a hero? No point rushing it, it could wait. "I will tell her when I get home."

"Well I am sure she will be very proud of you. And I know we will have a very happy client, thanks to you."

Dan smiled and walked to his car. He was looking for new clients and it looked like he had definitely found one.

CHAPTER TWO

Dan arrived at the Magistrates Court with just enough time to review his detailed submissions. The most important lesson he had learnt as a lawyer, *preparation is everything*. If a lawyer is to appear before any court, he/she must have spent time preparing their case. Anything could and often did happen in court and if you were not fully prepared; you were not doing the right thing by your client, the court, and yourself.

Dan found a quiet interview room and studied his notes. Fay Castle was 45 years old. Her husband had left her seven years ago, forcing her to fend for herself and her five children. Her husband had not paid a single cent in child maintenance payments despite the best efforts of the Child Support Agency.

Without any money from her husband, Fay had found it hard to survive on her Centrelink benefits alone, so she got a job and worked hard. However over the years she did not always tell Centrelink how much she had earned and she grew accustomed to the extra money. Fay fraudulently obtained $13,543 from the government in Centrelink payments over the years. Dan thought it best to refer to this amount as an overpayment, rather than a fraud.

Fay, like many of Dan's other clients who had been charged with Centrelink fraud, were nice people. They weren't your career criminal types, not your drug dependent types, not your alcohol fuelled violent types. They were generally nice people who thought it was OK to take money from the government when they were short of funds, and keep taking it once they had come to rely upon the extra money.

He had just finished reviewing his submissions when Fay arrived. Fay was a rough looking woman and it was obvious that she had led a hard life. Dan was glad to see Fay had her five children with her, with the youngest being nine years old. He usually didn't approve of children coming to court to see their parents being sentenced but, in this case, he felt it was necessary.

It would be much harder for the Magistrate to send Fay to jail with her young children looking on from the courtroom.

*

"All rise", shouted the Deposition Clerk, as the black robed presiding Magistrate, Milton Battersby slowly entered the back of the Court and sat down at the elevated bench.

Dan knew Milton Battersby quite well. Milton had been a Magistrate for many, many years and he was very close to the compulsory retirement age of 70. Milton was grey haired, small of stature and friendly to lawyers, rather than their clients. Although Milton was not overly endowed with intelligence, he was generally fair and consistent, which were the main qualities Dan respected in Milton. He liked the fact Milton was more inclined to verbally attack his clients, give them a real tongue lashing, rather than give them harsh sentences like jail time. Some Magistrates just wanted to punish defendants, Milton was not like that.

"In the matter of Fay Marjorie Castle – please give your appearances", His Honour Milton Battersby formally announced.

The Commonwealth Prosecutor was first to speak. The prosecutor was around Dan's age, with a non-descript average physique; short black hair and dark rimmed glasses. Dan thought he looked like Clark Kent from Superman. The prosecutor stood behind the Bar table and slowly and solemnly announced his appearance before the Court.

"Robin Banks, for the Commonwealth, your Honour."

Dan chuckled with everybody else in the courtroom. He had appeared on the other side of many cases with Robin and he always got a chuckle out of Robin announcing his name to the court. Apparently Robin's parents enjoyed some laughs as well. Dan liked a guy who could laugh at himself in the serious confines of a courtroom.

"Dan Grover from Chadwick and Grover for the Defendant, your Honour and Mrs Castle is sitting beside me," Dan announced.

"All right thank you – how is the Defendant pleading to these charges?"

"The Defendant is pleading guilty to all charges," replied Dan.

"Fine. I will hear from the Prosecutor."

Dan listened intently to Robin's summation of the facts of the case. Robin submitted that Fay Castle should do actual jail time, given the amount of money taken, that she had taken the money over many years, and to deter other potential offenders from illegally taking money from the government. Robin was able to take the emotion out of the case and just state the facts.

Robin's rationale for jail time was quite persuasive and Dan began to feel a sense of unease about his prospects of keeping Fay out of jail. He noted that His Honour was vigorously taking notes while Robin was talking. That was never a good sign.

"Thank you, Mr Banks, for your submissions – I would like to hear now from Mr Grover for the Defendant."

Just as Milton had finished saying these words and while Dan was getting to his feet to make his submissions, Wally Toomalomo the Deposition Clerk, whispered something to Milton. Milton then said, "Excuse me, gentlemen, but I have just been informed there is an urgent telephone call I must attend to. I propose to have a short adjournment while I take this call in my chambers."

"All stand", Wally Toomalomo said as Milton Battersby hurriedly left the courtroom.

Dan turned his head and smiled encouragingly at Fay who was looking at the floor and biting her nails. He had already told Fay that a possible outcome of today's sentencing was that she could be going to jail for a short time, but that he would do his very best to avoid that. He leaned over and reassured Fay that he had some cogent and compelling submissions to make on her behalf and the Magistrate had at this point, only heard one side of the story.

He then turned back away from Fay and started talking football with Robin. Robin was a Brisbane Broncos supporter while Dan was an avid Cronulla Sharks fan. They traded friendly barbs about the strength of their respective teams.

Dan paused for a moment to consider how Fay might be feeling about his friendly fraternization with Robin. The person who had minutes earlier made compelling submissions to the Magistrate that she should be sentenced to jail.

Lawyers, when you come right down to it, are hired guns – they are there to do the best job they can for whoever is hiring them at the time. There is nothing personal in a lawyer's work – he/she is just trying to achieve the best outcome they can for their client, regardless of the consequences for the person on the other side.

Dan was hopeful Fay would view his friendly conversation with Robin as just light banter. That she realised his fraternization with Robin would not have any effect on his ability or his desire, to provide her with the best possible legal representation and keep her out of jail.

"All rise – this Magistrates Court is now in session," Wally Toomalomo announced. Everybody in the courtroom stood to their feet, while Milton Battersby walked back in. Once Milton had sat down everybody else resumed their seats. Before Dan could stand to deliver his submissions, Milton began talking.

"Mrs Fay Castle please stand. Although the defendant has no previous convictions and is unlikely to reoffend, I must take into account the deterrent aspects of sentencing in this particular matter."

Dan was not sure what Milton was doing but he appeared to be sentencing Fay.

"With respect to these charges I sentence the defendant to two years in imprisonment, with that prison sentence to be wholly suspended after she has served six months in jail. I further order the defendant to …"

Dan had heard enough – he couldn't believe what he was hearing. He liked Milton but this was outrageous! He jumped to his feet and shouted, "Your Honour you appear to be delivering your sentence of the defendant without first hearing from the defendant."

Milton looked disorientated. "Oh, is that the case – I appear to have gotten ahead of myself. Mr Grover, please continue with your submissions on behalf of the defendant."

So much for reassuring Fay during the break.

Dan made his submissions with gusto but was concerned to see that Milton was not writing anything down. He had hoped that Milton would now be more lenient with his client given his guffaw.

After Dan had finished Milton said, "Thank you, Mr Grover, for your fine submissions on behalf of the defendant. Will the defendant please stand.

"Although the defendant has no previous convictions and is unlikely to reoffend, I must take into account the deterrent aspects of sentencing in this particular matter. With respect to these charges I sentence the defendant to two years in custody with that prison sentence to be wholly suspended after she has served six months in jail. I further order the defendant to repay the entire amount of $13,543 to the Commonwealth of Australia."

It was exactly the same sentence – his submission had meant exactly nothing. All his work and preparation was a complete waste of time – he may as well not have been there.

Fay was having trouble standing. Her legs were shaking. Her eyelids were flashing like distress beacons. Tears began slowly but stopped quickly on turning around and seeing her children.

Dan talked quickly to Fay about an appeal and said that he would approach Legal Aid about further funding. He reassured Fay that even if Legal Aid would not fund an appeal, he would do it for free.

At that instant Dan wondered if he would still have a legal firm in six months if he started doing unpaid legal work, but he felt a real sense of injustice here. Milton had obviously made his mind up about Fay's sentence before hearing from Fay, and that was wrong. On the face of it, it was a clear breach of natural justice.

Dan said his goodbyes to Fay and wished her well. He watched as Fay was led from the courtroom straight into police custody. He spent some time in the precincts of the court providing emotional support to Fay's children and to let them know that if they needed anything just to give him a call. Fay had already made arrangements for her children to be cared for by her mother, in the event things turned sour.

He walked out of the courtroom deflated that Fay was now in jail and that all his work on Fay's behalf had come to nothing.

Then he remembered the events of this morning and he called Gloria to hear some good news.

"Gloria, it's me."

"How did Fay Castle go?"

"Not as well as we had hoped, but there is a story to tell there."

"Yeah, well I have a story to tell you about Alyssa Paschetelle as well."

This was it Dan thought. This was what he was waiting for. To be encouraged after his difficult morning in Court.

"Well, she has patched things up with her husband and they have spoken to the police about charging you with kidnapping and assault."

"What?"

"Apparently you arranged for Alyssa's husband to have his jaw broken by a couple of bikies."

"What?"

"You then kidnapped the baby without her or her husband's consent."

"What?"

"I thought something was strange when Alyssa and her mother came here and collected the baby. Alyssa told me that her husband had been king hit and they were off to hospital to see if he was alright. I knew you wouldn't have hit him, so I asked what happened and they told me you got some bikies to bash him while the baby was still in his arms."

Dan was struggling to understand what Gloria was saying.

"But she wanted me to go and rescue her baby, after she had been punched, kicked and knocked to the ground by her husband."

"Well she isn't seeing it that way anymore. The police have called and they want to interview you."

"That's just great," Dan said incredulously.

"Wait, it gets worse."

"What do you mean worse, how could it get any worse?" Dan protested.

"The police officer who rang is a friend of my sisters. You know Doreen don't you?"

"Yes, I know Doreen," Dan answered abruptly.

"The police officer told me confidentially, that they have also tried to talk to those two bikies. They haven't been able to find them yet. However word on the street is that the bikies know the police are looking for them and they are not happy about it. Apparently the bikies are now looking for you and not in a nice way, given the heat you have brought on them with the police. He told me to tell you to watch your back, don't go anywhere alone for awhile."

Dan was struggling to comprehend what was happening.

"This day just keeps getting better and better," Dan said with sarcasm dripping from his mouth.

"Sorry, Danny, I know you were only trying to help the poor woman get her baby back. But did you really get those bikies to bash the guy?

"No, I didn't ask them to bash him. I did ask for their help but I thought they would just stand over him and maybe threaten him a little."

"Is there anything I can do?"

"No, Gloria, but thanks anyway. It might be best if we both took the afternoon off and shut the practice down for the rest of day."

"Sounds like a plan to me. I will lock up here.

"Danny, one more thing, your brother called and he asked me to remind you in case you had forgotten, that you are expected at his place tonight at 7:30pm sharp."

"No, I hadn't forgotten."

That was all he needed at the moment, to be reminded that he had to be at Claye's house at precisely 7:30pm tonight. That was a meeting he was not looking forward to.

CHAPTER THREE

Dan went home and unwound watching a football game he had recorded on the weekend. As he ripped open his second cold beer and sank once more into his soft comfortable couch, he pondered his day. A looming pay cut, a financial crisis that could shut down his legal practice before it really began, possible criminal charges for kidnapping and assault, not to mention a couple of violent bikies looking for him; and to top it all off, one of his nicest clients had just been sent to six months jail after the Magistrate had totally ignored everything he had said on her behalf.

At least, he thought, things could only get better from here. How could things get any worse?

Elise arrived home just as it was getting dark. Dan had managed to lift himself out of his mental quagmire and was preparing Cantonese stir fry chicken for their dinner. He usually arrived home too late from work to prepare dinner. Tonight he would surprise Elise.

In fact, he enjoyed cooking. He enjoyed creating something out of nothing. With his legal work he could toil hard to create the best case he could, yet all his best endeavours could be shot down by a few words from a Judge or Magistrate. With cooking he was at peace to create whatever he wanted and ultimately have something wonderful to show for it at the end.

"Well, how was your day?" Dan asked. "You are not going to believe the day I have had."

Elise didn't respond to Dan's questions but asked when dinner would be ready.

"It won't be long."

"I am just going to change. I will be back in a minute," Elise said.

Twenty minutes later they were seated together and Dan especially was enjoying his meal, chopsticks and all. Elise seemed preoccupied.

"Dan, we need to talk."

"Wow, that sounds ominous. Did I forget to empty the dishwasher last night?"

"Yes, you forgot to empty the dishwasher but what I want to talk about has nothing to do with the dishwasher."

"What do you want to talk about then?" Dan asked. He really had no idea what Elise wanted to talk to him about.

Elise stopped eating and looked at Dan. She took a moment before she said, "I don't know how to say this so I will just come out and say it."

Elise paused again.

"Ok," Dan said not sure if he really wanted to hear this.

"I don't know if I really love you anymore."

Dan also stopped eating. He had suddenly lost his appetite.

"There, I said it," The bombshell was dropped.

"What do you mean?"

"I have felt really low for several months now. I have just been listless and flat. I kept thinking why I am feeling so withdrawn and so down. Then I realised that I was not enjoying my life with you anymore. So the question, am I still in love with you?"

Dan gulped. It was all a huge shock for him.

"We just don't spend any time together like we used to. I get up and go to work, you're still in bed. I get home and you don't come home till late. We may eat together but then you go off and watch sport on TV."

Elise was on a roll now, she was no longer hesitating but unloading.

"We don't talk anymore, we don't go out together, we don't spend any quality time together and we don't seem to have any fun together anymore."

Dan wondered where all this was coming from.

"I thought we were getting on alright."

Elise looked at Dan and shook her head. "Is that all you have to say to me?"

"When I get home from work I am tired. It's a difficult job and I just need to relax for a couple of hours in front of the TV before I go to bed. Is that such a bad thing?"

"You know what worries me. I think you are shutting me out of your life. I rate last on your priorities of what's important in your life. You spend so much time at work and watching sport. Yet you find time to spend with your mates but not with me."

"You have your friends and I have my friends. You have your interests and I have my interests. I thought you liked not living in each other's pockets."

"I don't want to live in your pocket but you have been relegating me to a speck of dust on your jacket for some time now."

Dan wasn't thinking clearly. He was trying to get his head above water and recover from the tidal wave of emotion that had just engulfed him. He couldn't really make sense of it all at the moment. He eventually said, "What do you want me to do?"

"I just want you to think about what I have said and let's talk some more. I know this is difficult but I had to let you know how I am feeling."

"Yeah, well you have certainly timed this talk well, with the day I've had."

"It's not all about you all the time! You know that, Dan, don't you?"

Dan felt a sudden rush of adrenaline.

"I know that most of the time it is about you. What you like, what you want. I am always trying to please you, trying to make you happy. It's not about me because I am usually happy anyway."

He could actually see Elise's face flush after he said this. It always surprised him how quickly her angelic face could flush and flare with rage. Perhaps it had something to do with her Celtic heritage, soft freckles and vibrant auburn hair.

Elise flung both her chopsticks across the table at Dan.

"How dare you turn this back onto me," she retorted.

"Elise, just calm down."

"Calm down, are you telling me to calm down?" she demanded.

Dan immediately knew he should not have told Elise to calm down. He had learnt that telling her calm down was like throwing petrol on a fire.

He raised his hand in the air and apologized, "I didn't mean to upset you."

"Yeah right, you didn't mean to upset me. I come to you and pour my heart out and you turn it back onto me as though it's all my fault!" Elise yelled.

"Look I am sorry, I shouldn't have criticized you. I am just in shock. You may have thought about how you are feeling before now but for me, what you are telling me is all new. I just said the first thing that came into my head."

Dan reached over and touched her hand. Although her fist was still half clenched, she was showing the tell tale signs of calming down.

He put his arm around her shoulder and said, "Hey, come on it's me. I am absolutely positive we can work this out together. Just give me some time to process it all. You want to work it out, don't you?"

"Sure, that's why I bought it up, so we can work it out."

"Well I want that too. If we both want the same thing, then we will get it."

Elise appeared reassured and responded to Dan's hug.

"I am sorry, you know sometimes I just get so mad, so quickly."

"Yeah, I know."

Elise instantly jerked her head around to look at Dan.

Dan put his palms up, in a surrender position.

"You can get mad quickly, I know it, you know it. You're not perfect, that doesn't mean I love you any less. I love you despite your imperfections. Why I am sure if I think for long enough, I can come up with some imperfections of my own."

Elise smiled.

"Yes, well I can come up with a few of your imperfections right this minute, pride being one of them. And I can never have a serious conversation with you," Elise said.

"Let's not go there. I will think about what you have said and let's talk about it again later tonight," Dan replied, glad that the tension had dissipated.

"Thanks," Elise said as Dan picked up the chopsticks from the floor and placed them on the kitchen bench.

Dan asked quietly, "Would you like to do something together right now?"

"What?" Elise replied.

"How about a little action?" After all it had been nearly a week and that was something they definitely could do together.

"You think I am in the mood for sex, do you? Oh, brother!"

"Men!" was the last word Elise yelled as she stormed off.

"I was only joking; what do you take me for?" Dan yelled back at her.

Dan had seen countless TV shows where couples had engaged in wonderful wild sex immediately after having heated arguments. Yet this didn't seem to work in real life. It must be one of TV life's illusions he thought.

"And don't worry about the washing up, I'll do it even though I cooked tonight."

Elise was long gone.

*

As Dan drove to his brother's place after dinner, his mind replayed and rehashed the discussion he just had with Elise.

Where had it all come from? How serious was it? Was he to blame? What could he do to fix things?

He had met Elise while he was at university. Elise was two years younger than Dan and they met while she was working as a waitress at one of his favourite sporting clubs. Elise had just broken up with her boyfriend at the time who happened to be another law student.

Apparently, from what he could gather from Elise, her previous relationship had been quite volatile. She and her ex-boyfriend had argued often and the relationship ended when she caught him cheating on her. Elise was so angry that she spray painted the words, *I'm a two timing bastard* on her boyfriend's car and then posted the picture on his Facebook wall.

Elise had a quick fuse but he was happy to live with that. And it wasn't just Elise's innate beauty that drew him to her. It was something more; perhaps her soulful, brown eyes, which were the windows to her soul. Eyes that could inflame but also shine warmly and sparkle; eyes that looked for fun and adventure.

They had very divergent interests. Elise loved jazz, ballet and the theatre. Elise hated all sport, particularly rugby league which she thought was barbaric and brutal.

He hated jazz, couldn't stand ballet and was always bored at the theatre. He loved playing sport, watching sport and talking about sport with his mates. He particularly loved rugby league.

He had been a Cronulla Sutherland Sharks fan since he was six years old. He was not sure now what had attracted him to support the Sharks, perhaps it was the fact that they had never won the premiership. The Sharks were not able to win the competition even when the competition split in two during the Super League war, when the great game of rugby league imploded on itself.

His support of the Sharks was not made any easier by the fact Brisbane was a one team town, and the Brisbane Broncos unlike the Sharks, were one of the most successful teams in the National Rugby League.

Elise on the other hand was a budding artist. Elise worked as a waitress so she could afford to paint. She loved nothing more on a quiet Sunday than to spend all day in her makeshift art studio, painting and sculpting.

He encouraged Elise to pursue her dream of one day becoming a professional artist. However Dan was a Neanderthal when it came to art, he just could not see any beauty in it. He could appreciate the time and effort that went into creating a work of art but, no matter how hard Elise had tried, he could not feel any joy in looking at a piece of art.

He wondered if their differing interests and personalities, once a thing of humor and curiosity, had now turned into a cause for conflict and jealously.

CHAPTER FOUR

He arrived at Claye's home a little after 7:30pm that evening. Claye was eleven years older than Dan.

"Mate, you took your time getting here – late again, I see. How do you ever manage to get to the court on time?" was the first thing Claye said to him.

Dan was super sensitive to Claye's condescending tone, a consequence of having a rough day and an elder brother who always thought he knew best.

"It's only a couple of minutes past 7:30. I didn't know getting here exactly at 7:30 was so important to the wellbeing of the world!"

"Mate, I don't know how Elise puts up with you, you take offence so easily – I was just stirring you." Claye tended to say *Mate* a lot, whether it was to his only brother or to a complete stranger, Claye would always call them *Mate*.

"Listen, Claye, I am here because you asked me to come over to see you. I am not hard to get along with; I am extremely easy to get along with."

"Ok mate relax. I don't want to upset you, I just want to talk to you."

"I have just had a rough day."

"No worries, mate. How is Elise?"

"She is good."

He certainly didn't want to talk to Claye about his recent marital problems. Although Claye was his big brother, he was not someone Dan wanted to have heart-to-heart discussions with about his personal issues.

"Listen, mate, you know my oncologist was considering a donor stem cell transplant to treat my leukemia?"

"Yeah, I gave blood to see if I was a match," said Dan.

"Well, it turns out that you are a match, despite the odds of me getting a match with just one sibling. So my oncologist wants me to start on chemo straight away and then have the donor stem cell transplant."

"Claye, what are you saying?"

"Mate, the cancer has come back."

"I didn't know the leukaemia had come back, I thought you were in remission – I am sorry. Of course, I will….. Just tell me what you want me to do."

"I need you to come to the hospital when my doctor asks you to and donate some of your stem cells. They will then transplant your stem cells into me."

"No problems."

"I also need another favour. I need you to take on a sexual harassment investigation while I undergo this treatment. Will you do that for me, little brother?"

"Claye, of course I will." Dan thought for a moment then added, "What sexual harassment investigation?"

"Well, mate, you know I work for myself conducting corporate investigations. I have just received a request from one of my clients to investigate a sexual harassment complaint. Having to undergo this stem cell transplant will put me out of action for awhile. I can't do the investigation but I don't want one of my best clients to look elsewhere, I might lose them as a client. So I was hoping you would do it for me. After all, aren't you a hot shot lawyer now with his own legal practice?"

"I have never done any investigation work before, I wouldn't know what to do."

"It is easy, mate, you won't have any trouble and if you do have any questions, I am available for consultations."

"I am just not sure I have the time, as I really have to devote all my energies to build up my own legal practice at the moment. Can't you find someone else to do it?"

"Did I mention that it pays $300 an hour?"

"Mate, I am in," Dan said without any further hesitation. "You know I would do anything for you."

"Yeah thanks mate. I knew your generosity of spirit would come through once I told you how much it pays."

They both laughed.

"I will give you the details later."

With the business now out of the way, Dan was curious to learn more about the medical procedure Claye was about to embark on.

"What are the risks of this donor stem cell transplant?"

"Well, I have been told there is a 60% chance of being cured completely, a 20% chance of the leukaemia going but then coming back and a 20% chance of not making it out of the hospital. There is a common complication of the procedure called *graft versus host* disease, where the immune system your stem cells provide me doesn't recognize me or my organs, and it attacks them as being foreign. If that gets out of control I could be a goner."

"You seem to be taking this pretty well."

"Mate, I am scared to death. I am not so much scared of dying as of dying a slow and painful death. You know how Uncle Bevan suffered with cancer – well I don't want to go through the agonising and lingering type of death he went through."

Dan winced at the thought of his uncle's slow and tortuous demise.

"You know I am a Christian. I have made my peace with God; whether I die or not, it is up to him. But I am not ready to go just yet, so I am praying and expecting God to look after me. He has promised to never leave me nor forsake me, and nothing can separate me from him – so I am holding on tight to that promise."

Dan marveled at Claye's faith. He had wondered over the years if Claye was all show and no substance in his faith. After all, Claye could not seem to attract the female of the species and his relationships with other family members were sometimes strained. But here and now there appeared to be evidence that Claye's relationship with God was real and substantial. How else could he have the temerity to deal with the devastating news that his leukemia had returned and that he had one in five chance of dying soon with such confidence and poise?

"Mate, if there is anything I can do for you, just let me know." Dan usually avoided using the word *mate* as a way of showing Claye he did not conform to his ways. But now at this time he felt the need to include the word when he spoke to Claye; to show his elder brother that he would stand with him in this time of crisis.

"Anyway enough of me, how has your day been?" Claye asked.

"There have been a few ups and downs today, but nothing I can't handle." All of a sudden Dan's big day out did not seem so important anymore.

"But I do have to go. I want to catch Elise before she goes to sleep."

"Will you pray with me before you go?"

Dan was not a Christian. He was not against religion as such, but as a lawyer he was more of an evidence kind of guy. He wondered when Claye first became a Christian, how Claye could be so influenced by words without any evidence to back them up. He figured that Claye probably needed the crutch of religion to help him get through life.

"You want me to pray with you?" Dan asked uncomfortably.

He noticed Claye's look of concern at his question. He didn't want to hurt Claye. Not now, not with what he was going through. "Mate, if you want me to pray with you that's fine, just it's been awhile for me."

Claye put his hand on Dan's shoulder, closed his eyes and bowed his head.

"Father you give and you take away – blessed be your name. I am in your hands and I know you will look after me and see me through this ordeal I am about to embark on. Father, I want to thank you for my little brother Dan. I don't know how I could journey down this road without him. Although we have not always been close, he is here for me now when I need him. Bless Dan, really bless this talented man and help him in his journey towards a fulfilled spiritual life."

Dan said nothing. He could not believe that Claye, in his time of need, was praying for him.

At that moment for the first time in a very long time, he felt really close to his brother. He vowed there and then, to do everything he could to get Claye through this ordeal.

*

Elise was waiting up to talk with Dan after he returned home from Claye's place.

She was upset at the news that Claye's leukemia had returned and that the stem cell transplant he was about to undertake to save his life, could kill him.

Dan recounted the events of his day and Elise was suitably impressed with how he rescued the baby and concerned that he may face criminal charges over his good deed. He did not tell Elise about the bikies' apparent interest in finding him. It was best she didn't worry about that, what with everything else going on.

Eventually the conversation turned to their marriage issues.

"What do you think?" Elise asked.

"I am not sure what the answer is, but I do want to work things out."

"I think that we should spend more time together."

"What do you want to do together?" asked Dan innocently.

"You can't think of anything?"

"Well, I don't want to go clubbing anymore, I couldn't stand going to another art gallery and you know the ballet bores me to tears. I am not trying to be difficult but when you think about it, there aren't a lot of activities that we both enjoy doing together."

"What are you saying?" Elise asked with a concerned expression.

"Well, just spending more time together is not the answer is it? Isn't the answer more than that? Isn't it more fundamental than that?"

"Go on, I am listening."

"I am not sure what the answer is, all I know is that it requires some commitment on both sides. Have you still got that commitment?" Dan asked pensively.

"I am not sure. I know I am not happy in the relationship at the moment and I want to do something about it."

"What do you want to do?" Dan asked.

"I want to see a marriage counsellor," Elise announced matter of factly.

"Do we really need to? Are things that bad?" asked Dan.

"I don't know. I do know that our relationship has stalled. I think we need help."

As Dan struggled to find sleep that night, he reflected on the past 24 hours. He wondered what the next 24 hours had in store for him. Surely it would get better. It couldn't possibly get any worse, could it?

CHAPTER FIVE

Dan arrived at work and was relieved to see the office was still standing and hadn't been trashed by the *Vandals*. Dan balanced his coffee and almond croissant in one hand and tightly gripped his laptop in the other.

"How's it going, Gloria?"

"Good morning, Danny. Sleep well?

"I have had better nights."

Dan walked past Gloria to his office and before he could even unwrap his croissant or turn on his desktop computer, she was there standing in front of him, demanding to know what had happened the day before.

Dan gave Gloria the full story.

"So let me get this straight. You didn't tell the bikies to bash him."

"No, Gloria. I just told them what had happened. I hoped they would help but I certainly didn't ask them to hit the guy."

Gloria nodded.

"Also, they only hit him twice, I don't think that constitutes a bashing."

"You had better tell the police what happened before they come looking for you."

"Yeah, I will give the police a call and set up an interview."

"It's strange how quickly Alyssa got back with her husband. One minute they are fighting and the next minute she is back with him," Gloria observed.

"Women," Dan said raising both his hands in the air.

"You have a problem with all women, Danny, or just one or two in particular?" Gloria enquired, raising her eyebrows as though she was very interested in the answer.

"Gloria, if the world was full of women like you, it would be a much nicer place."

Gloria smiled. "Danny, you will go far my boy, very far."

"Straight to jail is where I will be going, unless I can sort this mess out."

They both laughed as Gloria turned and walked back to her work area. Dan chuckled as he heard Gloria snort twice like a moose on heat.

*

The day actually went well for Dan with the usual assortment of legal issues to resolve for people. As he left the office, he had been so engrossed in his day's work, that the two shiny black motor bikes parked in the bay next to his car did not even register with him as anything significant.

As he reached for his key, he felt a strong hand tighten its grip on his right shoulder. Dan wheeled around and recognized the shorter bikie with the rat's tail hanging from his bald head. No sooner had he turned around, than Dan felt rather than saw, a fist strike him in the solarplexes. It quite literally took his breath away. He immediately hunched over and coughed, breathing as hard as he could to get some air back in his lungs.

"Open up this heap, we want to talk to you in the car."

The voice was threatening and it came from the other side of the car. Dan turned around slowly and saw the tall bikie with the grey pony tail, the rat and snake tattoo, at his passenger door.

He unlocked the car and moved gingerly into the driver's seat. The tall bikie moved into the front passenger seat, while the shorter bikie sat directly behind Dan in the rear. He felt extremely uncomfortable and exposed, not being able to see the short bikie.

The older bikie, like last time, did all the talking.

"Dude, we don't want to hurt you, we really don't, not with you being a lawyer and all. But we don't want to get stung for some crazy assault bullshit either. So keep your big trap shut about us. I mean don't tell the cops, don't tell anybody about us, not even your pretty, little wife."

"My wife! What the hell has she got to do with this?" Dan blurted out.

"He is a lawyer, I thought he'd be shit smart," the older bikie said to the shorter one, who laughed on cue.

"Listen, dumb ass, we obviously know where you work. So I am letting you know, we also know where you live."

Dan didn't say anything. His stomach was really hurting, but all he could think about at the moment was Elise.

"Do I have to spell it out for you? If you say anything about us to the cops, you and your *ranga* wife will be shark food in the bay."

He was aghast. They not only knew about Elise but they had seen her as well. He tried to reason with them. There was absolutely no point being defiant in the position he was in.

"Listen guys, I won't say anything to anyone about you. My wife has nothing to do with this, can't we just leave her out of it."

"Can't do that mister lawyer," the older bikie said as he ran his hand up and down Dan's shirt in a menacing fashion. "But it's up to you, she will be sweet as long as you tell no one nothin'. Comprehenday?"

Dan decided to let the double negative pass censure.

Dan nodded. "I won't say anything."

"Good boy," the older bikie said smugly.

The short bikie then struck Dan in the back of the head with a cocked elbow, just as a parting shot. The bikies disappeared as quickly as they had appeared.

It took Dan some time to calm himself after his most recent encounter with the *Vandals*. He thought about going to the police there and then, but that was a risk he was not prepared to take. For the moment at least, until he could figure out a better plan, he would not tell anyone about the bikies.

Should he tell Elise? He felt it best not to tell her. It would only upset and worry her. Best plan now was to do what he was told to do and keep quiet, *tell no one nothin'*.

CHAPTER SIX

He pulled up outside a battered workers cottage in Spring Hill. It was a beautiful winter's afternoon, so Dan suggested the interview take place around a small table on the sunlit verandah.

He looked at Mia Wong in her jeans and tight fitting sweater. She was obviously very attractive but Dan was a professional; her attractiveness was irrelevant to his manner of dealing with her.

"Where do you want me to start, Mr Grover?" Mia asked.

"Look call me Dan. And at the beginning – from when you first started working for Dodsworth, Blainey and Parker".

"Ok, here goes. My ex-boyfriend and I came to Brisbane from Sydney a few months ago, looking for work. I had been working at the company for the last six weeks on a temporary contract which had just finished. My job was to do the administrative work for several of the accountancy teams, including the team Samuel Sanderson was in."

"How did you get on with Samuel?"

"We got on very well. I liked Samuel."

"Did you have any interest in him romantically".

"You mean sexually – of course not!" Mia exclaimed raising her voice.

"Look, there is nothing personal in what I am doing, I just have to ask certain questions," replied Dan. "So tell me about the lead up to what happened?"

"Well, work put on a function for staff last Friday evening and I really felt like winding down and having a drink. My boyfriend and I had just split up and so I was a feeling a bit down. To be honest I wanted to cut loose and party."

"What happened?"

"Everything was going well, I was enjoying myself. There was a whole crowd there just drinking, talking and dancing."

"Dancing?"

"Yes, there was a group of us there and someone turned the music up so we all started dancing."

"So you were enjoying yourself."

"Listen, I was having a real blast at the time. You know what it is like."

Dan pondered that it had been some time since he had been out partying. When was the last time he had a real blast? He quickly regathered his thoughts.

"Where was Samuel at this time?"

"He was dancing too, there was a whole crowd dancing."

"What time did the party wind down?"

"I am not sure of the time but it was late. At the end there were about five or six of us still raging. Then all of a sudden everybody just decided to go home. Samuel asked me if I wanted to stay on and have one last drink with him. So I stayed and the others left."

"Why did you stay? Why didn't you leave with the others?"

"I had nowhere to go. I mean, I could have gone home but there was nothing for me at home. I thought about kicking on and partying at a club but I had no one to go with. So I thought why not have a drink with the guy, after all I was feeling good and having a great time."

Mia paused and lowered her head.

"I suppose I let my guard down with him. But I thought I knew him. I trusted him."

"Tell me what happened."

"After everybody left, Samuel got a beer for himself and a glass of wine for me."

"How much alcohol had you had to drink by this time?"

"I can't remember but it could have been four or five glasses of wine."

"How much had Samuel had to drink?"

"I don't know."

"Go on."

"Not long after that last wine I began to feel really unwell. It's all a bit fuzzy from there. I must have passed out."

"What's the next thing you remember?"

"I remember lying in the back seat of a car."

"What happened then?" Dan asked as Mia had just stopped talking. She seemed lost in thought and on the verge of tears.

"The next thing I remember," Mia said in a soft voice, reaching for tissues and wiping her eyes, "was Samuel undressing me."

Mia paused again and Dan remained silent, waiting patiently for Mia to continue with her story.

"He then started touching me. I didn't want him to touch me but it was like my body would not react to my thoughts. I just could not move to stop him, or even say anything to him. I was trying to scream but no noise was coming out. My body would just not respond to my brain."

Mia was on the verge of sobbing.

"I felt violated about what was happening to me but I couldn't do anything about it. I felt trapped. I felt helpless."

"Would you like a break?"

"No, I want to get this over with," Mia responded as she reached for more tissues.

"What else do you remember?"

"The next thing I remember is waking up the next day, Saturday at my home."

"How did you get home?

"I don't remember."

"You remember Samuel touching you but not how you got home?"

"That's right."

"Alright, go on."

"I felt really sick. I had diarrhoea, vomiting and a pounding headache. I called a friend of mine, Jazz Carlon. Jazz has worked with women who have been abused. She thought I probably had my drink spiked by Samuel."

"Did you go and see a doctor?"

"No, I didn't want to see anybody."

"This is quite a serious allegation. Why are you not pursuing it through the police?" Dan enquired.

"A friend of mine had a bad experience with the police and I don't trust them. I don't want this to be just another police matter that drags on for years."

"What do you want to see happen to Samuel?"

"First and foremost, I don't want this to happen to anyone else. Also Samuel has done the wrong thing and he should be sacked. He is a sick and perverted person; he should be punished for what he has done to me," Mia said with rising levels of defiance and anger.

"How have you been affected by what happened?"

Dan waited patiently for Mia's reply. She appeared to be summoning up the strength to answer the question. Though the more time that elapsed and the more she appeared to think about her answer, the more upset she became.

In a tearful voice Mia whispered, "I feel deeply ashamed, repulsed, hurt, helpless and violated."

Mia paused.

"I can't wear the clothes I wore that night. I have trouble sleeping. I can't stop thinking about what he did to me."

Mia paused again.

"I trusted him and he took advantage of me. He treated me like a piece of dirt!"

"Have you received any counseling?" asked Dan.

"No, I can't afford it."

"Well, if you want me to – I can approach the company to see whether they will pay for some counselling for you."

"Thank you for that. That would be good if you would do that for me."

Dan noticed the faint trace of a smile as Mia tossed back a strand of her silky black hair.

"Will you need to see me again?" she asked.

"Probably, I will need to talk to Samuel and depending on what he says, I may need to talk to you again," replied Dan.

"That's ok, just give me a call. Thank you for being so patient with me today."

As he drove home that afternoon, he could not help but think about Mia Wong. If she was telling the truth, she had been shamefully taken advantage of by a trusted colleague. Why would she lie about something as personal and intimate as this?

Dan's attention was caught by a vivid orange sky. The sun had set and illuminated a string of nearby clouds, producing a visual feast for the eyes. It was a fairly common event for this part of the world, but for some reason at this particular time, the intensity of that blood orange sky deeply touched him.

CHAPTER SEVEN

As Dan came out of the elevator at Dodsworth, Blainey and Parker he saw Connor Mead. Dan was running about ten minutes late (caught in traffic again, he couldn't believe his bad luck) and he was sweaty, due to running from a downtown parking meter.

To the right of Connor, Dan noticed an athletic looking middle aged man and with him was a rather large, unattractive woman appearing to be in her early 40s.

Dan approached Connor Mead, thrust out his hand and said, "I am Daniel Grover."

Connor replied by introducing himself, Samuel Sanderson and Grace Sanderson, Samuel's wife. They all shook hands. Dan was taken aback at the strength of Grace's handshake.

Grace's eyes were also quite noticeable. They were small, blue and quite piercing. They reminded him of a Huskie's eyes, just a little bit frightening if you were not used to seeing them.

Connor was in his late 50s and well known in Brisbane legal circles. He had been running his own legal firm for 30 years and he gave the impression that he knew everybody and everything. Connor was a very large man over 193 centimetres tall, with a healthy head of dyed black hair and a booming voice.

"Now listen, Dan, can I call you Dan?" Connor did not wait for an answer.

"Can I talk to you about a few things in private before we begin?"

Again Connor did not wait for an answer, he just walked over to the window away from his client. Dan thought about saying *no, I don't want to talk to you in private*, but discretion got the better of him, and he slowly made his way over to the window to stand next to Connor.

"My client would like his wife to be present during your interview with him. Is that ok?" whispered Connor, though his whisper was as loud as a normal person's speaking voice.

"I don't really think that would be appropriate, with this matter involving serious allegations of sexual harassment," replied Dan.

Connor raised his voice to his normal level of loudness and exclaimed, "Why can't he have his wife there for support – you told him he could have a support person at his interview if he wanted to."

Dan glanced over at the Sandersons and it was obvious both of them heard what Connor had just said.

Dan tried to keep a lid on it and whispered, "I am conducting this interview and I would prefer that your client not have his wife present during the interview. In any event, I assume you will be his support person – he can have only one support person."

"Alright, but I think you are being very unfair to my client," replied Connor in an accepting tone which really surprised Dan. He had not expected Connor to acquiesce so easily when he didn't get what he wanted.

Connor then moved a step closer to Dan, clearly invading his personal space.

"Another matter is that my client has not been supplied with the particulars of the allegations that have been made against him and the questions you want to ask him. Natural justice dictates that before you interview him, you must first give him the specific allegations and put in writing the questions you want him to answer."

Dan had been warned by Claye that most lawyers had little to no experience with these types of corporate investigations and most just did not understand the concept of natural justice. He could tell from Connor's demeanor and the way he asked the question, that he expected full compliance from Dan. It crossed his mind at that moment, that Connor had raised the wife issue knowing full well Dan would not agree, but using his expected denial of that request to induce Dan to agree to this second request.

"Mr Mead, my understanding of natural justice is that it only applies where a final decision is to be made that could be adverse to your client's interests. My investigation is not a final decision. It is all about gathering the evidence and trying to find out what happened. If after the investigation has concluded the company believes it has grounds to take disciplinary action against your client, then at that time, I am sure your client will be supplied with the detailed allegations and particulars. Prior to our interview all he needs to know is that Mia Wong has made a complaint of sexual harassment against him.

"Also, I am not prepared to submit my questions to your client in writing – that would just give him an opportunity to invent a story and not tell the truth."

"Why you little upstart – how dare you lecture me about natural justice and how to conduct investigations! Do you not know who you are talking to?"

Connor's cheeks were now bright red and his voice was so loud that everybody waiting in the foyer could hear every word. All other conversations in the foyer had stopped and there was that uncomfortable silence that comes with bystanders being aware of a nearby conflict but pretending not to notice.

Dan was not going to be intimidated by Connor. He was after all a lawyer as well who probably knew just as much of the law on this issue as Connor. He was going to stick to his guns on this point, even if he turned out to be wrong.

"Mr Mead, I am a lawyer also and as I am running this process, it has to be conducted my way. Your client can refuse to speak with me if he wishes, in which case I will just have to rely upon what the complainant has told me."

The penny seemed to drop with Connor at that point. Connor was experienced enough to know his client needed to have his side of the story told and considered. There was no point alienating the investigator at this time – the investigator could be attacked later, if he found against his client.

"I didn't know you were a lawyer, you should have said so at the beginning. As long as my client's objections are noted in your report, I am sure my client will cooperate with the investigation today."

Dan then led Connor and Samuel to a small meeting room he had booked. The room had no paintings, or prints and no windows. It was to all intents and purposes like a small prison cell.

Dan commenced the interview by saying that he was electronically recording it, to which Connor produced a tiny digital recorder from his pocket saying that he intended to record the interview as well. Dan noted that Connor did not switch his digital recorder on when he put it on the table, which meant he probably recorded their earlier conversation without telling him. A covert recording of a conversation by one party to that conversation is not illegal, but not the done thing, especially when two lawyers were having a frank discussion.

"Mr Sanderson, I would like to ask you some questions about an allegation that has been made against you by Mia Wong that you sexually harassed her last Friday night. Firstly, can you tell me your current position?" asked Dan.

"I am a chartered accountant in the firm of Dodsworth, Blainey and

Parker," replied Samuel.

"Where did you work before coming here?"

Dan noticed Samuel hesitate – he must not have been expecting this question. Samuel glanced at Connor.

"What relevance is his employment history to this investigation?" asked Connor.

Before Dan could even answer this question, Connor looked at Samuel and said matter of factly, "Don't answer that question."

Wow, the interview had only been going for one minute and Connor was already interjecting and throwing his weight around.

"I am trying to investigate the allegations made against your client. I wouldn't ask a question if I didn't think it had or may have some relevance".

"Unless you can explain to me its relevance, Samuel will not be answering that question," Connor said with all the authority of someone who didn't expect his statements to be challenged.

Dan started grinding his teeth. He ran his fingers through his mop of thick brown hair. He had wanted to placate Connor and avoid a confrontation with him but he realized that unless there was a confrontation and he showed Connor once and for all that he would not be intimidated, the interview would be a complete shambles.

He looked straight at Connor. "I am not going to sit here and conduct an interview with you questioning the relevancy of every question I ask. Either your client answers my questions – which are not designed to trap him, just to find out what happened – or I will cease the interview here and now. My investigation report will then be based solely on what the complainant has told me.

"Now are we to terminate this interview and I make findings after hearing only one side of the story, or do you want to answer my questions? Is there a problem in Samuel telling me where he has worked before and what roles he has had in the past?"

"Alright, Samuel will answer your questions, but I want it recorded I am not happy for him to answer questions where the relevance of those questions has not first been made clear," Connor pronounced.

This corporate investigation work was not as easy as he expected. At least in a court you would have a Magistrate or Judge keeping lawyers like Connor in line (or attempting to do that). Here Dan was seeking to do his job and investigate the matter, while at the same time trying to keep Connor from hijacking the interview.

"I was a member of the Australian Armed Forces for 15 years. I then went to University and graduated in accountancy. My first accountancy job was for Spencer Rush Accountants, a relatively small firm. I worked there for 3 years before obtaining a number crunching position with a Market Research firm, Dooley and Associates. I worked there for 2 years before I obtained my current position," Samuel said.

"Thank you," Dan said looking straight at Connor before moving his gaze back onto Samuel. "I didn't think that would be a hard question for you to answer," Dan said shaking his head.

"In your current role what contact did you have with Mia Wong?" asked Dan, glad the interview was back on track.

"She was a temporary administrative officer. She did some of my unit's administrative work."

"How did you find her?"

"She was pleasant enough. I really didn't have that much contact with her myself."

"Were you interested in her romantically?" Dan enquired expecting to hear a blast from Connor.

"No way," exclaimed Samuel before Connor had time to fire up an objection. "I am a married man and I take my relationship with my wife very, very seriously. She means the whole world to me."

Samuel was convincing with this answer. Dan reminded himself that even though Connor was giving him a hard time, he should not put any antagonism he felt towards Connor onto Samuel. He could not get past the irony that Samuel was paying money to a lawyer to help him but that lawyer was actually hurting his case. Due to Connor's intimidatory tactics, Dan had to work hard to be open to the fact that Samuel may be a genuine guy, with nothing to hide.

"How did you come to have a drink with Ms Wong after work last Friday?"

"We were both at a work function and several of us stayed till late sampling the company's alcohol. When I went to go home with the others, she asked me to stay for one last drink. I tried to brush her off but she was persistent. She was alone and I felt sorry for her, so I agreed to have one last drink with her."

"Ms Wong told me that you asked her to have one last drink with you."

"That's a lie. She asked me to stay and have one last drink with her."

"What happened then?"

"She got sick. I took her home. Nothing else happened."

"Ms Wong claims that after everybody else had left the work function, you spiked her drink and then sexually assaulted her in the back seat of a car."

"For a start I didn't spike her drink. What did she say – I can't believe she is saying I did something like that to her."

Dan noticed that despite Samuel's words of outrage, he appeared quite calm and rational.

"Tell him what she said about her ex-boyfriend?" Connor interjected.

Dan thought about reprimanding Connor for asking his client questions but he decided to let sleeping dogs lie. The process called for Dan the investigator to ask the questions, not the respondent's lawyer.

"She told me she had just broken up with her boyfriend. She said he had hit her couple of times. The last time she obtained a Domestic Violence Order against him and the police threw him out of the house. She said the break up had been difficult and that despite the Domestic Violence Order specifying he couldn't come within one hundred metres of her house, he still had come over a few times to see her. She was scared of him."

"So tell me what happened – you were drinking together after everyone else had left?" Dan asked, seeking to regain control of the interview.

"We had a drink and then I went to the toilet. When I came back her behaviour changed completely. She seemed out of it. Her eyes were bloodshot and she was slurring her words. She told me she was feeling sick.

"I could see she was going downhill quickly, so I decided to take her home. I helped her downstairs to the basement car park where I had parked my car. I asked her where she lived but she couldn't tell me, so I looked inside her bag and found her license."

"Why didn't you just call her a cab?"

"She was not looking too good at this stage. She was floating in and out of cognitive thought. I didn't think it was fair to wash my hands of her and put her at the mercy of some unknown taxi driver. I will never do it again, but I went out of my way to take her home so she would be safe. I thought I was helping her; looking out for her."

"Tell him about the plastic bag. That is very *relevant*!" Connor interjected.

"When I looked inside her handbag for her license I noticed a small crumpled plastic bag. Inside the bag there appeared to be a couple of tablets. They looked like illegal drugs, you know party drugs."

"What did you think was happening?" Connor interjected again.

Dan knew Connor couldn't help himself; asking leading questions of his client to ensure that his client tendered all the evidence he had, to put his best case forward. However, he was interested in Samuel's answer to this question so he let it go.

"I wondered if she had taken some drug while I was in the toilet," answered Samuel.

"So what happened then?" Dan asked.

"I drove her home and I let myself in using a key I found in her handbag. I carried her to her bed, took off her shoes and left her there."

"Go on?"

"I placed a blanket over her so she wouldn't get cold.

"Tell him what she said to you as you were leaving," Connor again interjected.

"She mumbled something about wanting me to stay with her - to have sex with her. I didn't respond. I just got the hell out of there.

"Look, at all times I behaved appropriately around Mia Wong. I thought I was doing the right thing by taking her home and making sure she was safe."

"How has this complaint affected you?"

"This complaint has already caused me great embarrassment at work; mud sticks with a complaint like this and I believe my reputation will forever be tarnished by these crazy allegations against me. I feel devastated and wronged by this complaint. Fortunately for me my wife supports me, though she is very upset with Mia for making these untruthful allegations."

"Can you give me any reason why Mia would make up such a serious allegation against you?" Dan asked, anxious to hear Samuel's response.

"Honestly, I don't know what is motivating her. Perhaps she hallucinated after taking the drugs. Perhaps the trauma of her violent break up with her boyfriend got to her. Perhaps it's because I wouldn't have sex with her. I don't know, I wish I did."

"Alright, is there anything else you want to say?"

Samuel shook his head and said, "No."

Now the moment that Dan had been dreading. He realized that he could not complete this interview without letting Connor make some submissions and have the final say. After all, that is what he had been paid to do.

"Mr Mead, is there anything you want to add?" Dan asked quietly in the unlikely hope Connor may not hear him and they all could go home.

Connor didn't need to be asked twice.

"I have never been so appalled at the treatment of a client in my professional life," Connor announced with all the moral indignation he could summon.

"My client has been subjected to a scurrilous and totally baseless complaint and investigation without any proper regard for the law, his personal well being or his reputation. He is cross-examined without first knowing the full details of the allegations of what he was supposed to have done to this girl, his lawyer is not allowed to advocate on his behalf while he is being interviewed and his past is sought to be dragged up to railroad him into a conviction."

Dan looked down, put his hand over his eyebrows and rolled his eyes. Connor had to take a breath soon, surely.

"I want to make this point quite clearly – my client has at all times acted appropriately in his dealings with this woman and as there is no independent evidence to the contrary, he must be found not guilty.

"Also, as this alleged incident happened outside working hours, the police should be involved, not the company. If this *lady*, and I use the term loosely, believes that my client has sexually assaulted her, then the proper forum to determine her complaint is before the courts, not some tin pot corporate investigation."

Dan stared at the table and hoped Connor was coming to an end.

"I expect instructions from my client and his wife to institute defamation proceedings against this tramp. Therefore be aware that any decision reached by you and the company will in all likelihood be struck down by the court in our defamation action.

"Perhaps you should make the young woman aware of this fact, in case she feels in light of the proposed defamation action against her, that she should now withdraw her complaint against my client. It's obvious as the nose on my face that she is just after money."

Connor ended his tirade with a thud of his fist against the table. It was quite the performance.

Dan was initially numb, but recovered enough to shake everybody's hand good bye, open the office door and see Connor, Samuel and Samuel's wife leave the foyer via the elevator.

He sat back down; he had to settle his heart rate. He had just been subjected to an encounter with Connor Mead.

He reflected that Connor's *modus operandi* was clearly intimidation. Dan did not respond well to intimidation; he never did and never would. It was just something in his make up which rebelled against intimidation and bullying.

It would be easy to just dismiss Connor's submissions as intimidatory hot air, but he had made some relevant points Dan needed to check out. Also Dan had to work hard to ensure he treated Samuel with all fairness and not take a set against him because of Connor's disgraceful behaviour.

As he left the beautiful foyer of Dodsworth, Blainey and Parker, overlooking the Brisbane River, Dan made a mental note to never, ever become a lawyer like Connor Mead. Connor was so effused with his own self-importance that he had no other way of resolving conflict than by intimidation. He wondered if Connor was even aware of his own intimidatory behaviour, probably not. Empathy and self-reflection were just not part of Connor Mead's DNA.

CHAPTER EIGHT

The next day Dan went to see Claye at the Wesley Hospital.

The weather had turned bitterly cold, as cold as it could be in Brisbane. As Dan drove next to the magnificent Brisbane River, he could see many white tuffs on the river blown up by the ferocious westerly wind.

In reality Brisbane never got below 10 degrees centigrade in the daytime in winter but today with the wind chill factor, it was freezing. Dan's thick mat of brown hair was tossed about his face and he struggled to keep his hands warm as he walked to the hospital.

He entered Claye's room and noticed immediately that it was dark and that Claye was alone. He wondered why Claye had only a few lights on. There was a small chair on one side of his bed and a large recliner chair on the other side. Dan sat on the recliner chair and looked over at Claye.

Claye had an intravenous drip feeding into a catheter located at the top of his chest. Plus, Claye had several other tubes from his IV running into his wrist. He wondered how Claye could sleep with all the tubes that were being fed into his body.

Claye looked pale and unwell. He was asleep but woke up a few minutes after Dan arrived.

"Good to see you, mate," Claye said as he pushed the button on his bed to move it into a sitting up position.

"How are you feeling?"

"Well, I have been better."

"When is the stem cell transplant?"

"I am not sure. They have just been pumping me with chemo at this stage. The idea is to kill off the cancer cells before they do the transplant."

"I must say you are a pretty lucky guy to be able to get rid of your own defective stem cells and replace them with my superior breed," Dan said.

"Yeah, mate, I feel like a real lucky guy," Claye replied with more than a dollop of sarcasm.

"What's it like?" Dan asked out of curiosity, though with no real conviction. He actually didn't want to know too many of the details.

"Well, I am hooked to an intravenous machine 24 hours a day – I can't go anywhere without it.

"The chemo they are giving me not only kills the cancer cells but all the other fast growing cells in my body. Hence my hair is falling out.

"Nausea is always present, but they give me anti-nausea drugs, so that's not so bad. But the anti-nausea drugs give me diarrhoea, so I am always on the toilet.

"The worst thing for me at the moment is my mouth ulcers. My throat feels like it has razor blades in it and it is painful to swallow, not to mention I have lost my sense of taste.

"Also, the nurses check on you and take your blood pressure every couple of hours, so deep sleep is impossible. Seriously, mate, I wouldn't wish this on anybody."

Dan didn't know what to say.

"The only thing I can think of as being worse than what I am going through at the moment, is being a Cronulla Sharks supporter," Claye said in a deadpan manner but with the hint of a smile coming through at the end.

"Ahhh, mate," Dan said as he shook his head and laughed. "I was almost feeling sorry for you."

He was glad the topic of conversation had switched to football rather than Claye's cancer, and he was relieved Claye had not lost his sense of humour.

Dan said, "It's really disappointing they are playing so badly. Rugby league like any team sport is all about eliminating mistakes and building pressure; I can't see why the Sharks can't do that. You only have to watch the Melbourne Storm to see how they win games by building pressure."

"Mate, how is my case going? You haven't botched it have you?"

"It is an interesting case alright. Actually, I need your help on a few issues."

Claye sparked up on hearing this.

"The first issue is that I have two very believable people telling me completely different stories. There is no direct evidence to support either one of them. This may be a case of he said/she said and we have to leave it at that?"

"I have never investigated a case I could not solve," replied Claye . "In my experience there is always evidence to support one version as being more likely to be true, than the other version. Remember we don't have to determine the matter as a 100% certainty as to what happened. Unless the whole incident was videotaped we could never achieve that amount of certainty. All we have to do is decide the matter on the balance of probabilities – which version of events is more likely to be true."

"But it's just one person's word against the other, how can we take it any further?" asked Dan.

"Mate, that's why we have been called in. If the matter was easy to resolve – say they had an eye-witness, then they wouldn't need us to investigate it.

"What you have to do is look closely at the indirect evidence; that will lead you to who is telling the truth and who is telling lies. Particularly in sexual harassment cases, there is usually an absence of direct evidence, but there is always indirect evidence that will reveal what actually happened."

"What indirect evidence should I be looking for?"

"Things like recent complaint. What did the complainant say to the first people she saw after the incident happened, and what state of mind was she in at this time?

"Anything else?" asked Dan.

"Another point to consider is why would the complainant make up this complaint? In my experience women don't often make up sexual harassment claims against their male colleagues. Most people do not want to make a complaint against another work colleague, let alone make a serious sexual harassment complaint. Is there any legitimate reason why the complainant would invent these sexual harassment allegations?"

"Wow, Claye, you are not just a pretty face?" Dan remarked.

"Another important issue is pattern of behavior. By the time I investigate a sexual harassment complaint, if the respondent is guilty, he is likely to have harassed other women in the workplace previously. I have never investigated the first sexual harassment complaint against them. What is the respondent's pattern of behavior in dealing with other women in the workplace? Previous concerns or complaints against him can lead to the conclusion that if he has done it before, he is likely to do it again."

"Well, you really know your stuff in this area," Dan said. He was genuinely impressed. Perhaps he had underestimated Claye in other areas of life as well.

"Mate, I am a Grover; we are good at what we do."

Dan nodded his head. He really couldn't argue with that statement.

Bing, bing, bing, bing, bing.....

"Mate, there are a still couple of other questions I have for you, are you ok to talk about them now?" Dan asked. He was trying to ignore the piercing binging noise emanating from Claye's intravenous drip, which was wailing loudly for attention.

"Don't mind that noise; it goes on like that all the time. It just means that the chemo is finished or there is a blockage in the line. A nurse will be here to fix it soon."

"It's a bit hard to concentrate with that noise," Dan replied.

Just then Dan heard another machine go off in another room – *bing, bing, bing.....*

Fortunately, a nurse came and restored peace to Claye's room. One of the IV lines had become clogged and by flicking the line, the chemo was running freely again. Claye's intravenous machine was now quiet and happy.

After the nurse had left, Dan spoke. "I had an interesting and difficult interview with the respondent, mainly because Connor Mead was throwing his weight around."

"Who is Connor Mead?" asked Claye.

"He is a well known lawyer around town who thinks too highly of himself and too little of everybody else. Anyway, Connor did make a couple of points I want to discuss with you."

Just then another nurse came through the door and announced she had to take Claye's blood pressure. Dan stopped talking and watched. The nurse was obviously English by her accent.

"Dorothy, this is my brother Dan," Claye said.

"Pleased to meet you, Dan."

He nodded and smiled.

"Do you realize you have a very brave brother here? He never complains, just takes his medicine and smiles," Dorothy said.

He nodded again speechless. He was speechless because Dorothy's smile was particularly bright and cheerful, and because he had never ever thought of Claye as being particularly brave. The scales were falling off his eyes regarding his elder brother and he was seeing him in a whole new light.

As Dorothy was taking Claye's temperature and blood pressure, Claye turned to Dorothy and said, "Mate, don't worry about my little brother, he can talk, but I think your beauty has made him speechless."

Dorothy smiled, Dan blushed, and Claye chuckled having successfully embarrassed both of them.

Dorothy then turned to Dan and asked, "Is he always as incorrigible as this?"

Dan had seemingly lost the ability to speak by this time. He just nodded and grunted in the affirmative in response to Dorothy's question. Nothing more was said as Dorothy finished what she had come to do and left.

"As I was saying…"

"He speaks!"

"…as I was saying, I have a couple of issues that I need your learned guidance on.

"Firstly, the respondent allegedly slipped the complainant a date rape drug after work hours but on work premises, and then he allegedly sexually assaulted her in his car. Is it really a matter that we should deal with? It would appear to be more of a police matter, given the inappropriate conduct allegedly took place outside the context of work."

"If the complainant does not want to go to the police, I believe the company should investigate it. That's even if the inappropriate conduct occurred outside the context of work," answered Claye.

"Why do you say that?"

"As I understand the complaint, it involves a young female employee alleging a more senior male colleague took advantage of her and abused his position of trust with her. Now that such a serious complaint has been made, the workplace there can never be the same. For the benefit of the workplace, the company needs to know what happened and what they can do to address the situation.

"Also does the company really want someone like the respondent, assuming he is guilty, working for them if he is going to take advantage of their young female employees?"

"Ok, fair enough. Secondly, Connor Mead told me that his client was going to sue the complainant for defamation over the sexual harassment complaint she has made against him. How does that fit in with our investigation? I mean, I don't want to be caught in the middle of litigation just because I have been asked to investigate something?"

"Mate, the fact that the respondent may or may not sue a complainant for defamation is irrelevant to our investigation. We do our job properly to the best of our ability, regardless of any external pressure such as the threat of any legal action. What are we supposed to do, run away and hide with our tail between our legs because we might at some point be called to account for how we conducted the investigation?" Claye said passionately.

"Connor Mead virtually insisted that I tell the complainant that his client was going to sue her for defamation and that she be given the opportunity of withdrawing her complaint, rather than being sued. Should I do this?"

"No. The respondent's threat of defamation is probably just an attempt to intimidate the complainant to withdraw the complaint. We should not be party to that intimidation. If the respondent and his lawyers want to intimidate the complainant in this way, then let them do that themselves, without us having to do the dirty work for them."

"Ok, makes sense. What do I do now?"

"You should contact the workplace witnesses to discover the indirect evidence, put the respondent's version of events to the complainant and then get back to me," Claye said.

Dan nodded. There was a moment of silence between the two brothers.

"Mate, thanks again for doing this investigation for me. You've helped me out heaps by agreeing to donate your stems cells and now looking after this investigation. I don't know what I would have done without you, little brother."

"No worries, mate, I would have done the same for a blind beggar." At that moment he wanted to tell Claye how impressive he was, but he couldn't say those types of things to his elder brother.

As Dan left the oncology ward he could hear the continual wailing of many intravenous machines crying out for attention and he was glad he was healthy. Dan paused momentarily outside the hospital chapel, and without thinking, thanked God for his good health.

That was strange he thought. He had never really prayed before. Perhaps Claye was having more of an effect on him than he had realized.

CHAPTER NINE

The day arrived that Dan had been dreading. He was dreading it more than another meeting with Connor Mead, and that was saying something. Today was his first marriage counselling session.

Anita Blunt was the marriage counsellor. She was dressed modestly in plain colours (brown, beige, grey). There was nothing out there in Anita's appearance and she blended right into the landscape.

Dan was pleasantly surprised at how well everything went at marriage counselling. Rather than focus on their issues of concern, Anita had them focusing on why they got together in the first place.

Anita explained that when couples first get together there is this rush of excitement and electricity. It's all about making the other person happy. But after a few years the excitement and electricity fades and couples become much more self-centred. This may lead to unresolved conflict and anger, which may lead to bitterness and resentment.

Once there is bitterness and resentment in a marriage, it is difficult to save the relationship. Anything one person says or does is viewed by the other person as wrong, condescending or arrogant. They just don't want to be around that person any longer.

Bitterness and resentment in a relationship hides from view the very qualities that made couples want to live with each other in the first place. In Anita's experience people didn't change much. They can become set in their ways but their value systems, who they are and what they stand for, changes very little over time.

Anita told them the cornerstone to a successful relationship was the ability to resolve conflict, and the key to resolving conflict was putting the other person first. As soon as your focus was not to win the argument with your partner but to make them happy, everything changes.

This information came as a revelation for both Dan and Elise.

They were not lost in a barren desert of a bad relationship, they were just going through a dry patch. By being less self-centred and focusing more on what they could do for each other, all would be right with the world again. Could it be that simple?

As they drove home together Dan thought about Elise. She was like a tiger. Beautiful, fun loving, unpredictable, though not without claws.

He turned towards Elise and said matter of factly, "Do you know how beautiful you are?"

Elise smiled and responded, "Well, I don't really know about that."

"You are beautiful, inside and out. I am very lucky to have you in my life," Dan replied with some conviction.

Dan looked over to Elise and saw her blushing. Her auburn hair and complexion made blushing something that she just could not hide.

"I just wanted to tell you that. I know I have not complimented you very much lately," Dan said sincerely.

"Well, you shape up pretty well yourself. You're handsome, and I love your smile and sense of humour," Elise said smiling.

Dan returned the smile but was slightly embarrassed by the compliment. "I feel better already for coming here today," he pronounced.

"Can you guess what I am feeling right now?"

Elise unbuckled her seat belt and moved close to Dan. She kissed him and tenderly put her arm around him.

"Elise, I am driving," Dan said with mock indignation.

"So pull over, why not be spontaneous?"

"What, just pull over on the side of the road?"

"Why not, have you got something better to do?"

"I like the way you are thinking but we will be home in ten minutes."

"I thought you had some important interviews to get to after dropping me at home."

"I have, but they can wait. I have to do something more important than work. I have to spend some quality time with my beautiful wife."

Elise laughed and said, "Well, hurry up then, we don't want to lose the mood."

He put his foot to the floor and sped home. He definitely didn't want to lose the mood.

He rejoiced that he really had a tiger on his hands.

After his mid-morning manoeuvres with Elise, Dan pulled out of his driveway and hurried off to the local police station. As he drove down his street, he happened to notice a white Commodore parked nearby. As he sped past the Commodore, he saw that there was someone in the car but this person crouched down as he went by.

That was strange he thought. Why would someone sit in a parked car in a suburban street? And why would the driver crouch down so he could not see them?

His mind immediately turned to the warning he had received from the bikies and his forthcoming appointment with the police. He could be just imagining things but perhaps his sighting of the car was meant to be a warning to him, to keep his mouth shut. But how could the bikies possibly know he was on his way to be interviewed by the police?

He didn't like to be intimidated but at this time he had to think of Elise, not just himself.

Dan was of course running late for his interview with Senior Constable Mario Bartlett. He was older than Dan but not by much. His sky blue uniform was neat and creased to perfection. His light coloured sandy hair was cut short and precisely arranged, and he sported a perfectly trimmed moustache.

Senior Constable Bartlett turned on the video recording device in the sterile interview room and began the interview. He stated his name, asked Dan to do the same. He provided Dan with the required warning that anything he said could be used in evidence against him, asked Dan to provide some background details, such as his address and what he did for a living, and then got straight to the matters at hand.

"I am investigating a complaint that has been made regarding the kidnapping of a baby girl, named Emma Paschetelle a few days ago. I am also investigating a related matter being the assault of Emma's father. What do you know about these complaints?

Dan then recounted the story of how he came to rescue the baby, not kidnap her.

"So, for the record, are you saying that Alyssa Paschetelle asked you to retrieve her baby," Constable Bartlett asked.

"Yes, that was the clear impression I had from her."

"To physically assault and restrain her husband, if that was necessary to take the baby off him?"

"Well, we didn't have a long conversation about it. I had been told that he was very angry about the marriage break up. He had obviously been waiting for her. He slapped her, knocked her to the ground and kicked her while she was down. He forcibly took the baby from her. I formed the impression he was not a nice guy, but I honestly did not think at the time about how I was going to get the baby off him if he would not cooperate."

"How did you get the baby back?"

"I ran after Alyssa's husband as he ran from me. We eventually stopped at the shopping centre basement car park. I asked him to return the baby and he refused. He then started to walk away and I moved in front of him. He then pushed me out of his way and I stumbled and fell to the ground."

"Then what happened?"

"At that point two burly guys appeared from nowhere. They asked what was going on and I told them. Alyssa's husband then told them in no uncertain terms to get out of his way and one of them hit him twice, while the other took the baby and handed her over to me."

"Did you ask these guys to hit Mr Paschetelle?"

"No, I did not ask them to hit him and I did not want them to hit him."

"What did you want them to do?"

"I suppose I would have appreciated them asking Alyssa's husband to hand the baby over to me."

"Mr Paschetelle says that you told these guys to hit him."

"No, I didn't tell them to hit him. It was more a case of him swearing at them which I think, motivated them to hit him."

"Did you know these guys?"

"I didn't know them."

"Mr Paschetelle believes these two guys were bikies; members of the *Vandals*. Is that true?"

Dan hesitated before answering.

"They weren't wearing bikie colours – you know it's illegal these days – so it's hard to tell."

"What did they look like?"

"There was a tall one and a short one. They both had tattoos. One had long hair and the other one was bald. Look it all happened so fast, I am not sure if I could even identify them now, even if I saw them again."

"Are you sure about that?" Senior Constable Bartlett asked, apparently sensing that he may not be getting the full story from Dan.

He thought for a moment. There was no point dobbing the bikies into the police. He didn't appreciate being stood over by them, but for Elise's sake and his sake, nothing would be gained from describing them to the police at this time.

"Yeah, that's all I can help you with at the moment. I just can't remember anything more about them."

"Is there anything else you would like to say?"

"No, that's all."

"Alright, we will now complete the interview." Mario Bartlett turned off the video equipment.

"Mario, what's going to happen from here?" Dan asked pensively.

"I will take all the evidence to my superiors and they will decide if there is to be any charges laid or not. On the face of it, without the alleged bikies, it's really your word against the Paschetelles and I am not sure we would take their word over yours."

"Why thanks, Mario, I didn't know you cared?"

"We have had many call outs to the Paschetelles over the years and we know what they are like. They are volatile and constantly at each other's throats. They call us and then they make up and withdraw their complaints against each other, wasting our time. So confidentially, I don't think you have too much to worry about with this matter."

Well that was a relief. With Elise happy again and their relationship mending, the sexual harassment investigation earning much needed fees for his fledgling legal practice, and the bikies off his back with the unlikelihood of him or them being charged over rescuing Alyssa's baby; his life was once again going great.

Though he hesitated to use the word *great*. He had experienced enough of life to know that whenever anyone said their life was great, that things couldn't get any better; then within a very short time some part of their life was likely to be falling apart. Somehow that was just the way life worked. You couldn't boast about being happy, you just had to be happy.

CHAPTER TEN

After interviewing several Dodsworth Blainey and Parker staff members yesterday, Dan was glad that today he was out and about interviewing Mia Wong in the pleasant confines of the *Coffee Mug* coffee shop at Spring Hill. He actually arrived early, some five minutes before their scheduled 11:00am meeting time to secure a discreet table at the back of the coffee shop.

By 11:15am, Dan had finished his tall black coffee and his favourite lemon coconut slice, but Mia was nowhere to be seen. He was frustrated that Mia had not arrived, perhaps she was not coming. He checked his feelings of frustration, realising that in the past he had left people waiting for him.

Just then Mia arrived, looking bewildered and a little disheveled. She looked around the coffee shop and did not see Dan sitting at the back table. Mia ordered from the counter, then sat down at a table in the middle of the coffee shop. He looked at Mia. She was certainly attractive. Not super model attractive but nice, friendly attractive.

He stood up and motioned for her to join him at his table.

"Sorry I am late. As I walked here from my house I saw a car accident. I went over to check if everyone was alright. I actually saw some Brisbane Broncos players there helping out as well."

"Was anyone injured?"

"Not seriously. They were all a bit shaken but fine."

The waitress brought over Mia's coffee and there was a period of silence between them. It appeared pleasantries had finished.

"Mia, I need to talk to you about what Samuel said happened last Friday night."

"I don't know if I want to hear this," Mia said through a pained expression.

"We will see how we go. If you don't feel up to it at any stage, let me know."

Mia cautiously nodded her head.

"Samuel said that you asked him to stay on for one more drink after everybody else had left."

"No, he asked me to stay for one more drink," Mia said with some emphasis.

"Samuel saw a crumpled plastic bag in your handbag. He said the plastic bag contained some tablets, possibly party drugs."

"Oh my, God! I can't believe I am hearing this!" Mia exclaimed suddenly, shaking her head and raising her voice.

"This is….. I can't believe he would say that."

"Mia, I need an answer," Dan said quietly.

"An answer – of course I didn't have any drugs in my handbag. I don't do drugs. I just can't believe he would even make that up about me. Oh man, he is some piece of work!"

"Did you have a plastic bag in your handbag?"

"No."

"Samuel said that after he went to the toilet late in the evening, you started to lose it. Your eyes were bloodshot and you were slurring your words. You were not well. He then assisted you to his car and drove you home. He denies undressing you or touching you inappropriately in his car.

"He claims he was just looking after you and at all times he acted appropriately."

Mia's eyes were moistening and closing. Her hands had firmly grasped the table.

"He is lying. I don't know if I can stand to hear anymore of this," Mia said.

Mia was visibly agitated but Dan had to ask one more question.

"Samuel said that at your house, you asked him to have sex with you, is that true?"

"Oh my God!" Mia exclaimed.

She was almost hyperventilating.

He decided not to press Mia for a more accurate response.

He wondered if Mia was so naïve to think that she could fire such a serious complaint against someone and not expect that they would throw some dirt back at her.

"Mia, just to wrap up, can you tell me about your ex-boyfriend? I am only asking as Samuel said you talked to him about your ex-boyfriend and that you had obtained a Domestic Violence Order against him."

"What has my ex-boyfriend got to do with all this?"

"Samuel is saying that you told him your ex-boyfriend had been violent towards you. I suppose Samuel is implying that the trauma you may have suffered from your ex-boyfriend's violent behaviour towards you and your subsequent break up, could have contributed to you believing that Samuel has done something inappropriate to you."

Mia turned her head to one side and took several deep breaths. Eventually Mia turned back to answer the question

"Look, Brock and I had a difficult relationship. When he gets drunk he can get aggressive and smash walls. A couple of times he hit me. He had a difficult childhood. I know he was into drugs and in trouble with the police before he met me. But most of the time he was with me he was loving and generous. He was my first real boyfriend and we lived together for 12 months. Ultimately, I just could not take his erratic behaviour anymore and I ended it.

"The last time Brock was drunk he pushed me against the wall and threatened to bash me. I went to the police and got a Domestic Violence Order against him. End of story. My problems with Brock have absolutely nothing to do with what Samuel Sanderson did to me."

"Ok, thanks Mia. That completes the interview." Dan turned his digital recorder off and looked at Mia. She looked like a young lady who had been having a very hard time of life lately.

"You saw some of the Brisbane Broncos players, wow!"

Mia did not respond.

"Did you get any autographs?"

"No, I didn't see the point."

"I don't believe in getting autographs either. We don't get autographs from great doctors, or great scientists, or great politicians; so why do we get autographs from people good at sports? Why do we as a society put people on a pedestal just because they are good at sport, or music, or acting?"

"Great politicians?" Mia's demeanor visibly loosened and she broke into a faint smile as she posed this question.

"Well great politicians is stretching my point, but you see what I mean. Just because you are good at playing sport, singing or acting, why should someone want to get your autograph? Aren't there more important skills we as a society should value and be placing on a pedestal?"

"I agree with you but my father wouldn't. He is a fanatical Cronulla

Sharks fan in Sydney. He wouldn't like you criticizing rugby league players."

"Cronulla Sharks fan, well that is amazing. I am a Cronulla Sharks fan myself; have been since I was a kid."

"You do realize the Sharks have never won a premiership, don't you?"

"Yes, I am only too aware of that fact. But hey what a day, what a year, it will be when we win that first premiership. It will be something very special. I can't wait to proudly wear my Sharks jersey when we are premiers."

"Good things come to those who wait, my father always says. You stick with your team no matter what happens."

"Hey, that's what I always say! Your old man sounds pretty smart. It's good to know there are other like minded Sharks fans out there."

"As a Sharks fan living in Queensland, are you a cane toad or a cockroach?" Mia asked.

"A proud Queensland supporter," replied Dan. "You're not a cockroach are you?"

"Afraid so. What is it with you Queenslanders and the State of Origin anyway?"

"Let me explain." Dan moved to the edge of his seat and clasped his hands together. He took a few moments to compose himself before he began to dispense his words of wisdom.

"It all started many years ago when New South Wales with the aid of poker machine money, kept buying all of Queensland best players to play in their competition. Queensland would get beaten by New South Wales because New South Wales would use the ex-Queensland players as well as their own players. These defeats went on for year, after year, after year.

"Eventually Queensland was able to convince New South Wales to participate in a State of Origin competition, where you played for the State you were born in, not the State you were playing in. This led to teammates playing with each other in club teams one week, and then playing against each other in the State of Origin the next week. Many people thought the concept wouldn't work, mate playing against mate. But it did and how it did. As you know the passion in these contests has to be seen to be believed.

"Queenslanders in particular wake up with a smile on their face every time they beat New South Wales. This is because New South Wales always think they are better than us, they have this huge superiority complex. We have to keep beating them until they realize they are not better than us."

Dan having laid his proud Queensland heart out, then eased back into his seat. His mind wandered to the mascots of these two great passionate teams, pests. Unlikable, unkillable, tough and highly resilient pests, such as cane toads for Queensland and cockroaches for New South Wales.

"You realise you won't win the State of Origin series this year. We will be too good for you in the final game," Mia said with a glint in her eye.

"You keep dreaming. New South Wales can never match our team spirit."

"Really." Mia smiled again, this time it was more than an apprehensive smile, it was a relaxed, happy smile.

"Dan, can I talk with you about something off the record?"

It was the first time Mia had called him by his first name. They were getting on well and he was intrigued where she was going with this. What else could he say to her but, "Yeah."

"Over the last few days I have felt like I am being followed and watched all the time. Yesterday I ran through the underpass at the park terrified that somebody was out there, watching me.

"I have not seen anybody but there have been little things like the neighbour's dog barking a lot, my letterbox being left open and no one on the line when my phone rings. I didn't really think too much of it until I found a note this morning. It had been pushed under my door last night."

Mia opened her handbag and handed a piece of paper to Dan. He read the note which comprised of letters cut out of a magazine. The note simply contained the words:

Trollop

Leave town now or die

"Have you taken this note to the police?" Dan asked.

"I have called them about it but they didn't seem too interested."

"What did they say?"

"The police told me they would talk to Brock about it. They believe he was responsible for it. But why would Brock threaten me about leaving Brisbane? It doesn't make sense."

"Did the police saying anything else?"

"The police told me that they couldn't do anything for me until something actually happens. But what good is that to me, if the police won't do anything until after I am hurt or killed. I don't think the police are very interested in my problems."

"Can you move out of your house or get someone to come over and stay with you until this is sorted out?" asked Dan.

"I am new in Brisbane. I really only have one friend here. Jazz, is a single mother with three young kids to look after. Living with Jazz and her family would be very difficult and I can't ask that of her.

"Anyway, why should I have to move out of my own home when I have done nothing wrong?"

"What's the story with Brock?" Dan asked. He realized he may have been getting in over his head with this question but he had to ask it.

"I don't think Brock sent the note but I can't be sure. The DVO states Brock is not to come within a hundred metres of my place."

"Has he breached the DVO by coming over to your place since the order was made?"

"A couple of times he has come over to get his things without my permission but he has not been violent. He wants to get back with me."

"I am not sure what you can do about the situation, Mia, other than to be careful and call the police or a friend if you see anything out of the ordinary."

Mia turned to Dan. "I know I might be asking a lot of you Dan when I don't really know you, but you seem like a nice guy and I wouldn't ask if I didn't really need your help."

There she was using Dan's first name again.

"I would really, really appreciate if I could call you if something happens. I need someone to help me through this and I just don't want to involve Jazz. Will you help me? There may be nothing in this but it would help me sleep at night if I knew you were only a phone call away if something happened."

Dan knew better than to get involved in a client's personal life. Particularly where Mia was the complainant in a case he was still investigating. Dan instinctively knew that any friendship or help provided to Mia was dangerous and left him open to allegations of bias. In the circumstances there was only one answer he could possibly give Mia.

"Sure, happy to help."

There was something about her which made it impossible for him to provide the logical, rational answer of *No*. She looked vulnerable, concerned, in need and he just had to help her out.

Mia reached out her hand and touched his wrist and said, "Thanks Dan, thank you so much. I know you have gone out on a limb for me here, I really appreciate it."

The suddenness of her touch made Dan take a deep breath. All of a sudden he felt his heart beating rapidly. He was shocked to feel this way.

After what seemed an eternity, Mia slid her hand from Dan's wrist, touching his hand on the way back to the table.

"Well I have to go now, good-bye."

He did not say good-bye, he was still in shock but he did find the strength to nod his head and smile as Mia was leaving.

All of a sudden he felt excited at the prospect of seeing her again; of not knowing what would happen if he did see her again.

Wait a minute. Had he forgotten he was married?

He decided not to think about Mia and how excited he had felt about the prospect of possibly seeing her again. After all, he didn't even know Mia. He was just helping her out. He probably would never see her again anyway.

CHAPTER ELEVEN

Dan found Claye wandering the hallways of the oncology ward holding onto his new best friend, his intravenous drip on wheels. It looked as though Claye's grip on the IV unit was so tight that he was holding onto it for dear life, perhaps he was.

"Claye, how are you feeling?"

"Mate, good to see ya. How's our little investigation going?"

"I have pretty much wrapped it up. I just need to tie up a few loose ends with you and then do the report. But first, how are you going?"

"Well, I am almost finished my chemo. It won't be long now till I need your stem cells. I hope you are looking after them for me."

"Yeah, they are doing just fine at the moment."

"The nurses will let you know when they need you to come in and donate your stem cells."

Dan nodded then changed the subject.

"As for the investigation, I have talked to everyone and I am reasonably certain about what happened but I want to run it past you first. Get an objective point of view."

"Why, are you having trouble being objective?"

Why did Claye ask that?

"No, of course not! As this is my first investigation I would like to run it past you, that's all."

"Alright, let's have it."

"The complainant, Mia Wong, told a friend of hers about the complaint the day after it happened. The friend, Jazz Carlon, states that Mia was in a distressed and agitated state at the time.

"In terms of recent complaint, Mia ticks that box well and truly."

"There appears to be no logical reason why Mia would make this complaint unless it was true. The respondent, Samuel Sanderson, has suggested it is because he rejected her request for sex. However, the only evidence of Mia actually asking Samuel for sex comes from Samuel. There is no corroborating evidence."

Claye nodded as though taking it all in.

"Samuel also suggested Mia might be suffering trauma associated from her recent break up with a violent ex-boyfriend. While this is a possible theory, there is no evidence to back it up.

"I interviewed ten women at the workplace. Some women think Samuel is sleazy and others quite like him. Although the pattern of behavioural evidence is conflicting, overall it does suggest a concern with the way Samuel treats women."

Dan stopped momentarily to get his breath.

"Samuel said that he found a small plastic bag which he believes contained party drugs in Mia's handbag. He believes that she drugged herself.

"Mia denied possessing any party drugs or taking any drugs. Mia was in absolute shock when I told her what Samuel had said about her taking drugs."

Dan again paused in his story as he prepared to announce his verdict.

"Therefore, having carefully considered and evaluated all the evidence, I believe it is more likely than not, that Mia is telling the truth with respect to her complaint against Samuel Sanderson. There is just no logical reason for her to make up this complaint."

Claye did not respond, but seemed lost in thought.

"What do you think?" Dan asked.

"Mate, I think you have done a fantastic job with this investigation. You have left me in no doubt that the complainant's version of events is the one that is more likely to be true. Well done!"

"Well it was elementary really. I just followed the evidence trail. Mia was a particularly impressive witness."

"Good job."

"Claye, our finding against his client is really going to upset Connor Mead. You know he might come after us in court."

"What do you mean us, *paleface*? It's you he will go after, not me."

"You know some people think blood is thicker than water," Dan said dryly.

"If one of the consequences of making the right finding is being sued, then so be it. We can't be intimidated by lawyers or threats of legal action. We are not doing our jobs, if we are going to be worried that the person we find against, isn't going to like us. We must determine the truth of the matter regardless of the consequences.

"In life, the consequences of lying are always worse, than the consequences of telling the truth," Claye said with conviction.

He wasn't sure if he agreed with Claye on that point. Sometimes in life you had to lie to protect yourself or other people who may be hurt by the truth.

"Mate, there is one thing I need to talk to you about, it's quite concerning actually."

Dan's ears pricked up at this comment. He had not told Claye about his agreement to help Mia, or the excitement that role seemed to grip him with at the time, or the fact he found it hard not to think about her. He wasn't keen for Claye to know about that. She probably would never call him anyway.

"What's on your mind, Claye?" Dan said as casually as he could muster.

"Mate, those Cronulla Sharks of yours just keep losing. Mate that team could not play their way out of a paper bag. You might as well believe in the tooth fairy as she will bring you more joy than the Sharks. How can an intelligent, good looking guy like you continue to support those losers?"

Dan sighed. "Mate, all they need is a competent and consistent front office, a good coach and to recruit players other clubs actually want, not also-rans. You will see they will come good next year – I have a really good feeling about next year."

"Sure mate sure, they will come good next season," Claye whispered raising his eyebrows. "By the way how is Elise?"

"She is good."

"You both getting on alright?"

"Yes, why do you ask?"

"Well, I was just praying the other night and I felt this real ache to pray for both of you. It was as though God was telling me both of you were on his mind."

Dan was cut by this remark.

"Mate, on my laptop last night I saw this Christian skit on You Tube. It was performed in Knoxville, Tennessee in 2006 to the song *Everything* by Lifehouse. You have to see it. It is the most amazing skit I have ever seen! It makes me cry every time I see it. It graphically shows God's love towards us and how he protects and pulls us back to him, even if we stray away from him and do our own thing. Seriously, mate, it is awesome!"

"Yeah, when I get a chance to have a look at it I will," Dan said as convincingly as he could.

"Ok, mate, I am feeling a bit tired. Keep looking after those stem cells for me."

Dan left the hospital feeling uneasy with Claye's words. He did not really believe in God. Yet he felt concerned that God was supposedly telling Claye to pray for him and Elise.

*

"Umm, that was good!" Gloria exclaimed as she licked her fingers clean.

"Thanks for that, Danny."

"You're not worried about eating something like that?" Dan asked.

"I know it's not good for my thighs, but life is too short not to enjoy the things you really like doing. And I really like doing jam donuts!"

"Gloria, now that I have your undivided attention, can you catch me up on what has been happening in the office while I have been out investigating?"

"It's been pretty quiet actually, though today I heard that Legal Aid has knocked back funding for Fay Castle's appeal."

Dan hung his head. "That's a blow. I wonder why they knocked her back, she has merit."

"Can she pay for her own appeal? Gloria asked.

"No, she has no money. She is a single parent just trying to survive in today's economy."

"Yeah, I know what that is like," Gloria said nodding.

"Well, I will have to do the appeal for her for nothing," Dan said after some thought.

"We can't afford that."

"I can't let her rot in jail."

"We are behind on the rent already. Danny you can't afford to do legal work for people who can't pay, no matter how good the cause."

"Things will work out, Gloria, they always do.

"How do they always work out?"

"It's a mystery," Dan said as he smiled.

"Anyway, this sexual harassment investigation is going to pay some big dollars," Dan said as he moved from their tiny amenities room to his small office.

"Dan, before you go, can I talk to you about something?"

"Sure, Gloria, fire away."

"My sister, you know Doreen? She told me she saw you this morning at the *Coffee Mug* in Spring Hill. She said and I am using her words now, *Dan seemed pretty tight with a pretty young Asian woman.*"

Dan felt the blood draining from his face.

"She was quick to get that report in," Dan said with feeling.

"Of course I told her that you must have had your reasons for being there with the young woman and it was all part of your work. Doreen seemed unconvinced though. She said that it looked like the two of you were an item."

Gloria hesitated and waited for Dan to say something.

"What are you trying to say to me, Gloria?"

"You have such a wonderful marriage, Danny, and Elise is such a nice person. I am worried about you, that's all. I don't want you to fall into any traps. I don't want you and Elise to get hurt."

"Gloria, let me put your mind at rest. I was meeting the complainant in the sexual harassment investigation I am doing. There was nothing in it. Honestly, it was just a professional meeting." He felt his heart skip a beat.

He was pretty much telling the truth. Yet he still felt like a kid being caught with his hand in the lolly jar.

"My husband told me the exact same thing when I accused him of cheating on me all those years ago. I can still hear his words, *honestly there is nothing going on between me and my secretary, it's all professional.*"

"Gloria, I am not your husband."

"I know that but I don't want to see history repeat itself. You know it ended our relationship."

"But I always thought your husband died when you were together. Didn't he slip on some rocks and fall off a cliff while you were bushwalking?" Dan asked.

"He did die that way but that was after I caught him cheating on me with his secretary. His death was tragic, of course, but his constant cheating and repeatedly lying about it to my face; that really hurt me. It left a gaping hole in my heart that I have not been able to fill even to this day. He hurt me so much."

"Geez, Gloria, if I did not know any better I'd say you pushed him off the cliff yourself," Dan said.

He knew he should not have said it, even to suggest it in jest was inappropriate but he was not thinking clearly.

However instead of being offended, Gloria looked him straight in the eye and with an expressionless face said, "What if I did, he would have deserved it."

He was astounded with Gloria's response. He was trying to process it. She didn't just admit to killing her husband, did she?

Before Dan could respond he heard two quite noisy snorts which morphed into several moose mating calls. Gloria was in fits of laughter and pointing at him.

"I had you going then, didn't I, Danny boy?"

Dan smiled and chuckled to himself.

"Yes, Gloria, you had me going there."

After a few minutes Gloria's infectious laughter eventually subsided.

"Danny, if you say it was all above board, then it was all above board. I know I can trust you and that you tell me the truth, unlike other males I have known. I am sorry to have raised it with you, but I just wanted to put Doreen at ease. I knew there would be a logical explanation for it all."

At that Gloria walked back to her reception area, while Dan sat down at his cluttered desk and tried to work on his sexual harassment report. He felt gutted to mislead Gloria like that, but what else could he do. To tell the whole truth would only have complicated matters way too much.

CHAPTER TWELVE

It was raining lightly, and around 7:30pm when Dan arrived home. He was tired after a big day. All he wanted to do was eat dinner and relax watching the Ashes from England. The Ashes are a century old cricket rivalry between Australia and England. England invented the gentlemen's game of cricket but Australia perfected it by playing it like football; hard, tough, uncompromising and with a will to win no matter what the cost.

Beating England in cricket is what Australian's love to do, it is part of their DNA.

As Dan walked in the house Elise came to meet him and greeted him with a peck on the cheek.

"You're late, where have you been?"

He was surprised at Elise's abrupt question.

"Today I interviewed the complainant in the investigation I am doing for Claye, then I went and saw Claye. I have spent the rest of day working on the investigation report."

"Don't put that umbrella down," she said motioning to Dan as he put his umbrella beside the door. "We are going out tonight."

"What, I don't remember anything about going out tonight."

"I decided to be spontaneous again. You remember spontaneous, don't you?"

"Yeah," Dan said uncertain as to what was happening. He liked spontaneous but not tonight. Tonight he was exhausted.

"I have booked a table for us at *Comos*. So let's go, I booked the table for 8:00pm and I don't want to be late again."

He registered Elise's dig at him about being late all the time. Can't people give him a rest about that? He never intended to be late but sometimes things just happened, like traffic jams appearing out of nowhere.

Comos was fine dining. Dan liked food but he was not a fine dining advocate. Their food was always elaborately presented in very small quantities and the cost was outrageous. Elise should know he didn't like going to *Comos*.

"Look, I am really exhausted. Couldn't we order some Thai food and stay in? It's raining and it might be nice to stay in and cosy up together."

Elise didn't seem to appreciate Dan's counter idea and her mood changed quickly. "What's on? What sport do you want to watch, rather than go out with me?"

Dan was on the defensive and a bit put out that Elise had taken his stay at home idea so badly. He did want to watch the Ashes but he could watch it later in the night after spending some time with Elise at home. Why had she gotten so mad with him so quickly?

Still he knew better than to tell Elise that he had planned to watch some sport tonight; he knew that would stir her but he couldn't help himself. If she wanted to have an argument with him for some reason, he would accommodate her.

"Well, I was planning to watch the Ashes tonight."

"You and your sport! I have gone to all the trouble to organize a pleasant evening out with you and you would rather watch cricket. I just don't understand why you even want me around!"

"Look, you are taking this all out of context. I am tired, I have had a hard day and it's raining. All I did was suggest that we could stay in and eat. I can always watch the cricket later tonight. I don't know why you are getting so upset about this."

"You honestly don't know why I am getting so upset about this. Let me make it crystal clear for you. I have been working hard all day at work and then I come home and do washing and ironing. After that, all I wanted to do was spend some quality time with my husband over a nice meal and a couple of glasses of wine; have someone else wait upon me for a change. But for some reason my husband doesn't seem interested in doing that with me. That is why I am upset!"

He could see Elise was upset. He could not understand how Elise could be so great with him as she was at the end of the counselling session and then get so angry with him as she was here, all in the space of a couple of days. He had done nothing other than to make a counter proposal, yet she had flown off the handle as though he was the most insensitive husband in the world.

No point continuing this argument. Like their other arguments it had come out of nowhere, when he was least expecting it.

"Look no problem, let's go out," Dan said to appease Elise and resolve the conflict.

"There is no point going out now. I am not in the mood; thanks for that!"

Before Dan could reply, Elise marched out of the dining room and up the stairs to their bedroom and slammed the door shut.

He gave Elise a few minutes to cool down. He then made his way up the stairs and gently opened the bedroom door.

"I know what you are after. Me too, I am right in the mood for it now," Elise said.

"Come on let's go," pleaded Dan who chose to ignore Elise's latest sarcastic remark.

Elise was hesitating.

"Come on, you have already booked it."

"You won't spoil the evening by being all sullen and not talking to me?"

"No, we can talk about anything you want, even your pet subject the Sharks if you want. Hey the girl I interviewed today ran into some Brisbane Bronco players, you won't believe what happened." Dan knew that Elise knew he was only joking.

Elise smiled and the redness drained from her face, "No, I would rather not talk about football, or cricket or any other sport tonight if that's fine with you."

"No problem."

Dan drove like a madman, sparking several safety rebukes from Elise but he made it to *Comos* on time; he was determined they would not be late.

CHAPTER THIRTEEN

Dan had just gotten into bed and was dozing off to sleep when the call came. It sounded like his mobile phone was about to explode, the way it went off.

"Who would be calling you at this hour of the night?" Elise asked as Dan fumbled for his phone.

Dan ignored her question as he had an inkling who it might be.

"Hello," Dan said scratchily into the phone.

"It's me, Mia. Look, I am really sorry to ring you so late but I just saw a man outside my house. I screamed at him and he ran off. I am really freaked out. Can you come over?"

Dan didn't take long to make the decision. Mia sounded frantic.

"Ok, I will be there in 10 minutes."

"Thanks."

Dan terminated the call, got out of bed and started getting dressed.

"Who was that?" demanded Elise who was now wide awake as well.

For a split second he thought about telling Elise the truth.

"That was the hospital. Claye has had a bad reaction to one of the chemo drugs they are giving him. They want me to come straight over."

"Oh no, that's terrible. Do you want me to come with you?"

"No, stay here and get some rest. I know you are tired. I will call you on the mobile if anything happens. Look, they always expect the worst; it's probably nothing. He is one tough old bird that Claye. I saw him this afternoon and he was fine."

"What did they say, how bad is he?"

"Look, they didn't really say much. I will know more when I get over there and find out the full story."

"Alright, but ring me as soon as you know something, ok?"

"Sure. Hey, do you know where my shoes are? I can't find them."

"They were all muddy from the rain and you traipsed through the house with them when we came home from the restaurant. I put them in the laundry so you would clean them before wearing them again. Can you quickly clean them before you go, I don't want the carpet to get any dirtier?"

Dan dressed quickly and at the last minute splashed on some cologne. It was just a spur of the moment thing.

"Alright, see you later."

"Call me ok, call me. What, no kiss good-bye?"

Dan promptly moved to Elise's side of the bed, pecked her on the cheek and started walking downstairs towards the laundry. As Dan was leaving, Elise shouted out to him, "Is that cologne you're wearing?"

"It's for the nurses." What else could he say?

Dan found his shoes and quickly started scraping off the mud. Unfortunately, the mud was caked on.

He then hurried out to the garage where he got into his Subaru Impreza and sped off to Mia's house. Dan liked sports cars but on a suburban solicitor's wage, he could not afford a new one. However he had the next best thing, a second hand Impreza.

As he drove out of the driveway and turned into the street, his mobile phone rang. Again the piercing ring tone of the phone startled him, as did the vibrations it made in his pocket; it was Mia. He pulled over to the side of the road and answered the phone. He did not trust himself to drive late at night in wet conditions, while having a conversation with someone like Mia.

"Hello."

"Dan, where are you?"

If Dan thought Mia sounded frantic on the last call, she was positively jumping out of her skin on this call.

"I am on my way, what's the problem?"

"My lights have just gone out. Someone is still out there, I am sure of it, and now they have killed my lights. I am freaking big time, please hurry."

"Have you called the police?"

"Yes. They said all their patrol cars are busy right now but they could be here in an hour. I told them to get stuffed. I could be dead in an hour."

"Have you called the power company? The electricity could be out due to the rain."

"No, I haven't called them but I can see other lights on down the street."

"Ok Mia, I have to hang up now. I will be there very soon. Make sure everything is locked."

"Hurry, Dan, please hurry!"

*

Dan was starting to get worried now. He had tried not to think of Mia, but at times he could not help himself. In all this Dan had not actually believed Mia was in any real danger. But now with her seeing someone outside her house and the power to her house being deliberately cut, he was concerned about her welfare and possibly his own.

It wasn't long before he parked his car in Mia's driveway. It was very dark inside. He knocked on the door and yelled, "Mia, it's me, Dan!"

He heard soft footsteps running to the door and it being unlocked. The door opened narrowly at first and then it swung wildly open. Mia threw herself around him; Dan liked her touch. He was still not sure why he liked her touch so much.

It took some strength on Dan's behalf to delicately pull Mia off him.

"Are you ok?" Dan asked.

"I am petrified but I feel a whole lot better now you are here."

"Where is your meter box?"

"I don't know."

"Have you got a torch?"

"Yes, I have one here." Mia had a torch in her hand and she gave it to Dan.

"I am going outside to check the meter box. Lock the door behind me."

"You're not going to leave me?"

"Mia, it will be fine. I need to check the meter box and then I will be back."

Dan used the torch light to navigate around the house until he saw the meter box. He carefully looked around before opening it. He didn't want to be knocked on the head by someone while he was concentrating on the switches inside. He could see no one, nor could he hear anyone. In fact, it was deathly quiet.

As quietly as he could, he opened the meter box lid. Unfortunately, the lid had rusted and it made a terrible screeching noise when it opened. It sounded like a cat being strangled, not that he had ever heard a cat being strangled.

He looked around again, certain that if anybody was moving around outside, they would have heard him open the meter box. He carefully surveyed the area around where he was with the torch. Satisfied that there was no one near him, he looked at the switches in the meter box.

He saw that the safety switch had been tripped and that explained why all the power was off. He flicked the safety switch back on and he saw the lights illuminate in Mia's house.

He shut the meter box lid quickly this time, to try and minimize the screeching sound, but it sounded even louder. He then walked briskly to Mia's front door shining his torch on every corner and crevice of the yard; he saw nothing out of the ordinary.

"Mia, it's me again, open the door."

Mia opened the door and again flung herself into Dan's arms in a very strong bear hug. He was pressed tight against her velvet dressing gown. He could smell and feel the freshness of her soft hair as it was swept across his face.

He again moved Mia gently off him and said, "Let's go inside."

Once inside the safety of the house, Mia asked, "What's happening?"

"The safety switch in your meter box was off, so I flicked it back to the on position, that's all."

"Did someone cut my power off?"

"Well, the safety switch is designed to go off and shut your power down if there is fluctuation in the power levels at your house. The safety switch could have been tripped by a fluctuation in your power caused by a bad electrical device, or it could have been turned off by someone deliberately. The fact that you saw someone outside your house probably leads me to the conclusion that it was turned off deliberately."

"Do you think he is still out there?"

"I don't think so. I had a quick look around and I didn't see anybody."

Mia sighed as though a weight had been lifted off her shoulders.

"Thanks, I really appreciate you coming over like this. Can I get you a beer, cup of tea or something?"

"Yeah, tea would be good."

"How long can you stay?"

"Well, I can stay for awhile."

"Great."

Dan moved into the kitchen with Mia who began making a pot of tea. "Tell me about the guy you saw earlier tonight. Did you get a good look at him?"

"I was getting ready for bed and I went to the bathroom to brush my teeth and that's when I saw him looking at me through the bathroom window. He was standing near the fence."

Mia pointed through her kitchen window to the back fence which was several metres from the house.

"What did he look like?"

"Well it was dark, but I could definitely make him out. He was wearing a dark jacket and jeans. I couldn't see his face but he was wearing a cap of some description.

"Anyway, I yelled at him and he took off. It was really freaky.

"Then the lights went out. That really spun me out, let me tell you. And now you have come and rescued me."

While she said this Mia reached out and touched his arm. He felt unable to move and Mia only removed her hand when the kettle turned off after boiling.

"I know I am asking a lot, but could you stay overnight? I mean, I don't know what's going on. With someone in my yard, turning the power off and that note threatening to kill me. It's really starting to get to me."

Could he stay the night? Should he stay the night? The smart thing would be to get the hell out of there.

"Sure, I can stay the night."

In the end he figured she needed his help. He wasn't going to leave her in distress.

"So, Mia, who do you think it is?"

"Can we sit on the couch and talk, it is more comfortable than these kitchen chairs?"

As they moved into the living room and onto the couch, Mia opened one of the curtains and peered out onto the street.

"Mia, I don't think anyone is out there now, particularly as my car is in your driveway."

"I suppose you're right, but I am still freaked."

There was some silence as they sipped their tea.

Dan waited for Mia to answer his question about who she thought was doing this to her but she did not respond, she seemed lost in thought.

"The guy obviously wasn't Brock as you would have recognized him." Dan said this as more of a statement than a question.

"No, I don't think it was Brock."

"You're not sure?"

"I didn't see his face; it was dark and he was wearing a cap."

"But was he the same build as Brock, you know height, weight etc.?"

"He was big like Brock, but I don't think Brock would hurt me like this.

Look I don't want to talk about Brock."

"Is there anyone else other than Brock who may want to stalk you in this way?"

"No, there is no one else. Unless … you don't think Samuel Sanderson could be involved?"

"Unlikely, did he look like Samuel?"

"Well he was about Samuel's size, perhaps a little bigger, but I couldn't really tell. I only saw him for a second."

"It's a mystery then," Dan said in a lighter tone.

"I think I will have to leave Brisbane," Mia announced matter of factly.

"Where will you go?"

"I am not sure, but I will probably go back to Sydney. My father is there and I have some friends there as well. I don't think I can take this anymore."

He didn't show it but he felt disappointed. He knew Mia was making the right decision to leave, but his heart sank a little anyway.

He had felt electricity surging through his body whenever Mia touched him. He had not felt this way in a long time. He remembered feeling this way in High School when he had his first crush on a girl, Sarah Crabtree. It was not a feeling he could control, it was a feeling that controlled him.

But he was a married man; he should be able to control his feelings, shouldn't he?

"Did you grow up in Sydney?" Dan asked, trying to take his mind off how he was feeling towards Mia.

"Yes, I was born in Sydney. Cronulla, if you must know."

"I have never been to Cronulla but I will get there one day."

"You should go, it is beautiful there on the beaches. My father owned a pharmacy in Cronulla until he retired a few years ago. My mother died in a car accident when I was six, so my father raised me. I am an only child."

Mia hesitated, flicked her hair and then went on with her story.

"Because of my father I grew up around sport, particularly football. I am not an avid fan like he is, but I like watching rugby league and I enjoy going to the games."

"Wait a minute. My mind can't compute what you just said. You're obviously female, young, attractive and yet you like watching rugby league and you enjoy going to the games. Are you for real?"

"Yes, you are looking at someone who enjoys rugby league. I like watching other sports too, like rugby, 20-20 cricket, basketball, even soccer."

"Be still my beating heart," Dan said as an actor on a stage.

"Come on, you must know other women who like sport?"

"No - you're the only one."

Elise and the other women he had dated just didn't get it. They didn't get sport. The fierceness of the contest, the skill under pressure, the sense of belonging to the team, the uncertainty of the result, the celebration in victory; these were foreign concepts to the women that Dan knew.

The women that Dan knew resented sport because of the time and passion it took from its fans like him. He wondered what it would be like to actually be close to a woman who shared his sporting passion, rather than it being a source of constant criticism.

"That's enough about me, what about you. Are you married?"

"I am married. Six years we have been together."

"How wonderful for you."

"We are working through some problems at the moment. The zing has gone out of our marriage." He felt bad saying that the moment he said it, but he could not take it back.

"As you know, I am a lawyer. I have my own legal practice."

"What about your family?"

"I have one brother, Claye. He is eleven years older than me and, unfortunately has been diagnosed with leukemia. At the moment, Claye is in hospital receiving chemotherapy in preparation for a donor stem cell transplant. In the process of destroying his cancer cells they will be destroying his stem cells and immune system. That's where I come in as I am the donor for him. They will shortly be harvesting my stem cells to give to Claye, to help him to recover from this shocking disease and its treatment."

"I am impressed, you not only save damsels in distress but you also are saving your big brother as well."

"It's nothing really, all in a day's work."

"No, it's more than nothing, it's very brave and very loving."

Mia's eyes welled up with tears and she began to cry softly. "I have no one who would do that for me."

Dan reached out and slowly put his arm around her shoulder to comfort her.

Mia snuggled her face on Dan's neck and he felt the softness of her cheek. Mia moved her face up to his cheek and instinctively he turned his face to meet her. For a second they hesitated, before their lips surged together and they kissed.

It was as though nothing else mattered in the rest of the world. All he could think about was kissing Mia. Her kiss was soft yet strong, it was full yet not overpowering; it was passionate.

The kissing continued on and on as they held each other tightly. Then his hands seemed to move of their own volition. He caressed her hair, her neck, her back, as far as he could reach behind her. He then moved his hands slowly around to the front of Mia's soft, sweet smelling body.

He hesitated but there was no reaction or concern from Mia. In fact before he had fully realized what was happening Mia had clasped his hand in hers and she started gently and slowly guiding his hand around her body.

Then out of nowhere their passion was loudly and shockingly interrupted.

Dan's mobile phone went off the wall, or so it seemed to him. There it was in his pocket vibrating and calling out to him in ear piercing decibels. He stopped, and put his hand up to Mia, motioning to her that he had to get this.

Dan was breathing deeply, taking long slow breaths. He saw from the caller ID, it was Elise.

"It's my brother. You know the one in hospital."

As he stood and walked out to the verandah, he marveled at how easy it was for him to lie. Perhaps all these years he had had this hidden talent of being able to lie convincingly. A lawyer with a hidden talent for lying; he couldn't help but give a faint chuckle at that thought.

"How is he? You said you were going to call." It was Elise and she sounded concerned.

"Yeah, sorry about that, I forgot. He is alright now but there is still some concern about his condition."

"When are you coming home?"

Dan hesitated before answering this question. He was conflicted. Something told him he should leave now, but he wanted to stay. In the end he made a quick call.

"They have asked to me to stay the night."

"You are staying the night?" Elise sounded disappointed and deflated.

"Yeah but I will be back first thing tomorrow morning."

"Why can't you come home now?

"Look, it's a bit complicated and I'd rather not get into it right now. I will be needed to donate the stem cells very soon and it could even be tonight."

There was nothing like adding some truth to a lie to make it more believable.

An uncomfortable silence ensued between them before Dan said, "Look I have to go now. I will call you if something happens."

Dan heard Elise terminate the call. His breathing had returned to normal, but his mind was racing. Elise didn't say *love you*; she always ended a call with those words; that was strange.

The whole thing was strange. What was he doing here with a girl much younger than himself, who had just come out of a violent relationship? Not to mention that she was the complainant in an investigation he still had to complete.

But most importantly he was married.

Is this who he was? Who he wanted to be?

In all these questions he knew that the answer was clearly, no. Yet there was a force, something pulling him towards this girl. His body craved her touch.

"Dan, are you alright?" Mia asked from the doorway.

"Yeah, it was just the hospital. My brother has had a bit of a turn."

"Can you still stay, or do you have to go to be with your brother?"

After pretending to give the matter some thought Dan answered, "I think I should stay with you. I can't really do anything for Claye tonight. I will go and see him in the morning."

"Hey," Dan said to Mia who had moved to be standing very close to him.

"Hey," Mia said looking into Dan's eyes.

"I think we need to cool it for a bit for a whole bunch of reasons," Dan said.

"What reasons?"

"I don't think it is right for me to start something with you, while I am still trying to work things out with my wife. I hope you can understand where I am coming from?"

Mia's eyes squinted and her lips turned up. However, after a few seconds her face relaxed and she sighed.

"I can understand, perhaps with all the emotion running around here tonight we got a little ahead of ourselves. It's fine, don't worry about it."

"Thanks, Mia."

"If things don't work out with your wife, perhaps you could come to Cronulla and see me."

"Yeah, that sounds like a plan."

"Are you happy to sleep on the couch? I don't have a spare bed and I am not sure if I could trust myself if we had to share a bed."

"The couch will be fine," he answered.

"Ok then, will you be here when I get up this morning?"

"Probably not, it will be better if I make an early get away once the sun comes up."

"Thanks, Dan. You are a great guy. I will send you a postcard from Cronulla."

"Yeah, all the best, Mia, I look forward to getting that postcard. When will you be leaving?" Dan asked.

"As soon as I can get the removalists organized. Probably in a couple of days."

"Mia, I don't know if I can spend the night here again."

"It will probably be only a few days or a week before I leave for Sydney and I might spend my nights at a motel. Tonight has really scared me, but I don't want to be the one to come between you and your wife, so it's ok. Do what you have to do with your wife, but remember me if it doesn't work out with her."

"Mia, you are something else, you know that."

"Something else, is that how you describe me? Ouch!" Mia seemed hurt by his description of her.

He was trying to give her a compliment, not offend her.

"By something else I mean you are *hot*, not that it's just looks that are important. I mean you clearly have the looks but it's more than that. What I am trying to say…"

Dan stopped talking as Mia burst out laughing.

"I know what you mean, I was just stirring you."

Dan smiled. She certainly had him going there. Well done, she was good. An attractive, caring, sport-lover who liked joking around with people; what more could any guy ask for?

Dan recovered. "I knew you were stirring me – I was just playing along with you."

"Yeah, right," Mia said still laughing.

At that Dan closed the curtains, took his shoes off and watched Mia head to her bedroom and shut the door. He snuggled up to some fluffy blankets and tried his best to catch some sleep on the couch.

As he drove home in the early daylight hours, he reflected about what had just happened. He liked Mia, he really did. But to destroy his relationship with Elise as well as fracture other friendships and family relationships for her when he barely knew her; that would be crazy. Yet there was something about her that he really liked, something that attracted him to her.

Should he tell Elise the truth? Dan decided not to. He had shared a single moment of passion with Mia that was all. Mia would be moving to Sydney in the next few days and so why tell Elise? It would only upset her.

*

Over the next couple of days Dan had no contact with Mia as he threw himself into finishing the investigation report.

He had been thinking about Elise. If the zing had gone out of their marriage, then he needed to do everything he could to put it back.

He remembered the Counsellor's words about trying to focus on pleasing the other person and not being selfish. He would put her needs above his.

What was he thinking when he agreed to help Mia? What on earth was he thinking when he kissed her?

Well all's well that ends well, he thought. No one knew about his liaison with Mia and nothing bad had come of it. He was fortunate in that respect.

He felt guilty about straying from Elise but now he would recommit to her.

As he finished his work and skipped out of his office to his car, he was happy. Not only had he the State of Origin to look forward to tonight, but also he would soon be putting the pieces of his marriage back together and saving Claye's life by donating his stem cells.

Even a New South Wales win in tonight's game couldn't dampen his spirits. Well, it would upset him, but not for too long!

CHAPTER FOURTEEN

Queenslander! Queenslander! That was the Queensland rally cry, and Dan and his mates Macca and Robbo were shouting it out from the comfort of Dan's home. The Blues (New South Wales) were attacking the Queensland line with five minutes to go. New South Wales were already up by 4 points and if they scored another try, it could be curtains for the Maroons (Queensland).

Then it came. The Blues' winger lunged for the try line but he was knocked over the sideline by some gutsy and determined defence. Queensland would get the ball back from the resultant scrum.

"I knew we would hold them out," yelled Macca as he jumped to his feet, pumping his fists.

"We need to get the ball down the other end," said Robbo stating the obvious.

Robbo was good company but Dan wondered why he was always a bit negative during football games. For some reason he never expected his team was going to win.

"There is still plenty of time, no need to panic," Dan said as calmly as he could to reassure Robbo and himself.

Queensland comebacks were legendary. Every Queenslander knew that when it came to playing the Blues, you never, ever gave up. So many times the Blues had thought they had won the game but Queensland came back to beat them at the very end. It got to the stage where even the Blues supporters were expecting to be overrun in the last minutes of any game.

Just then the Queensland five eighth slipped a magic ball to the fullback who ran like the wind. He was tackled just short of the try line but somehow he managed to pass the ball to his winger who scored wide out.

Dan, Macca and Robbo all shouted the same word in unison, **"TRY!!!"**

There was much hugging, high fiveing and fist pumping!

"He will get this, even though the kick is from the touchline," Robbo announced. Dan and Macca laughed; even pessimistic Robbo was caught up in the euphoria they were feeling at the moment.

Just then Dan heard knocking on the front door. Dan ignored it. Surely no one would be coming to see him during a State of Origin game.

He remembered early on in his marriage to Elise, her sister had rung him during a State of Origin game to ask for some legal advice. He couldn't believe it. He was only too happy to provide his sister-in-law with free legal advice but he was gobsmacked that she called him in the middle of a State of Origin game. It had never really occurred to Dan until that time, that some people in Queensland were not interested in and indeed did not even watch State of Origin games.

"Oh he has missed it, I knew he would miss it," lamented Robbo as the conversion sailed just wide of the goalposts.

"Ladies and gents, fasten your seatbelts we are going into extra time," announced Macca, licking his lips in anticipation that the game and the euphoria were not ending, but only just beginning.

Then Dan heard it again, only this time the knocking was much louder and sounded more urgent than last time. What was going on? He knew the visitors could not be for him, not during a State of Origin game.

"Elise, there is someone at the door, can you get it?" Dan called out.

"You get it, you're downstairs and can you keep that racket down? I can't hear myself think up here."

"I can't get it at the moment, we are just about to start extra time," Dan replied.

Dan heard Elise's footsteps down the stairs and the front door open.

"Dan, there are some people here to see you," Elise said as she entered the TV room.

"Look it's extra time at the moment, can you look after them for a few minutes?"

"No, it's the police and they want to see you," Elise said quite forcibly this time.

Elise's forceful words had the desired effect; she had the attention of Dan, Macca and Robbo.

"Ok, I will see them. Are they still outside?" Dan asked as he turned his head back to watch the TV.

"They are in the hallway waiting for you, they wanted to come inside," answered Elise.

"Alright, tell them I will be with them in a minute," Dan replied.

"Thanks," Dan added as Elise was walking out the doorway.

"Why don't you invite them in to watch the game?" asked Macca.

"Because he is worried they have come around to arrest him for being a loser," Robbo volunteered.

"A loser?" queried Macca.

"Yeah, you know a Cronulla Sharks fan," replied Robbo.

Both Robbo and Macca were in fits of hysterical laughter at this comment.

"How long did it take you to think that one up, Robbo?" asked Dan in a deadpan voice.

Robbo's and Macca's laughter halted abruptly as a Maroons' player kicked out on the full, meaning the Blues' would get a full set of six tackles ten metres from the halfway line in Queensland territory. Serious defence was needed to keep them out of range from kicking an easy field goal.

Queensland were hitting hard and knocking Blues' players back in the tackles. There was a field goal attempt by a New South Wales player that just missed. The tension on Queensland had eased. Queensland would get the ball back on their 20 metre line. Dan thought now was a good a time as any to quickly meet his new guests. He had absolutely no idea what they wanted.

He walked smartly to the hallway. He saw two people dressed in civilian clothes. A male taller than Dan, he was at least two metres tall. The second person was a female about his own height. Elise was not around and he assumed she had gone back upstairs.

The male police officer was middle aged, receding hair line and dressed in plain clothes, jacket, t-shirt, jeans and cowboy boots. The police officer held out his hand and introduced himself as Senior Detective Michael Sloan from the Brisbane City Criminal Investigation Branch. Detective Sloan then introduced his female partner as Detective Sarah Little. Dan reached out and shook Detective Little's hand; she seemed strangely familiar to him. He had probably seen her in court.

"Look, officers I suppose you are aware the State of Origin is on at the moment. It's nearly finished, extra time, can you wait till it's over?" Dan asked.

"The State of Origin, I have heard of that, who is playing?" Senior Detective Sloan asked innocently.

Dan could not believe his ears. He was stunned. A Brisbane Detective asking who was playing in the State of Origin. Since the inception of State of

Origin in 1980, it had only ever been Queensland versus New South Wales. He thought everybody in Queensland knew that, even football haters like Elise knew that.

"Sorry, he is from South Australia," Detective Little said to Dan, obviously aware of Dan's pained and confused expression.

Well that explains it. Only Queensland and New South Wales have rugby league as their main football code. In the other States of Australia the dominant football code is Australian Rules.

"Look, I have to get back to the game. What is this all about?" Dan said hurriedly.

"Well, Mr Grover, we are sorry to have interrupted your sport watching but we need you to come with us to the police station to discuss a very serious matter," Senior Detective Sloan said abruptly.

"Look, the only place I am going to right now is back to the TV room to watch the end of the game. It's in extra time, so I won't be long. If you want to wait fine. If not, leave me your card and I will call you tomorrow. Why are you here anyway, you could have just rung me?"

He could hear Macca and Robbo *hooping and hollering*, something important must have happened in the game and he missed it. What a disaster!

He turned and began walking away when he heard Senior Detective Sloan say loudly and deliberately, "Mia Wong has been murdered."

Dan stopped in his tracks, turned around and with a perplexed expression he faced Sloan. "What?"

"You heard me," replied Sloan. "We found your business card in her handbag, so we need to have a chat."

Just then Macca and Robbo went right off. Dan could hear shouting and screaming from nearby houses. Macca put his head around the corner and said excitedly, "We won, yeeeeeeeeeeees!"

"It was never in doubt. I always knew they were going to win," Robbo added cheekily.

"What's wrong, you don't look so good?" Macca asked looking at Dan.

"The police have just given me some bad news. I have to go to the police station with them. They want me to go right now. Hey, do you mind telling Elise. Someone from one of my cases has been murdered; no one she knew."

"*Geez, Louise!* Ok, we will tell her. Won't we Robbo? We just want to stay for the trophy presentation, then we are off," said Macca. As always he was right to the point.

"That's fine, see you guys later."

Dan jumped into the back of the unmarked police car. He was in shock. He could not believe what he had just heard. He had only seen Mia a couple of days ago.

"What happened to her?" asked Dan.

"We don't want to get into that in the car, we will explain everything at the station," replied Sloan.

Dan was actually grateful for the quiet in the police car as it gave him time to think.

Mia dead; he could not believe it. She was such a lovely person. Who could have done such a terrible thing to her?

He would have to tell the Police about the threatening note Mia had received. Also, he would tell them about Mia seeing a stalker outside her house and then her lights being switched off.

But should he tell them that he spent the night at Mia's house? What about the moment of passion he had shared with Mia?

Should he get a lawyer to be present during his interview with the police? Surely he was not a suspect, so why would he need a lawyer to be present?

Poor Mia. He found it hard to think clearly as the horror of her murder began to seep slowly into his consciousness.

CHAPTER FIFTEEN

Dan was left waiting near the duty officer's desk at the Brisbane City Police Station for what seemed an eternity. Unfortunately, the police station didn't have any heating in the public area. As Dan had left suddenly, he hadn't taken his coat. He was positively shivering when Detective Little came out from behind a security door and asked him to follow her.

"Have we met before?" Dan asked innocently.

"Yes, I believe we have," answered Detective Little.

"You don't remember me? Well, that is flattering," she added.

He did not answer the question as he could not remember where or when he had known Detective Little. He definitely knew her but he just could not place her. During his legal career Dan had met many police officers.

He was led to a small windowless interview room where Senior Detective Sloan was waiting for him, sitting behind a small table. Sloan sat across from Dan, while Detective Little sat at the head of the table.

"Now, Mr Grover, we want to ask you some questions about Mia Wong. As we have told you earlier this evening, we are investigating her murder. Can you tell us about your relationship with the deceased?" asked Detective Little.

"Before we start can you tell me what's going on? I mean what happened to Mia Wong, when did it happen, where did it happen, how did it happen?"

"Mr Grover, we will get to that in good time, but first we need to ask you some questions before you ask us your questions," replied Senior Detective Sloan.

"Alright, for the past two weeks I have been working for my brother, Claye Grover, in his corporate investigation business. Mia Wong was the complainant in a sexual harassment complaint that I was investigating for his client Dodsworth, Blainey and Parker, Chartered Accountants."

"What was the complaint?" asked Detective Little.

"I had agreed that my investigation would be kept confidential. I am not sure I can break that confidentiality commitment without my client's consent."

Sloan looked disapprovingly at Detective Little and shook his head. He then turned to Dan and announced, "A young woman has been murdered, you understand what that means don't you. Every minute we delay investigating her murder, reduces our chances of successfully catching her murderer. You want us to wait to receive what could be vital information because you signed a piece of paper saying you would keep this information confidential?

"Lawyers! Seriously, do you ever want to see justice served or do you just look out for yourselves and your clients regardless of the consequences?"

Dan had thought about this point while waiting at the police station. He didn't want to break his confidentiality agreement. But at the end of the day Mia had been murdered and he wanted the police to catch her killer. So he had decided to tell the police about Mia's complaint and his investigation, as long as he could put his confidentiality concerns on the record.

"As you have made your point so eloquently Detective Sloan, I will tell you what I know. I do want justice for Mia. I do want you to catch her killer."

Perhaps more than you know, thought Dan.

"That's *Senior* Detective Sloan."

Dan ignored Sloan's reprimand about using his incorrect title.

"Mia Wong complained that one of her work colleagues, Mr Samuel Sanderson, spiked her drink while they were drinking after work on a Friday night, a couple of weeks ago. Ms Wong claimed that Mr Sanderson then sexually assaulted her in his car.

"I investigated Ms Wong's complaint and determined, on the balance of probabilities, that what she had complained about did happen."

"When did you last see Mia Wong?" asked Detective Little.

"A week or so ago Mia told me in confidence about a threat that had been made against her. In fact, she showed me a piece of paper that had been slipped under her door. The note said something like, *Trollop leave town or die.* The wording appeared to be in letters cut out of a magazine.

"A couple of nights ago, Ms Wong rang me and said she saw an intruder in her yard and that her electricity had been cut off. She was frantic.

"I arrived at her house approximately ten minutes after she rang me. I went to her meter box and found that the safety switch had been flicked off. I flicked the switch on and her power came back on. That was it, nothing else happened."

"Did you see the intruder?" asked Detective Little.

"No."

"How did she describe the intruder?" asked Little.

Dan hesitated trying to recall Mia's description of the intruder. "He was a large guy around my height, I think. He was wearing a dark coloured jacket, jeans and a cap. Mia only saw him for a split second before he ran off into the darkness. She did not see his face."

"Did anything else happen that night?" asked Sloan.

"No, nothing else happened that night."

"How do you know that for sure?" queried Sloan.

"Because I stayed the night with her."

"Ok, now we are getting somewhere," Sloan said nodding towards Detective Little.

"I stayed the night at Mia's request as she was petrified. I slept on the couch."

"You slept on the couch. That is your evidence, is it?" repeated Sloan.

Dan was surprised at where Sloan was going with this. There was no way Sloan could know about their moment of passion.

"Yeah, I slept on the couch, why is that hard to believe?" Dan asked.

"Nothing of a romantic nature happened between you and Ms Wong? You were just what, good friends were you?" queried Sloan.

"There was no romance, sex, sexual relations, whatever you like to call it, between Miss Wong and I. I don't know how else to say it to make it clear to you that I am telling the truth. I had only just met her."

"But why did she call you over, I mean you weren't a friend of hers were you? Weren't you an independent investigator investigating her complaint?" asked Sloan.

It appeared as though Sloan was onto him somehow and Dan didn't know what he knew or how he knew it, but he could not change his story now. Hopefully Sloan was just giving him a hard time because he didn't like lawyers.

"We were not friends." It hurt Dan to say that.

"Ms Wong was new in town. She literally didn't know any other males in Brisbane except her ex-boyfriend, and she didn't want to call him. I felt sorry for her. I had all but finished my investigation report. I saw someone scared and I answered their call for help. That was all there was to it from my point of view."

There was silence before Dan added, "Also, she was moving back to

Sydney within the week."

"What can you tell me about Ms Wong's ex-boyfriend?" asked Sloan.

At last Sloan had moved his line of questioning away from him.

"His name is Brock. I think they had been living together in Sydney and then a few months ago they moved to Brisbane for work. Apparently, she took out a Domestic Violence Order against him because he pushed her up against a wall and threatened her. She said that he had hit her a few times before this."

"Did Ms Wong believe Brock was behind the letter and intruder incident?" asked Detective Little.

"I did ask Mia that and she said she did not believe Brock was harassing her. Though, I think she said the intruder was of a similar build to Brock."

There was a pause in the questioning.

"What happened to Mia?"

Detective Little looked at Sloan who nodded.

Detective Little then replied, "Mia Wong was found dead in her home yesterday afternoon after we received an anonymous phone call."

"How did she die?"

"That has not been finally determined but it looks like she was beaten about the head with an object."

"Oh, that's horrible. Do you know why she was killed?"

"No, we have no idea. That's why we are talking to her friends, neighbours and associates, to ascertain who she was and whether she had any enemies."

There was a moment of silence as Dan struggled to take in what he had just heard.

"Have you got any idea, Dan, who Mia Wong's murderer might be?" asked Detective Little.

Dan was sure he had heard her voice before. Particularly when Detective Little had called him Dan. He had heard her say his name before, but where, when?

"I don't really know, I mean, I didn't really know Mia Wong that well. I am aware of only two possible suspects. Brock, Mia's ex-boyfriend would appear to have violence issues.

"The other possible suspect is Samuel Sanderson. I believe he did sexually assault Mia, so I suppose he has the capacity to physically assault her. I don't know what he would gain by killing Mia, except perhaps revenge for complaining about him. That seems a big revenge to take on somebody. Though I think he's definitely worth questioning."

There was then a period of silence where Detective Little stared at Dan, while

Senior Detective Sloan rumbled through papers in a manila file on the desk.

Dan felt uncomfortable, so he stood up and stretched his legs.

"Sit down, Mr Grover, you are not going anyway. I have pulled your file from the computer. It makes interesting reading," Sloan said.

"What do you mean?"

"For starters you are wanted for questioning in relation to complaints of deprivation of liberty, kidnapping and assault occasioning grievous bodily harm. They are quite serious charges, Mr Grover."

"Look, that was all a big mistake. I was interviewed about those charges by Senior Constable Mario Bartlett a week or so ago. He told me it was all over, there was nothing in it."

"That's not what the computer says," replied Sloan.

"Well the computer is wrong," Dan said forcibly. He was feeling under attack and he just wanted to leave.

"Is the computer also wrong about your alleged links with dangerous bikie gangs?"

"Yes, it is wrong."

Sloan was smirking and shaking his head. He was making it patently obvious that he didn't believe a word of what Dan was telling him.

"Well, Mr Grover, I don't think you can help us any further at this time. We will be in touch. You may go now if you wish," Sloan said quite out of the blue.

Dan was glad his questioning was over so suddenly. He was on his way out the door when he heard Sloan say, "Mr Grover, there is one last thing, I almost forgot about it. How do you explain Ms Wong's diary blog which she entered the day she was murdered?"

Dan stopped in his tracks. Blog, what blog? He didn't know Mia kept a diary blog.

"In her diary blog Ms Wong confesses her love for you and apparently you two had just been at it like rabbits. I quote,

> *We really went for it last night, it was amazing. I literally could not breathe. After all the jerks I have been with, could Dan be the one? Dan said he might leave his wife and come to Sydney to be with me. That would be awesome!!*

"Now come back, sit down and tell us the truth. This is a murder investigation, not an episode of *Neighbours*!" demanded Senior Detective Sloan who was sounding quite pleased with himself.

Dan wasn't sure what to do. Obviously Sloan had deliberately left this question till the end to trap him, to catch him off guard.

He paused and said, "Don't believe everything you read Detective Sloan; particularly what you read in a woman's blog."

Dan kept walking out of the office. He wasn't coming back to continue the interview unless they were going to arrest him.

"*Senior* Detective Sloan", yelled Sloan, sounding less pleased with himself.

The fact that he and Mia had kissed passionately was really nobody's business but his own. He could not see how his kissing Mia or any feelings she may have had for him could possibly affect the police investigation.

Dan's thoughts turned to who did kill Mia. It had to be related to the threatening note, the intruder and the power being turned off. But who was it?

Poor Mia such a young life, cut short so brutally.

Outside the police station Dan turned his phone back on. Almost immediately it rang. He saw it was Elise.

"It's me, what's going on? I have been trying to call you. Macca said that a friend of yours has been murdered."

How did Elise know to call anytime he was thinking about Mia? It was like she had a sixth sense.

"The complainant in that sexual harassment complaint I had just investigated for Claye has been murdered. The police are just interested in talking to anyone who knew her."

"What could you tell them?"

"Not much. I just told them about the investigation."

"Are you alright?"

"Yes, I am a bit shaken up though. I will tell you all about it in the morning."

"Where are you now?"

"I'm in the city."

"Do you want me to drive into the city and pick you up?"

"No, it's late, I'll catch a cab. Don't wait up for me."

Dan terminated the call. He actually wanted to walk the streets for awhile to process what had happened. He needed some time alone.

He was tempted to tell Elise there and then about kissing Mia but he decided discretion was the better part of valour. Elise didn't deserve to hear something like that on a telephone call. Perhaps he would tell her everything tomorrow.

CHAPTER SIXTEEN

"Your bacon and eggs are ready," Elise yelled from the kitchen.

"Thanks can you bring it out to the deck? I will be down soon."

Dan had little sleep last night. His mind was racing all over the place. He had decided not to tell Elise the full story. His main priority now was to try and work things out with Elise, and telling her he had kissed Mia would not help. That would only make things worse.

The winter sun was out in full blast. The sky was a deep blue colour. There were no clouds.

Dan looked out over the trees near his deck and listened to the birds. He could hear and see beautiful rainbow lorikeets, blustery noisy miners, yodeling magpies, laughing kookaburras, imposing sulphur-crested cockatoos, sweet singing butcherbirds and of course nasal sounding crows.

No matter where you went in Australia one bird was always there, the crow.

"So tell me what happened last night at the Police Station? Who was murdered?"

"Her name was Mia Wong."

"What did you tell the police?"

"I told them what I knew," Dan said matter of factly.

Elise didn't say anything, she just looked at him. A look that said she was very interested in what he had to say next, but she was not going to ask him to go any further, that was his decision.

He then told Elise what had happened with Mia, the note, the intruder, all of it except of course their moment of passion.

"Why did you do it?"

"Excuse me?"

"Why didn't you get one of your friends to help her?"

"Oh, that thought did cross my mind but Mia would not have known them. She needed someone she knew and trusted."

Elise didn't seem totally convinced.

"What night did you go over to her place?" asked Elise.

"A few nights ago," Dan said casually.

"But you have been home or we have been out together, every night for the past week," Elise replied.

"Actually, it was the night I was called to the hospital to see Claye. I was at the hospital when she called me on my mobile." He didn't like lying to Elise but he was committed to this path.

Elise was looking at him now as though in some type of trance. Her face was totally expressionless and drained of any colour.

"You actually stayed the whole night at her house?"

"She was petrified. I slept on the couch."

Dan again looked for Elise's reaction. Her stony face was wilting and tears were starting to well up in her eyes.

"Why didn't you tell me about all this at the time?" Elise asked in a stilted voice.

"What can I say; I just never got around to it. It only happened a few nights ago."

Tears were running down Elise's cheek. They had started one at a time but the dam had burst and now they were streaming down her face.

He reached out to put his arm around Elise to comfort her, but she recoiled from his touch. He was surprised.

"Is that all you want to tell me?" Elise asked as if summoning all the fortitude she could muster.

That pricked Dan's attention. He had not seen that coming. He didn't say anything but looked at Elise in an inquisitive manner.

Just then it happened again. His mobile phone went off screeching, vibrating; demanding to be answered.

Dan didn't want to answer the phone, he wanted to throw it off the deck and smash it into pieces. He quickly checked the caller ID and remembered the number as being from the hospital. He answered the phone.

"Dan Grover."

"Mr Grover this is Nurse Manager Burmiester. The time has come to harvest your stem cells on behalf of your brother Claye. We need you to come to the hospital as soon as possible."

"Can I come in this afternoon?'

"No, we really need you in now."

"Alright, I will be there as soon as I can."

"Thank you, Mr Grover."

Dan terminated the call and looked at Elise. She had stopped crying. She looked like she was deep in thought a million miles away.

He had been self injecting for a week to promote his stem cell growth. He knew the harvest day was coming but the call to come in, so suddenly, still surprised him.

"Elise it's the hospital. I have to go there now, so they can harvest my stem cells and give them to Claye. We can talk again this afternoon if you want."

Elise gave Dan no response. She didn't even acknowledge she had heard what he said.

"I've just got to call Gloria to rearrange some appointments for this morning, then I will have to go."

"Do what you want Dan. It's your life."

He was puzzled by Elise's words but he didn't have time to think about their meaning.

He quickly called Gloria, finished his breakfast, cleaned up the dishes (it was the least he could do) and made tracks for the hospital.

CHAPTER SEVENTEEN

That evening Dan arrived home and was relieved to discover a note from Elise saying that she was out having dinner with Barbara, her sister. He really didn't want to talk to Elise about Mia anymore. He showered, dressed and left for work the next morning before Elise woke up.

On Friday afternoon Dan arrived home exhausted. He was feeling the effects of donating his stem cells the previous day and he had been working hard on Fay Castle's appeal that afternoon.

That evening neither he nor Elise seemed interested in rehashing their conversation from Thursday morning. They ate dinner quietly together before they embarked on their usual Friday evening rituals. Dan lay on the downstairs sofa to watch Friday night football, while Elise worked in her art room.

Dan dosed off during the football, he often did that on Friday nights. He woke up to banging, quite loud banging.

He heard it again. It was the door, someone was at the door. He heard Elise moving around upstairs and he called out, "I'll get it."

He went to the door wondering who would be knocking on his door late on a Friday night.

"Mr Grover, it is a pleasure to see you again," Senior Detective Sloan said in a manner that conveyed too much pleasure for Dan's liking.

"You remember my partner, Detective Little?"

Dan smiled and nodded in Little's direction.

He did not allow them to pass, despite Sloan's attempt to walk straight in.

"To what do I owe the pleasure of seeing you again so soon, Detective Sloan?" Dan asked.

Sloan immediately grimaced at Dan's failure to acknowledge him as *Senior* Detective Sloan, but he let the comment pass.

"Aren't you going to let us in?"

"Well, no. I am really tired, I am watching Friday night football and I don't want to speak to you right now. Don't you ever see people during business hours?"

"That's a policeman's lot I suppose, we are always on duty. The bad guys never rest, Mr Grover," replied Sloan.

"Let's make an appointment. I can come down tomorrow morning, Saturday morning at 10am. No, actually, I will be busy tomorrow morning." He remembered he had planned to take Elise out for brunch tomorrow morning and he wasn't about to put her off because of some cop who refused to work normal hours.

"It doesn't matter, Mr Grover, we don't care about your busy schedule of football watching. We have come here to see to your wife."

"My wife, what are you talking about? My wife doesn't know anything about Mia Wong." He was groggy having just woken up but now all of a sudden he was very much awake.

"Well, we beg to differ on that point, Mr Grover. Now if you will just let us pass." At this point Sloan moved past Dan pushing him to one side. Dan followed Sloan into the house and Detective Little followed Dan.

"Look, I am sure we can work this out tomorrow, or Monday, or sometime. I will come down and talk with you at the police station. But there is no point talking to my wife. She doesn't know anything about Mia's murder."

Sloan ignored Dan and proceeded along the corridor.

"Furthermore, she does not have to answer any questions if she does not want to and tonight she does not want to." Dan was trying to be reasonable about this but frustration was getting the better of him.

Elise had come downstairs and Sloan made a line directly for her, while continuing to ignore Dan. Dan grabbed Senior Detective Sloan's jacket to get his attention and he quickly turned around and raised his voice at Dan, "Are you attempting to hinder a police officer in the pursuit of his duties?"

"No, but I want to talk to you. You know I know the law. You know you have no right to be in my house without my permission. You know my wife does not have to talk to you. You should know my wife does not even know Mia Wong. So why are you here creating this scene?"

"Why am I creating this scene? I thought you as a sharp lawyer, Mr Grover, would be able to work out what is going on."

"I have no idea!" exclaimed Dan. He wasn't lying, he had no idea what was going on.

"I will tell you what we are doing here, Mr Grover. If your wife does not immediately come down to the police station to talk to us voluntarily, then we will be arresting her."

"What?" Dan said unable to fully comprehend what Sloan had just said.

"You should get your hearing checked, Mr Grover. Everybody else heard what I said," replied Sloan.

"Listen to me. She is not going to talk to you. I will come and see you tomorrow morning."

Senior Detective Sloan turned to Elise and said very slowly and deliberately, "Elise Grover, I am arresting you for the murder of Mia Wong. You do not have to say anything in your defence, but if you do say anything, it may be used against you in a court of law. Do you understand?"

Elise didn't say anything but nodded her head meekly.

"You can't be serious!" Dan said with a look of incredulity that would have done John McEnroe proud.

Dan still couldn't get his head around what was happening. Perhaps he was still asleep and dreaming. He shook his head to try and wake himself up but to no avail, all he did was hurt his head.

"Sloan, what are you doing? Are you crazy, my wife doesn't even know Mia, let alone have a reason to kill her? Look, as I said, if you want to talk to me I am available. We can go right now if you want to."

"It's nice of you to be willing now, to give up your precious time watching football. But we did not come here to talk to you, we came for your wife."

"On what basis are you arresting her?"

Sloan ignored Dan and moved to grab Elise on the arm.

"You can't just come in here and arrest my wife and not tell us why."

"In fact, we can do exactly that and we are doing that. We don't have to give someone a reason why we arrest them. You should know that being a hotshot lawyer."

"Can I get some things?" asked Elise meekly.

"No, your husband can bring things in for you later. Let's go now!" demanded Senior Detective Sloan.

"I really need to go to the toilet," Elise pleaded.

Sloan shook his head.

Elise bowed her head. She looked very unhappy but resigned to her fate.

"Surely, Sloan, that would be ok. I will go with her so she is not alone," volunteered Detective Little.

"Alright, one minute and that's all. I will wait here in the corridor for you. Also give Detective Little the clothes and shoes you were wearing on Tuesday afternoon, we need to analyse them."

After visiting the toilet Elise retrieved her denim jeans, a long sleeved shirt, her chocolate coloured jacket and the shoes she was wearing last Tuesday afternoon and gave them to Detective Little.

"Are these all the clothes you wore?" asked Detective Little.

"Yes," replied Elise.

"Have these clothes been washed?" asked Sloan who had been handed the clothes by Little.

"Yes."

"Why did you wash them?"

"Because they were dirty."

Sloan didn't seem overly impressed with Elise's answer. "Alright, let's go."

At that Elise headed off with Senior Detective Sloan and Detective Little. Dan noticed that Elise was not protesting her innocence and in fact she appeared to be resigned to her fate.

He was dazed, stunned. He still had some idea that he was only dreaming this nightmare.

As Elise was leaving, Dan yelled out to her, "Don't tell them anything. Stay silent till I come and see you."

Then he shouted, "Sloan, she won't be answering any questions without me being present."

He wondered what was going on. What could the police have on Elise that would be strong enough for them to barge into his house and arrest her? They should have arranged for her to surrender herself into custody if they had evidence against her, not come into her home and arrest her in the middle of the night.

Elise had a temper but she wouldn't hurt anybody. What the hell were they arresting her for? Dan felt like he had been one of the main players in the Mia Wong story and yet he obviously had no idea what was going on.

How was Elise involved at all? She didn't even know Mia Wong's name until he told her about Mia yesterday morning.

*

It took Dan only fifteen minutes to arrive at the Brisbane City Police Station. He informed the police officer on duty that Elise had just been arrested for murder and he was not only her husband, but also her lawyer. Dan stressed that his client should not be questioned by the police without him being present during any interview, and that he needed to see her immediately.

Three hours later and Dan was becoming quite agitated. The duty officer had given Dan a variety of excuses why he could not see her. Initially, the duty officer told him that Elise was unavailable as she was being processed. Later he was told because of overcrowding in the cells, they had no secure rooms where he could see her. He was even told at one stage that they were going to move Elise to another police station. Apparently some operation had been conducted that night and the cells were full of people charged with drug and prostitution offences.

Dan approached the duty officer for the fourth time. He fought hard to control his mounting anger and frustration.

"Mate, I have to see my wife now. I have already been waiting here for three hours and I am really worried about her. It doesn't matter where I see her, as long as I see her. I know you are just doing your job, but unless I see her now, I am going to have to file a complaint with the CMC."

"It's got nothing to do with me. I am just relaying to you what I am being told," said the duty officer from behind the counter. He seemed to be amazed that Dan would be so upset with him.

"Just give me your name and number," Dan said as he pulled out his phone. "I mean, I will get to see her sometime. Your delaying me just means you will have a complaint lodged against you personally, as well as the detectives you are in cahoots with."

"Let me go and see what the situation is now," the duty officer said as he sighed and opened a security door.

The duty officer gave Dan the impression that he was doing him a big favour by checking on the situation with Elise again. He was amazed at the hardened attitude of the duty officer. It had taken a direct threat to file a complaint against him personally with the Crime and Misconduct Commission, before he would go and see for himself what was happening with Elise; and then to act as though he was only doing Dan a favour. He wondered if the duty officer would be so uncaring if he was on the other side of the counter.

After about five minutes the duty officer returned and said, "As I have said before, we have no secure rooms available for you to talk to your wife, but if you want, you can have a few minutes with her in the cell she is in. She has three other women in her cell."

"Fine, let's go," said Dan. He was past caring where and how he saw Elise, he just needed to see her.

The police officer led Dan into the back of the police station, along a corridor until they came to the holding cells. He noted that the cells were quite full.

The police officer stopped at the very last cell which contained four women. Dan looked around for Elise and saw her sitting on a metal bench by herself with her head in her hands.

The duty officer announced, "Grover, a visitor for you", and then he left.

Elise rushed over to Dan. They held hands through the bars of the cell.

"Are you ok? I have been trying to see you for the last three hours but they wouldn't let me in."

"Actually, it's not too bad. I have learnt a few things from the girls in here already."

"Learnt a few things?"

"Yes, they speak a different language to me. They use words I have never heard before. I really have led a sheltered life."

He was relieved that Elise was taking her incarceration reasonably well. He had feared the worst, given the submissive state she was in when she was arrested.

"Have you talked to the police?"

"No, I haven't told them anything. They were most upset. I think that Detective Sloan is a misogynist. The way he was speaking to me; it was like he believed I was an idiot just because I was a woman. Saying things to me like unless I talk to him, I will never get out of here. I mean how can he get away with making threats like that?"

"You have done well not telling *Senior* Detective Sloan anything."

"So what happens now, when do I get out?"

Dan looked around and although they were speaking softly, there was no doubt that some of the other women in the cell were listening to their conversation.

"They will take you before the Magistrate this morning. Given that it's a murder charge, the Magistrate really has no discretion. He can't grant you bail this morning. But I will be working on a Supreme Court bail application over the weekend and I will file it on Monday or Tuesday. We should get a bail hearing in the Supreme Court by Thursday or Friday."

Elise collapsed suddenly. Her legs had given way and she was now sitting on the floor holding onto the bars. He had thought Elise was holding up remarkably well, but it was all a front for her cell mates and Dan.

"You alright?" asked Dan concerned.

"I don't understand. I won't be going home this morning?"

Dan squatted down. "Unfortunately the Magistrate you will see this morning has no power to grant you bail on a murder charge," answered Dan trying not to sound like he was just explaining the rules to a card game.

"Only the Supreme Court can grant you bail."

"Why can't we go to the Supreme Court this morning, why do we have to wait till Friday? Like that's a week away."

"The Supreme Court doesn't sit on Saturdays and we have to give the prosecution a couple of day's notice of our bail application."

"I have to stay in here for a week?" asked Elise trying to come to grips with the reality of the situation.

"I know it is not ideal, but with a murder charge the earliest we can arrange to have your Supreme Court bail application heard would be Thursday." Dan was torn between trying to reassure Elise and lift her spirits, at the same time he didn't want to promise something he could not deliver.

"A week! I can't believe I will be in this cell for a week."

"They will probably move you to the Brisbane Women's Correctional Centre with the other female inmates who don't get bail. I will come and see you there tomorrow."

"You mean I will have to spend a week in an actual jail with convicted criminals?"

"Technically, yes, but hopefully they will keep the convicted criminals away from the prisoners on remand like yourself."

"That cheers me up. I feel a whole lot better."

"At least when you go to the Correctional Centre we will be able to talk privately in our own interview room. I really need to find out what evidence they have against you and hear what you have to say, before we make the bail application. We can't talk here."

"But I want to tell you what happened now. Don't you want to know whether I did it or not?"

"Did it or not, what do you mean? You didn't even know Mia, did you? Don't answer that. Let's wait till the Correctional Centre."

"Don't lawyers on TV always say they don't want to know if their client did it or not?"

"They do, but they usually aren't married to their clients. On TV, trials are just a game, in real life they are deadly serious. I can't defend someone unless they tell me their version of events and I believe them."

"That's good to hear because I didn't murder anyone."

"Of course you didn't. That would be absurd."

Dan and Elise embraced through the bars.

"Hang tough, I will get you out. See you Sunday."

CHAPTER EIGHTEEN

Dan waited in the coffee shop across the street from the Police Station. He had devoured three tall blacks each with a dash of milk, an almond croissant and two slices of raisin toast before he saw her. She was walking away from the coffee shop and at a brisk pace as well. He spilt the remnants of his last coffee on his shirt as he moved quickly to catch up with her.

She was walking up Roma Street, so he hurriedly skirted down a side street and then stood in front of her on the footpath. She was too busy looking at the footpath and consumed by her own thoughts to notice him. So there was nothing for it but to chase after her and put his hand out in front of her face to force her to stop and pay attention to him.

"Sarah Crabtree. Well, it's been a long time," Dan announced.

"Hey, it's you. I didn't think you remembered me."

"To be honest, I didn't at first. But last night I woke up in the middle of the night and your name just popped into my head. Sarah Little is Sarah Crabtree. Amazing what your subconscious can do."

"It's very flattering to be remembered by your subconscious, but I am off duty now and I am going home." Sarah started to move off.

"Sarah, could we catch up for old time's sake? I could buy you coffee."

"Look, with the situation your wife is in at the moment, I don't know if that is a good idea."

"Sarah, I am flying in the dark here and I really need your help."

Sarah hesitated. Dan said only one more word, "Please!"

"Alright, there is a coffee shop called *Bonfires* in the Mall. I will meet you there in 10 minutes."

"Thanks, Sarah, see you there."

Sarah kept walking in the same direction she had been travelling previously, even though that was away from the Mall. Dan walked in the opposite direction to Sarah, towards the Mall. He wasn't crazy about the idea of having more coffee, but given he had little sleep last night he figured the coffee would do him more good than harm.

Dan was sitting at a table at the rear of the coffee shop when Sarah walked in. She looked good, with her light blonde hair sweeping down over her shoulders. Sarah took off her trench coat and sat facing Dan with her striped buttoned shirt, neat tan slacks and brown flat soled shoes.

"I have to say you look good. I mean it, you look really good," Dan said.

Sarah smiled and said, "I bet you say that to all your old girlfriends."

"Truth is, I don't have that many old girlfriends."

At that point the waitress arrived and Sarah ordered a flat white on soy, while Dan ordered his fourth tall black.

"You have changed."

"Yes, thank goodness. I had some work done, lost some weight and dyed my hair. What do you think?" Sarah said playing with her blonde locks.

"I like it. Blonde hair really suits you. Wasn't your hair brown before?"

"I had short brown hair before, but I didn't like it. I really wanted to make a few changes in my life."

"Seen any of the old gang around?" Dan asked.

"No, I must admit that I have lost contact with everybody in my class. I suppose it's because I haven't been going to any of the high school reunions. What about you?"

"I have been to a few reunions but not for a couple of years now. I don't know what it is about high school reunions but I don't seem to like them anymore. It's like meeting all these people you have nothing in common with, except having been in the same class as them many years ago.

"I mean, I was friendly with people at school but all these years later meeting up with them again, it's like meeting strangers. And do you bring your partner, I mean they don't know anybody but people like to see partners there."

Sarah smiled but said nothing.

"I see you are married," Dan said looking at Sarah's rings.

"Married? Oh no, not married. It's a long story actually. In fact, I am divorced."

"Divorced?"

"Yes, a few years ago now."

"Must have been rough for you."

"It was rough actually. Hamilton was a bit of a letch."

"Hamilton?"

"Yes, Hamilton Clyde-Little. He is an art dealer in Sydney. We met and started living together soon after I left school. Unfortunately, he couldn't keep his hands to himself and he is now living with his third wife."

"I am sorry."

"Don't be, it's probably the best thing that could have happened to me. I got hitched to his wheelbarrow way too young. Now that I am single again I am loving it."

"Do you remember our time together?" asked Dan.

"Of course, women don't forget those things. I really liked you and you dumped me. I was heartbroken because of you. I should still hate you." Dan was pleased to see Sarah laugh out aloud when she said this.

"I had hoped you still had fond memories of me because of Tarnook Crescent."

"I have never forgotten you or Tarnook Crescent."

Sarah was Dan's first real girlfriend. After he had summoned the courage to finally ask her out, they dated for several months while in high school. During this time they had made out passionately but had not gone all the way. Dan was a little frightened that Sarah was happy to go all the way with him and encouraged him to do so. In the end, Dan decided that he didn't want to have sex with Sarah, or anyone else in high school; he would wait for the right girl at the right time. Consequently, he broke up with Sarah.

Sarah didn't take their separation particularly well. She refused to speak to him for months and sometimes he caught her following him and just staring daggers at him.

One night he was at a party at Tarnook Crescent. Sarah was drinking and making an exhibition of herself. He made the mistake of asking her if she was alright. Sarah none too politely told him to go jump off a cliff, or words to that effect.

He was about to leave the party when he heard yelling and laughter coming from an upstairs. He made his way to the source and found a group of guys lined up outside a room. When he asked what was happening, one guy told him that a skank named Sarah was getting on with everybody who wanted to have a go with her.

That wasn't like Sarah, something was wrong. He pushed the door open and muscled his way in, much to the chagrin of the guys who had cued up outside.

He found Sarah on a bed partly undressed with one guy on top of her and another few guys watching, drinking and laughing.

"Get out!"

The guy on top of Sarah screamed, "I am not finished yet."

Dan didn't know these guys, but what they were doing to Sarah was not right. He could either leave or do something about it.

If he did something, it was likely he would be bashed by the mob and then they'd continue with Sarah. If he did nothing, then he could avoid being bashed but what about Sarah? She deserved better than this degrading behaviour.

Really the decision was not too hard for Dan. If he had a chance to do the right thing, he would do it. So he went for it.

Dan tackled the guy on the bed so hard that he heard the guy's ribs crack, as he hit him with his shoulder. He was up on his feet quickly, before the other guys had a chance to react. He yelled at them to get out and pushed, shoved and herded them out of the room.

These guys were older than Dan but his actions surprised them and they were compliant. Perhaps it was the sight of the tough guy Dan hit crying that really shook them up. He had them all rounded up and out the door, with the door locked, in what seemed like only a few crazy seconds.

Sarah was in a daze on the bed. She appeared only partially coherent. He wasn't sure if she was pleased to see him or not.

His next task was to get Sarah and himself out of the house which was going to be difficult, given the guys he had surprised were probably still in the house and none too pleased with him.

His plan was simple, he called the Fire Brigade. It wasn't long before the wailing engines of the Fire Brigade could be heard screaming down the street. In the confusion he helped Sarah to her feet and walked her out to his car and drove her home.

He told no one what happened. Not her parents, his parents or any of his friends. A few days later he received tickets to the Broncos in the mail. Attached to the tickets was a note which simply read:

> I will never forget what
> you did for me.

*

"Sarah, I need your help. Can you tell me what evidence you have against my wife?"

"You are aware I am not supposed to talk to you about the matter."

"I understand the legal position but I am asking more as a friend than a lawyer. I really need to know what evidence you have against my wife, as I just don't understand what is going on here. I mean as far as I am aware, Elise didn't even know Mia Wong."

Sarah looked straight at Dan. He could tell that she was unsure what she should do.

"I won't tell a single soul, it will just be between you and me, just like Tarnook Crescent. Please Sarah, I need your help," Dan pleaded.

"Alright, I will tell you. But you can't tell anybody you got this information from me."

"Yeah, that's fine Sarah. I give you my word, I will tell no one."

"Your wife has been positively identified by a neighbour as arguing with Mia Wong on her verandah, on the day she was killed. Your wife was also seen entering Mia Wong's house later that same day."

"That can't be right. How can the neighbour be so sure it was Elise?" asked Dan.

"The neighbour was concerned enough by the argument she witnessed, that she took down the make and registration number of the woman's car. The neighbour had one of the registration number's missing and it took us a couple of days before we traced the car back to the one owned and driven by your wife.

"Also, since your wife has been in custody, we have shown her picture to the neighbour in a photo board line up and she has positively identified your wife as the woman she saw at Mia Wong's house twice on the day she was murdered."

Dan wondered how on earth Elise even knew Mia, let alone knew where she lived. And why Elise would visit Mia twice on the day she was murdered. It didn't make any sense to him.

"The murder was reported by an anonymous female caller and the phone call has been traced back to Mia Wong's house. The call was made at 4:54pm. The neighbor saw your wife enter Mia Wong's house shortly before this time."

Dan's face had lost all its colour. He could not comprehend what was happening or what he was hearing. Was he asleep, was this some elaborate nightmare?

"There was no sign of forced entry and this would lead to the conclusion that Mia Wong knew her attacker.

"We have interviewed the other suspects you told us about, Brock Shepard and Samuel Sanderson. We believe from discussions we have had with Mia's friends that she would not let either of these two gentlemen into her house. Also both guys have watertight alibis."

"What about the note I told you about? The note threatening Mia's life unless she left town, have you found that?"

"No, we made a thorough search of Mia's premises and we did not find any threatening note."

"But just because Elise was there, and I don't know yet how she got there or what she was doing there," Dan paused.

"I mean, her being there does not mean that she committed the murder," Dan pronounced.

"A preliminary investigation of the clothes your wife was wearing at the time of the murder has found minute traces of blood. We have yet to confirm that the blood belonged to the victim. But we think the blood we found will belong to the victim, particularly because the clothes have been washed several times with bleach and the shoes have been scrubbed clean. Why would your wife wash her clothes with bleach and scrub her shoes clean if she had nothing to hide?"

Dan was numb, he could not move; the evidence was too overwhelming for him. He just had not expected it to be so strong. He had hoped that Senior Detective Sloan was just playing games with him; that Sloan arrested Elise to get at him.

"Dan, your wife had motive, capacity and opportunity."

"But what about motive, there is no motive," Dan said at last thinking clearly.

"It would appear from Mia Wong's blog, that you were having an affair with her. Your wife found out about it, argued with Mia and then later that day went back to make sure the affair would stop."

"But we weren't having an affair."

"Then why would she write that you were having an affair?"

"I don't know."

"You admitted to spending the night with her."

"Sarah, I really appreciate what you have told me, but I don't want to get into an interview situation with you right now, maybe later.

"Look, I know I can't convince you of this but you do not know my wife, I do. There is no way in this world Elise would even contemplate murdering someone, let alone actually murdering them. It is just not possible despite what the evidence may say. She is not a violent person."

"Are you sure about that Dan?" Sarah asked.

"Yes. We have been together for six years. I know her. She can be bit fiery at times but basically she is a decent and caring person."

"Do you really know her? Sometimes we can think we know someone but in reality we never really know them. Never really understand who they are or what makes them tick."

Sarah had become quite emotional. She quickly wiped away a solitary tear before refocusing.

"I shouldn't be telling you this but do you know about Elise's criminal history?"

"What criminal history?" asked Dan incredulously. "Elise hasn't got a criminal history."

"Ok, I shouldn't have mentioned it."

"Sarah, don't leave me hanging here. Our whole conversation is confidential."

"It would be illegal to tell you about her previous criminal history."

"Please, Sarah!"

Sarah was quiet for a few seconds while she looked at Dan.

"Alright. She has previous history for willful damage, assault and possessing a weapon in public with intent to cause fear."

Dan's mouth dropped. He could not believe what he was hearing.

"Our records indicate that she caught her boyfriend having sex with another woman in his car. She went ballistic. She took a tyre lever from the boot of her car and smashed in all the windows on her boyfriend's car, while he and the other girl were still inside. They were in fear for their lives, such was the ferocity of her behaviour and the threats she made to kill them."

"I was under the impression that she had just spray painted his car with the words, *I am a two timing bastard.*"

"No, it was much more serious than that."

"What sentence did she receive?"

"The court records show that she received a suspended prison sentence, community service and probation."

Dan's head was spinning. Could he be wrong about Elise? Could he have lived with her all these years and not really known her, as Sarah had suggested. He needed time to think it all through.

"Hey, I have to go. But can I get your mobile number, just in case I need to talk to you again?"

"Sure." Sarah then hesitated and asked, "By wanting to talk to me again, you mean about the case?"

"Yes, about the case, only about the case. Sarah I only have one priority at the moment and that is to get my wife out of jail."

Sarah handed Dan a Police Service card with her mobile number on the back.

"Sarah thanks, I really appreciate it. I think we are even now."

"No, we are not even yet, not by a long shot. I will never forget what you did for me. If I can help you again, let me know."

They both left and walked different directions down the Mall.

He was in shock. He reminded himself that every case had two sides and he had only heard one side of the story. After all, Elise had told him she was innocent and he had believed her.

He tried not to think of Elise as a murderer, he really did, but the evidence against her was overwhelming!

CHAPTER NINETEEN

Dan felt winter's chill as he stepped out of his car and walked along the bitumen car park at the Brisbane Women's Correctional Centre.

After signing in and going through security, Dan was led down an outdoor pathway to a small interview room. A few minutes later Elise arrived, escorted by a burly female corrections officer. The corrections officer left as soon as Elise entered the room.

"Elise how are you? I have been worried about you."

"Yeah, I'm fine."

He knew that Elise was the type of stoic person who could be in the throes of being eaten alive by a Great White shark and still say she was fine. She was someone who hardly ever complained or wanted attention focused on herself.

"The good news is after we finish this morning, I will work on your Supreme Court bail application and file it tomorrow. We should have a bail hearing in the Supreme Court in a few days."

"Seriously, still a few more days!

Dan had never seen Elise like this before. She was dressed in a grey prison issued tracksuit, her hair was unkept and she had dark rings under her eyes.

"I am working on it, believe me. But before I file our bail application I need to hear what happened."

Dan didn't tell Elise about the information he had received from Sarah Little. He wanted to see what Elise told him before he started asking questions.

Elise sighed. It was as though she was physically and emotionally preparing herself to finally tell her story.

"Well, that night we went out for dinner at *Comos*, I just had a feeling you were not there; that you had something else on your mind. Anyway, when you got that late night phone call on your mobile from the hospital, I don't know why, but I was suspicious.

"I rang Claye to see how he was. Claye said he was not feeling too good but there was no emergency with his health. He had not asked the hospital to call you.

"I then made a split second decision to follow you. You had lied to me about the phone call and I wanted to know why."

Dan gulped.

"I wasn't sure if I was going to catch you but when I turned down our street, I could see your car parked on the side of the road. I followed you to Spring Hill."

Dan began squirming in his seat. Right here and now he was not sure he wanted to hear the rest of Elise's story.

"After I parked my car I saw a young woman literally jump into your arms, not once but twice. I saw you and her going for it, before the curtains were closed and the lights went out.

"I called you to get you out of there but you obviously had other things on your mind at the time.

"I stayed there sitting in my car on the side of the road for what must have been hours. I am not sure how long I was there. I was numb. I was in shock. Why would you be doing this to me? What had I done to you?"

Dan wanted to jump in and tell Elise the full story. He had to work really hard to restrain himself because he needed to hear Elise's story before he told her his story. He needed to hear what she saw, what she did and what she was feeling at the time.

"The next day I was a mess. I just couldn't comprehend that you would do something like that. I really wanted to know how long it had been going on and where it was headed. I thought about talking to you but you were not around and I didn't want to have that conversation over the phone. Anyway, I couldn't be sure you were not going to lie to me again."

Dan flung his arms out, he couldn't help himself any longer. "That's not fair. I would not have lied to you." His mind convicted him of what he said before Elise could.

"Are you telling me you would not have lied to me? Claye seemed pretty certain that the hospital had not called you. I am pretty certain you did not go to the hospital that night, despite what you told me. You lied to my face, yet you would have told me the truth had I asked you about it later?"

"There is more to the story than what you think," Dan said raising his arms.

Elise did not respond.

Dan sighed. "I am sorry. I should not have interrupted you."

"Anyway, I didn't know what to do. Then I thought why not go to the horse's mouth and ask your girlfriend. I knew her address. If I talked to her I might get the truth."

He closed his eyes.

"So I went to her house and knocked on the door and introduced myself. It is an understatement to say she was surprised to see me. She wouldn't let me in and she wouldn't even give me her name."

Elise was looking straight at Dan while she was talking. He couldn't bear to look at her for more than a few seconds at a time.

"We talked on her front verandah. The conversation didn't last long. I wanted to know what was happening and she would not give me a straight answer. She just told me to go and ask you. She was acting weird and agitated right from the beginning.

"I became frustrated with her evasive answers. She seemed to be telling me that nothing had happened between you.

"In the end all I asked of her was to give me a commitment that she would never see you again. She told me she was leaving town in a few days. I said great, so give me a promise that you will never see him again. That should have been easy. She would not give me that commitment. She would not promise me that she would never see you again."

Dan pondered Elise's words. Mia had really cared for him, perhaps more than he had realized.

"In fact, she hinted quite strongly that you were considering leaving me to run away with her."

Dan looked at the ground.

"I did yell and scream. I told her to stay the hell out of our lives. An elderly lady who lived next door came out on her verandah and asked if she was alright. At that I just left.

"I drove around for awhile, I don't know how long, perhaps an hour or so. I ended up at the Botanical Gardens. It occurred to me that I had really lost my temper with her from the beginning. I thought if I went back and talked to her nicely, calmly, woman to woman, she might answer my questions."

Elise rocked back in her chair and stared at the ceiling. Dan was all ears.

"I have no idea what time it was but it was late afternoon. I went back to her house and knocked politely on the door. I tried the door and found it was not locked. I opened the door and called out, *Hello.*

"As the door was not locked I figured she must be home. So I walked slowly inside the house calling out *Hello*. I walked into the lounge room and then I saw her lying on the floor. I thought she had fallen or collapsed. I bent over to see how she was.

"Her head was partially hidden between a sofa and a coffee table. I found her lying face down in a pool of blood. I moved her slowly so I could see her face. It was then that I saw her head had been smashed in. It was awful!"

Elise paused for a moment, shut her eyes and tried to regain her composure.

"I felt for a pulse but I couldn't find one. I could see from her limp body and the damage to her head that she was dead. There was nothing I could do for her. I felt sick. I just wanted to get the hell out of there.

"I got halfway to the front door when I felt really guilty. I couldn't just leave her there and do nothing. I called 000 from the phone in the house. I didn't give my name as I didn't want to get involved. I wasn't involved, I had just found her body.

"I didn't want to talk to the police about why I was there. I couldn't help her, so it was easy to convince myself there was no need to get involved."

"Why didn't you tell me?" asked an incredulous Dan.

"I did try and tell you on Thursday morning when you were talking to me about your interview with the police, but I decided to listen first. When you didn't tell me the truth about your relationship with her, I thought if you could keep a secret from me, I could keep a secret from you. It was childish of me I know, but I was not thinking clearly at the time."

His mouth had run dry but his body was bathed in perspiration.

"Elise, nothing happened that night other than a kiss. Your phone call broke it up. We agreed to stop after the kiss and I slept on the couch.

"I told Mia that my focus was to restore my relationship with you. I did say that if things didn't work out between you and me, then I might go and see her in Sydney. But that was it, it was all pie in the sky stuff."

"Are you honestly telling me that you did not sleep with her?"

"Yes, I am telling you that loud and clear. I am telling you the truth. You know me."

"I don't think I know you at all. I thought I did but I am not sure anymore."

"Elise, I have to ask you a few questions about what happened."

"I don't think I can answer any questions today, my mind is spinning and I have a pounding headache."

"Alright, that's ok; we will talk again later. You know I am doing everything I possibly can to get you out of here."

Dan and Elise didn't hug. Elise got up first and turned away. He placed his hand on her shoulder and she didn't reach for it but kept walking out the door and down the path. He sat there for a moment and tried to make sense of it all.

He wondered how it had come to this. A young woman he had kissed had been brutally killed and now his wife was charged with her murder.

He believed Elise, but it was obvious that she didn't trust him. He had lied to her. She had good reason not to trust him. Their relationship was now more tenuous than ever. He had to regain her trust. With that thought firmly planted in his mind, Dan fired up his old Subaru and headed out of the prison car park.

CHAPTER TWENTY

It was a bright, sunny day, perfect late winter weather as Dan drove through one of the most expensive suburbs in Brisbane. The tree lined streets of Clayfield were picture perfect.

The homes were huge and had all manner of expensive cars parked in their spacious driveways. The house blocks were very large, considering they were so close to the city. Many contained tennis courts, swimming pools, gazebos and massive Poinciana and Jacaranda trees.

Dan drove up the meandering driveway and parked in the allocated visitor's spot. He was impressed. The house was all white and it was built in the grand old Queenslander style. From the surrounding gardens, tennis court and verandahs, it was obvious this house was imposing and impressive.

He walked up the stairs to the verandah and was met by a young boy about ten years of age and an old ginger labrador.

The labrador, despite its obvious old age, still had thoughts of grandeur and stood his ground near the doorway growling and barking at Dan as though his life depended on it.

"Don't move or he will bite you!" exclaimed the young boy.

Dan doubted the old labrador had any teeth left and he had intended to call the dog's bluff by continuing along the verandah to the front door. But given the boy's instruction he thought it best to play it safe and not proceed any further.

"I am here to see your father, is he in?" asked Dan.

"He is home but he is working and he can't be disturbed while he is working," replied the boy.

"I am a friend of his and I wonder if you could go and get him for me. My name is Dan."

The labrador was still barking incessantly and Dan could not make out what the boy had said to him in reply. But the boy had said something to him and he was not moving.

He figured he would just walk to the door anyway and take his chances with the dog. He noticed the boy was wearing a Manly Warringah Sea Eagles cap which was very rare in Brisbane. Manly are the team everybody in rugby league loves to hate no matter what other team you supported – like Collingwood in the AFL.

Like all Cronulla fans he particularly disliked Manly. The Cronulla Sharks had only made two grand final appearances in their history and both times they were beaten by Manly.

"You don't support Manly do you?" Dan shouted to be heard over the incessant barking.

The boy looked at him as though he was unable to understand what Dan was saying to him.

Dan pointed to the boy's head and then made a whirling gesture with his hand like *that's crazy*.

"Stop! Be quiet, be quiet!" the boy shouted at the dog. The dog was clearly reluctant to take instruction from the boy but downgraded his noise level from loud barking to guttural growling.

"You don't support Manly do you?" Dan repeated as the noise level abated somewhat.

"Sure, I support Manly. They are the best team in the comp."

"Manly," Dan said incredulously. "How could you support Manly, everybody hates Manly?"

"What team do you support?"

"Sharks, I support the Sharks." Dan said as he pumped a closed fist in the air.

"The Sharks, they are crap!"

Dan wondered how everybody, including ten year old boys, could be so dismissive of the Sharks. They weren't a bad team. It's just they had never won the premiership.

Just then a woman came to the door and rescued Dan. She said something to the boy and he and the dog disappeared.

She walked over to Dan put out her hand and said, "I am sorry about that."

Dan grabbed her hand and shook it.

She said, "My name is Cheryl Banks, I see you have met Sandy and Monty."

"Hello, I'm Dan and I am here to see Robin. I am a friend of his. Is he in?"

"Yes, he is out the back in his office working. Does he know you are coming? He doesn't like to be disturbed while he is working."

"Yeah, I have heard that. I did text him that I was coming over this afternoon. He texted back, said it was fine and gave me his address."

As Dan walked through the house he immediately noticed that the house was clean and well kept. There didn't appear to be a speck of dust in the place, despite the ten year old boy and an even older dog.

Wait a minute. Cheryl had called the boy, Sandy. Surely not! Surely Robin had not named his son, Sandy Banks. After all the ribbing and gratuitous ridicule he would have endured because his parents had named him Robin Banks. Surely Robin had not called his son Sandy Banks.

Eventually they came to the end of the house and to a room with the door shut. There was a large sign on it which read:

DO NOT ENTER

Cheryl knocked gently on the door before opening it and saying, "Robin, a friend of yours is here to see you."

"Show him in," came a voice from the room.

Cheryl pulled back from the doorway and motioned for Dan to enter the room.

"Thanks," Dan said to Cheryl as he moved past her and shook hands with Robin, who was getting up from his desk.

"You called your son Sandy, Sandy Banks. No wonder he is a Manly supporter, the poor kid," Dan said with mock concern.

"It's nice seeing you again Dan. I am sure you haven't come all this way to criticize me in my own home about my son's name."

"Actually, I have something very important to discuss with you but it just hit me that you called your son Sandy Banks, after all you must have gone through with your name."

"I am not sure where you are getting your information, but it is inaccurate. My son is Montgomery Banks and our dog is called Sandy. My wife thought there was some humour in naming our light coloured dog Sandy."

"Oh, I see," Dan said.

"As for Monty being a Manly supporter. Well he loves his football and I asked him when he was younger which team he wanted to support; he liked the Sea Eagles mascot, so he chose Manly. I am not a father who insists or expects his son to follow the same team as he does. In fact, I think a healthy rivalry is good for a father and son relationship. Monty supports the Sea Eagles, you know I support the Broncos, and Cheryl supports the North Queensland Cowboys; we all have some fun with it."

Dan looked around Robin's office; unlike the rest of the house it was a mess. There were papers strewn all over the place, the desk had several large files that were open and on top of each other, there was a laptop on the floor and the rubbish bin was in clear view and full to overflowing.

"I must say you have done pretty well for yourself Robin, affording this house on your prosecutor's wage."

"My prosecutor's wage would not pay for my Saab convertible's premium fuel, let alone this house. Cheryl's parents have some serious money and they bought this house for us. Cheryl receives regular installments from them through a family trust fund, so we can afford life's little necessities."

"Yeah, I can see that," Dan said as he looked out the office window to the tennis court, gazebo and manicured lawns.

"So what can I do for you? You mentioned something in your text about having a job for me."

"I heard that you have left the Commonwealth Prosecutor's Office and have begun working for yourself as a barrister. I must say you have nice digs for a barrister."

"Yes, I have just jumped in the deep end and made the change from working for somebody else to working for myself. I haven't been able to secure a room yet in a barrister's chambers in the city, so I am working from home at the moment."

"Robin, let me say at the outset I have always admired your work. Being on the other side of the Bar table from you, I have seen how you have succinctly and cleverly cross-examined witnesses and been able to influence magistrates, judges and juries. I believe you are very competent and in a short time you will become a much sought after barrister."

Robin was blushing. Dan had not seen this from him before. He had only known Robin as another lawyer doing his job with the occasional friendly banter about sport. He had not seen Robin as a real person who might blush at hearing how talented he was.

"Anyway, enough of the buttering up. What do you want me to do for you?" asked Robin.

"Let me start from the beginning. My brother Claye has leukemia and is currently in hospital having a donor stem cell transplant. I am the donor by the way. He is actually using my stem cells, my immune system to beat his cancer once and for all."

"Heaven help him," Robin said dryly.

Dan ignored Robin's remark. "Claye runs a corporate investigation business where he is contracted by companies to investigate allegations of workplace misconduct. Given that Claye is in hospital, I agreed to conduct a workplace investigation for him."

Dan noticed Robin was already looking bored. That vacant look that barristers often get when they are not interested in what is being said.

"I conducted an investigation for Claye where the complainant alleged that she was sexually assaulted by a work colleague."

"In the workplace?" Robin asked appearing to be more interested now.

"Not exactly. She and a work colleague were drinking after a workplace function when he spiked her drink and later sexually assaulted her in his car."

"Were the police involved?"

"No, the complainant did not trust the police."

"Were there any witnesses? How do you know if the complainant was just imagining everything or worse, that she was making the whole thing up?"

Dan did not appreciate the question. Mia was not someone who made things up, or was she? He really didn't know Mia that well.

"There was indirect evidence around recent complaint, consistency of versions and pattern of behaviour which led me to accept her version of events as being more likely to be true."

"So where do I come in?" Robin asked.

"The complainant Mia Wong came to me just before I had finished writing the investigation report. She showed me a note that threatened her life unless she left Brisbane. She felt that she was being followed and watched. She was very scared. She had only recently moved to Brisbane and she didn't have anyone else she could ask to help her, so I agreed to help her out."

"What do you mean, *help her out*?"

"I agreed to help her out, if she felt scared or threatened at any time."

"So you agreed to help her out on an unrelated matter to your investigation, while you were still completing your investigation. Weren't you worried about bias, that your report could be tarnished by an allegation that you were biased towards the complainant?"

"Yes, that thought did cross my mind, but I was nearly finished the report and she desperately needed help and there was no one else to help her."

"The police, other friends of hers, or friends of yours, could not have helped her?"

"She was not confident the police could or would help her, and I could understand that."

"I presume she was a good looker."

"She was ok," Dan said wanting to downplay Mia's appearance and the idea he had only helped Mia because he was attracted to her.

"Go on," Robin said.

He could see that he was now pricking Robin's interest.

"I received a call from Mia late one night. I went over to her house and discovered that someone had flicked her safety switch off and she had no power. Mia had earlier seen someone lurking in the shadows of her yard. She was really scared, she was petrified.

"In summary, I flicked the safety switch on for her. I didn't see anyone loitering around the house. I stayed the night."

"You what?" asked Robin leaning forward anxious not to miss the answer to his question.

"Mia was really scared. What was I supposed to do?"

Robin did not respond. He just looked at Dan.

"I did not sleep with her. We made out a little and that was all."

Robin twisted his lips and raised his eyebrows. He did not say anything.

"That was all! There was nothing more to it than that. Anyway a day or so later the police rock up to my house and tell me that Mia has been murdered in her own home.

"I was in shock. I gave the police all the information I had, except for leaving out the kissing part. I figured that was not relevant to their investigation. It's personal."

"So you lied to the police who were conducting a murder investigation?"

"Look, in hindsight, I probably should have told them about making out with Mia but I just didn't think it was relevant at the time."

"You mean you didn't think anybody would find out about it?"

"I suppose that thought crossed my mind as well."

"Go on."

"Well a couple of days later the police came knocking on my door again and this time it's not me they want to talk to. They end up arresting Elise, my wife, for Mia's murder."

"Hold on – what did you say?"

"The police believe Elise killed Mia in a fight over me."

"What do you believe?"

"I don't believe Elise murdered Mia."

"Why do you believe that?" Robin asked casually.

"I have been married to Elise for six years. I know her well, or at least I thought I did. She can get angry at times and she does not think much of me at present, but she is not someone who lies or is capable of murder. She is capable of some verballing, especially towards me, but she is basically a very caring person. Violence is not part of her DNA."

"Jealously is a powerful motivator. People change when confronted with extraordinary circumstances. You should know that, Dan, from your legal aid work."

"Elise does have a previous criminal conviction for assault. Apparently, before she met me, she smashed the windows in of a car that belonged to her boyfriend at the time. She found him cheating on her with another woman."

Robin grimaced with the news.

"It does get worse in that her boyfriend and the girl were in the car at the time Elise smashed the windows in. Apparently she threatened to kill them."

"Come on, Dan, you expect a jury to buy that she is not the violent type?"

"I was surprised to hear what happened with her ex-boyfriend. But I have lived with this woman for six years. I have seen her cry when she sees a hurt animal and she just can't watch TV shows depicting children being hurt or abused. I am sure the car incident was just a one off spur of the moment thing when she was young, a teenager. And she didn't actually hit anyone, only the car."

Robin shook his head.

"I have been thinking about it and the likely perpetrator is the person Mia saw in her yard. The person who switched her electricity off and sent her the threatening note. Elise couldn't be this person as she didn't know Mia until she followed me to her house."

"Do we have any evidence of that?"

"I can provide evidence of that, from what Mia told me and showed me."

"The police don't have the threatening note?"

"No, they didn't find it."

"Did you see the intruder?"

"No."

"So the only corroboration for the existence of the threatening note is from you, Elise's husband. There is no corroboration of Mia seeing an intruder, except what she told you which is technically hearsay.”

“I actually saw the threatening note, so that evidence is not hearsay. Also, I told the police about the threatening note before Elise was arrested. This proves that I did not make up my evidence about the note to protect Elise.”

“There is the possibility that Mia’s murder had absolutely nothing to do with the stalker and the threatening note.”

“Elise didn’t do it, Robin, and I need your help. I am too involved to represent her myself and I would like you to represent her.”

“You should not even think about representing her, as her husband, not to mention you are a witness,” Robin said with authority.

Robin leaned back in his chair and clasped his hands against the back of his head. “Look, Dan, I am honoured you have asked me but I have not been in any murder trials before. I have only just begun to work at the private Bar. There are many more senior barristers than me that you could choose.”

“I know you are inexperienced with murder trials but I also know you are very capable. I want to work with you on this as your instructing solicitor. I can’t just sit by and let Elise get convicted. I need to be involved in the case.”

“So, what you are saying is that more experienced barristers than me would quite rightly not allow you to be as involved in this case as you would like to be. But as I am inexperienced in serious criminal matters, you hope that I would not be so principled.”

“Yes, that’s about it, and you are good. I wouldn’t have picked you unless you were competent.”

“I need some time to think about this, Dan.”

“I have a Supreme Court Bail Application set for tomorrow at 2:00pm. I am afraid we don’t have much time.”

Robin swung around in his chair to face away from Dan and look out over his tennis court and manicured lawn. After what seemed like an eternity, Robin returned his chair to face the desk and he looked straight at Dan.

“I must be crazy agreeing to this, but for a criminal barrister the zenith of your career is a murder trial. I can’t let it pass. I may never get another one. Alright, I will do it but if I feel you are not thinking rationally or objectively, you will replace yourself as instructing solicitor with another solicitor, agreed?”

“Agreed.”

“Right, we need to get cracking straight away. What have you got for me?” asked Robin.

“I have a brief for you in my bag which contains a signed statement from

Elise. I took the liberty of compiling it for you before I came over."

"I can't believe my first case as a private barrister is a murder," Robin said shaking his head, looking at the papers Dan had handed to him.

Dan looked rather sheepish as he lowered his head and then raised it to face Robin.

"Robin, another consideration for me in deciding that you would be my first choice as Elise's barrister is that I felt your fees would be much less than those of more experienced barristers. I mean this being your first private case, I was hoping your fees would be something that an ex-legal aid lawyer like myself could afford."

"Forget the fees, we will work them out later. This is a murder trial. If I win this case I will have a reputation that will allow me to charge whatever fees I like in the future."

"That's the spirit. A competent barrister who is not worried about fees. Your reputation is going to go ahead in leaps and bounds after this trial. You will be fighting off all manner of drug dealers, paedophiles and rapists."

Robin chuckled as he began reading the Brief of Evidence that Dan had prepared.

CHAPTER TWENTY ONE

Dan made his way through the throng of people queuing up at security and proceeded directly to Courtroom 4. He found Robin pouring over his submissions in a nearby interview room.

"Would you like to see Elise before court?" Dan asked.

"Yes, I would like to meet her."

In the Queensland judicial system there are separate barristers and solicitors. Solicitors can do court work but usually solicitors take instructions from clients and instruct barristers to represent their clients in court. Often clients do not meet their barrister until the morning of the court case.

Dan and Robin made their way down to the holding cells beneath the Supreme Court.

Elise was wearing a simple white dress and black heeled shoes that Dan had brought in for her to wear. Her long auburn hair was tied up in a bun and she was wearing little to no makeup.

"Elise, this is Robin Banks, he is the barrister who will be representing you in the bail application today," Dan said.

Elise raised her eyebrows at Robin's name.

"I know he has a funny name, but I have worked with him before and he is very good," Dan said sincerely.

"Thank you, Robin, for taking on my case. I can't tell how much I am looking forward to getting out of jail today and being home again," Elise said.

Robin raised his hand. "Before we go any further, Elise, you need to be aware that getting bail today isn't certain, in fact it is probably only a 50 - 50 proposition at best."

Elise quickly turned to Dan and with the blood rushing to her face, she raised her voice and said, "I thought you told me that I would be getting out of here today!"

"It's a decision for the Judge. We can't be certain what he will do. What I promised was that Robin and I would do everything we possibly could to get you out of jail today. We have thoroughly prepared for today's hearing and we expect it will go well, but we can't guarantee anything."

Elise put her head in her hands. Dan felt sorry for her but he was only repeating what he had already told her several times this week.

"What type of committal hearing do you want us to arrange in the event you don't get bail today?" asked Robin.

"I just want to get out of here as soon as possible. Whatever it takes to get my trial heard quickly is what I want. It upsets me that you have stopped me from talking with the police. Once I tell my story, I reckon this whole nightmare will be over. The last thing I want to do now is get caught up in some legal process which keeps me in jail, when I have done nothing wrong."

"Elise, I understand where you are coming from, but the legal process is designed to afford you rights which ultimately will be of benefit to you," Robin said without any emotion.

"Do you, Mr Barrister, do you understand where I am coming from? Do you have any idea where I am coming from? Do you have any idea what it is like to be frog marched out of your own home in the middle of the night? To be kept in jail with women who would bash you as quickly as look at you? To have your every movement monitored and watched? To have people look at you like you are dirt, no more than a common criminal? To have no idea when, if ever, you will be able to wake up from this living nightmare? I don't think you have any idea where I am coming from."

Rather than being upset, Dan was relieved to see Elise having a go at Robin. She was showing some spark, some fight for her own survival that she would need to get through this ordeal.

Dan leaned over so that he was close to Elise and he spoke softly. "Robin and I will do our best for you today. We can't begin to know the ordeal you are going through at the moment but know this; we are on your side, we will do anything and everything we can to get you out of here, be it today or down the track."

After a few moments of silence, Elise turned to Robin and said, "I'm sorry, I am just scared and missing my home. I appreciate all you are doing for me."

"Alright then, no harm done, we will see you in court," Robin said as he hurriedly left Elise with Dan trailing behind him.

Dan turned and said, "Hopefully you will be home tonight and we can have a candle lit dinner on the deck."

"I hope so, I hope so."

*

Dan and Robin sat on the left hand side of the bar table while the Department of Public Prosecution's prosecutor and his instructing clerk sat on the right hand side. Out in front and up a level sat His Honour Justice Bradley Milles, with his Associate sitting in front of him and lower down. To the side and behind Dan was the dock where Elise sat.

Courtroom 4 was like any other courtroom in the Supreme and District Court complex. It was wood paneled, with an unpainted high concrete ceiling, large video monitors mounted on the walls and air conditioning vents running through the floor. The Queensland Coat of Arms was barely prominent above the elevated Judge's seat.

Like all modern court rooms it had computers and electronic recording devices installed.

All in all it was a pretty inhospitable place to be for anyone who did not work there.

Dan took notes as the DPP prosecutor outlined his case. The prosecutor started with the evidence and then pleaded with His Honour not to let a dangerous and perverse criminal like Elise out onto the streets.

Give me a break, Dan thought. The prosecutor doesn't know anything about Elise.

The prosecutor said nothing really compelling just the same old submissions about serious crimes being perpetrated by serious criminals who should be kept locked up until the trial, for the protection of little old ladies everywhere. Dan thought the prosecutor's monotone regurgitation had actually turned Justice Milles off his submissions.

Robin rose to his feet and began his submissions by emphasising that although Elise was seen at the murder scene around the time of the murder, she was not seen committing the murder. Robin asked His Honour if visiting someone was a crime, let alone an act that should deprive them of their liberty pending a trial.

Robin invited His Honour to consider Elise as a young wife who just happened to be in the wrong place at the wrong time, no more than that. That Elise was in a stable long term relationship with a solicitor of some standing known to this court, that her previous convictions were many years ago and were a spur of the moment thing, due to the impetuosity of youth.

Robin asked Justice Milles to consider the psychological damage someone like Elise could suffer at being confined with hardened criminals for months or even years before the trial of this matter might take place.

Dan liked what he heard from Robin. It was, after all, Robin's first submission on behalf of a defendant; he usually worked on the other side of the Bar table.

His Honour Justice Milles leaned forward slowly, looked in Elise's direction and said, "This is a difficult matter I will need a little time to come to my decision. I will adjourn for one hour and then come back and deliver my determination."

His Honour slowly rose out of his seat and left as everybody else stood and bowed in deference to him.

Dan asked Robin, "Well, how do you think it went?"

"It went well, better than I had hoped actually."

"Yeah, I thought it went well, the Judge seemed to be taking onboard your submissions. Well done, by the way."

"Thanks, just doing my job."

"Why do you think he needs an hour to make his decision?" asked Dan.

"It could be that he is impressed with our submissions. He does not want to keep Elise locked up pending the trial and he needs time to justify that decision, given the seriousness of the murder charge against Elise. Or it could be that he has someone to see over afternoon tea and he would like an hour off."

The corrections officer who was sitting near Elise got Dan's attention and let him know that Elise wanted to talk with him. Dan moved over to Elise and she asked him, "What is going on?"

"The Judge is having a break. We hope he is writing a decision granting you bail. Why else would he need so much time? It all looks good. Robin did a good job and the Judge appeared to be very interested in what he was saying as opposed to what the prosecutor was saying."

"Dan, I have been thinking. I want you to know that I believe you when you tell me you weren't having an affair with that poor girl."

"Thanks, Elise."

"I do appreciate the help and support you are giving me."

"That's ok. Remember, no matter what the outcome is today, I am going to be with you in this to the end. It's you and me, right?" Dan pumped his fist for affect.

Elise smiled and grabbed his hand.

"We are taking her back to the holding cells now," the corrections officer said as Dan and Elise held hands. Dan let go first and watched Elise being taken back through the internal doors which lead to the secure lift taking her to the basement holding cells.

*

"All rise!"

With these two words Justice Bradley Milles re-entered the court.

The courtroom was deathly quiet. Everybody from the Judge's Associate to the corrections officer, to the journalists and other people sitting in the public gallery, and of course Dan, wanted to clearly hear His Honour's decision in this matter.

"At the outset let me say I have been extremely impressed with defence counsel and the way he has made submissions on behalf of his client. It is obvious to me that Mrs Grover is, for all intents and purposes, a lady of good character with no involvement in criminal matters for many years. She is a young woman who very much misses her home environment."

Dan didn't like where His Honour was going with this. When judges or magistrates rapt the defendants at the beginning of their sentencing remarks, it usually meant they had bad news to tell them at the end of their sentencing remarks.

"However..."

There it was that terrible word *However.*

"However, I cannot go past the gravity of the indictment presently before the Court and the substantial mandatory term of incarceration which will accompany that indictment, if it is proven beyond a reasonable doubt in this judicial system. Hence, having fully considered this matter from every angle and giving it the full magnitude of my deliberations, I am convinced that my only real option to properly serve justice, despite my personal feelings of sympathy towards the accused, is to determine that she remain incarcerated until the indictment has been fulfilled."

With that His Honour quickly left the courtroom before everybody could stand and bow.

There remained an eerie silence in the courtroom after Justice Bradley Milles had left. No one seemed to know quite what had happened.

Dan a criminal lawyer understood what His Honour had just said but he knew Elise probably would not have. Why do Judges speak in such language that no one other than lawyers can understand them? Anyway that was a question for another time. Certainly he wondered why it would take Justice Milles an hour to come up with those few words of wisdom.

Dan turned to Robin to confirm the bad news before he would break it to Elise. How would she react, he shuddered at the thought.

Robin had his head bowed and he looked up and mouthed the word, *Sorry*. He did not say the word he just mouthed it. The courtroom was still eerily quiet.

Dan turned around and saw Elise's puzzled expression. He walked over to her and by the time he had reached her, after only a few steps, her expression had changed to one of complete horror and anguish. Elise began sobbing before Dan said anything to her. In reality, he didn't know what to say.

"It's a disappointment. But it's a journey we are on and disappointments along the way don't determine the ultimate destination. The trick is to recognize this as just a battle, a skirmish along the way. The ultimate prize is to win the war. Make no mistake we will win the war, you will be found not guilty."

As a lawyer he knew he could not promise anything. He particularly could not promise someone they would be found not guilty. Who knew what a twelve person jury would or would not do? But for the time being, his days as a by-the-book lawyer were coming to an end and the time for being a husband of a wife who desperately needed him to support her were coming to the fore; he couldn't be emotionless or cautious about this anymore.

"Stay strong and keep your head up in there until we can get you out."

Elise didn't say anything but she grabbed Dan's hand while sobbing quietly.

"It looks like it's over, we will have to go now," the corrections officer said.

"Just give us a few more minutes, please," Dan pleaded.

The corrections officer did not reply but remained seated.

Dan hugged Elise and she melted into his arms.

He couldn't help thinking that he had been the cause of all this turmoil and suffering. He had to make things right.

After a few minutes the corrections officer stood up and seemed determined to go. Rather than cause a scene Dan whispered to Elise to remember that she was not alone in this, he was with her too.

At that Elise was escorted by the corrections officer out of the courtroom.

Robin came over to Dan and said, "I don't know about you but I could use a beer. Why don't we go to the tavern and discuss where to from here over a few cold ones?"

"You paying?" Dan responded quickly with a sly grin.

"Yes, I will pay, though at the rate you're paying me, this job will end up costing me money." Robin laughed quietly as he gathered up his papers which were strewn all over the bar table.

"Actually, Robin, I don't think I will. Thanks all the same."

"Come on, there is no point beating yourself up over the decision," Robin persisted.

"I just don't feel like it at the moment. I will call you tomorrow."

Dan was aware that he and Robin needed to debrief about what had just happened and discuss where to from here, but he just couldn't stomach having a drink with him today. He was too upset.

As he left the confines of the court complex he felt a sudden and strong urge to pray for Elise. He had not experienced anything quite like that before. He was not sure what was happening but he rationalised his feelings as just being traumatized by the prospect of Elise spending the next few months in jail, not to mention the rest of her life!

CHAPTER TWENTY TWO

Dan moved quickly down the long corridor of the hospital's Intensive Care Unit, even though he had no real idea where he was going. He was relieved to see a familiar face at the nurse's station.

"Hi, Dorothy, remember me, Dan Grover? I am Claye's brother. I just had a call from someone here letting me know that Claye is not doing too well."

"Yes, I remember you. You are the quiet one of the brothers."

Dan and Dorothy both chuckled awkwardly remembering their last meeting.

"How is he?"

Dorothy's face changed from smiling to dead pan in an instant.

"Unfortunately, your brother has had an adverse reaction to the stem cells he received as part of his transplant."

"What do you mean?"

"With respect to these types of transplants there is always a risk that the donor's immune system is too strong. The donor stem cells may kill the disease but also may attack the patient's vital organs.

"As with any cancer treatment, everybody is different, every cancer reacts differently to treatment, there is no exact science.

"Unfortunately, the donor's immune system has begun to attack Claye. Claye's Hematologist and Oncologist has admitted Claye to the ICU so that we can give him the specialist around the clock care he needs at the moment."

"How bad is it?"

"All I can say as a nurse with some experience in this area is that it is quite serious."

Quite serious, that didn't sound too good. With all the work he had put into Elise's bail application over the last week he had not really had much time to even think about Claye. Claye can't be that bad, can he?

Dan walked quietly into Claye's room and noticed that he was asleep. He sat down a few metres from Claye's bed, careful not to come too close to him.

His thoughts turned to his childhood and the good times he and Claye had had together. In situations like these you remember the good times, rather than the bad times; of two boys playing together in the back yard without a care in the world.

"Mate, mate can you hear me?"

Dan was in another world playing cricket with Claye and he could hear Claye calling out to him. Just then he realized Claye was speaking to him in this world, not in his memory world.

"What's wrong with you?" Claye said abruptly, in a raspy voice.

"Just off in memory land."

"For a moment there I thought you had croaked on me," Claye said.

"So, Claye, how are you? You seem to be back to your old self."

"I'd be really good if it wasn't for your stem cells, they are literally killing me."

"Sorry about that. But you had to know my cells would be superior to yours in every way. You sound alright, are you feeling ok?"

"Not really. I feel so sick I can't eat, can't drink. I can't even swallow without pain. Not that I can really taste anything anyway."

"Well look on the bright side, you always wanted to lose a few kilos, now it is happening for you."

"Yeah, I should patent this diet. Guaranteed to work, only problem is that you are in constant pain and feel nauseous all the time."

"I am sorry I haven't been to see you for awhile, I have been busy."

"Mate, what's happening out there?"

"I won't bore you with the full story, but you know that investigation I did for you the other day, well the complainant has been murdered. The police talked to me as they found a diary blog she had written which they believe indicates that she and I were having an affair. We weren't having an affair but, long story short, the police have charged Elise with the murder."

"What?" Claye gasped as he said this and he went into a long and painful coughing stint.

He thought about calling the nurses but decided against it as Claye eventually came around.

"That's exactly what I said when I was told they were going to charge Elise with murder. Unfortunately, Elise didn't get bail, so she will have to stay in jail until the trial which will be months away."

Claye appeared to be speechless, which was something Dan had not seen before.

"Mate, I would like to ask your advice on a couple of matters if you are up to it?"

"Mate, anything," Claye said still spluttering and trying to stop coughing.

Claye moved his bed via his remote control to a sitting position and gave Dan his full attention.

"How is Elise holding up? It must be terrible for her."

"Not the best at the moment."

"What can I do for you, mate? Ask me anything."

"The complainant, Mia Wong, I don't know too much about her or who might want to do this to her. She was a lovely person. In terms of an investigation into who might have killed her, where do you suggest I should start?"

"I suppose the key is getting to know her better, to get an idea about who could have murdered her. Perhaps you could talk to her friends and family. But the police should have done that already."

"The police seem to have jumped on the bandwagon pretty quickly that it was Elise. I am not sure how much time they have put into investigating other suspects."

"Mate, for me not knowing too much about anything to do with this matter, I would concentrate on the work colleague. From what you have told me about him, if someone is devious enough to spike a young woman's drink, sexually assault her in his car and then convincingly lie about it, he is a very unreliable character who may be capable of anything.

"Check into his previous workplaces. As I told you before, we never investigate someone who has committed their first act of sexual harassment or assault. There is always a trail to find other sexual harassment victims. Maybe this is not the first murder for our guy."

"Good thinking, I will do that."

Dan stopped talking. He was uncertain how to approach Claye about the other topic he wanted to discuss with him.

"Mate, anything else you want to talk to me about?"

"Well out of the blue, I have started having these random thoughts about God. I always believed God was just a figment of your imagination, but I am not so sure now. You seem to have a faith in God that is real, despite your problems. Why do you believe in God?"

"Mate, I believe in God because a little voice in my heart tells me he is real."

"But if God is real, why would he let you suffer like this? Why would he let Elise suffer like she has? Why would he allow Mia Wong to be murdered?"

"Mate, that is a good question.

"My belief is not based on what God has given me or not given me. In other words my faith in God is not dependent on my personal circumstances.

"I do not know why some people go through hardships, while others don't. I do know that God loves me and that nothing or no one can separate me from him.

"All Christians run into trouble from time to time. But God rewards those who persevere, who do not throw away their faith just because things in their life are not going the way they would want them to go.

"I know that God wants me to be a blessing to others. This is what sustains me; his love and my desire to pass on that love to others."

"When did you get to be so religiously insightful?"

"Mate, I have been lying in bed for weeks without being able to eat, drink, breathe, pass wind or do anything without discomfort. I could die at any moment. It is amazing how having a life threatening disease like cancer can help you see things more clearly."

"Thanks Claye, I mean it, thanks."

"Hey, on your way out could you ask that nice nurse Dorothy, to come in and see me. Tell her I need some attention."

"Sure thing, Claye."

Dan walked straight out of Claye's room to the nurse's station where he saw Dorothy.

"Hey just been to see Claye and he seemed in good spirits, not like he was on death's door."

"Claye has a strong personality. He is a character, a trooper. He picks himself up when people visit him. Even with the nurses he is always polite and joking. But he is very sick."

"Claye asked if you could go in and see him. Apparently he wants some attention."

Dorothy smiled.

"Thanks again for all that you are doing for him. Please let me know if his situation changes."

As Dan was leaving he paused and watched Dorothy walking briskly towards Claye's room. He marvelled at how little he really knew about his big brother. They had never been very close. Perhaps that should change.

CHAPTER TWENTY THREE

Dan was driving along Coronation Drive next to the mighty, muddy Brisbane River, when a violent thunder storm exploded all around him. He could see the dark clouds rolling in threatening to strike, as he left the hospital. He had felt the wind whipping up from nowhere and he had smelt the sweet scent of rain in the air. He knew what was coming but had hoped to make it back to his office before the thunder storm unleashed its full fury.

Thunder sounded like an almighty whip being cracked in the sky. Lightning lit up the darkness. Even though it was only 4:00pm the massive dark storm clouds had strangled all the sunlight out of the day and car lights were illuminating everywhere.

Then rain came in all its ferociousness. Dan's windscreen wipers were at full speed, yet they were struggling to keep up with the torrent of rain that was now hurtling down. He was concentrating intently as the road was clogging up with parked cars and overflowing storm water drains.

He felt the vibration of his phone before he heard it ring, due to the din of the thunder storm. Dan had no choice now, he could not continue driving in these conditions and talk on his phone at the same time. He abandoned his plan to drive through the surging storm. Best to pull over and wait this one out.

He had difficulty finding a safe place to pull over on the side of the road but eventually he did. By the time he could answer his phone, the call had cut out.

He looked at the phone number that had been calling him and he recognized it as the mobile number given to him by Sarah Little.

He wondered why Sarah would be calling him. It must be important. He was about to hit redial on his phone when all of a sudden it sprang to life again.

"It's Robin, can you talk. Sounds like you're in an air raid shelter."

"Yes, I can talk. It's just a bit hard to hear you over the noise of the thunder storm."

"I can see the storm coming in but we haven't had any real activity here at Clayfield yet."

"You will soon, I think it is coming your way. What's up?"

"I have just received the prosecution statements and evidence for the committal and I have found something important. Can you come over?"

"I am on my way, be there in 10-15 minutes depending on the storm."

Dan terminated the call made by Robin and worked his phone to find Sarah's number. He rang the number but only received voice mail. He was reluctant to leave a message on Sarah's phone. He was aware she had not left him a voice mail message on his phone.

He decided to brave the storm again and carefully maneuvered his old Subaru back onto the road. He wondered what important evidence Robin had found in the committal documentation and if it related to Sarah's missed call.

The thunder storm had moved on by the time Dan arrived at Robin's house. The powerful storm had ripped through Clayfield, leaving a trail of debris haphazardly strewn across the once leafy Clayfield street where Robin lived.

"Quite a storm we just had passing through here," Robin said.

"Yeah, there is debris everywhere."

"I bet the airport copped a hiding."

Enough of the small talk thought Dan.

"You said you found something important in the prosecution evidence?"

"Yes I did, it was tucked away in the middle of these papers."

Robin held aloft a handful of papers and waved his arm over a mass of other documents completely covering his desk.

Dan looked at Robin expectantly. Robin seemed to be having another thought and was a million miles away.

"Are you going to tell me or do I have to work it out telepathically?" Dan asked.

"There are two things actually. The first is a finger print report in relation to a glass vase that was owned by the victim. The report indicates that Elise's finger prints were found on the glass vase.

"I initially thought this report was included in the evidence as the police were trying to establish Elise was in the victim's house. Because she has not talked to the police, they only have the neighbour's evidence that she was at the victim's house.

"However, when I dug further through the documentation, I found a supplementary statement by Detective Sloan, the arresting officer."

"Actually that's *Senior* Detective Sloan. He gets a bit touchy about people referring to him only as Detective Sloan," Dan said seriously but with a sly grin on his face.

"Anyway, from Senior Detective Sloan's statement it appears that the glass vase was found under a sofa across the room from where the victim was found.

"This really spiked my interest in this vase. I called the prosecutor and was told that the glass vase was not initially found by the police when they reviewed the crime scene. Apparently the vase was only found some weeks later when crime scene cleaners were called in to clean the place.

"It was only after I pushed the prosecutor as to the significance of the glass vase that he dropped the bombshell."

Dan was on the edge of his seat. He suspected he would not like the bombshell but he needed to hear it.

Robin said nothing. He had created this tension then paused for effect, a typical barrister tactic.

"Are you going to tell me or is it one of those mental telepathy things again!" Dan added without trying to hide the frustration in his voice. This whole case was beginning to get to him, big time.

"Hold your horses, give me a chance to tell the story," Robin seemed miffed at Dan's abrupt attitude. Like most barristers, he enjoyed a little theatre now and again.

"After some intuitive digging on my behalf, the prosecutor told me that this particular glass vase is the likely murder weapon. It had the victim's blood splattered all over it and its shape is consistent with the blows the victim received to the head."

Dan didn't like the sound of that. Elise's finger prints on the murder weapon, how did that happen?

"But wait there's more. The prosecutor also told me that he had just received another statement from Senior Detective Sloan, which I do not have, indicating that he has recently talked with Elise about the glass vase. Sloan states that Elise denied touching the vase or having any knowledge of the vase.

"Apparently, after Sloan informed Elise that her finger prints were on the vase, she changed her story and admitted that she touched the vase but could not account for why she touched the vase or how it came to be under the sofa across the room."

"Sloan should not be talking to Elise. We have made it quite clear to the police she should not be spoken to about these matters without her legal representatives being present."

"I did make that point rather forcibly to the prosecutor and he just said that it has happened and couldn't do anything about that now. Of course, I can jump up and down about that at the trial, but there is little I can do about it at the committal. You can't trust these guys. We should have told the DPP we needed to cross-examine the prosecution witnesses at the committal."

"It's easy to make the correct calls in hindsight; we didn't know about the vase then," Dan said. "Elise was adamant she wanted the trial as soon as possible and we couldn't do that if we had to wait six months for a committal hearing with cross-examination."

"Regardless of Sloan trying to paint Elise as a liar, how did her finger prints get on the murder weapon?" Robin asked.

"I have no idea. We can ask her about it at tomorrow's committal hearing."

"You realize this puts a whole new complexion on this case. Prior to this evidence, Elise was placed at the scene of the crime and that was all. There was some evidence of motive but really the case against her was purely circumstantial. Now with Elise's hands all over the murder weapon and her lying to the police about it, we are in a world of pain," Robin said convincingly.

"Look Robin, this situation does look bad for Elise, but we haven't heard from her yet. I know her, she did not commit this crime; I will bank my life on it."

"Think long and hard about that statement you have just made, my friend, as you will have to stake your career on her innocence. The finger print evidence means you will have to testify and that could mean your career as a lawyer could be in jeopardy, given you lied to the police about your interaction with the victim. It is possible that if you testify you could be charged with hindering a police investigation, and of course any criminal conviction could result in you losing your right to practice as a lawyer."

The ramifications of this case were continuing to hit him over the head with a sledgehammer.

What did Claye just tell him?

God rewards those who persevere, who do not throw away their faith just because things in their life are not going the way they would want them to go.

Well, he and Elise certainly were in trouble here. Dan humoured himself with the thought that there was certainly room for God to work in his life. He had enough problems to keep God busy for some time.

But was God real? If only he could get some positive news, rather than negative news all the time, it might be easier to believe!

"You alright?" Robin asked.

"Yeah, just lost in thought. Thanks, Robin, you have done well. See you tomorrow at the committal. Hopefully things will be clearer for us all then."

*

Dan sat in his car outside Robin's house and punched Sarah's mobile number into his phone.

"Sarah, it's Dan Grover here."

"Hello, Dan. I can only talk for a few minutes."

"Sarah, you rang me about something?"

"I just wanted to give you a quick heads up about a glass vase that has recently been found at the home of Mia Wong. We believe it to be the murder weapon. Preliminary investigations reveal your wife's finger prints are all over it."

"Our barrister has already picked up on that piece of evidence, but thanks for the heads up."

"I just felt you needed to be aware of it before the committal."

"Yeah, somehow it was hidden away in the prosecution's material."

"Have you changed your mind about your wife? I mean the case against her looks very cut and dry."

"Things don't look good at the moment but I have not had a chance to speak to her yet about the vase. I still can't see her doing it."

"Alright Dan, I have to fly. Take care on the roads out there after the storm; there is debris everywhere."

"I will. Thanks again, Sarah, I really appreciate your help."

At that Dan moved his Subaru into first gear and gently pulled out onto the once pretty Clayfield street where Robin lived. He was careful not to hit any rain sodden vegetation or tree branches that had crashed onto the road during the storm.

CHAPTER TWENTY FOUR

There were only two chairs in the tiny interview room so Dan stood up and let Elise and Robin sit down across from each other. Dan stood to the side of the small table, between Robin and Elise.

There was a period of short, uncomfortable silence before Robin spoke.

"Elise, let me explain what is happening today. Today is the committal hearing, where the prosecution will hand to the Magistrate all the evidence they have against you. In the weeks since the bail hearing they have provided some of that evidence to me and I will get more material this morning.

"As your instructions are to get a trial date as soon as possible, we have agreed with the prosecution, that we will not cross-examine any of their witnesses this morning. Consequently, the committal hearing will not take very long, possibly ten minutes. The Magistrate will accept the documents from the prosecution and then ask you how you plead. You can plead guilty, not guilty or enter no plea. The Magistrate will then commit your matter to the Supreme Court. Do you have any questions about the process?"

"Yes, what's the point of having a committal hearing if it is only going to last a few minutes?"

"A committal hearing is a procedural step for Magistrates to determine whether serious criminal charges will be committed for trial in the District Court or the Supreme Court. Most of the time Magistrates will commit matters for trial to the higher courts because they do not have to decide the guilt or innocence of the accused, they just have to be satisfied a jury could convict the accused on the available evidence. With respect to your charge, there is enough evidence to be satisfied a jury could convict you.

"That doesn't mean a jury is going to convict you of the charge. Once we get to the Supreme Court, the onus will be on the prosecution to convince a jury of your peers beyond a reasonable doubt, that you have committed this crime. In my experience that is quite a difficult thing for the prosecution to do. So don't be concerned about the Magistrate today committing your matter to the Supreme Court. That has no real bearing on our ultimate prospects of success in the Supreme Court."

Dan wasn't sure if Elise understood Robin's answer, or if she felt satisfied with it. In any event, Elise did not ask Robin any more questions.

Robin continued, "I need to clarify a couple of issues with you in relation to the prosecution material I have just received."

Dan felt his heart beating faster. What if Elise did do it, what if Elise admits to it here and now, that she murdered Mia? He wasn't sure he could cope with that.

"The police have found the likely murder weapon. It is a glass vase that was owned by the victim. The police allege that the murderer picked up the glass vase and struck the victim repeatedly about the head with it."

Dan was watching Elise closely. Her expression was one of numbness. There was no outrage at the violence against Mia, or overt sympathy for Mia.

"Elise, the evidence from the prosecution is that your finger prints were found on the glass vase, the murder weapon. Can you tell me how your finger prints came to be on the vase?"

Dan's senses were on high alert.

"I don't know how they got there.

"As I told the police, I have been trying to forget about what happened. It is not something that I want to remember. It was horrific."

Elise paused and looked at Dan, and then back at Robin.

"I have been trying to put the horror of finding the body out of my mind for weeks; and to suddenly now have to try to and recall everything that happened is difficult, confronting and painful for me. Honestly I can't really remember the glass vase."

"The prosecution's evidence is that the glass vase was found under a sofa across the room. Can you account for how it got there?"

"No, I can't explain how it got there. My focus at the time was to turn the poor girl over and see how she was.

"The vase didn't really mean anything to me until the police came and asked me about it a few days ago."

"Why did you talk to the police about it? I understood from Dan that you and he had agreed that you would not talk to the police about this matter?"

"The police officer, Detective Sloan came to the jail and asked to talk with me. I wasn't sure if I should talk with him as Dan had told me not to talk to the police. But Detective Sloan said that he only wanted to ask me a couple of questions and my answers to these questions could clear the whole thing up.

"I thought it's only a few questions, why not talk to him if it means I might get out of here sooner? I didn't think I had anything to hide from the police."

"What did you tell Detective Sloan?"

"Detective Sloan said they had a witness who saw me at the victim's home around the time of the murder. I did not dispute that.

"Then Detective Sloan asked me if I had picked up a glass vase in the victim's house? I told him that I did not touch any glass vase.

"Detective Sloan then asked me if I could account for my finger prints being found on the vase. I acknowledged that if my finger prints were on the vase, then I must have touched it.

"It was only then, that Detective Sloan told me that the glass vase was the murder weapon."

Dan was still watching Elise intently.

"Detective Sloan asked me if I could account for how the glass vase ended up underneath a sofa and I told him I couldn't remember anything about that."

"It is very important you do not speak to the police again, certainly not without Dan or I present. There is no point speaking to the police as they already believe you murdered the victim, or they would not have charged you with that offence. Despite what the police may tell you, now that you have been charged, they will only talk to you to strengthen their case against you; not to weaken their case and let you go."

Elise nodded meekly and accepted the scolding from Robin.

"The problem we face now is one of credibility. The prosecution will tell the jury that you have lied to the police about the vase. They will say that you told them you did not touch the glass vase, but after you were told the vase contained your finger prints, you changed your story to fit the evidence," Robin said.

Elise put her head down and softly sighed.

"It's not the end of the world. Witnesses often remember traumatic events in stages and need prompting to recall certain parts of what happened, especially when they have been trying to forget what happened," Dan said with a view to lifting Elise's spirits and putting some context to the discussion.

"So how are you going to plead today?" Robin asked eventually.

Elise appeared concerned by Robin's question. She looked at Dan and then back at Robin.

"Not guilty!"

"How you plead is a matter for you. It's entirely your decision. It's not a matter where Dan and I can tell you how to plead, you must make up your own mind," Robin said.

Dan sensed Elise's concern had not diminished.

Dan turned to Robin and said, "Elise has said she didn't do it and so she will be pleading not guilty."

Robin backtracking said, "I didn't mean to imply that I thought Elise is guilty, I was just alerting her to the requirement that she alone must make the decision which way she pleads."

Elise looked at Dan and then at Robin. Elise said quite distinctly with as much force as she could summon, "I did not kill her! I did not kill her! I will be pleading not guilty."

Dan was pleased with Elise's response, not that he ever really doubted her. Well perhaps he doubted her a little bit, but now he was fully back onboard.

"Ok, good. Let's go and get you a trial date," said Robin with all the conviction of a coach.

"Can you tell me when that trial date might be?" asked Elise.

"I believe we should get a trial date in October or November."

"But that's still another couple of months away," Elise said more than a little distressed.

"You are on the home stretch now. Just be a little bit more patient and it will all be over," Dan said as he reached out and touched her shoulder.

Elise grabbed Dan's hand and they embraced.

Dan whispered, "Stay strong, the journey is coming to an end."

*

After Elise had left, Dan and Robin said nothing to each other. They made their way to the court where the committal was to take place and found a nearby interview room.

Dan was the first to speak.

"Well, what do you think?"

"Honestly?"

"Yes, honestly."

"Elise's finger prints on the murder weapon certainly create problems for us. The fact she initially denied touching the vase to Sloan is also a problem for us. The fact that Elise can't explain how the murder weapon came to be hidden under a sofa across the room also is a problem."

"Yeah I know all that, but what do you think?" pleaded Dan.

Robin rubbed his chin and said, "I don't think she did it. I mean, why would she call the police to report a murder that she had just committed and then run away from the murder scene? It just does not make sense."

"Great, we are on the same page," Dan exclaimed.

"But we have an awful lot of work to do to convince a jury to be on the same page as us. We really need to hone in on the written threat made to the victim before she died and provide the jury with other possible perpetrators. That's where you come in Dan. Get me some other bad guys to put before the jury."

"Mate, we are definitely on the same page. I already have a couple of bad guys in mind."

The committal hearing did in fact last only ten minutes and ended with Elise pleading not guilty and her matter being remanded for trial to the Supreme Court.

Dan had only two, possibly three months to investigate this murder. The thought of Elise being imprisoned for life for a crime she did not commit was almost too painful to bear. He would not rest until he found out who killed Mia Wong.

Poor Mia, such a young life so tragically and brutally cut short.

CHAPTER TWENTY FIVE

That rocky road slice was great. Dan licked his fingers, sipped his coffee and stared out the window at *Bonfires*.

Dan's tastes ran heavily to sugar and sweet things and he loved nothing more than rocky road slices, lemon coconut slices and blueberry muffins. He wondered how long he could indulge his sweet tooth before the excess calories caught up with him.

As usual, his daydreaming, or reflections on life as Dan preferred to call it, had taken him out of reality and he had not seen her until she was right on top of him.

"Hello, is there anybody in there?" Sarah said.

"Yeah, I was just reflecting on the important things in life," Dan replied.

"Oh, you mean food."

"Yes, real food like rocky road slices and blueberry muffins."

"Wow, you do think deep thoughts don't you?"

"Take a seat, what are you having?"

"I will have," she hesitated for a few seconds while speed reading the menu. "I will have a skinny latte."

"Nothing to eat?"

"No."

"You are sure about that? What about a muffin or a piece of banana cake? How about a rocky road slice, now I can recommend those puppies."

"No thanks, I am trying to watch my weight. You know I have put on a few kilos since I was at High School."

"You look great. You don't need to worry about your weight. Now me, that's a whole different story."

"Oh, men don't have to worry about their weight like women do. It's not fair."

Well she was right there, Sarah Crabtree or Sarah Little as she was now known, was right. Society placed much more pressure on women to conform to a particular body shape and size than men.

Dan purchased Sarah's skinny latte and returned to the table where she was sitting. He could not help but be impressed by her appearance. She really had blossomed since high school.

"Sarah, thanks for coming to see me. I need your help again."

"What can I do for you? I mean ethically."

"I am looking at other suspects in this case who may have committed the murder, other than Elise. The main two other suspects, as I see them, are Brock Shepard and Samuel Sanderson." Dan looked at Sarah for any sign of acknowledgement or disagreement.

"Dan, I want to help you, I really do, but I can't do anything that would be ethically wrong. That would put my employment with the police service in jeopardy."

"I understand, Sarah, and I don't want you to do anything you are uncomfortable with, but any information you might be able to give me would be appreciated. I mean, I am only asking for information that will come out at Elise's trial anyway. I certainly won't be telling anyone, and that includes my barrister, that you have given me any information. You will have complete anonymity from me."

Sarah stroked her hair. It appeared that she was thinking, trying to find a way to help him but retain her integrity in the job. She then stopped suddenly, sipped her skinny latte and said, "Alright Dan, it will be our secret. I will help you where I can. What do you want to know?"

"Can you tell me more about the alibis of Brock Shepard and Samuel Sanderson? You told me last time they have watertight alibis. There was only sparse reference to their alibis in the committal material."

Sarah looked up to the ceiling and then returned her gaze towards Dan and said, "Let me say at the outset that my boss, Senior Detective Sloan, believes your wife murdered the victim."

"What do you believe?"

"This is only my second homicide case. I am very, very inexperienced so what I believe is not reliable."

"But what do you believe?" Dan asked as he pressed Sarah for her opinion.

"Maybe we have missed something. Certainly we missed finding the murder weapon. But from the evidence we have, I believe that there is no other logical conclusion other than your wife murdered Mia Wong."

Dan sighed.

"But why would she call the police to report the murder if she had just committed the murder, it doesn't make sense," Dan stated impassionedly.

"Senior Detective Sloan and I did discuss that hypothesis after we matched your wife's fingerprints to the victim's phone. The conclusion we came to was that your wife must have known that she was seen, or likely to be seen, entering the victim's house at the time of the murder, possibly by the neighbour she had encountered earlier in the day. Assuming she may have been seen entering the victim's house at the time of the murder, she called 000 to report the murder to make it appear as though she had just found the body.

"We thought it was quite a smart move on your wife's behalf because if she was not identified by the neighbour, she also could not be identified as the triple 000 caller. But if she was identified by the neighbour and subsequently arrested, she could point to the fact that she called triple 000 to provide support to a story that she had only found the body and then went onto report it."

Dan was gob smacked!

Though as a lawyer he was trained in maintaining the party line, no matter what arguments were put up against it.

"I hadn't really thought about that exotic answer, I had been taken with the more obvious explanation. That she reported the death because she found the body and felt morally obliged to report it."

"You see that's another thing. She felt morally obliged to report the murder, but she did not feel morally obliged to stick around and wait for the authorities to turn up," Sarah said with some feeling.

"Sarah, I am not here to debate the case with you. We should save that for the trial."

Sarah stood up and was ready to leave.

Dan reached out his hand and touched Sarah's hip. "Sarah, please don't go. I really need your help."

Sarah sat back down.

"Look, I don't feel comfortable talking to you about all this."

"If you can't help me, that's ok, but if you can tell me anything I would really appreciate it."

Sarah looked at Dan. He had clasped his hands as if praying for mercy.

"Ok, I will help you but I must be out of my mind."

"Thanks," Dan replied.

Sarah pulled out a small notebook and began reading from it. "Brock Shepard was drinking at the Breakfast Creek Hotel from 1:00pm until 5:30pm on the day Mia Wong was murdered. Your wife reported the murder at 4:54pm and our pathology people put the time of death at some time after 4:00pm. Brock was drinking with several people during the day who all can remember seeing him there. Particularly, Brock was remembered by the bartender on duty this day and she can positively remember Brock being at the hotel from 1:00pm till around 5:30pm."

"But the Breakfast Creek Hotel is only 5 minutes or so from Spring Hill on the Inner City Bypass. Brock could have left the Hotel and committed the murder and returned in less than 15 minutes."

"Sloan and I did look at that point. We discounted it because the bartender was sure that Brock was sitting at the bar all afternoon and was not absent for more than a few minutes to go to the toilet. She told us she particularly remembered him as being a loud, talkative drunk who proceeded to get more aggressive and obnoxious during the day, culminating in him being thrown out of the hotel around 5:30pm."

"Still, Brock could have disappeared for 15 minutes in a crowded bar, it has to be possible."

"It is possible but unlikely given the bartender's evidence and the fact his cognitive ability to plan and execute this murder would have been impaired by the large amount of alcohol he ingested during the day."

"I have been told that Mia took out a Domestic Violence Order against Brock in the weeks before her murder. I assume you looked at that."

"Yes, the DVO allegations were that Brock had pushed the victim against a wall and was holding her by the throat. That obviously concerned us but when we questioned him, he denied the allegations. We noted the court file indicated that Brock was going to contest the DVO allegations."

"So it was only ever a temporary DVO?"

"Yes."

"But what about Brock's previous criminal convictions? They must have caused you some concern?"

"Brock has no previous criminal convictions."

"No, that can't be right. I have been told he has a criminal history for violence and drug offences. Have you checked in New South Wales?"

"I don't know who you have been talking to but I can tell you categorically that Brock Shepard has no criminal convictions either as an adult or a child in

Queensland or New South Wales."

They both paused for a few seconds. Dan because he didn't want to have an argument with Sarah, that was not why he was there. He desperately needed her help.

"Can you tell me about Samuel Sanderson's alibi?"

"Samuel Sanderson called in sick from work on the day in question at about 8:00am. He attended a doctor's surgery at 2:00pm, where he complained of having the flu and he was prescribed medication. A bankcard transaction slip confirms Mr Sanderson purchased the medication at 2:35pm at a pharmacy in Chermside. Mr Sanderson stated that he then went home and spent the rest of the day in bed. Mr Sanderson's wife has confirmed that she was with her husband all day, at the doctors, at the pharmacy and at home."

"Can you tell me whether Samuel Sanderson has any previous convictions?"

"Mr Sanderson has no previous criminal convictions of any kind."

"Thanks Sarah, I really appreciate what you have shared with me. I will not tell anybody about our little chats."

"Will there be more chats?" Sarah asked.

"I don't know. Hey, is there any likelihood that someone off the street could have done this?"

"No, we discounted that likelihood pretty quickly. Nothing of value appears to have been taken from the house, so robbery is unlikely. Why would the victim let in a stranger? The crime looks like a crime of passion, of feeling against the victim, in that the victim was hit many more times around the head than what was necessary to kill her."

Dan was downcast, the news Sarah was giving him was not helpful to Elise. He had nothing more to ask Sarah, so he was quiet.

"You're not still supporting that hopeless dolphin team are you?" Sarah asked with a hint of a smile.

"They are not the dolphins, they are the Sharks. And yes, for your information, I am still supporting them and they are still disappointing me. Next year though, they will come good. They have to. I think they will make the semis next year."

"You're hopeless. Why don't you support the Broncos like everyone else in Brisbane?"

"The Broncos are my second team. But the Broncos make the semi finals every year and win the premiership every couple of years. Where is the joy in that? Broncos' supporters always expect to win, hence they don't experience overwhelming euphoria when they do win, only disappointment when they lose.

"You can only experience real joy, if you have experienced real pain."

Sarah looked puzzled. "You're crazy," she said shaking her head.

"I mean, at school when playing sport I never wanted to be picked on the best team; the team with all the star players on it. I always wanted to be on the other team that was expected to get beaten by the star team. In that way the joy of winning was multiplied when the underdog team beat the star team. There is no greater joy than a team of battlers beating a star team."

"But a star team will always beat a team of battlers," Sarah said.

"Well that is nearly always true," replied Dan.

"So in effect, you are really a masochist who enjoys being regularly beaten up."

"No, I don't enjoy being beaten, but I really enjoy winning against the odds."

"Well you are against the odds in this case, but if anyone can beat the odds, you can."

"Thanks, Sarah," Dan said with some feeling as they both got up to leave.

"I will be seeing you."

"Not if I see you first," Sarah replied as they both laughed and headed their separate ways up and down the Mall.

CHAPTER TWENTY SIX

Dan sifted through the online search for Wong in the White Pages personal section and eventually found the name he had been looking for. Mia's father still lived at Cronulla.

He contemplated calling Joseph personally but in the end he decided to travel to Sydney to meet him face to face; it was worth the extra expense. His best chance of talking with Mia's father was just turning up at his home unexpectedly.

He liked Sydney. After all, what wasn't there to like about a city built on a magnificent harbour, with great weather, that had showcased the best Olympic Games ever and was the spiritual home of rugby league?

By the time he had stepped out of the taxi he could well and truly hear and smell the ocean. He had never contemplated moving away from Brisbane, but if he did, Sydney would be the place. He also liked Melbourne with its great sporting arenas so close to the city and he liked Hobart with its historical charm. Of course, there was also tropical North Queensland with its beautiful beaches and rainforests. Too difficult to decide; he would just stay in Brisbane and visit the other places.

Dan had the taxi stop at the start of Kookaburra Lane. Joseph Wong's house was number 23. He walked nervously to the front door. It was quite a large house, larger than he had expected. He noticed that the garden was in immaculate condition but the house itself seemed a little dilapidated.

He rang the door buzzer, but there was no response.

After a few fruitless minutes of ringing the door bell, he decided to have a look around. He moved to the side of the house and pushed a gate ajar that opened onto a backyard.

Joseph Wong certainly had a green thumb, the garden was beautiful. There were all types of flowers and shrubs, as well as small ceramic sculptures of angels and the like, strategically placed around the lawn. The centerpiece was a large fountain which had water cascading down a stone wall.

"Hey, what are you doing here? You're trespassing!"

It was a man's voice and it sounded like it was coming from his left. He looked to his left and saw several large paper bark trees with many *old man's beard* plants floating in the sea breeze as they hung off the branches. Dan couldn't actually make out that anybody was there.

"I have told the Jehovah's Witnesses before, I don't want anybody knocking on my door, so please leave."

"I am not a JW. But I am here to see a JW," Dan said, quite pleased with his little pun.

"No JWs here mate, so see you later."

"I am here to see Joseph Wong."

Dan still could not make out the man talking to him. He figured he must be standing behind the paper bark trees.

Just then Dan sensed movement to his right and, from behind a pair of perfectly straight ghost gum trees, a short, pot bellied, casually dressed man moved out to stand near him.

"Sorry, I thought you were over here," Dan said pointing to his left.

"A common mistake to make, especially in this garden with the fountain and it being so close to the ocean, sounds can be distorted."

Dan put his hand out and stepped towards Joseph.

"Hello, my name is Dan Grover, pleased to meet you."

Joseph instinctively put his hand out to shake Dan's hand, but then as if struck by a bolt of lightening; he snapped his arm back to his side.

Dan knew this reaction was coming.

"Mr Wong, I have travelled from Brisbane today to see you. Please accept my sympathy for the loss of your daughter Mia, she truly was a wonderful person."

"You haven't come all this way just to tell me how sorry you are for my daughter's death?"

"No, that's right, but I would like to talk to you about your daughter's death. I believe the police have charged the wrong person and, with your help, I would like to find the person who really murdered Mia."

"The police have told me that Elise Grover murdered my Mia. Are you any relation to her?"

"Mr Wong, I am her husband. But please know that…."

Dan stopped mid sentence as he saw Joseph raise a large garden fork. He hadn't noticed the fork before. Joseph's complexion appeared to be turning redder and redder by the second and his face and neck were now so red he looked like he was going to explode. So much for the mild-mannered pharmacist-next-door image.

"Get out! Get out now!" Joseph shouted, raising his garden fork in an aggressive fashion.

"Mr Wong, can I call you Joe? Well perhaps not."

Joseph advanced towards Dan, holding his garden fork like a spear.

Dan was retreating now and speaking at the same time.

Joseph moved quickly to the back of the house and unlatched a door to what appeared to be an outdoor entertainment area. A large black dog, which looked awfully like a pit bull, ran straight at Dan.

He was now in full retreat mode. He could call Joseph later and try and talk to him. As Dan turned around at speed, he tripped over and fell, knocking over a nearby angel sculpture. Both the angel sculpture and Dan hit the ground heavily. The angel sculpture's wings fell off as it made contact with the ground. Dan was more fortunate in that he only grazed his head when it came into contact with one of the broken off angel's wings on the ground.

In any event, it was pandemonium with the pit bull having a head the size of Tasmania, barking hysterically several inches away from Dan's head. Dan curled up into a fetal position covering his bloodied head with his hands. Bits and pieces of the ceramic angel were scattered everywhere.

"Roger, come here, Roger," Dan heard Joseph shout.

Roger? Who calls a pit bull Roger?

Roger went back inside the fenced off area and Joseph walked over to where Dan was lying on the ground.

"What have you done to my angel? You will have to pay for that," demanded Joseph.

"Don't worry about that, look what your angel has done to me," Dan said as he showed Joseph the blood flowing from the gash on the side of his face.

"That angel didn't move. It's an object. You're the one with blood on his hands," Joseph countered.

Dan looked at his bloodied hands and couldn't help himself, he began to chuckle at the absurdity of the situation. He did indeed have blood on his hands in his altercation with the ceramic angel.

He looked up and he could see Joseph was smiling as well. Soon both men were beside themselves in fits of laughter as they egged each other on to even more depths of laughter, more than Dan knew he had inside himself.

Finally, Dan stopped and said, "I wouldn't mind a cup of tea."

"How about a cold beer?" replied Joseph.

"Sold," said Dan. And with that Dan followed Joseph inside his house past Roger, who was now quite friendly towards him.

Joseph gave Dan a couple of band-aids which he applied after washing his face.

No sooner had he sat down on a large black leather couch, than Roger raced over and jumped up beside Dan, nestling his extremely large neck and face in his lap.

"Looks like Roger likes you," Joseph said as he handed Dan a bottle of ice cold beer in a stubby holder.

Dan lightly patted Roger's enormous head. What else could he do? This was Roger's domain.

Joseph spoke first, "The police have not told me too much about what happened. What can you tell me?"

He told Joseph the full story, being careful not to leave anything out.

Joseph was motionless. He seemed to be concentrating intently on what Dan was telling him.

"I believe that someone other than my wife killed Mia. Someone she was familiar with, who she willingly let into her home. At the moment I am investigating the possibility that Mia's ex-boyfriend Brock murdered Mia and I would like to talk to you about Brock, if that's ok."

"Brock, yes he could have done it. I never liked him."

"What can you tell me about Brock?"

"Mia met him while he was still a drug addict. I think he was doing community service for some crime he had committed."

"Are you sure Brock was convicted of a crime in New South Wales? The police have told me that he has no convictions for any crimes in New South Wales or Queensland?"

"I am sure. He was convicted of several crimes. Apparently he bailed his father up once with a knife to his throat. I also found out from a friend of Mia's that Brock had been in prison for awhile. Mia always tried to downplay Brock's criminal past to me, but I was able to find out information about him from other family members and friends."

"I wonder why there would be no criminal record of Brock Shepard's behaviour?"

"Did you say Brock Shepard?"

"Yes, that's his name isn't it?"

"No, his name is Brock Utley. Mia said he changed his name to Shepard soon after she met him. He had this thing against his father and he didn't want to continue to be known as Utley."

"Well that might explain why no criminal record has been found. What was Brock like?"

"Brock had a troubled life as a child and teenager. His father would beat him up for no particular reason.

"Brock ran away from home when he was 12 or 13, something like that, and he lived on the streets for several years. Living on the streets got him into drugs and the criminal activity that goes with trying to feed a drug habit.

"By the time he was 17 he had been in and out of juvenile detention many times and, from all accounts, was an alcoholic.

"At one point Brock was doing community service at an animal refuge where Mia was volunteering. Mia met Brock and saw him as a project; to improve his quality of life and get him off alcohol and drugs. Eventually their relationship turned into a romantic one and they began to live together."

"Did you approve of Mia living with Brock?"

"No way! Seriously Mia was much too good for Brock. But Brock was the quiet, brooding, handsome type and Mia was convinced he was the one for her."

"Did Brock ever hit Mia?"

"I suspect he may have but Mia never told me that he did. If I had of known that he hit her, I would not have let Mia live with him. That was not how she was raised, to accept violence from men."

"Did you know that Mia had broken up with Brock?"

"Yes, she did call and tell me that. She just said she couldn't take living with him anymore. I think he was finally out of her system. I certainly wasn't going to convince her to get back with him."

"Did you know she was moving back to Sydney?"

"No, I didn't know that. The last time I talked to her was a couple of weeks before she was killed."

At that point Dan had finished his questions. Rather than just get up and leave, he felt the need to just sit there quietly for awhile.

"One of the truly great disappointments in my life is that I never took the time to tell Mia how much she meant to me. She was my only child. She meant everything to me. The last time I held her in my arms was months ago."

There was another period of silence.

"I have trouble now even remembering her beautiful smile."

Joseph stopped talking and sighed. Dan could see that Joseph was fighting back tears.

Dan didn't cry. Rugby league was the toughest football code in the world and you'd never see those guys cry. Real men never cried. Yet here and now, listening to Joseph's heartfelt words, he felt his eyes moistening. Joseph was the real deal; he was not putting on a performance.

Physical contact also did not come naturally to Dan, especially with other men. Yet at this moment, he gave into a force much greater than he had felt with men before. A force that made him move over to where Joseph was now quietly sobbing and put his arm around him to comfort him.

"I'll find Mia's killer, I will do that for you. Give you some justice for her."

"I don't need you to find Mia's killer, I want you to bring her back to life," Joseph pleaded.

"I am sorry, I can't do that, mate, I can't do that."

By the time his taxi had arrived, Dan had cheered Joseph up with stories of the glory days of the Cronulla Sharks. They didn't have many glory days to share, but they both appreciated the common bond.

He promised to keep in contact with Joseph and let him know what happened at Elise's trial.

Joseph pleaded with Dan to come and visit him again next time he was in Sydney.

Dan looked back fondly at the great garden Joseph had built as the taxi sped him to the airport.

CHAPTER TWENTY SEVEN

Back in Brisbane, Dan wasted no time in calling Sarah with the news that Brock Shepard had been using an alias and that his real name was Brock Utley. Sarah promised to check out Brock Utley's criminal history and meet him in a couple of days at their usual rendezvous point.

Sarah was there first this time and she ordered Dan a tall black with a dash of milk and a lemon coconut slice. She gasped when Dan walked into *Bonfires*.

"What happened to you, go a couple of rounds with Mike Tyson?"

"No, it's nothing, just a couple of stitches."

"Please explain."

"I interviewed a witness and while I was there I tripped over a statute of an angel in his garden and cut my head open. It's not as bad as it looks. The doctor just put a few stitches in it."

"You really are aggressively investigating this matter," Sarah said.

"You know who you remind me of?" Sarah asked rhetorically. "A Cronulla Sharks player after his warm up."

"That's funny, that is really funny," Dan said with disdain.

Sarah, though, did think her joke was funny and she chuckled away for some time.

"Back to business, what did you find out about Brock Utley?" Dan asked.

"How did you find out about Brock's alias?" Sarah answered with a question.

"Just some basic investigative work. As a detective you wouldn't understand that concept."

"Ouch!"

Dan and Sarah sipped their coffees, before Dan broke the silence.

"Thanks for the coffee and the lemon coconut slice. By the way how did you know I like tall blacks with a dash of milk and lemon coconut slices?"

"Just some basic investigative work."

Dan looked puzzled.

"You ordered the exact same thing last time, dummy."

"Did I? I suppose I must have," Dan said putting his coffee down and shaking his head.

"Sarah, what can you tell me about Brock's previous convictions?"

"I can tell you if someone has no criminal convictions, but when they have a criminal record I can't legally just give that information out, it is confidential," Sarah said.

"From that I can deduce that Brock Utley has a criminal record?" Dan asked looking at Sarah intently.

Sarah did not respond in any way.

"Perhaps the best way of doing this is for me to make a statement and you tell me if I am wrong. In that way you are not providing me with information, so much as correcting me from having incorrect information."

"Alright, fire away."

"I have heard Brock Utley spent time in jail, is that right?" asked Dan.

Sarah didn't say anything.

"I have heard that Brock has several assault convictions, including one serious assault involving his father."

Again Sarah said nothing.

"I understand Brock has drug convictions."

Again Sarah said nothing.

"I believe Brock may have assault convictions involving females."

"Not females as such," Sarah said.

"Brock has an assault conviction against one female."

Again Sarah said nothing.

"I assume Brock has an assault conviction against Mia Wong."

"No, the victim was not Mia Wong."

"The assault took place more than two years ago, before Brock met Mia."

There was no answer from Sarah.

"I assume that this woman was in a relationship with Brock when he assaulted her."

Sarah did not respond.

"I expect that Brock would have been under the influence of alcohol with respect to both assaults against his father and his ex-girlfriend."

Again, no answer from Sarah.

"Sarah it seems to me, that Brock could be our man. He has obvious violent tendencies against people he is in relationships with, who he believes have hurt him. Alcohol either gives him courage or takes away his self restraint. On the day Mia was killed Brock was consuming alcohol, large quantities of alcohol."

"We were surprised to find Brock had a criminal history including violence under another name. He told us he had never used an alias. We actually found some traffic convictions of his in the name of Shepard, so we accepted what he told us. Given his criminal convictions and deception, Sloan asked me to look into Brock further, which I did."

Sarah took a sip of what looked like another skinny latte; as usual, she had not ordered anything to eat.

"I found Brock yesterday in a detox clinic. It appears he has taken Mia's death to heart and vowed to his family *to get off the grog for good*. Brock says he has not touched a drop of alcohol since Mia's death.

"Brock told me that he had hoped to get back with Mia. Apparently he had planned a surprise for her. He showed me an airline booking where he paid for two tickets to Sydney in his name and Mia's name. The purpose of the Sydney trip was for him and Mia to see her favourite band in concert.

"Brock also showed me the two concert tickets he had purchased, which were quite expensive. The trip to Sydney and the concert tickets were booked and paid for a few weeks before Mia's death and the concert took place a couple of weeks after Mia's death."

Dan took a few moments to take this information in.

"Brock could have purchased the tickets as a ruse, to put you off the track. He could have planned the whole thing. Buying the tickets before Mia was killed doesn't really prove anything."

"Sloan and I agree that the prior purchase of the airline and concert tickets and the sudden change in Brock's behaviour *to get off the grog for good,* do not by themselves prove that Brock didn't kill Mia. But when you combine that behaviour with his alibi, it's pretty telling. Also we don't believe Brock is the type of person who is capable of thinking through a crime of passion like this and planning it all out."

"But maybe Brock didn't pre-meditate the murder. Maybe he went over to see Mia to tell her about his surprise and she rejected him. Brock was already intoxicated and he just snapped and killed her in a moment of alcohol fuelled rage," Dan added.

"I suppose that could have happened, but could Brock have gone back to the hotel he was drinking at and just act normally after killing Mia like that?

"Also, he really appears to have taken steps to turn his life around since Mia's death. Is that the action of a murderer?" Sarah responded.

Dan didn't answer the question but just looked out the coffee shop window.

"What are you going to do now?" asked Sarah.

"I am going to do some investigating of Mr Samuel Sanderson."

"Good luck with that and if I was you I would wear some protective headgear before I did any more investigative work. It seems to be dangerous to your health and detrimental to your good looks," Sarah added with a smile.

"Ha ha, gee you're funny today, Sarah."

"Well gotta go, more bad guys to catch."

They got up together and moved away from the table. Dan followed Sarah through the maze of tables. Momentarily, Dan's attention was taken with Sarah's flowing blonde locks dangling delicately over her shoulders. At that instant another customer pulled her chair out in front of Sarah and Dan forcing them to stop suddenly. Sarah was able to stop before Dan, who overbalanced and grabbed hold of Sarah. For a few seconds Dan held Sarah in his arms, before he gently let her go.

"Sorry about that, I couldn't stop in time," Dan said.

"You weren't paying attention were you?"

"No, I wasn't. Sorry, it won't happen again."

He thought Sarah looked a little sad when he said it wouldn't happen again, but perhaps that was his mind playing tricks on him.

"See you later and thanks again, Sarah, for everything."

"My pleasure," Sarah said as she walked off up the Mall while Dan walked off in the other direction.

He looked back and to his surprise she stopped and turned towards him. Sarah smiled and waved before disappearing into the crowd.

CHAPTER TWENTY EIGHT

Dan had spoken to Elise several times over the phone and in person, keeping her updated about the case. He could only see Elise during regulated daytime visiting hours, so it was quite a balancing act for him to visit Elise, work on her case and continue to keep his own legal practice afloat.

After the initial shock at not being granted bail, Elise had settled reasonably well into jail routine. She had an end date in sight and Dan noticed she was now resigned to making the best of things. However, during the last phone call he had with Elise she sounded worried and said she had something very important to discuss with him. He didn't want Elise to explain her concerns over the prison telephone service, so he arranged to visit her the next day.

As Dan entered the interview room used by visiting lawyers to see their clients, he wondered what Elise's concerns were. Why all of a sudden she had something important to tell him? He hoped that she was safe in jail. The women's prison system was not nearly as bad as the men's, but prison, even a woman's prison, was not a safe place.

After a perfunctionary hug, Dan studied Elise as she sat down across from him.

"Are you ok? I was worried about you?"

'Yes I am fine. I have made a few friends, that seems to work around here."

"I need to tell you about my conversation with Mia's father Joseph. It turns out he is a really decent guy and I was able to get some information from him about Mia's ex-boyfriend Brock. Apparently, his real name is Utley not Shepard."

"I think you have already told me about this."

"Well ok, but did I tell you that the police have discovered that Brock Utley has previous history for violence in relation to his father and another ex-girlfriend of his?"

"I didn't know that. Does that mean the police will drop the charges against me?"

"No. They have re-interviewed Brock and they still don't believe he murdered Mia."

"So your whole trip to Sydney was a complete waste of time?" Elise said with some feeling.

"No, I don't think so. Just because we can't get the police to change their minds doesn't mean we can't get a jury to believe Brock could have done it."

Dan looked at Elise and she didn't seem too impressed.

"I mean Brock could have murdered Mia. He had thoughts of getting back together with her, which she didn't share."

"You'd know all about that wouldn't you?" Elise said harshly.

Dan ignored the comment.

"He gets up the courage to tell her about a surprise he has for her by consuming copious amounts of alcohol. He goes over to her place and she lets him in as it's only Brock. He plays the get back together card with the surprise. She rejects him, turns her back on him and then he hits her and continues to hit her because he is drunk and she has finally spurned him."

"Why would she let him in if he was drunk?"

"I don't know, I wasn't there," Dan said wondering why Elise was being so negative. During his last visit she appeared quite appreciative of what he was doing.

"You wanted to see me?" Dan enquired.

Elise squirmed in her seat.

After a few moments of silence Dan said, "I don't want to rush you but I have a mountain of work waiting for me back at the office."

Elise continued to look uncomfortable.

"Barb came and saw me yesterday."

"That's great. So your sister came and saw you," Dan said more as a question.

"Well, she has been talking with Dave. You remember Dave, the banker guy she has been going out with for the last six months?"

"Yeah, I have met Dave. What are you getting at?"

"This is difficult for me."

Dan looked at Elise and he could see it was difficult for her to say what she wanted to say. But he still had no idea what she wanted to tell him.

"Elise, just tell me what the problem is," Dan pleaded.

"Barb and Dave believe that you should not be representing me. They think you are too close to all of this, being my husband, my lawyer and a potential witness. They think given your relationship with Mia and me, you can't be objective or effective."

Dan said nothing. He didn't like what he was hearing.

"They also think you should be using an experienced barrister not a relatively junior one. They did some digging and discovered that this is Robin's first case as a private barrister."

"What do you think, Elise? I mean Barb and Dave can have their opinions but you have been in this from the beginning. What do you think?"

"I had been thinking about it for some time, even before Barb and Dave raised it with me."

Dan was broadsided again by Elise. He continued to be surprised by her.

He had absolutely no idea she was thinking this way.

"Do you think you would be better off with some solicitors and barristers you don't know, than with Robin and I?"

"Maybe, certainly Barb and Dave think so."

He didn't respond but shifted his gaze from Elise to the ceiling.

"We didn't do too well in the bail hearing.

"Also, it would give you more time to work on your own legal practice," Elise added.

"So what do you want to do?" Dan asked biting down on his lip.

"I am not sure. Certainly it will cost us a lot more money if we have to hire an experienced legal team. One of the girls in here said a top legal team could cost us $15,000 a day, just for the trial."

"Don't worry about the money. We will sell the house or extend the mortgage if we have to," Dan said.

"Honestly, what do you think? Would I better off with a different legal team?"

He hesitated and thought for a moment before speaking. He wanted to tell Elise to stop taking advice from her sister, her sister's new boyfriend and the other female prisoners she was meeting at the foodhall and just listen to him. But he knew deep down that there was some merit in the advice they were giving Elise.

Perhaps he was too close to it all. In fact, he was right in the middle of it all.

But he had discovered useful information about Brock that the police didn't know about, he had established a useful contact in Sarah, and Robin was very good, albeit inexperienced in serious criminal matters. There were pros and cons either way.

"Maybe you would be better off with a more experienced legal team. That is probably the smart thing to do. But I just know so much about this case and I am desperate to get you out of here. I think Robin and I are the guys you want in your corner. However, it is your decision and whatever decision you make, I will accept it. No matter what you decide, I will always be here for you."

Dan noticed Elise biting on her lip and she had tears welling up in her eyes. "Some of the girls in my cell block have given me the names of some lawyers they recommend."

Dan winced. "Do you want me to check them out?"

Elise pulled out a crumpled piece of paper from the back pocket of her grey track suit pants. As Dan reached out for it, she hesitated before folding it back up and putting it in her pocket. "No, let me sleep on it and I will call you back in a day or two," Elise said.

"Alright, I will continue working on the case until I hear from you that you want me to stop."

They stood and hugged briefly before Dan left.

CHAPTER TWENTY NINE

Dan was now on the trail of Samuel Sanderson. He had gone as far as he could with Brock Shepard without interviewing Brock himself. There was no point in speaking to Brock personally, as Brock was unlikely to just admit he had killed Mia. All Dan and Robin needed to do was establish to a jury that Brock could have murdered Mia. They didn't need to prove that Brock had actually murdered Mia. They only had to raise a reasonable suspicion that someone other than Elise had murdered Mia.

In terms of investigating Samuel Sanderson, he began his investigation at Dooley and Associates, Market Researchers. Samuel had worked there only a couple of years ago.

Dan was, not surprisingly, running late for his prearranged interview with Fiona McNamara who was the Human Resource Manager at Dooley and Associates. There was just no place to park in the city these days and he had to drive around for some time to find a street park. He wasn't going to pay the exorbitant parking fees that were charged by privately owned parking stations if he could avoid it.

Dan entered the high rise building that housed Dooley and Associates. A petite receptionist watched Dan come towards her and she smiled.

"Hello, my name is Dan Grover and I have an appointment with Fiona McNamara. I am a little bit late." Dan shook his head and then said, "Parking in the city, it's hopeless isn't it?"

The receptionist nodded and said, "Yeah, tell me about it."

"Ms McNamara will be with you in a few minutes, Mr Grover, please take a seat." The receptionist motioned Dan to some large lounge chairs to the side.

Dan eased over to the lounge chairs and made himself comfortable. He was happy to see today's newspaper on a glass coffee table. As Dan was a sports fan, he started reading the newspaper from the back, rather than the front. Unless there was something really important or exciting happening in Brisbane or the world, the sports pages were always of more interest to him than the first few pages.

Dan was fully engrossed in his third sports article when he heard a raised voice coming from the receptionist's desk.

A giant of a man, at least 208 centimetres tall was standing right over the tiny receptionist demanding to see her CEO.

"I'm sorry but the CEO is unavailable at the moment, perhaps you could leave your name and phone number and I will ask her to call you back?"

"No, I damn well won't leave my name and number. I have already left my name and number several times and I never get a call back. I want to see your boss now!" the burly man said raising his voice to an even louder level.

"Well, sir, if you leave your name and number with me, I will give it to our CEO, personally, and tell her of your concerns."

"You're not listening to me. That's the trouble with the younger generation, they never listen. I don't want to leave a message. I want to see someone. I have just come into work and I have nowhere to park my car as people from your firm have parked in the car spaces allocated to my firm.

"This has happened before and I will be damned if I have to go out and try to find a park on the street again. It's a 2 hour limit on the street anyway. I am not standing for it anymore! I am not taking it anymore! I want to see your CEO! Go and get her for me now!"

Wow, this guy was really quite intimidating. Dan expected the receptionist to run off and not come back, but she didn't.

"Sir, I can appreciate your concern, I really can, but our CEO is just not available at the moment. She is in a presentation with one of our largest clients and she has left me specific instructions not to disturb her."

The huge man moaned like he was going to explode.

"Get me someone else in authority. I want to see them now!"

Dan again thought the young receptionist would run off and get somebody, anybody brave enough to front this huge guy.

"I can see if I can find someone else for you to talk to but I know that most of our senior management team are in the same presentation. If you would like, I can send an urgent email to all staff, alerting them that they should not be parking in your company's car spaces under any circumstances. And telling them to immediately move their cars if they have parked their cars in your allocated spots. I will also leave an urgent message for the CEO to discuss this matter with you the minute she is free.”

The very large man stood there for a few seconds glaring at the receptionist and then suddenly he reached into his coat pocket. Dan was on tenterhooks by this stage and was not sure what was going to happen next.

What was the guy reaching for? Was it a gun, a bomb? Would he be able to tackle this huge man mountain and disarm him? A million thoughts passed through his head. Including an observation that no one from Dooley and Associates had come out to support the young receptionist and she had been left to deal with this angry man mountain by herself.

The very large man then pulled a piece of paper from his coat pocket and flung it at the receptionist.

“These are the registration numbers of the cars parked in our spaces. Have them moved immediately, or I will be putting this matter in the hands of my lawyers.”

Dan pondered that lawyers were always the stick that people threatened each other with. No wonder lawyers had a bad name in the community.

“My name is Robert Button and I am on floor 2. You had better get someone to come and talk to me about your firm’s deplorable behaviour before the day is out or there will be hell to pay!”

As the extremely large man lumbered down the internal stairs to Dan’s right, he noticed the receptionist sigh and slump back in her chair.

“How are you feeling?” asked Dan.

“I have a headache. I am shaking all over and I just want to go and lie down,” the receptionist said.

“I must say, your handling of that gorilla was pretty impressive. What is your name?”

“Chelsea.”

“Chelsea, that guy was very intimidating; and the way you stood up to him and took on his problem and solved it by yourself, without subjecting anyone else to his rage; that was very impressive.”

“I feel sick.”

“You were awesome. But I would get onto that all access email about the cars parked in his company’s parking bays as soon as possible.”

“Yeah, I just need a few minutes to recover.”

“Mr Grover, I presume. I am Fiona McNamara.”

Dan’s attention turned to a plump middle aged woman with short black hair, wearing a dark skirt and tightly buttoned mauve coloured shirt.

Dan nodded and Ms McNamara said, "Come this way."

He followed Ms McNamara through a small corridor to an elongated meeting room. The meeting room was dominated by a large oval shaped table with modern chairs. As with most modern chairs, they looked good but were quite uncomfortable.

"What can I do for you, Mr Grover?"

"Call me Dan."

"Alright, what can I do for you, Dan?"

"I am a lawyer investigating a matter involving a former employee of yours, Samuel Sanderson. I am after some background information about Mr Sanderson. How did you find him as an employee?

"I don't know if I can answer that question on privacy grounds."

"Its not really a privacy issue. I am not seeking any personal information about Mr Sanderson, just corporate information."

Ms McNamara did not seem to be convinced.

"I am investigating whether Mr Sanderson has a pattern of behaviour or not, of sexual harassment or abuse of female employees."

"We are one of Australia's leading market research companies. We don't employ people who sexually harass other staff."

"Does that mean that you never had any complaints about Mr Sanderson while he worked here?"

"No, I am not saying that. Please don't put words into my mouth, Mr Grover."

"I am sorry. What can you tell me about Mr Sanderson?"

Ms McNamara hesitated.

"Look, Mr Grover, I do not feel comfortable in giving you any information about Mr Sanderson other that he worked here for about 18 months and left of his own volition. I am not prepared to provide you with anymore information about Mr Sanderson's time here without first checking with our lawyers."

Here we go again, using lawyers to end the discussion.

"This is really important. A young woman has been murdered. Can you at least tell me off the record, if you had any concerns about Mr Sanderson's behaviour while he was working here?"

"No, I am sorry. I can't give you any information about Mr Sanderson without first checking with our lawyers. I will get back to you."

It was obvious he wasn't going to get anywhere with Ms McNamara today.

"Alright, thanks for your time, Ms McNamara. I look forward to hearing from you."

Ms McNamara escorted Dan to the foyer and then she disappeared as quickly as she had appeared.

He walked over to the elevator and pressed the down button. As he was waiting for the elevator he turned around and saw Chelsea looking at him and smiling.

"How did you go with Ms McNamara?" Chelsea asked.

"Not as well as I had hoped," Dan replied.

"Hey, wait a minute, I forgot to give her my contact details. She was going to get back to me about something."

On the back of his business card Dan wrote;

I need information about Samuel Sanderson. Please call me.

Chelsea gladly took the business card from Dan. He noticed her pleasant demeanor change when she read his note.

"Did you know him?" Dan asked Chelsea.

Just then Fiona McNamara appeared again as if from nowhere.

She went straight to Chelsea and said, "What's this email you sent about me parking my car in someone else's car space? I don't appreciate…"

Ms McNamara stopped mid-sentence as she turned and noticed Dan.

"Mr Grover, you are still here?" Ms McNamara asked more as an accusation than a question.

"I remembered I had forgotten to give you my contact details. I have just given my card to your receptionist."

"Your contact details?" Ms McNamara seemed confused as to why Dan would be giving her his contact details.

"You were going to get back to me after you consulted your lawyers," Dan said.

"Ah yes, that's right I was too. I am so busy these days, one meeting leads into another, you know how it is."

Dan knew how it was. Ms McNamara had no intention of ever getting back to him or consulting her lawyers about this matter. She had just said that to fob him off.

"Anyway, I would really appreciate if you could get back to me. It's literally a matter of life and death," Dan said this to Ms McNamara, but more for Chelsea's benefit.

As Dan waited for the elevator to arrive, he turned again to Ms McNamara and said, "I heard something of the car park issue while I was waiting for you. You should go and talk to that guy Robert Button, he was quite rude and obnoxious."

Just then the elevator arrived and Dan stepped in.

Before the elevator door had closed Dan heard Ms McNamara say to Chelsea, "I think I will do that. I will go and see Robert Button whoever he is, and give him a piece of my mind."

Dan smiled.

CHAPTER THIRTY

Dan was apprehensive as he drove to the women's prison to meet with Elise.

The more he thought about the situation, the more he was coming around to the idea that Elise would be better served with independent legal representation.

Elise deserved to be represented by the best and he had to admit that he and Robin were not the best lawyers going around. Though they were probably the most committed lawyers Elise could find. But was commitment better than experience?

Elise was the client. He could not insist on representing her just because he wanted to be the one to get her off. After all wasn't that just being selfish?

He reaffirmed in his own mind that no matter what the decision, he would continue to support Elise in any way he could.

He raised his eyes to the sky and quickly asked God to help Elise make the right decision. He felt embarrassed and silly but he also felt slightly reassured in offering this short sharp prayer.

After their standard greeting of a short hug, Dan took a few seconds to really look at Elise. How has she come through it all he wondered? After everything that had happened she was still the same Elise.

In fact he thought she looked better than the last time they had met. She still had dark circles under her eyes, but today she looked more assured, somehow more at peace with herself.

"I must say you are looking good. If anyone can wear a non-descript, over sized, drab, grey prison tracksuit and still look good, you can."

"Thanks. It's been awhile since I have had any compliments."

"It's been impressive the way you have handled yourself ever since this nightmare started. It would have been easy for you to drop your bundle, but you haven't; you have kept it all together."

He reached out his hand and grabbed Elise's hand.

"Before you give me your decision, let me say that I support you 100%.

In fact, I think you should get independent experienced legal representation.

"I really should have raised it with you before. I suppose I was just blinded by my desire to get you out of here.

"Rather than spend too much time on the lawyers your friends at the foodhall have recommended, I have taken the liberty of compiling my own set of names. I have already rung a few of the barristers to check their availability."

Dan noticed that Elise was shaking her head.

"I mean we can still consider the barristers and solicitors your friends at the foodhall told you about if you like. That's not a problem."

"You talk a lot don't you?" Elise asked.

"Sorry. I was just trying to make this conversation easier for you."

They shared a moment of silence before Elise spoke.

"I met another one of your girlfriends in here the other day."

"Girlfriends? I don't think so," Dan replied, greatly concerned by Elise's statement.

"Yes, she told me you were fantastic. You really did it for her."

"I don't know who you could possibly mean."

"She said that you moved heaven and earth for her. I suppose that means you really rocked her world."

"I don't have many ex-girlfriends and none of them, to my knowledge, are in jail."

"Who said she was an *ex*-girlfriend?"

"Honestly, I don't know who you are talking about!"

"She didn't know I was your wife when she was talking to me. So she had no hesitation in telling me that you, Dan Grover, were one of the nicest blokes she had ever met."

She paused and stared straight at him.

"Apparently, she has only known you for a couple of months."

Dan's head was literally spinning. He was trying so hard to comprehend what Elise was saying that white spots were beginning to appear before his eyes and he felt a migraine starting. Where was this coming from?

He could not respond.

"Well, at last you are speechless," Elise said after a few moments.

Then she laughed. She threw her head back and laughed out loud.

Dan didn't know what was happening but he was relieved to see Elise laughing. Soon he was joining in and laughing as well. Though he had no idea what was going on.

"Are you going to tell me the name of this mystery woman?" Dan eventually asked. "Because I just don't know who you are talking about. Honestly."

"Fay. Fay Castle is her name."

"Oh, Fay Castle, how did you meet her?" Dan said exhaling and wiping the sweat from his brow.

"We both like books; we met in the prison library. One day we got to talking and she tells me her story. She said she was on the end of a very rough decision and was sentenced to jail. Although Legal Aid would not fund an appeal, her lawyer refused to give up on her."

Elise took a deep breath and then continued with her story.

"Yesterday Fay rang me from the outside. Her appeal was successful and she has been released. Apparently her lawyer used brilliant arguments to win the case for her on appeal. She couldn't stop raving about him. She offered him some money but he refused to take it."

"Well she has been through a fair bit being imprisoned and separated from her children. Really, she doesn't have much," Dan explained.

"I asked her the lawyer's name, as you know I was looking to get someone really good to work on my case. I got the surprise of my life when she said that her lawyer was none other than, Dan Grover."

"You got the surprise of your life finding out that I was a good lawyer?" Dan pondered out loud, as he was processing what he had just heard.

Elise chuckled again, while Dan feigned to look hurt.

"Anyway, it's pretty clear to me now that I want you to represent me. If you believe Robin is the best option for me, then I am happy with him as well."

"What about Barbara and Dave?"

"Who? It's you and me against the world. We are the ones in this fight, they aren't."

"Amen, to that," Dan said.

"Amen? Are you sure you want to bring God into this?" Elise asked.

Dan nodded slowly and said softly, "Somehow, I think God is already in this."

"Well you are the lawyer. I will trust your professional judgement on that," Elise replied.

They hugged and kissed for some time before Dan tore himself away.

At the doorway Dan stopped and turned towards Elise.

"I am so sorry for getting you into this mess."

"Don't worry about that now. Just get me out of here."

Dan did not say anything. He just nodded, turned and strode purposefully away.

CHAPTER THIRTY ONE

Between the football and cricket seasons there was little sport for Dan to watch. All he could find on TV was the World Darts Championships. England was supposed to dominate but they lost in the first round, leaving Australia as one of the next favourite teams to win.

He enjoyed a beer and was falling asleep watching the final darts match when his mobile phone went off.

"Hello, its Chelsea here, from Dooley and Associates. Is that Dan Grover?"

Dan being half asleep was a little slow on the uptake, and thought the voice on the phone said she was *Chelsea a drooling associate.*

He thought of some of the girls he had met during his youth in bars and clubs, and no one named Chelsea came to mind. During a rebellious phase in his late teens Dan did drink to excess, but he could not place the name Chelsea anywhere where he may have had too much to drink.

"Sorry, I can't," were the only words Dan could get out.

"It's me, Chelsea, from Dooley and Associates. We met last week. You came to the office asking about Samuel Sanderson."

"Ah, Chelsea, the brave receptionist, I remember now."

"I wasn't that brave, just doing my job."

"Just doing my job. Rubbish! You were terrific the way you handled that giant. Hey, did Fiona McNamara ever go and pay our very large friend a visit?"

Chelsea giggled and said, "You're a bad man, Dan Grover. Ms McNamara went to see Mr Button and I haven't heard a peep out of her since. Apparently, the way he behaved towards me was like a love sick puppy compared to his ballistic behaviour towards poor Ms McNamara."

Dan smiled. You reap what you sow – what goes around comes around.

"Chelsea, to what do I owe the pleasure of your call at this late hour?"

"Its only 10 o'clock, it's not that late is it?"

"Actually, us oldies go to bed at around 10 o'clock."

"Oh, I am terribly sorry, I didn't realize you were that old."

Dan had meant the *oldies* term to be a joke but Chelsea had taken it literally.

"I am fine, just dozed off watching TV. How can I help you?"

"I understand you are interested in information about Samuel Sanderson. Is that correct?"

"Yes."

"Why do you want information about him?"

"It's a long story but I wanted to know if anyone in your firm had any trouble with him while he was working there."

"What have you been told already?"

"Fiona McNamara was not helpful. She said your firm would not employ anybody who would commit sexual harassment and she would not comment on Samuel Sanderson for privacy reasons. I think she was just fobbing me off."

"You have to realise that Ms McNamara is only doing her job. Dooley and Associates are the biggest and best market research firm in Australia. Ms McNamara and the other managers don't want the firm's reputation tarnished by allegations of sexual harassment."

There was silence then on the phone for what seemed like an eternity, though it was probably only for a few seconds.

"Chelsea, if there is anything you can tell me about Samuel Sanderson I would appreciate it."

More silence ensured.

"Look, Chelsea, all I am asking for is some information. At the moment it's just between you and me. What do you say, can you help me?"

"We had a researcher working for us by the name of Kathleen Brown. She was a university graduate and she had only been working here for about two months when she complained that Samuel Sanderson had sexually harassed her."

"What happened?"

"I don't really know what happened, just that Kathleen complained to Ms McNamara about Samuel Sanderson. Kathleen told me that Ms McNamara wasn't really interested in her complaint."

Dan had been half asleep, now he was wide awake. Samuel had form for sexual harassment in more than one workplace.

"Anyway, Kathleen left the firm a few days later."

"Where is Kathleen now?"

"We did keep in touch for awhile, but I honestly don't know where she is now."

"Do you have her phone number?"

"After your visit I rang Kathleen and told her you were at the office asking about Samuel Sanderson. I asked Kathleen if she wanted to talk with you about what had happened to her.

"Kathleen said under no circumstances would she talk with you. She told me it had taken her two years to get over what happened and she wasn't about to relive that nightmare again for anyone. Sorry, but she has moved on."

"I understand but I really need to talk with her. It's extremely important."

"I hadn't talked with Kathleen for a long time before the other night and she was pretty adamant she didn't want to talk with you."

"Chelsea, I realise you are stuck between a rock and a hard place, but it's possible Samuel Sanderson could have murdered someone. This person is a young woman who used to work with Samuel. This young woman complained about Samuel sexually assaulting her. I believed her story about Samuel Sanderson."

Again there was a further period of long silence.

"Chelsea, I am impressed with you as a person by the way you stood up to the hulk the other day and also for providing me with this information; you didn't have to do that but you did. If you could only see your way to giving me Kathleen's telephone number, I will take it from there. I won't tell her or anyone that it was you who gave me her number."

"She will know it was me as I just called her about what happened."

"Yeah, she will probably guess it was you. Can you put aside the fact she could be upset with you in light of the serious situation we have here, the murder of a young woman like yourself?"

More deathly quiet over the telephone.

"I dunno, I don't normally betray my friends' confidences."

"Chelsea, sometimes you just have to do the right thing regardless of the consequences. That's what sets strong people and leaders apart from others; their preparedness to do the right thing regardless of the consequences. They have integrity."

"I don't think I am a strong person or a leader."

"Don't sell yourself short, Chelsea. With your integrity, you can be whoever you want to be."

More silence. Dan could literally hear himself breathing.

"Alright, I only have her mobile number. I will give you that but don't say you got it from me. I don't have her address. Kathleen doesn't want anyone to know where she is living."

"Thanks, Chelsea. I really appreciate your help."

Could this be the break he was looking for? Could Samuel Sanderson's pattern of behaviour stretch to murder? Certainly Kathleen has not been murdered but then she has moved and left no forwarding address.

Why does Kathleen not want anyone to know her current address? Was Kathleen running away from Samuel? Did Kathleen receive a threatening letter?

Will Kathleen talk to him? How should he approach Kathleen?

He would need to think carefully about the answer to those last two questions.

CHAPTER THIRTY TWO

At precisely 7:00pm he rang Kathleen Brown's mobile phone number.

"Hello," Dan heard a female answer.

"Hello, my name is Josh and I am calling from Albury McNabb market research. I was wondering if you could spare a few minutes to take part in an important survey I am conducting today."

"Look I don't really have any time to spare, I am sorry."

"Before you go can I just tell you that the survey will only take five minutes and we are offering a free three month subscription to any Australian published magazine of your choice. It's really a great reward for five minutes of your time."

There was a pause and Dan could feel the female he was talking to weighing up whether to take part in the survey. He hoped he was talking to Kathleen Brown.

"What's the survey about?"

"Online shopping."

"Ok then, if it is only going to be five minutes. I used to work for a market research firm many years ago and I know how hard it is to get people to take part in these telephone surveys."

"Thank you. Which market research firm did you work for?"

"Dooley and Associates."

Yes, it was Kathleen Brown. He pumped his right fist.

"Before we start, do you need to hear our privacy charter?"

"No, I don't have time for that."

"Please be aware that our conversation today may be recorded and monitored for quality assurance purposes. Is that a concern for you?"

"No."

"Well let's begin. On average, how often do you shop online? Less than once a month, once a month, once a week, once a day, or more than once a day?"

"Probably about once a week."

"On average, how long do you spend online each time you shop? Is it more than two hours, between two hours and one hour, or less than one hour?"

"I spend on average between one hour and two hours when I shop on-line."

"Can you tell me tell me what type of items you buy on-line? They can be classified as clothing, cosmetics, personal apparel, jewelry, food, tickets, or other items. You can choose more than one item here."

"I buy clothes and tickets, and I have bought items such as a hand bag. How would you classify a hand bag?"

Dan had no idea, but said the first thing that came into his mind. "Oh, that would be personal apparel."

"I also bought a second hand car on-line. Where does that fit in?"

"That would be other items," Dan said, making it up as he went along.

"You must have a big catch all list in other items. Won't that affect the integrity and accuracy of the survey data?"

Dan thought for a moment. "I am really at the lower end of the food chain at Albury McNabb. I only work here on a casual basis. The survey questions were prepared by one of the managers and my job is just to get the data. I leave it up to the powers-that-be to analyse the data."

"Yeah, I have been there and done that, Josh. Yours is not to reason why but to do or die."

That was a close call. He decided not to engage in any further banter with her but just proceed as quickly as possible with the prepared questions.

He completed the survey by asking Kathleen questions about why she shopped on-line, how she became aware of where to shop on-line, what advantages she saw in shopping on-line, and what were the disadvantages of shopping on-line.

Dan was glad the survey had finished with no further questions from Kathleen. After all he reasoned when he compiled the survey questions, most recipients of surveys were just trying to complete them as soon as possible. Hence Kathleen would be unlikely to ask him too many questions, if any, about the survey. Although she had previous experience working as a researcher.

"Thanks for your answers, we have come now to the personal particulars part of the survey. Do you live by yourself, live with a partner, live with a partner and children, or live with other adults?"

Dan felt Kathleen hesitate.

"I am not really comfortable telling you my personal circumstances."

"As you will appreciate from your time working in market research, we need the personal particulars of our sources to properly collate and analyse the data for our client. Without personal particulars our research value is severely limited."

"Ok, I know you keep this information secure and confidential."

"Absolutely."

"I live alone."

"Can you tell me your yearly income: is it over $150,000 a year, between $150,000 and $100,000, between $100,000 and $50,000, or less than $50,000 a year."

"Between $50,000 and $100,000."

He noticed the immediate response from Kathleen and he assumed she was now answering these personal particular questions rapidly, to end the survey as quickly as she could.

"Can you give me your age?

"Twenty–five."

Now for the big question. "Can you tell me your address?"

There was a moment of silence before Kathleen responded.

"I am not comfortable telling you my address. No offence, Josh, but your client doesn't really need to know where I live and I would like to keep it that way."

"I can appreciate your concern but we have now finished the survey and your address is only needed so my manager can authorize your magazine subscription and we can send it out to you."

More silence from Kathleen.

"If you have any concerns about the validity of the survey I am happy to provide you with the phone number of my supervisor and you can call her to verify our privacy charter."

More silence from Kathleen before she said, "Ok then, what's your supervisor's name and phone number?"

Dan had prepared thoroughly for the interview with Kathleen. Its whole purpose was to obtain Kathleen's address. He had to get her address to see her personally; a phone call to her would just scare her away.

What he had not prepared for was Kathleen actually asking him for his supervisor's name and phone number. Whoever asks to speak to a supervisor when answering survey questions?

Although he was caught unprepared by the question, he could not delay answering it. He looked at the phone he was holding and said the first thing that came into his head.

"Phone booth 1300, 3200 triple 1."

"I am sorry did you say your supervisor's name was phone booth?"

"Uh, Fran Booth, is my supervisor. She is at a conference today but you can call her tomorrow. You know how it is, worker's work and supervisor's attend conferences and seminars."

"Yeah, I know how it is alright."

More silence.

"Which magazine subscription would you like? We have Finance Australia, Business Review Weekly, Cosmopolitan, Cleo, and many others to choose from. Even Fishing Australia and Rugby League Week are available."

"To tell you the truth, Josh, I am a Queensland girl living in Melbourne. They are aussie rules mad down here. There is virtually no rugby league news in the newspapers. I wouldn't mind getting Rugby League Week, even though the season has finished, it will keep me up-to-date with player movements."

"Ok, fine Rugby League Week it is. Well that finishes the survey, thank you for your participation," Dan concluded.

"I am sorry there is one more thing, I don't have your name or address. You can ring my supervisor tomorrow and give her your details and we will then try and match up your name and address with the subscription you want. Or you can give me your details now and the whole subscription thing will be sorted out and you should get the latest issue of Rugby League Week in a week or so."

More silence.

"My name is Kathleen Brown and I live at Unit 3, 29 Burnett Place, Hawthorn, Melbourne."

"Do you support the Hawthorn Hawks?"

"I support the Hawks. In Melbourne you have to support some aussie rules team, it's just part of life down here. But I miss going to see the Broncos play at Suncorp Stadium."

"Actually I am a Cronulla Sharks supporter." Dan couldn't help himself.

"Oh Josh I feel sorry for you. Really you support the Sharks. Why?"

"I suppose I am a true believer. They will come good one day."

Dan heard a disbelieving groan emanate from the other end of the phone.

It was time to terminate this conversation.

"Anyway thanks for your help. That now completes the survey."

Dan put down the telephone receiver and breathed easier. Kathleen was still very sensitive about giving out her address several years after working for Dooley and Associates. Why?

CHAPTER THIRTY THREE

It was a bitterly cold day in Melbourne, with a freezing wind howling up and down the unit block.

Dan was taken by surprise when the door opened suddenly, after he had pressed the buzzer a fourth time.

A young woman answered the door bell. She was casually dressed as one would expect for a Saturday afternoon in a sloppy joe, track suit pants and joggers.

"What can I do for you?"

"My name is Dan Grover and I really need a few minutes of your time."

Dan noticed that Kathleen's eyes had already started to glaze over as though she expected him to try and sell her something, or perhaps worse, complete a survey.

"I have travelled from Brisbane to meet with you Kathleen."

Now that got her attention. At that moment Dan noticed Kathleen had deep set hazel eyes and they were intently fixed on him.

"I am a lawyer investigating the murder of a young woman in Brisbane several months ago. One of the suspects in the case is a man called Samuel Sanderson. I have reason to believe you have some information about Mr Sanderson which could help my client."

Dan noticed Kathleen's demeanor change from pleasant to scared but he just wasn't prepared for her slamming the door on him. As if in slow motion he saw Kathleen reach for the door and slam it shut. He wasn't about to put his arm or foot in the door's path and all he could do to react was to move his whole body backwards. He moved so quickly that he overbalanced and fell over, twisting his knee and grazing his wrist and elbow on the unforgiving concrete surface.

"I am sorry, but please go. I don't want to talk to you or anyone ever again about Samuel Sanderson," Kathleen said through the closed door.

"I wouldn't have come all this way to talk with you if it was not a matter of life and death. Please give me just a few minutes of your time. We can keep everything you tell me confidential."

"How did you find me?"

Dan pulled out the latest issue of Rugby League Week from his bag and he slid it under the door to Kathleen.

"There is an interesting article in there on the Brisbane Broncos new signings. Sorry, I read it on the plane."

Kathleen slowly opened her door and it looked like she was going to throw the magazine at Dan.

Perhaps she felt sorry for him as he was sitting near her doorway windswept, dishevelled and bleeding from his fall. Perhaps she had had enough of keeping silent and she now felt the need to tell someone about what had happened to her. Whatever the reason, Kathleen opened the door and motioned for Dan to come inside.

As Dan limped inside Kathleen said, "Stay there and I will get something to cover your cuts. I don't want you bleeding on my carpet."

"Thanks," Dan said, "I appreciate your concern."

*

Dan was feeling slightly uncomfortable seated on Kathleen's couch with his bandaged right leg stretched along the couch and his left leg hanging over the side. He had though warmed up thanks to Kathleen's central heating and a steaming mug of piping hot chocolate she had made for him.

"Can we talk about Samuel Sanderson?"

Kathleen stared vacantly out her lounge room window.

"I had only been working there for a few days when Samuel seemed to go out of his way to be friendly towards me. He would email me jokes and take me out for coffee. He was the perfect gentleman.

"Then one night after a few of us had been working off site, we ended up at a bar. I didn't notice when the others left but at one point in the night I remember we were alone. I had drunk a fair bit by this time."

Kathleen hesitated at this point in her story.

"Samuel was good looking, funny and I liked him. Perhaps I led him on, I was very intoxicated."

Kathleen stopped her story again. This time Dan had to prod her to keep going.

185

"What happened?"

"We were drinking alone at a table a little bit away from everyone else and he started touching me. I didn't know what to do. I suppose I was naïve. I just froze. I didn't confront him or tell him to get his hands the hell off me. I wanted to tell him to stop taking liberties with me but I didn't want to upset him.

"Then all of a sudden he reached over and kissed me. I was in shock. I didn't know what to do. I let him go on with it for a few seconds, then I pulled away. As I pulled away he grabbed my arms and pulled me back towards him.

"I told him he was hurting me and to let me go. But he didn't let me go, he continued to pull me back to him and he tried to kiss me again.

"The more I struggled with him, the tighter he grasped my arms and the more he hurt me. It was as though he was not going to let me go and I had better submit to him or he would hurt me."

Kathleen's voice was wavering.

"It was really painful and really scary. In the end, I managed to knee him in the groin. He relaxed his grip on me and I started screaming and kicking."

Kathleen was demonstrably upset and in tears as she relived those terrifying moments.

"One of the security men at the bar came over and asked me if I was alright. I said I was fine, but I was not fine. I was hysterical. It had all happened so quickly. The security guard must have seen the state I was in and he called a taxi for me. The security guard escorted me out of the hotel and sent me on my way home."

"Did you tell anyone about what happened?"

"I did tell a couple of girlfriends. I also told work. I even lodged a complaint there about him."

"What happened?"

"My workplace wasn't interested in my complaint. They saw it as my word against his, and of course, I couldn't deny I was drunk at the time."

"Why did you leave Brisbane?"

"A week or so after I lodged the complaint, I am not sure now of the timelines. But I remember receiving a letter which threatened my life unless I left town. The letter was really scary stuff. It was one of those you see in the movies which used printed letters from newspapers and magazines to make up the words."

Dan's eyebrows twitched at the mention of the threatening note.

"I was really scared, petrified. The note was slid under my door late one night when I was home. I had seen the evil in Samuel's eyes at the bar and I knew what he was capable of. So I just up and left Brisbane. I did all I could to hide my new address from him."

Dan was breathing heavily, his heart was pounding. The note that Kathleen received was the key to Samuel being involved in Mia's death. For Mia received a similar note, he had seen it.

Dan asked the next question as casually as he could. "Do you still have the note?"

"No, I couldn't stand having it around me, it put chills up my spine every time I saw it. I threw it out years ago."

Dan dropped his head in disappointment.

"Can you remember exactly what the note said?"

"No, I have tried to forget about it. I think it just said I would die if I didn't leave town."

"Is that all?"

"Yeah, that was all. No wait, I think the note referred to me as a harlot or something like that."

"Could it have been a trollop?"

"That's right it was a trollop. I remember thinking, who uses the word *trollop* these days."

"What do you mean, when you say you know what Samuel is capable of?"

"It is hard to explain and perhaps its just a woman's intuition, but I truly believe I was fighting for my life that night. He was like an animal, he not only wanted to have sex with me, he wanted to hurt me."

"Did you go to the Police?"

"No, I was just so scared. I just wanted to get out of town as quickly as I could. Who would believe me anyway?"

"Would you be prepared to come back to Brisbane to tell a court what happened to you?"

Kathleen was quiet for sometime before she spoke.

"I am sorry. I truly am, but I am not putting myself at risk again. I have made a good life for myself down here. It was very difficult for me to tell you what happened. I imagine it will be even more difficult to tell my story in a courtroom.

"I have paid the price to live without fear. I left all my family and friends behind in Queensland. I just can't live with fear again and I would be doing that big-time if I went to a court in Brisbane and testified against Samuel Sanderson."

"I really appreciate you talking with me, Kathleen. I understand your decision about not wanting to testify."

He knew they could subpoena her to come to court, but what was the point of that? It would only upset Kathleen and possibly put her in danger. Who knew what she would tell the court if she was forced to testify against her wishes.

"I am sorry I cannot be of more help. But I need to feel safe. It has taken me a long time to feel safe again and I just can't throw all that out the window."

"Ok, I will leave you my mobile phone number. Please call me at any time if you remember anything else or would like to talk some more."

At that Dan gave Kathleen his business card and asked her to call him a taxi. Dan was back and warm in sunny Brisbane within a few hours.

CHAPTER THIRTY FOUR

Spencer Rush Accountants occupied the 2nd floor of a trendy renovated building in Teneriffe. The accountancy firm was quite small with only seven partners, so to compete against the big, national and international accountancy firms they called themselves a *boutique* practice. Boutique meaning that they specialized in certain areas of accountancy practice and their specialization meant they could match the larger firms in these areas, but at a reduced price.

However the boutique label meant their premises had to be trendy and make a statement, not stodgy and conservative. Hence their premises at Teneriffe was not like your usual accountant's office. Their grand old building was beautifully crafted out of cut sandstone and it was originally built in 1894 as the hardware emporium of *Tobin & Sons*.

As Dan walked into the restored building, he wondered what it would have been like to enter this building in its heyday at the start of the 20th century. No doubt, people would have been milling around everywhere, talking with each other and discussing the latest news. No iphones, Facebook, or Twitter; in those days people would have to talk with one another face-to-face to hear the news of what was happening.

As Dan was admiring the interior decor of the reception area, a middle aged woman pleasantly asked if she could help him.

"Yes, I have an appointment with Siobhan Corke, your practice manager," Dan replied.

After about five minutes, Siobhan Corke appeared and led Dan away to her office overlooking the Brisbane River. Siobhan was in her late 30s, tanned, with shoulder length cropped dark hair. She was immaculately dressed with gold jewelry dripping off her neck, wrists and fingers.

"Mr Grover, what can I do for you?"

"I am investigating a matter involving a Mr Samuel Sanderson, a former employee of yours. I was wondering how you found him at your firm. Whether there were any complaints about his behavior, especially towards female employees.”

Siobhan Corke’s demeanor changed from pleasant to one of concern. “Well, Mr Grover, we did have some issues with Mr Sanderson and it was because of those issues that we let him go.”

“You fired him?”

“Not exactly, we suggested to him he should resign or we would sack him. In the end we had some discussions with his lawyer, but he decided just to leave voluntarily, rather than fight being sacked.”

“Can you tell me what the issues were?”

“I can’t tell you specifics but generally we felt that he was not respectful of personal boundaries. He was someone who was not prepared to follow rules and he was quick to take advantage of young, naïve staff members.”

“In other words, you are telling me he was a slimeball?”

“I wouldn’t use such graphic words, but we had concerns about the strength and fortitude of Mr Sanderson’s character.”

“Did you ever meet Mr Sanderson’s wife?”

Dan was not sure why he had even asked that question, but he figured you could never have too much information.

“Yes, I met her a few times at staff functions. I must say she appeared a little odd to me. Her eyes were like glass when she was speaking to you; it felt like she was looking right through you. She was not someone I felt comfortable being around.”

Dan had felt a similar concern about Grace Sanderson. Perhaps he thought she had to be a little odd to marry and continue to live with a sexual predator like Samuel Sanderson. Dan pondered what would make a woman want to live with someone like that?

“Mr Grover, are you ok?”

“Yes, I am fine. I was just admiring your beautiful offices.”

“We are very proud of them, they are heritage listed you know.”

Dan shook himself away from Siobhan’s dazzling smile and said, “Just getting back to Mr Sanderson, I really need to know whether any of your staff made any sexual harassment or sexual assault complaints against him.”

“Several women came and saw me and expressed their concern about Mr Sanderson’s treatment of them but in reality we really only ever had one formal complaint about him.”

"Can you tell me about that complaint? It would really help me out."

"I didn't want to get into specifics. But I suppose I don't really owe Mr Sanderson anything and I would be very concerned if he is still sexually harassing women."

Dan liked Siobhan Corke. Unlike Fiona McNamara, she seemed to be more concerned about people's welfare, rather than the firm's reputation.

"The formal complaint came from one of our administration workers, Amanda Peterson. I have made some notes about her complaint. Let me get the file."

Siobhan Corke walked over to her filing cabinet and pulled out a large manila file.

"Amanda complained that Samuel took advantage of her on an audit they had conducted together in Toowoomba. It was a two day assignment and after they had dinner together, they apparently consumed alcohol for some time in Mr Sanderson's hotel room.

"Amanda said that she liked and trusted Mr Sanderson and she was not completely shocked when he tried to kiss her. She told me that she kissed Mr Sanderson back. Apparently, Mr Sanderson then started to grope her and at that stage Amanda was having second thoughts about what she was doing.

"Amanda told me that Mr Sanderson had taken some of his clothes off, and was in the process of removing her clothes, when she told him to stop. She said she had been fine with some intimate contact with Mr Sanderson but she did not want to get naked and have sex with him.

"Her complaint was that Mr Sanderson refused to stop. Amanda became very concerned when he grabbed her and appeared to be forcing her to have sex with him. Amanda felt it was only her mobile phone ringing and her ability to answer that incoming call that stopped Mr Sanderson from raping her."

Siobhan took a deep breath.

"Amanda was very upset and emotional when she confided in me about what had happened. She was unsure about what to do. I suggested she lodge a complaint and I would arrange for it to be investigated.

"Amanda did lodge a formal complaint against Mr Sanderson, but the investigation report was inconclusive. Mr Sanderson told the investigator that they both were very drunk at the time. He said that all his physical contact with Amanda was by consent and he was the one that stopped, not her. Mr Sanderson said that Amanda wanted to have sex with him but in the end he decided he couldn't do that to his wife. He suggested to the investigator that

Amanda's complaint against him was motivated by her desire to get back at him for rejecting her sexual advances."

Dan noted the similarity of Samuel's defence in this complaint to his defence of Mia's complaint.

"The investigator concluded as it was her word against his; he could not determine that the complaint was substantiated. Consequently, we could take no action against Mr Sanderson with respect to this particular complaint."

Siobhan closed the file and looked out towards the river.

"Amanda was, to say the least, very upset with the investigation report. She was also upset with our firm for not taking any action against Mr Sanderson.

"She was particularly livid at Mr Sanderson portraying her as some type of prostitute. At one point Amanda told me she was going to lodge a complaint with the police of attempted rape against Mr Sanderson.

"About two weeks after Amanda told me she was going to the police, she just disappeared. I have not seen or heard from her since."

"What do you mean disappeared? How could she just vanish? Did she resign?"

"No, she just didn't show up for work for a few days. I rang her mobile and it had been turned off.

"I rang her mother. Her mother told me she had not heard from Amanda for some time and she didn't know where she was. Amanda's mother didn't seem too worried about her and she told me that Amanda was an independent, head-strong, young girl.

"I assumed that Amanda, to use the colloquial expression, *got the shits with everyone* and left town to start afresh."

"She didn't contact you for her pay or anything?"

"No, but we did pay all her entitlements into her nominated bank account."

"Is there anything else you can tell me about Samuel Sanderson?"

"You don't think something bad has happened to Amanda do you? I mean, I hadn't really thought about it too much."

"I don't know. It could be Amanda just moved to a new town and didn't want to let anyone know where she was. It has happened before. Can you give me Amanda's mother's phone number and address? I would like to check it out further."

"Certainly. I feel really bad now that I've not chased this up before. Is there anything else I can do?"

"No thank you, Siobhan. You have been more than helpful."

As Siobhan Corke led Dan out to the foyer of Spencer Rush, he noticed that she was not dazzling that smile around anymore. Indeed, Siobhan continued to look quite concerned as he made his way down the stairs.

CHAPTER THIRTY FIVE

Amanda's mother lived in Corinda. As Dan drove to Corinda vivid memories came swirling back to him. He had been living in Brisbane during the disastrous 2011 floods.

Dan's house was not affected by the floods but he was a proud member of *the mud army*; thousands upon thousands of volunteers who went house to house, street to street, suburb to suburb, to clean houses and businesses decimated by the flood.

There were two powerful, yet contrasting images of the 2011 floods bobbing around in Dan's mind as he drove through the suburbs of Chelmer, Sherwood, Graceville and other flood affected areas on his way to Corinda.

First, the absolute devastation the flood brought to many, many people in Brisbane and throughout Queensland. His first clean up job was in Corinda and although he had read of the flood damage and seen it on TV, what he had read and seen had not prepared him for the absolute devastation he found.

Everything was covered in grey mud; everything. A smelly, slimy, sticky mud. The stench was overwhelming. Everything people owned had to be thrown away. It was literally rotting on the footpaths. And it was the same, house after house, suburb after suburb.

The second overpowering memory was one of mateship and camaraderie that he had rarely seen before. Out of the absolute devastation of the floods arose a sense of oneness, which lies dormant in people until a disaster happens. Thousands of people from Brisbane and indeed all over Queensland and Australia came to the flood affected areas of their own volition and helped out. There were traffic jams as people tried to get into affected areas to help out.

A tall, thin lady opened her door to Dan. He thought she was probably in her mid 60s, with puffy eyes and a haggard appearance. She wore a loose fitting dress and long dangling earrings.

"Hello, my name is Dan Grover, I was wondering if I could talk to you about your daughter, Amanda."

"Who are you?"

"I am a lawyer and I am investigating the death of a young woman."

"A young woman?" The lady's demeanor changed dramatically from one of curiousity to one of deep concern.

"Mia Wong was her name. I am investigating a possible link between Mia Wong and a man called Samuel Sanderson."

"My name is Rose Peterson, Amanda's mother. Won't you come in?"

Dan followed Rose into her modestly decorated high set chamfer board home.

"Can I get you anything?"

"Coffee would be good."

Dan sat down in a comfortable but dilapidated looking sofa in the lounge room.

Rose brought coffee over for Dan and herself as well as some homemade cookies.

"I shouldn't but maybe just one for the road," Dan said as Rose offered him a cookie. After all, he thought, Rose might be offended if he didn't take at least one.

"What do you want to know?"

"I have been to Spencer Rush, where Amanda used to work. They told me that she disappeared after making a complaint of sexual harassment against Samuel Sanderson. I was just wondering if you know where Amanda is, or anything about her complaint against Samuel Sanderson?"

Rose looked at the ceiling and then straight at Dan. She sighed and moved to the front of her chair before replying.

"Amanda disappeared about five years ago now. I don't know too much about her complaint against Samuel Sanderson, other than she was very disappointed in the reaction she got from her workplace.

"Amanda and I were never very close and she would only tell me what she thought I needed to know about her personal life, which was not much.

"She felt shafted by her workplace and she went to the police. From what I can gather the police were not overly interested in her complaint either. Apparently this Samuel Sanderson guy used to work in the military or the police, something like that, and they believed him over her."

Dan was very interested in what Amanda's mother was telling him. So interested, that he was munching on his second cookie before he had realised it.

"Amanda was very depressed about it all. One day I tried to reach her and couldn't. She had disappeared, vanished. I called the police. They checked her phone records, credit cards and bank accounts, and none of them had been touched for weeks. She didn't have much money and she was heavily in debt.

"The police weren't able to locate her. I made the mistake of telling the police that Amanda had been very depressed about not being believed in her complaint and they immediately put her disappearance down to suicide.

"Although the police say there is no evidence of foul play, I believe in my heart that she was murdered."

"Did she have any enemies?"

"None that I know of. I mean, she was a very head-strong, young girl. She probably put a few people offside with the things she might have said, but I know of no one who disliked her enough to murder her."

"Do you know if the police talked to Samuel Sanderson about Amanda's disappearance?"

"They told me they did talk to him. Apparently he told the police that he didn't know anything about Amanda's disappearance. The police said he told them that she had probably just run off, as she was embarrassed about lying to everyone about him. I got the sense from the police that he was quite smug about the whole thing."

Rose put her coffee mug down and looked straight at Dan.

"What do you know about Samuel Sanderson, what has he got to do with your case and is it relevant to Amanda?"

"In my case, a young woman was murdered after making a complaint to her employer that Samuel Sanderson had sexually harassed her. There could be a connection between that case and Amanda. I don't know for sure but there is a distinct possibility the two cases are connected.

"Do you know if Amanda ever received a threatening note before she disappeared? Something like leave town or you will be hurt."

"Amanda never told me that she had received a threatening note like that but she could have.

"She has been murdered by that Sanderson guy, hasn't she?"

"I don't know. It's possible," Dan answered softly.

Rose bent over and quietly sobbed into her hands.

Dan moved over to Rose and put his arm around her. After a few minutes when Rose had regained her composure he said, "Thank you so much for sharing Amanda with me. What you have told me has been very helpful."

"I don't know how I have helped you. I would like to hear what happens with your case, especially if it is relevant to Amanda."

"Certainly Rose, I will let you know what happens. Here is my card, if you want to talk about anything at all, just give me a call anytime."

"After all these years of not knowing what has happened to Amanda, I really need to know something, anything, so I can lay her memory to rest."

As Dan drove back to work he pondered the information he had received in the last few days. It all seemed to fit a pattern of behaviour where Samuel Sanderson could have murdered both Amanda and Mia. However, there was a distinct lack of direct evidence linking Samuel to both crimes.

Dan needed to think about what to do and discuss his next move with Robin, after all the trial was not far away now.

CHAPTER THIRTY SIX

Dan was busy working at his desk when Gloria waltzed into his office.

"You're not going to believe who just rang wanting to make an appointment to see you?" she said excitedly.

Dan looked up vacantly, hoping Gloria would just tell him the answer.

"Guess," she said.

Damn, he would have to play her game.

"The Queen?" suggested Dan.

"No, think about it Danny. Who would you least expect to want you to represent them?"

"Prince Charles?"

"No, be serious."

"Look, Gloria, I am really busy what with Elise's trial and my other legal work. Can you just tell me?" Dan asked.

"You're no fun these days. It's all work with you now," replied Gloria as she marched out of Dan's tiny office.

"Aren't you going to tell me?" Dan yelled to her as she resumed her position at the front desk.

Gloria came rushing back into Dan's room.

"Alyssa Paschetelle, can you believe it? The woman who made that complaint to the police about you kidnapping her baby."

No, Dan couldn't believe it.

"Anyway, she has split from her husband again and she had the temerity to want you to represent her. She said something about she wants a fighter and you are the baddest fighter she knows," Gloria said giggling to herself.

"Now don't go all moose on me, Gloria," Dan said starting to smile himself.

At that Gloria lost control and started snorting and making several moose mating calls.

"What did you tell her?" Dan asked, after Gloria had settled down.

"I told her I would ask you. But you are not going to act for a client that accuses you of wrong doing, let alone kidnapping her baby."

"Actually, Gloria, I want you to ring her back and tell her I will act on her behalf."

"Why would you want to do that?"

"Because I want to get something in writing from her that will exonerate me once and for all, from rescuing her baby. You always need a back up, Gloria."

"Smart move."

"In the process of acting for her in the family law matter, I might also be able to obtain an indemnity from her husband."

"I thought the police had dropped those charges?"

"They told me they were not going to proceed with the charges, but you never know Gloria, you never know. The police could easily change their mind and charge me. Best to get something in writing from the Paschetelle's, if I can, to use as leverage with the police if they ever change their mind.

"Elise's trial is starting next week, so book Alyssa in to see me this Thursday."

"Aye, aye Captain," Gloria said as she mockingly saluted Dan.

"By the way, how is Elise going in jail? I feel just terrible that she has been charged with murder and has to wait for the trial in jail. The poor thing."

"Actually she has surprised me. She could have dropped her bundle in there but she has shown real steel. She has shown character to keep it all together."

"I told you, Danny, she is a real treasure. You should never let anything come between you and her. Certainly not that girl you were seeing in that worker's cottage in Spring Hill."

"Mia Wong is dead Gloria. For your information I wasn't seeing her. Anyway, how did you know she lived in a worker's cottage in Spring Hill?"

"Ah, I know from somewhere. I think it was the newspapers."

"I don't remember Mia's actual address or house description being in the newspapers."

"Doreen must have told me. Doreen lives in Spring Hill."

"But that was months ago."

"I have a good memory, Danny. You should know that by now."

He knew Gloria had a good memory but that was stretching things.

"Danny, I just settled that last conveyancing contract we got in. That will be quite a good earner for us," Gloria announced, quickly changing the subject.

"Thanks Gloria, I could not have kept this practice afloat without you."

"Think nothing of it, Danny. Just remember you can rely on me to do whatever needs to be done."

At that Gloria turned on her heels and skipped out of Dan's office.

*

When Dan arrived home that evening, he found a police service card in his letterbox. On the back of the card was a message from Sarah asking Dan to ring her.

"Hey Sarah, what's up?" Dan said into his phone.

"I was just wondering how it was all going. I haven't heard from you in awhile."

"It's going fairly well," Dan replied.

Although Sarah had been very helpful and had risked her job to assist Dan, he couldn't help but be circumspect with the information he had discovered about Samuel Sanderson. No point alerting the authorities to it before trial. The information would have a much greater effect if they surprised the prosecution lawyers with it at the trial.

"Fairly well, what does that mean exactly?"

"Well…."

"Come on Dan, it's me, Sarah. I know you have been getting around."

"Sarah, you have been brilliant, but I can't in all fairness to my client, tell you our case before the trial."

"Your client. You mean of course your wife."

"That's right. It is difficult for me as a lawyer, husband and possible witness to be effective in all my roles."

"What about friend?" Sarah asked.

"Yes, friend is an important role as well. I sincerely hope we are still friends."

There was a moments silence between them.

"You still think she didn't do it, don't you?"

"I am more convinced now she is innocent than when we last spoke about it."

More silence between them, till Sarah spoke up.

"I realise you have probably been doing it tough, so on the eve of the trial so to speak, I thought I would cheer you up and invite you out for dinner. What do you say?"

Dan was not sure.

"Even Shark's supporters have to eat," Sarah volunteered

Dan was tempted, but then he thought better of it.

"No, I don't think so."

"Look I'll shout you, how's that? I know how tight you are."

"I am not tight with money."

"You drive around all day looking for a street park rather than pay for parking, and you are not tight?"

"Well, that's different. I am not tight with my friends."

Dan decided to change tack.

"Sarah, it would not be a good look, especially for you, if someone saw us eating dinner together on the eve of the trial. The defendant's husband and lawyer eating dinner with one of the prosecution's main witnesses. That would not be good for your career."

"Come over to my apartment then. No one will see us there."

Dan hesitated.

"Apartment 15, 112 Treloar Lane, Holland Park," Sarah volunteered her address.

"Sarah, I might give that a miss as well."

"It's only dinner, Dan, nothing else."

"I appreciate the offer, I really do. I don't want to upset our friendship but now with the trial about to start, I really have to focus all my energies on the trial. Also, I am acutely aware what happened last time I was invited over to a woman's place at night."

"Ok Dan, no problems. I was just seeing how you were; catching up. By the way, have you thought what you will do if your wife is found guilty?"

"What do you mean?"

"Have you thought what you are going to do? Will you stay with her or get a divorce? I mean she could be in prison for the next 15 years."

"No, I haven't really thought too much about it. I am just expecting her to be found not guilty."

More silence between them.

"All the best Dan and may justice be served."

"Yeah thanks, Sarah. I will *see you* in court."

At that comment they both chuckled. Dan was about to terminate the call when he thought of something he needed to ask Sarah.

"Hey Sarah, one last thing. You said you knew I had been getting around. What did you mean by that?"

Silence was the response, until Sarah said, "Joseph Wong rang and abused Sloan for arresting the wrong person for his daughter's murder. He believes Brock Shepard should have been charged. Apparently he gave Sloan a hard time over it. Turns out he has been talking to you about who we charged. He told Sloan that you went all the way to Sydney just to talk to him."

"Nice guy, Joseph Wong."

"I am not sure Sloan agrees with you on that."

"It wouldn't be the last time Senior Detective Sloan and I disagree on something.

"Thanks again Sarah, I mean it."

At that Dan terminated his call with Sarah and began to prepare one of his favourite meals, Australian Tiger prawns with squeezed lemon and rocket on a crusty bread roll.

CHAPTER THIRTY SEVEN

Dan arrived at the hospital just as the nurses were changing their shifts. He cleaned his hands using one of the many hand washing units located in the hospital corridors.

He found Claye sitting in his easy recliner chair reading the newspaper.

"I'll have a hot herbal tea and a sweet biscuit thanks. I am leaving the hospital today so I don't have a completed menu for you to take," Claye said without looking up.

"Well that's a relief, the staff were about to go on strike if you stayed here any longer."

Claye looked up quickly from his newspaper with a stunned expression until he realised it was Dan speaking.

"Little brother, I didn't expect you to be here on time. I expected you to blow in sometime this afternoon."

"Are you packed and ready to go?" Dan asked the question but he knew Claye was a very organised person and he would have been packed and ready to go well ahead of time.

"Mate, just let me say a few goodbyes and then let's hit the road out of this joint!"

Dan loaded his car with Claye's hospital possessions which had accumulated during his long stay. He noted that flowers were not part of Claye's hospital possessions. Flowers were banned in the oncology wards due to the risk of bacterial infection posed to patients with low immunity from the decaying plant material in the water.

"I bet you're glad that's over," Dan said as he sped off with Claye.

"Actually, it's not over. I am well enough to be discharged from hospital but I am still having outpatient treatment. I have been told it could take me twelve months to fully recover."

"How are you feeling now?"

"Not bad, but I tell you I never want to go through that again, ever!"

Claye put his hand on Dan's shoulder and said, "Hey thanks, mate, your stem cells have saved my life. I owe you big time."

"Forget it, I am glad I could help you out.

"By the way Claye where are we headed, home?"

"Actually I would like to go to the beach. I have been longing to go to the beach everyday since I have been in hospital. I still don't have much energy but I would really like to go to the beach for an hour or so, before we go home."

"Mooloolaba ok, or do you want to go somewhere closer to home say, Redcliffe or Sandgate?"

"Let's drive to Mooloolaba Beach. It will look amazing this time of day. It's so great to be out of hospital."

Claye put his head back to rest as Dan drove towards the Sunshine Coast and the rolling surf of the beautiful Mooloolaba Beach.

Suddenly Claye snapped his head forward and asked, "How's Elise?"

"She is going as well as can be expected."

"How is the case looking?"

"It's looking good. I've discovered information about the victim's ex-boyfriend and particularly about her ex-work colleague that will blow the charges against Elise right out of the water."

"Dan are *you* ok?"

"I am surviving. Though I am starting to develop some phobias."

"Such as?"

"Sometimes I imagine I am being followed. You know being watched. It's probably just paranoia. This case is really getting to me."

"What do you mean? Do you think someone is watching you?"

"It's hard to explain but sometimes I just feel like I am being watched. I look at cars in the rear vision, just to check whether I am being followed. I look at people on the street and wonder if they are watching me."

"You are paranoid."

"That's not the worst of it. For the last couple of weeks I have even taken to jamming a little piece of paper in the door when I leave the house, so I can tell if someone has broken into my home while I have been out. You know the paper will drop to the floor when the door is opened."

"Have you been to the police? I mean someone could be following you and watching you."

"No, I don't want to talk to them without any proof. Besides I have been very busy."

"Mate, for a smart bloke you act pretty dumb sometimes. Go to the police, tell them about it. At the very least they will take note of it; if something does happen it's important they have a record of it now."

Dan thought for a moment and then added, "It's a pity you are my big brother because occasionally you give such wise advice. Obviously as a little brother I am sworn never to take my older brother's advice."

"Oh come on," Claye said as he laughed and playfully punched Dan in the arm.

"A mosquito, someone let a mosquito in the car and it landed on my arm.

"Boy you have lost some power in your punch."

"Hopefully, I have only lost my physical punch, not my mental punch."

Dan raised his eyebrows and said tongue in check, "From what I can see your mental faculties are as per usual."

At that comment Claye punched Dan in the shoulder again.

"A fly, a fly got in the car and it landed on my shoulder."

They both laughed and laughed, until Claye started coughing uncontrollably. At that point Dan stopped the car and watched as Claye *threw up* on the side of the road.

Claye looked gaunt and he was stick insect thin. The intense treatment he had been through had taken a terrible toll on his body. Dan knew Claye was getting better but it was clear he was not out of the woods yet.

CHAPTER THIRTY EIGHT

It was a stinking hot afternoon when Dan once again pulled into the Brisbane Women's Correctional Centre car park. He had his car's air conditioning on full blast. He was assaulted by hot air as he opened his car door and walked along the boiling bitumen car park to the prison entrance.

Dan was meeting with Robin and Elise to take her final instructions before the trial. He arrived early so he could have some personal time with Elise.

"Well, hello stranger, haven't seen you for a few days," Elise said as she entered the small interview room.

"Yeah, sorry about that."

"You are apologizing to me. Admitting you have done something wrong. Wow."

"I feel bad about not seeing you these last few days."

"You are a changed man, Dan Grover, and I like it."

Dan hesitated as Elise looked straight at him.

"How are you going really? Will you be able to make it through the trial?" Dan asked.

"It hasn't been easy. In fact, at times, it has been really hard. It has helped though knowing you are on my side."

Elise was pale but holding it together. Several months inside a women's prison had hardened her up quite a bit.

"I think you have done remarkably well holding it all together in here. Exactly how have you done that?"

"I have kept my head down and made a few friends. Actually, the prison chaplain has been very good to me. He even gave me a copy of the Bible. I thought I might as well read it as I have nothing else to do.

"I was really angry at you, the world, God, for putting me in here. But you know for the first time in my life, I have the time to contemplate the important things in life. I can't really explain it, but whenever I read the Bible or think about God I feel stronger, somehow more empowered, more at peace."

Elise reached out and touched Dan's hand.

"Perhaps when all this is over we could go to church together?"

"I would like for us to do that together," Dan said.

"Is this a private meeting or can anyone join in?" asked Robin who appeared out of nowhere.

"Come on in, Robin. Elise and I were just having some private time before we discussed the trial," Dan said.

"I got your text about blowing the prosecution case out of the water, so let's hear it," Robin said as he threw his briefcase of papers onto the small table.

"You haven't said hello to Elise yet."

"Sorry Elise, I have been working so hard on this case, that I was fixated on the smoking gun Dan has found for us."

"Two *sorrys* in one day, one from a husband and one from a barrister. Remarkable. I wonder if that's ever happened in the history of the world before now," Elise said with a smile. Dan also saw the humour in it.

Robin looked at Elise in a perplexed manner and then he looked at Dan for clarification.

"Don't worry, Robin, it's a private joke between Elise and I," Dan said.

"Anyway, I wouldn't call it a smoking gun, more a complete picture of how Elise should be found not guilty."

"Don't make us wait, give us the full story," Robin said eagerly.

Dan then recounted in great detail all he had discovered in the last few weeks.

"Very good work, Dan, that's more than we could have ever hoped for," Robin said.

"We will need Kathleen Brown to testify, especially to describe the note she received." Robin said.

"There is a slight problem in that Kathleen has destroyed the note. Also she is still very concerned about appearing in court and revisiting her ordeal with Sanderson. Kathleen made it quite clear that she did not want to testify or be involved any further in our case."

"We can just subpoena her. Her evidence is too crucial to ignore."

"She is very scared and who knows what she will say if we force her to testify against her will."

"I don't see anyway around it. We have to get Kathleen Brown to testify."

"Perhaps we could try and have her testify via telephone or video link."

"Yes, that could work; depends on what Judge we get, but testifying via video link due to serious concerns about safety may just work. Good thinking, Dan, I knew you were not just a pretty face."

Dan smiled at Elise and put his hands up as if to humbly say, *I am too good, I can't help it.*

"One other thing we can attack is the strength of Samuel's alibi, his wife. Samuel has obviously got a problem that while intoxicated he likes to force himself onto women. His wife must know what he is like, why does she continue to live with him and support him, such as providing him with an alibi? We should think seriously about having a crack at her in the witness box," Dan suggested.

"I don't know about that. We have no evidence as such to put to her, that she has lied to protect him in previous cases or in this case. All she has to do is say that she knows he is a *slimeball*, but on this particular day this *slimeball* was home with me. Questioning her could backfire on us.

"I think it is best if we leave her right out of the trial."

"Ok, you are the barrister. You run the trial how you think best. I will bow to your great experience in these matters."

Robin and Dan exchanged glances. Elise picked up on the implied jab about this being Robin's first murder trial.

"Let's discuss the other witnesses," Robin said. "They will start with Senior Detective Sloan."

"Unless either of you have any concerns, I intend to vigorously pursue Sloan in the witness box."

Elise looked puzzled.

"That means he will get stuck into him when he testifies," Dan clarified.

Elise nodded in agreement as did Dan.

"Next they will call Detective Little. Same approach for her. I intend to vigorously pursue her or as a lay person would like to put it, get stuck into her when she testifies.

Elise nodded in agreement.

Dan appeared not so certain. "Look, I don't think she will have much to say against us and I wonder whether we should attack every prosecution witness just for the sake of it."

Robin and Elise fired questioning looks towards Dan.

"Detective Little has been very helpful to me in this case. I don't see any reason to make an enemy of her now."

"Alright, I will go easy on her depending on what she says. Is there any other prosecution witness I should be careful with?"

"No, I think you should rip them all to shreds," Dan said pulling apart an imaginary rope.

Robin smiled. He knew the art of cross-examination was not an easy art to master. One had to attack the credibility of the other side's witnesses, without getting the jury offside. If the testimony of a witness survived cross-examination, then it always had a very powerful effect on the jury. So it was a matter of outsmarting and outmaneuvering a witness to catch them out in some mistake or inaccuracy. If they were lying or inaccurate with respect to some small piece of information, could the jury trust them with more important information?

Cross-examination was indeed a difficult skill to master but Robin had always shown an aptitude for it and if the truth be told, he enjoyed it. He enjoyed the position of power he held in questioning witnesses – controlling them, and he enjoyed the game of pulling apart their evidence. The only thing he did not enjoy was losing but that was all part of the game.

The fact that many witnesses did not like him after he cross-examined them, was something he could live with. In fact he thought it was a trait that all successful lawyers particularly barristers had; they were not sensitive to whether people liked them or not. They were in it for the power, the fight, the win, sometimes even the truth. They weren't in it to make friends. If they were in it to be liked, they weren't going to be an effective advocate.

*

"Now I need to talk to you both about whether either of you will testify," Robin said.

"Firstly Dan, if you do testify, you will have to admit that you misled the police about the extent of your relationship with Mia. The Crown Prosecutor will seriously attack your credibility and your professional reputation will be in tatters."

"Geez, Robin, don't sugar coat it for me," Dan added.

"Also, as I have mentioned to you previously, your testimony could lead to criminal charges being brought against you of hindering a police investigation.

Further the Legal Services Commission is likely to take a dim view of any criminal convictions against you. Ultimately the Legal Services Commission

209

could seek to disbar you from practising as a solicitor because of your criminal conviction and because you engaged in a romantic relationship with someone whose complaint you were investigating at the time. I am sure that would be a breach of ethics."

"I wouldn't call it a romantic relationship," Dan said, deliberately not looking at Elise. "We kissed that's all. I mean, it's not like I am a mass murderer."

"In any event you could lose your reputation, your legal practice and your career if you testify."

"But I have to testify to Mia being stalked and threatened. Mia can't do it, so I have to."

"Yes, it would be preferable for you to testify."

"Is there some way Dan can avoid testifying? I don't want to see him lose everything." Elise asked.

"Dan doesn't have to testify. However, if Dan doesn't testify then that will weaken our case," Robin answered.

"Elise, don't worry about me. I will be alright. Whatever it takes to get you out of here, I will do. I am testifying," Dan said reassuringly.

"The other concern is that the Judge may not let you instruct me at the trial and also provide evidence," Robin said.

"What do you mean?" asked Elise.

"Witnesses are not allowed to hear the evidence of other witnesses before they testify; this ensures they don't invent stories to fit in with what the other witnesses have said. If Dan is to testify he will have to give evidence at the end of the trial. The Judge may not let him sit in court to instruct me during the trial because he will hear what the other witnesses are saying before he testifies."

"Dan, I want you sitting next to me during the trial. And I don't want you to lose your career over me."

"Elise, I need to testify. If I perish, I perish, but I must set right what I have put in motion here. I can't take the risk of you being convicted and spending the rest of your life in jail. My reputation, my practice and my career are insignificant in the whole scheme of things."

Dan was worried that he would lose his reputation, his legal practice and his career, but he had new priorities. Perhaps he had not given Elise everything of himself during their marriage, but that was going to change.

"What do you think, Robin?" asked Elise.

Robin thought for a minute and then said, "We really need Dan to testify.

The jury needs to hear from him exactly what Mia was going through at the time of her death. That she was being stalked and threatened. We can't get that evidence before the jury except through Dan."

"But I don't want Dan to lose everything."

"I will only lose everything if I lose you."

Elise smiled and reached out for Dan's hand.

"But I want Dan to be with me, I need him to be with me during the trial."

"We will explain the situation to the Judge at the beginning of the trial and with any luck, he will let Dan instruct me and provide evidence.

"Now what about you, Elise? We need to discuss whether you should testify," Robin said.

"Of course I am testifying," Elise said, slightly bewildered.

"Quite often defendants do not testify at their trials. This is because prosecutors are well skilled in the art of cross-examination and they will use all their skills to attack your credibility in the witness box. If they manage to trap you in an untruth, or make you look silly or uncaring before the jury, then they have won.

"For example, when you spoke to the police about the glass vase, you initially told them you had not touched it. Later, when they told you your finger prints were found on the vase, you changed your story and admitted to touching the vase."

"You have only talked to the authorities once about what happened and already they have caught you out, so to speak. If you testify you will probably be caught out several times and thus provide material for the prosecutor to attack your credibility before the jury."

Robin paused to allow Elise to take in what he had said before he continued.

"There is another concern with Elise testifying. Because we have to attack the character of the prosecution witnesses, the prosecution will be able to highlight Elise's criminal convictions. We can't raise Brock's previous criminal history and then object when the prosecution raises Elise's previous convictions. If she testifies, the jury will get to hear about her attack on her ex-boyfriend."

"Robin, I can appreciate the problems for Elise if she testifies, but she has not told her side of the story yet. I think the jury really needs to hear her story," Dan added.

"Of course I am testifying. If I am going down, I am going down all guns blazing," Elise said with more than a hint of desperation. "We are going to win this case, aren't we?"

"We have a good case but in a trial situation you can never be sure of what is going to happen," Robin said cautiously.

Dan could see that Elise did not respond well to Robin's conservative answer. Elise's shoulders had slumped and she was staring at the table, not making eye contact with them. He was surprised how quickly her fighting mood had changed.

"Elise, we are going to blow them out of the water!" Dan said standing up and using his hands to convey an explosion.

As they stood to leave, Elise came over and briefly hugged Dan and kissed him. There was no lasting physical contact, but he recognized that Elise was in a difficult place right now and her emotions were probably all over the place. If that was the best she could give him, then so be it.

"See you tomorrow," Dan said softly as he left. "Get a good night's rest."

"Yeah, like that's going to happen."

Dan smiled and said, "Just think about football. That always sends you to sleep."

"I think I will need more than thoughts of football to get me to sleep tonight."

"Hey, I almost forgot. I brought you a couple of dresses to wear at the trial."

Dan handed over a large shopping bag containing the dresses.

"Nothing too sexy I am afraid. I didn't want to have any of the men in the jury having a heart attack when they see you."

"Thanks, I will look at them later," Elise said in a halted voice, clutching the shopping bag close to her chest.

At that Dan and Robin walked out of the interview room and left Elise.

As they were walking back to their cars Dan turned to Robin and asked, "Honestly, what do you think of our chances?"

"Honestly, I think they are good. The only thing that really concerns me, other than your career taking a hit, is Elise's fingerprints on that vase and how it came to be found across the room under a sofa."

"Robin, I am touched you are concerned about my career ending. I didn't pick you for such a sentimental guy."

"I am not sentimental. But if you get disbarred, think about it, who is going to brief me. I have only just started at the private bar. You are my best source of work right now. If you get disbarred, my new business venture will take a big hit.”

“Geez, Robin, you are all heart.”

“Isn’t that what you want in a Barrister? The ability not to be affected by emotion, but to doggedly seek out the pertinent facts and persuasively present them.”

Dan had to admit it, Robin had a point there.

The two men reached the prison car park together and opened the doors to their respective vehicles, Dan in his old Subaru and Robin into his new Saab. Both men immediately gasped as they felt the hot air trapped inside their cars. They wound down their respective windows to release the hot air, cranked up their air conditioning units to maximum and sped off.

Dan couldn’t believe it, but the trial would soon be upon them.

CHAPTER THIRTY NINE

It was another stinking hot day, 35 degrees centigrade and 70% humidity. Dan was soaked with sweat by the time he had run from his downtown car park to the Supreme Court complex. He was determined not to be late and in fact arrived a few minutes before Robin. Robin cut quite the figure moving through the crowd in his grey wig, white jabot and flowing back gown.

Dan had discovered at the pre-trial hearing that Her Honour Justice Mary Hooper had been allocated their trial. He was ecstatic as Judge Hooper had been a favourite university lecturer of his. In fact, he had been one of the first solicitors to brief her when she entered the private bar after her university days.

Before the trial began Dan and Robin met with the prosecution team. Unfortunately for them the prosecution team in this case was led by none other than the legendary Chad Gabriel. He had a well founded reputation of working hard and playing hard. Winning at all costs seemed to be his motto.

Since becoming a lead prosecutor, Chad Gabriel had the awesome reputation of not losing one trial he had contested. Though this statistic was a little unreliable as he made sure that he settled all the cases he thought he might lose. After all a judgeship was not too far away, as long as he kept his impressive statistics and maintained a high profile in the legal community.

*

The first order of business after the jury had been selected was for Robin to seek the Judge's permission for Dan to instruct Counsel for the accused and also to provide evidence.

"Your Honour this is a very unusual case in that the husband of the accused is also my instructing solicitor. My client has made her instructions quite clear, that she wants, indeed needs, her husband to be with her in Court for support and for legal reasons. However, her husband, my instructing solicitor, Mr Dan Grover will need to give evidence on behalf of the accused in this trial. Hence I am alerting Your Honour now to the situation I have outlined and seek Your Honour's permission for Mr Grover to undertake both the roles of instructing solicitor and witness for the defence."

Dan watched Her Honour Justice Mary Hooper intently. He hoped that she would recognize him. At one point he was sure she did look at him and smile.

"This is most unusual, Mr Banks. Can't your client instruct another solicitor to represent her interests other than her husband?"

"I am afraid not, Your Honour. They have limited means and do not qualify for legal aid. Mr Grover has been extensively and indelibly involved in this case since day one."

"What do you think of this unusual request, Mr Gabriel?"

"Maam, I have no objection to Mr Grover acting as instructing solicitor during the trial and providing evidence on behalf of the defence."

Dan was surprised that Chad Gabriel had not objected. He wondered why he had been so civil about the request. That was not at all like his win at all costs, take no prisoners, hardnosed reputation.

"Well then as Mr Gabriel has no objections, I will not stand in Mr Grover's way of being present in Court, instructing Mr Banks and later providing evidence on behalf of the defence. Of course, Mr Grover, I do not need to remind you that you are not only a solicitor bound by the Law Society's ethics but you are also an officer of this court, and hence I expect, no demand from you, absolute ethical behaviour."

"Thank you, Your Honour," Robin said.

As Robin sat down, Dan whispered to him. "I didn't think it would be that easy. Why did Gabriel agree to our request so readily?"

"Because he wants the jury to see you as part of Elise's legal team. He knows as well as we do that when you give your evidence, you will be admitting to unethical behavior. He is just setting you up for a fall before the judge, the jury and ultimately the Legal Services Commission."

"Gee and here I was thinking he was a nice guy."

"Believe me, his reputation for never losing a trial is not based on thin air. He is a very formidable opponent. We can't relax around him for a second."

Dan turned around and smiled at Elise who was sitting in the dock a few metres behind him. He gave her the thumbs up signal to signify that they just had a win. Elise managed a forced smile back and then turned her attention to

Chad Gabriel who was beginning his opening address to the jury.

"Ladies and gentlemen of the jury, you have been given an important and sacred task to perform this week. It will be your responsibility to provide justice to a young woman whose promising life was cruelly cut short by a tragic and brutal death.

"It is the crown's contention that this beautiful young woman, Mia Wong, was repeatedly and mercilessly bashed to death in her own home by the accused, Elise Grover.

Chad Gabriel turned towards Elise and paused for effect.

"The crown does not hold this contention lightly. It did not pluck this belief out of thin air. No ladies and gentlemen, the crown is convinced in the certainty of this belief because the evidence clearly and squarely points to the accused, now sitting before you in the dock."

"You will hear evidence that the defendant's husband, Mr Daniel Grover, had an affair with Mia Wong. You will hear evidence that the accused went to Ms Wong's home and had a heated argument with her about her husband's affair."

Dan kept his head down. Nevertheless he could feel the jury members staring at him disapprovingly.

"You will hear evidence that later that day the accused returned to Ms Wong's home. After Ms Wong let the accused into her home, the accused cowardly struck Ms Wong from behind with a glass vase owned by Ms Wong. The accused then repeatedly bashed Ms Wong about the head with the glass vase in a horrific crime of passion."

While saying these last words, Chad Gabriel repeatedly raised and lowered his left arm – role playing the ferocity of the murder to the jury. He stopped, wiped a drop of perspiration from his forehead and looked intently at the jury.

"Ladies and gentlemen, you will hear forensic evidence that the only fingerprints found on the glass vase belonged to the accused.

"The glass vase was found hidden under a sofa across the room from where the victim was murdered. When questioned about the glass vase, the accused denied any knowledge of it. When it was put to the accused that her fingerprints were found on the glass vase, the accused changed her story and admitted she touched the glass vase but could not explain why she touched it."

Chad Gabriel again paused, allowing the jury to catch up with the points he was making and to ensure the jury were ready to absorb the end of his opening address.

"Ladies and gentlemen, you may be asked by the defence to suspend belief in this case. How else can they get you to disregard the evidence? Don't be fooled by rabbits suddenly appearing out of hats, just concentrate on what the evidence is telling you. Concentrate on what you can see, what you can hear and what you can touch.

"In this case, all the evidence points to a jealous wife, an angry wife, a calculating wife who callously called triple zero to report Mia Wong's death, after she had killed her. Then the accused fled the scene and scrubbed her clothes to clean the victim's blood off them. I ask you to carefully consider, are these the actions of an innocent woman?

"Ladies and gentlemen, do not be fooled by any red herrings that may be thrown in desperation by the defence. They will point to this shadow and that shadow as possible perpetrators of this crime. Please always bear in mind your responsibility to the unfortunate young woman and her family. Her death should not be in vain. She, more than anyone here in this courtroom today, deserves justice. And you are the only ones able to give her that justice. Such is the sacred and important task that you must undertake over the next week of this trial."

Dan almost wanted to stand up and applaud. Chad Gabriel was good, very good. He could see the jury members watching his every move, hanging on his every word. All Dan could do now was hope Robin could match Chad Gabriel's rhetoric and highlight to the jury that there was indeed another side to this sad story.

Dan's hands were sweating. He was nervous, but also excited. He couldn't wait for the real battle to begin. The scene had now been set for the trial to start in earnest.

CHAPTER FORTY

Dan watched as Sloan quickly made his way to the witness box and took the oath. Sloan did not look at all anxious and in fact he looked like a man without a care in the world.

"Senior Detective Sloan, can you outline for the Court your involvement in this case?"

"Certainly, I was called to review a crime scene where a young woman had been found bashed to death. An anonymous call had been received by emergency services reporting the death of this young woman at 4:54pm.

"The young woman had been bludgeoned around the head. The resultant pathology report indicates that she was struck with a blunt object to the back of her head, then she was subjected to 10 or 11 forceful blows to the side and front of her head.

"A glass vase was found hidden underneath a sofa across the room, some distance from the deceased's body."

"Objection! The Detective can comment on where the glass vase was found but he can not testify as fact that the glass vase was deliberately hidden," interjected Robin.

"I tend to agree with Mr Banks, what do you think Mr Gabriel?"

"Thank you for your assistance Your Honour, I will rephrase.

"How far was this glass vase found away from the victim's body?"

"Across the room, about four metres away."

"And it was found in full view?"

"No, it was found underneath a sofa. In fact, the glass vase was so far away and so concealed that its presence in the lounge room was not picked up by an initial crime scene search of the premises."

"What is the significance of the glass vase?"

"Forensics have confirmed that the glass vase was the murder weapon."

"Where did the glass vase come from?"

"We have established from photographs and the deceased's ex-boyfriend, that the glass vase was owned by the deceased and normally rested on a coffee table quite close to where the deceased's body was found."

"What is the significance of the glass vase in terms of the accused?"

"The defendant's fingerprints were found on the glass vase. No other finger prints were found on the murder weapon."

"What else of importance did you find at the deceased's residence?"

"There was no forced entry into the premises. Nothing was stolen. The accused let her attacker into her home."

"Anything else of importance?"

"We conducted a sweep of her laptop and found a recent entry into her diary blog."

"What did this entry say?"

"I have printed a copy out for the court. It says,

We really went for it last night, it was amazing. I literally could not breathe. After all the jerks I have been with, could Dan be the one? Dan said he might leave his wife and come to Sydney to be with me. That would be awesome!!

Elise let out a shrill shriek. Dan realized that Elise was probably hearing these words for the first time. He kept his head down.

"Exactly when was this entry made to the victim's diary blog?"

Sloan paused for effect and then in a voice that was very clear and controlled but with a touch of emotion, he said, "It was entered by Mia Wong at 9:15am on the morning, of the same day, that she was bludgeoned to death."

"Who is Dan?"

"Dan is the accused's husband, Dan Grover."

"Did you ask Mr Grover about his relationship with the victim?"

"Detective Little and I interviewed Mr Grover soon after the victim's death. Mr Grover denied having any romantic involvement whatsoever with the victim. Though Mr Grover did admit to visiting the victim and staying overnight at her house, on the night prior to her murder."

"Mr Grover denied having any romantic involvement with the victim, even after you put her diary blog to him?"

"Yes, that's correct."

Dan noted Chad Gabriel's repeated questioning of Sloan on this point so the jury would not miss its significance.

"At what time of day did Ms Wong die?"

"The pathologist puts her time of death between 4:00pm and 5:00pm."

"How did you come to charge the accused with this vicious murder?"

"When conducting house to house interviews Ms Wong's neighbour gave us certain information implicating the accused."

"Did you speak with the accused and did she assist you in the investigation of this crime?"

"We tried to talk with the accused but on the advice of her husband, she refused to cooperate with our enquiries."

"I object. How can the detective know *why* my client did anything? He is not a mind reader as well as a policeman, is he?" Robin interjected.

"I know your client refused to speak to me on her husband's advice, as I heard him tell her not to speak to me. Also when I did try to speak to her, she told me she could not speak to me because her husband had told her not to."

"I think the detective has answered your objection, Mr Banks. Please continue detective," said Her Honour.

"After we arrested Mrs Grover, I asked her about the glass vase and she said she didn't know anything about a glass vase. In effect, she denied touching it.

"I informed Mrs Grover that her fingerprints had been found on the glass vase. Then she changed her story and admitted touching the vase but she could not remember why she would have touched it. In effect, she lied to me about touching the glass vase."

Dan expected Robin to object to the lying tag Sloan had attached to Elise, but he was strangely quiet.

"I asked Mrs Grover to account for why the glass vase was found under a sofa some distance from the deceased's body and she could not tell me how that came about."

"Why did you believe Mrs Grover brutally murdered this poor young woman?"

"Well in my experience murder usually has three elements. Motive, opportunity and capacity. Mrs Grover was very angry at Ms Wong for sleeping with her husband. Mrs Grover went to Ms Wong's home and found she was alone. Ms Wong let Mrs Grover into her home and the accused took advantage of the opportunity she found herself in, hitting Ms Wong with a glass vase she found nearby. Ms Wong was killed in a rage; she was struck many more times than needed to kill her. It has all the hallmarks of a very emotional killing."

"Thank you, Senior Detective. No further questions."

"Your witness, Mr Banks."

Dan waited for Robin to stand up and begin his cross-examination but he was still seated writing some notes.

"Mr Banks, do you want to cross-examine this witness?" Her Honour asked.

"No questions, Your Honour," Robin replied.

All of a sudden Dan was finding it hard to breathe. In fact he almost overbalanced and fell off his chair.

"No only joking, Your Honour, I do have a couple of questions for this witness."

"Well get to it, Mr Banks, and I would appreciate no more joking in my Court."

Dan agreed. That type of joke nearly gave him a coronary.

"Duly noted, Your Honour.

Now Detective Sloan ..."

"That's *Senior* Detective Sloan."

"That is right how silly of me, must have been a mental block.

"Senior Detective can you tell me how long you have been a detective?"

"I have been a Senior Detective for two years, a Detective for ten years before that. I have been in the police force for 18 years both here and in South Australia."

"Do you consider yourself to be a competent and experienced detective?"

Sloan had been around too long and testified in too many trials not to be wary of such a leading question.

Dan noticed Sloan hesitate with his answer.

"You haven't got an answer for me, Senior Detective Sloan?" Robin asked, also noting Sloan's initial reluctance to answer the question.

Sloan had no option, he had to answer the question and he had to provide a positive answer.

"No, I have an answer for you. It's just that I don't like to blow my own trumpet. I am very experienced police officer and I do consider myself to be a competent detective, as do my superiors who promoted me to the rank of Senior Detective two years ago."

"Well witness, let's take a closer look at some aspects of your investigation shall we, to see if they were performed competently.

"Firstly, did I hear you say a crucial piece of evidence in this investigation, i.e. the murder weapon, was not found by you or your investigation team when the crime scene was first examined?"

"Yes, that is correct."

"So it was just missed?" Robin asked waiving his hands in the air.

"Yes, initially it was."

"When and how was it found?"

"It was found by crime scene cleaners approximately two weeks after the murder."

"Two weeks after the murder, it was found by cleaners. Does that seem like good detective work to you, Senior Detective Sloan?"

"It was missed initially, which is regrettable, but the main thing is that it was found."

"My concern Detective Sloan, is that two weeks had elapsed before this vital piece of evidence was found. That the murder weapon was found by accident, by cleaners who were cleaning the crime scene. Presumably after you Detective Sloan, had given the all clear for the crime scene to be cleaned."

Dan noticed that Sloan had given up correcting Robin as to his proper title.

"My concern, Detective Sloan, is that the integrity of your investigation has been compromised.

"My concern, Detective Sloan, is that you have made a big show of the vase being *hidden*. I think you said that in your evidence, it had been hidden under the sofa some metres from where the deceased's body was found."

"I mean, for all we know one cleaner could have found the vase under another piece of furniture and then kicked it away under the sofa where another cleaner found it. Who knows who had access or who entered the property during those two weeks!"

Sloan began squirming in his chair.

"Well no, we had the crime scene secured for those two weeks."

Sloan bit his lip. He knew he had made a mistake giving that answer as soon as he had said it.

"Oh, Senior Detective Sloan," Robin said with gusto turning to face the jury.

Robin was back to calling Sloan by his full title, to highlight to the jury just how incompetent he was.

"Please tell me how you secured the crime scene for those two weeks? With duct tape and a note telling people please don't enter? Perhaps you posted a large photograph of yourself looking angry and pointing your finger, with a caption saying *stay out*? I am sure that would have scared the real murderer away."

Robin was playing the jury and attempting to have some sport with Sloan. Gabriel was too slick a prosecutor to stand for it and he was soon on his feet.

"Your Honour, Senior Detective Sloan is obviously a hard working and long standing policeman who has dedicated his life to protecting people like you and me. Does he have to be ridiculed like this, in this court of law?"

"I agree, Mr Banks, please cross-examine the witness and remember you are in a court and not on a stage. Witness, please answer the question."

"What was the question?" replied Sloan who was starting to look rattled.

"The question was how did you secure the crime scene for those two weeks?" Robin said.

"Well of course we had official police tape, signs warning people to stay out, we had police officers and forensic experts coming and going all the time and we also had both sets of neighbours on alert to call us if they saw anybody who was unauthorized enter the premises."

"Witness, surely you would agree with me that it was possible in those two weeks for someone to enter the crime scene undetected and place the murder weapon, the glass vase, under the sofa where the cleaners supposedly first saw it."

"Yes, it is possible but I think it is highly unlikely that anybody..."

"Witness you have answered the question. I was only looking for a yes or no response."

Sloan was experienced enough to know that Robin was only looking for a yes or no answer but he wanted the jury to know that he thought it highly unlikely that anybody would have entered the house and planted the murder weapon under the sofa.

"Detective Sloan you received information from Mr Grover at the beginning of your investigation that the deceased was being stalked and threatened by someone, is that true."

"Yes."

"What steps did you take to investigate this important piece of information?"

"We could not find any evidence to support Mr Grover's assertions. We talked to neighbours, friends and family members of the deceased and they did not know anything about the deceased being stalked and threatened."

"Isn't it possible that the deceased didn't want to alarm friends and family, and that was why she sought support from Mr Grover?"

"That is possible, but unlikely."

"Just because neighbours, friends and family may not be aware of a recent and imminent threat, that doesn't mean it does not exist."

"I suppose I was concerned about the veracity of what Mr Grover was telling me because he had obviously lied to me about not having a romantic relationship with the deceased."

"In terms of the romantic relationship, you really have no idea what form that took do you? I mean you don't know if it was just words, a kiss, or what form or intensity it took?"

"I believe it was intense enough for the accused to kill the deceased."

Dan could tell that Robin didn't see that one coming. Elise gasped as if out of breath. He turned to comfort her with a forced smile.

"Getting back to your investigation of Mr Grover's information, you didn't take his information seriously did you?"

"I was concerned that Mr Grover may have been lying to us about the threats and the stalking, to protect his wife, to throw us off the track with our investigation."

"But didn't Mr Grover provide this stalking information to you before his wife was charged?"

"That's true but Mrs Grover could have told her husband about the murder after she had committed it and then arranged for him to provide false information about threats and stalking to the police when he was questioned."

"But you have no evidence that the accused said anything to Mr Grover about the death of the deceased, do you? That is all conjecture, isn't it?"

"I have no direct evidence that the accused told her husband about her murder of the deceased, though I believe this happened."

Elise let out another loud gasp. She then began to cough uncontrollably. Dan turned around and offered her a plastic cup of water and another encouraging smile.

"Your Honour, surely we have had enough of this witness's opinions. I ask that his opinion which is not backed up by any evidence be deemed inadmissible and the jury be told to not take such an opinion into account when they are deciding this matter."

"Mr Banks, you asked the question and the witness answered it. I will not direct the jury to disregard the answer to your question just because you didn't like it."

A thought flashed through Dan's mind as to whether Robin was really up to it. Cross-examination was hard, particular when dealing with an experienced police officer.

"You are satisfied, as an experienced and competent detective, that you thoroughly and appropriately investigated Mr Grover's information about the deceased being threatened and stalked?"

"Yes. Some enquiries were made but the two men Mr Grover gave us both had watertight alibis.

"Also, Mr Grover's credibility in my mind was shot when he misled us about not having a romantic relationship with the victim."

"Are you calling Mr Grover a liar?" Robin angrily demanded.

At that point Dan grabbed Robin by the arm.

"Forget about defending me. We have to concentrate on Elise. Ask him about Brock and Samuel."

Robin composed himself. One of the secrets of good cross-examination was never to lose your temper. When you lose your temper, it becomes personal. You do not think clearly and more importantly you lose the jury.

"I put it to you Detective Sloan that Mr Grover provided you with two possible suspects in this case. A Mr Brock Shepard the deceased's ex-boyfriend and a Mr Samuel Sanderson, the deceased's workplace colleague. Is that correct?"

"Yes, Mr Grover told us that the deceased had taken a DVO out against Brock Shepard and she had lodged a complaint of sexual harassment against Samuel Sanderson."

"Did you thoroughly investigate these two men?"

"Yes, we interviewed each man and thoroughly checked their alibis. Brock Shepard was at the Breakfast Creek Hotel drinking all afternoon and was seen by friends and the bartender there. Samuel Sanderson was on a sick day from work, but his wife was with him the whole day."

"Well, Detective Sloan, let us delve a little deeper into these two suspects and see whether your thorough investigation has matched my own investigation.

"First Brock Shepard. Is it true your initial check of his criminal history disclosed no prior offences?"

Sloan looked surprised by the question. He hesitated.

"It's a simple question witness," Robin said looking at the jury. "It should not be a hard question for an experienced police officer like yourself to answer."

"Yes, a check in Queensland and New South Wales under the name of

Brock Shepard revealed he had no prior criminal offences only traffic offences. However, we later discovered that he had changed his name from Utley to Shepard. A check of his criminal history in New South Wales under Utley then revealed he had prior criminal convictions."

"How did you come to find out his real surname was Utley?"

"My partner, Detective Little, came up with that information. I am not sure where she got it from."

"Wouldn't a question to Mr Shepard or a call to his family have revealed his correct name from the very beginning?"

"We asked Mr Shepard if he had ever used an alias and he told us he hadn't."

"It wasn't good detective work though was it? You could have undertaken a more thorough search of Mr Shepard."

"We got the right result in the end."

"Anyway Detective Sloan, what did you discover about Mr Shepard's previous criminal history?"

"He had previous criminal history for assault and drug offences."

"So how did you investigate Mr Shepard?"

"We talked with him and discovered that prior to the victim's death, he had purchased airline tickets in his name and in the name of the deceased to travel to Sydney to see a concert which was to take place a few weeks after the deceased's death. Given this information and his strong alibi, our investigation team discounted him as a legitimate suspect."

"Detective, my investigation team has discovered that Brock Shepard had been living on the streets of Sydney since he was 12 years old and was involved with drugs and other criminal activities. By the time he was 17 he was a chronic alcoholic, he violently assaulted his father and he seriously assaulted a young woman who was living with him in a defacto relationship.

"We also found out he assaulted the deceased several times during their relationship. The deceased ultimately took out a Domestic Violence Order against Brock Shepard to protect herself from his violence and to ensure he stayed away from her. In her application to the court the deceased alleged that Brock Shepard pushed her against a wall at their home and held her there by her throat.

"Doesn't all that add up to a legitimate suspect, Detective?"

"When we spoke to Brock Shepard he had voluntarily entered a detox centre. He was particularly upset about Ms Wong's death," Sloan answered.

"Also his alibi is quite strong. The bartender told us she particularly remembered him as being a loud, talkative drunk who proceeded to get more noisy and disruptive during the day, culminating in him being thrown out of the hotel about 5:30pm."

"Surely Brock Shepard, while he was at the hotel, could have found twenty minutes to slip away and murder the deceased."

"From all reports, Brock Shepard is not a guy who plans things. He is more of a spur of the moment kind of guy who wears his heart on his sleeve. We don't believe he could have planned the murder by slipping away from the hotel, murdering the deceased and then come back to the hotel and act like nothing had ever happened. "

"Still Brock Shepard could have just gone to Ms Wong's house with good intentions, say to tell her about his surprise for her. She could have rejected him and, under the influence of alcohol, lashed out and killed her violently and passionately. I understand his previous assault convictions were all alcohol fuelled."

"After considering all the evidence I don't believe Brock Shepard killed the deceased."

"But it is a possibility isn't it? It could have happened?"

"Yes, it possibly could have happened but I don't think ...."

"That's fine Detective, I just needed one of those yes or no responses."

Dan turned to Elise and smiled. Elise was having trouble coping, but there was little he could do about that beyond providing her with an encouraging smile every now and then.

"Now Detective Sloan, let's turn our attention to Mr Samuel Sanderson. On what basis did you rule him out as a suspect in this case?"

"On checking Samuel Sanderson's criminal history we discovered that he had no previous convictions. On checking Samuel Sanderson's alibi, his wife was quite sure that he was with her all day. On that basis we eliminated him as a serious suspect in this case."

"Detective Sloan were you not concerned that the deceased had complained to her employer that Samuel Sanderson had spiked her drink and sexually assaulted her?"

"That information was concerning but ultimately it was only an allegation which Mr Sanderson denied."

"But it was more than that. Mr Grover fully investigated the matter and found on the balance of probabilities, that Mr Sanderson had in fact drugged

Ms Wong and sexually assaulted her in his car."

"With respect sir and I know you are only doing your job," Sloan said with more than a touch of arrogance, obviously enjoying the moment he was about to have. "Mr Grover was having an affair with Ms Wong at the time he was investigating her claims, so it would have been improper and irresponsible of me to rely upon any findings he made against Mr Sanderson, in his so called independent investigation report."

Dan put his hand to his head. Who could have imagined so much damage could come from his one moment of passion?

"Alright witness, what do you know about Kathleen Brown?"

Robin moved straight to discuss Kathleen Brown to recover the high ground. One had to remember the jury was always watching what was said and done in the courtroom.

"Sorry, I don't think I have ever heard of Kathleen Brown."

"No, I didn't think you would know about Kathleen Brown. Let me tell you her story."

"Your Honour, this is the murder trial of Elise Grover, she is on trial for murdering Mia Wong. Do we really have to sit here and listen to a story about a person named Kathleen Brown, of whom we know nothing?" Chad Gabriel was on his feet and flashing a pained and exasperated expression to Justice Hooper.

"Mr Banks, why are you telling this witness a story about someone the prosecution and this witness has never heard of?"

"Your Honour, Kathleen Brown's evidence in this matter is crucial for the defence. Her evidence will point the jury away from my client. I should be allowed to put her evidence to relevant prosecution witnesses for comment, before she provides her evidence for the defence."

"Fine, Mr Banks, you may proceed."

Robin looked chuffed at having a win over the smarmy Chad Gabriel.

"Kathleen Brown is in hiding. Kathleen Brown is scared for her life."

"Get on with it, Mr Banks. Now is not the time for speech making," quipped Her Honour.

So much for Robin's win over Chad Gabriel. Her Honour's remark rightly brought Robin back to reality.

"Detective, Kathleen Brown used to work for Dooley and Associates as did Mr Sanderson. Kathleen Brown says..."

Robin read from a statement Dan had recently obtained from Kathleen

Brown which graphically illustrated her fearful story.

Robin finished reading the statement and looked up at the jury.

"After being viciously sexual assaulted by Samuel Sanderson, Kathleen Brown lodged a complaint of sexual assault with her employer. After lodging that complaint she received a note threatening her life if she did not leave Brisbane, immediately.

"Ms Brown took that threat seriously and in fear of her life she left town, making sure Mr Samuel Sanderson did not know and could not find out where she went. Even to this day she still continues to conceal her whereabouts.

"Detective Sloan are you concerned about Kathleen Brown's experience with Samuel Sanderson?"

"I am concerned about her for sure, but if she left town covering her tracks, how were we supposed to find out about her?"

"If my investigation team can find out about her, why couldn't your investigation team find out about her? You are an experienced and competent detective aren't you, Detective Sloan?"

Sloan did not answer the question.

"How can amateur investigators find out about her and professional investigators like yourself, not know anything about her?"

Sloan remained silent.

Dan conveyed a mock expression of hurt to Robin and whispered, "Who are you calling amateur investigators?"

"Detective Sloan, let me tell you about Amanda Peterson.

"Amanda Peterson worked for Spencer Rush Accountants five years ago. Ms Peterson filed a complaint with her employer that she was sexually assaulted by a workmate, none other than Mr Samuel Sanderson."

Robin then told Amanda Peterson's distressing story from the beginning.

"Soon after Amanda Peterson complained to the police that Mr Sanderson attempted to rape her, she disappeared off the face of this earth. Her bank accounts, credit cards, mobile phone and personal affects have never been touched.

"Ms Peterson may have committed suicide with her body somehow not being found after all these years, or I submit the more likely scenario, is that she has been murdered."

The courtroom was deathly quiet. Dan thought that literally he could hear a pin drop such was the level of studied attention being paid to what Robin was saying right now.

"Senior Detective Sloan you didn't investigate Samuel Sanderson properly did you?

There was no immediate answer from Sloan. Eventually he just mumbled, "I don't agree with you."

"In fact, you were quite derelict in discharging your responsibilities to the deceased in properly and competently investigating her murder."

"We did properly investigate this murder."

"Senior Detective Sloan, seriously, how can you say that?"

Chad Gabriel was quickly on his feet. Even he had been spellbound by the stories he had just heard but he had recovered and it was game on again for him.

"Your Honour, Mr Banks is badgering this witness. Mr Banks has asked him the same question several times and each time the witness does not provide the answer Mr Banks wants, he badgers the witness again."

"Mr Banks, I agree with Mr Gabriel. Please refrain from badgering the witness."

"Yes, Your Honour, perhaps I got a little carried away."

"Do you have much more for this witness as I am about to recess for the day?"

"I have but one more question for this witness.

"Senior Detective Sloan, given the information you have now heard regarding a concerning pattern of aggressive and violent behaviour towards young female co-workers by Samuel Sanderson over a period of years; surely your opinion in relation to him has changed, in that he must now be a person fairly and squarely under suspicion for the murder of Mia Wong?"

Robin asked the question more as a statement of fact than a question. There really could only be one answer Sloan could give.

"No."

"No, how can you possibly sit there and say, no?" Robin said with some feeling and more than a little exasperation. He had done everything but hit Sloan over the head with a baseball bat, to get him to admit real concerns regarding Samuel Sanderson in this case.

"No, this information has not changed my view that Samuel Sanderson did not murder Mia Wong. Perhaps, if what you are saying is true, Mr Sanderson maybe someone who is prone to sexually assault young women, but he did not murder Mia Wong."

"How can you be so sure of that, Senior Detective Sloan?"

"Because whoever murdered Mia Wong was a *woman*, not a man."

"What?"

"You heard me Counsel. It was a woman who committed this murder, not a man."

To say pandemonium then broke out in the court would be a gross understatement.

Robin was speechless. Dan repeatedly said to anyone who would listen, *what the hell is he talking about?* Elise stood up, sighed and then collapsed, falling out of the dock onto the floor just behind Dan and Robin. Dan and the corrective services officer rushed to her aide.

Members of the public and reporters who had been following the case from the public gallery were talking loudly amongst themselves trying to work out what was going on. Her Honour was beside herself trying to restore order and seek medical attention for Elise.

In fact the only calm person in the courtroom was Senior Detective Michael Sloan who allowed a small smile to grace his face during the commotion.

Sloan knew exactly the pandemonium he would cause with his last statement and he was quite enjoying the power he felt in being able to cause such chaos in what was usually a hostile environment for police officers.

Eventually order was restored and Elise regained consciousness. Her Honour was relieved to find out that Elise had only a small bump on her head, but was otherwise uninjured.

"Well, I think this is an appropriate time to recess for the day. We will resume at 10:00am tomorrow morning. I remind the witness that he is still under oath and he is not to discuss his testimony with anybody until he has finished testifying. Court adjourned."

Dan turned to Elise and they hugged briefly.

"What's going on?" Elise said very concerned.

"I don't know, I honestly don't know but we will find out tomorrow. Don't worry we have made some real inroads in the prosecution case today." Dan said these words as calmly as he could. He did not want to give Elise any insight into how worried he was actually feeling at this moment. It was quite possible their whole defence had been obliterated by that one statement from Sloan.

Anyway, they would know more tomorrow. Hopefully Sloan didn't know what he was talking about, and that was entirely possible. Still Dan had a sinking feeling that Sloan was not stupid enough to make a bold statement in court like that without being able to back it up. But how? How could he back up his statement that only a woman could have killed Mia? Anyway no point worrying he thought, best just to stay calm.

Dan watched as the corrections officer escorted Elise away through the side door in the courtroom, that led to the secure lift for the holding cells in the basement of the court complex.

He then turned to Robin and said, "What just happened?"

"Dan the man, I don't know, I honestly don't know. I did notice that Chad Gabriel seemed to be quite pleased with himself. It must have been a tactic of his, to let Sloan's evidence on this point come out in cross-examination for more effect."

"Well, it certainly worked."

"All we can do is wait and see what Sloan says tomorrow. Go home and get a good night's sleep," Robin said.

Yeah, a good night's sleep, like that was going to happen. The Sharks had more chance of winning next year's premiership than he had of getting a good night's sleep.

Dan walked slowly out of the courtroom and down the lift to the foyer, and then out onto the street, towards where his car was parked. It was the slowest, saddest and loneliest walk he had ever made.

CHAPTER FORTY ONE

By 8:30am the next morning it was already hot and humid. A thunderstorm was looming.

Not unlike the destructive thunderstorm Dan had witnessed in the courtroom yesterday. How could Sloan be so certain the murderer was a woman? Why was this evidence not discovered before trial? How could it be true?

His thoughts turned to Elise and how she must be feeling. He had assured her that they would blow the prosecution case out of the water, yet the prosecution was obliterating their case. Her liberty, her sanity, her relationships, her whole life was suddenly hanging by a very loose thread.

As soon as he arrived at the court precinct Dan made his way down to the holding cells.

There were a few moments of uncomfortable silence between them.

"How's it going?" Dan asked eventually breaking the silence.

There was no response from Elise.

Perhaps Elise hadn't heard him. She was looking at him but not really acknowledging him.

"Did you get any sleep last night?" he asked again. "I know I didn't."

Still no response from Elise. He wondered if she was alright mentally. Perhaps she was still in shock from yesterday.

"You sure made a graceful exit yesterday. I gave it a 9.5; I mean with the double twist and half pike entry it was one of the best dives I have ever seen in a courtroom."

He knew that humour was sometimes a risky way to communicate with Elise, especially in serious situations, but he needed something. He could see the faint trace of a smile emanating from the side of her mouth. Her soft brown eyes made contact with his and he caught just the hint of a sparkle in them.

"You only lost points for landing on your head, if not for that I would have given you a 10; a perfect score."

Elise's mouth widened to a full length smile. He loved her smile. It was as though her whole face lit up.

"I thought lawyers were supposed to be serious and straight laced; how the hell did I come to marry you?"

"Just lucky I guess."

"Dan what's going on?" Elise asked with the smile suddenly vanishing from her face.

"To tell you the truth, I don't know. Sloan obviously has some reason for testifying that the murderer was a woman but we won't know that till he resumes his testimony this morning.

"I mean, the prosecution should tell us their case at the committal, or certainly before the trial. Robin and I have not seen this evidence before, so we don't know what is going on. Maybe the prosecutor is just playing games with us. If he is playing games then it will reflect badly on him before the jury.

"How are you holding up?"

"I wasn't too good last night and I have a splitting headache already this morning."

"You are doing great just to be here ready to go this morning."

"I am sorry I fainted yesterday. I don't know what happened. One minute I was hanging on every word and the next minute my mind just went blank, it just shut down on me. The next thing I remember is you kneeling beside me asking me if I was ok. The jury must be thinking I am a drama queen, putting on a performance like that."

"I think the jury saw you as a normal person yesterday. Your fainting was a perfect way for the jury to see you as a real person who they can identify with. Actually it would be good if you could faint again today, but this time add a little bit more noise, and some blood would be nice."

Elise playfully punched Dan in the arm. He smiled. He would take a playful punch from her anytime.

"Listen mister, my job is to sit in the dock quietly; there will be no histrionics from me in the court today, not if I can help it. Your job by the way, in case you have forgotten, is to get me out of here."

Dan nodded politely. He hadn't forgotten. Elise's situation and his role in her incarceration played constantly on his mind.

"Hey, I have brought you something." Dan handed Elise one of her favourite cardigans.

"Thanks, it does get cold in there."

"But wait there is more."

Dan reached into his bag and pulled out a small gift wrapped present and handed it to Elise.

"It's not my birthday."

"I know but I just wanted to give you something, something special from me to you."

Dan watched as Elise carefully unwrapped the small present.

It was a handwritten poem.

As the sand is to the sea
So are you to me.
When you laugh you do not laugh alone.
When you cry you do not cry alone.
When you fight you do not fight alone.
When you stand you do not stand alone.
As the sand is to the sea
No much more than that, you are to me!

Dan watched as a solitary tear escaped down her cheek.

"I hope you like it. It is a bit corny. I just wanted to tell you…"

Elise didn't wait for Dan to finish talking. She reached out and hugged him, before whispering, "I love it, it is beautiful."

*

"All rise," Justice Mary Hooper's Associate shouted as Her Honour made her way into the courtroom.

Sloan was already sitting in the witness box before Her Honour arrived to start today's proceedings.

"Mr Banks, you may continue with your cross-examination of this witness."

As Robin stood to his feet the courtroom was eerily silent. There could not have been a greater contrast from the pandemonium of yesterday afternoon to the stillness of this morning.

"Witness you testified last night that you believed the person who murdered Mia Wong was female. Is that correct?"

"Yes."

"On what evidence do you base that belief?"

"On the evidence of Tom Johnstone," Sloan replied.

"Who is Tom Johnstone? I have never heard of him."

"Tom Johnstone is a Dental Surgeon who happened to be jogging past the deceased's home around 5:00pm on the day she was murdered. Mr Johnstone says that he saw a woman leave the deceased's house at this time."

"But how do you know that the woman Mr Johnstone saw leaving the deceased's home was the murderer?"

"Because he saw blood splattered all over her clothing."

Dan heard Elise gasp as though she was struggling to breathe. He turned around quickly and she signaled to him that she was ok.

"Can Mr Johnstone identify this woman?"

"No, apparently she pulled the baseball cap she was wearing down over her face so she could not be recognized."

"If Mr Johnstone did not see this person's face how can he be sure she was a woman?'

"You will have to ask him that."

"Believe me Detective I will be asking Mr Johnstone that."

"Detective Sloan can you explain to this court why Mr Johnstone's evidence has not been provided to the defence before now?"

"Your Honour," Chad Gabriel was on his feet before Sloan had time to think about the question, let alone answer it.

"Your Honour, if my learned friend wishes to oppose Mr Johnstone's evidence being admitted in this trial, then the appropriate time for him to raise his objection is when Mr Johnstone is called to give his evidence. It is not appropriate for my friend to cross-examine Senior Detective Sloan on this legal issue."

"Mr Banks, I tend to agree with Mr Gabriel on this point."

"I will withdraw the question, Your Honour. I only have one set of questions remaining for this witness."

Dan had discussed with Robin ending his cross-examination of Sloan with these particular set of questions. Juries tended to remember the last words a witness said, so Robin had to end his cross-examination with Sloan taking a decisive hit to his credibility.

"Detective Sloan were you informed by Mr Grover that you were not to question his wife about this case, without her lawyer being present?"

"Well, that may have been said but was Mr Grover acting as her lawyer or her husband at the time?"

"Were you told by Mr Grover or not, that the accused was not to be questioned about this matter without legal representation?"

"Well there was some confusion at the time of her arrest…"

"Witness just answer the question plainly without trying to sidestep it. Were you told this, yes or no?"

"Yes, it was mentioned."

"Can you tell me why some weeks after my client was arrested, you violated her rights by questioning her about the glass vase, without her legal representatives being present?"

"The fact that your client's fingerprints were found on the glass vase only came to light some weeks after she was arrested. As soon as I obtained this information I put it to the accused, so she could explain how her fingerprints came to be on the murder weapon."

"But you could have asked my client your questions regarding the glass vase with her legal representatives present, couldn't you Detective?"

"I suppose in the euphoria of obtaining such a crucial piece of evidence, I might have overlooked notifying her legal representatives. But I must stress that the accused spoke to me voluntarily, she could have just refused to talk to me."

"You were looking to trick her weren't you? You were trying to catch her out with this fingerprint evidence, weren't you Senior Detective Sloan? That's why you didn't call Mr Grover and arrange for him to be present at your interview."

"No, that's not the case at all."

"In fact, you induced my client to answer your questions, by telling her if she answered your questions about the glass vase, then she might be released. Isn't that so Detective?"

"No, that is a lie."

"You're a lie *Senior* Detective Sloan!"

"Your Honour," Chad Gabriel was on his feet and looking as though he had just taken a hit to the groin, such was his pained expression. "This is outrageous conduct by the defence."

"Mr Banks, you should know better. I will assume such a distasteful comment was a slip of the tongue. If I hear any similar disparaging comments from you I will assume that you had planned them. In that case I would have no compulsion reporting you to the Bar Association for improper conduct. Do you understand me, Mr Banks?"

"Yes, Your Honour. I apologise to the court for my comment."

"Is that the end of your cross-examination of this witness, Mr Banks."

"Yes, I have no further questions for this witness," Robin said as he sat down.

"Any re-examination Mr Gabriel?"

"Just a few questions Your Honour."

"Senior Detective Sloan, did the accused have the opportunity of speaking with her husband or some other legal advisor, before she spoke to you about the glass vase?"

"Yes, the accused could easily have called her husband or some other lawyer and spoken to them before answering my questions about the glass vase."

"When the accused spoke to you about the glass vase, in your opinion did she do so voluntarily?"

"Yes, she wanted to speak with me."

"One final question, was the victim sexually assaulted at the time of her death?"

Robin jumped to his feet. "Your Honour, I object. The prosecution cannot introduce evidence during re-examination. They can only ask questions to clarify what was said during cross-examination."

Chad Gabriel was still standing. "My learned friend quite vigorously cross-examined Senior Detective Sloan on why he didn't suspect two men, Brock Shepard and Samuel Sanderson of committing this heinous crime. My question is just shedding more light on that line of questioning.

"I agree with Mr Gabriel. You may answer the question witness," Her Honour said dispassionately.

"Mia Wong was *not* sexually assaulted," Sloan said.

"No further questions, Your Honour."

Dan watched as Senior Detective Sloan stood up and walked past him out into the public gallery where he took a seat directly behind Chad Gabriel and the prosecution team. They had landed some blows to Sloan's credibility but they had not knocked him out of the ring. Indeed, from Sloan's smug appearance and his warm smiles to the defence team, he doubted that Sloan even felt the blows they had landed on his credibility.

Of much greater concern to Dan now was the possible body blow that a Mr Tom Johnstone could land to their case. They had male suspects to provide to the jury, not female suspects!

CHAPTER FORTY TWO

"Your Honour the prosecution calls Tom Johnstone to the stand."

"Your Honour the defence objects to this witness providing evidence in this trial."

"Ladies and Gentlemen of the jury, I would ask that you leave us for a short time as I deal with the legal issues surrounding the evidence of Mr Johnstone. It is not appropriate that you hear these legal issues as they may be prejudicial to the facts on which you need to be clear to determine your verdict in this matter," Her Honour explained to a confused jury.

After the jury had left the courtroom, Robin stood and addressed Her Honour.

"This is a murder trial. My client could lose her liberty for life. Hence evidentiary rules must be obeyed to ensure her trial is fair. The prosecution can't be producing witnesses at this late hour. It is just unfair and prejudicial to my client for this witness to provide evidence against her, when we have just found out about this witness five minutes ago."

"Mr Gabriel, why should I let this witness testify?"

"Your Honour, this is indeed a murder trial. Hence every last piece of relevant evidence should be presented to the jury for their consideration. To leave out a vital piece of evidence might prevent them from solving the jigsaw puzzle of this case. It is absolutely vital the jury properly consider all relevant evidence for justice to be done.

"Mr Johnstone lives in Townsville and he first contacted the police over the weekend. I only found out about his existence after the trial had started.

"There has been no conspiracy here to hide evidence from the defence. Indeed we are more than willing to make Mr Johnstone available to the defence to test his evidence.

"One final point, Your Honour, is that Mr Johnstone's evidence is largely rebuttal evidence. Mr Johnstone cannot identify the murderer, his evidence is simply that the murderer was a woman. Hence, the significance of Mr Johnstone's evidence is extenuated if the defence asserts that a man could have murdered the deceased.

"Given the cross-examination of Senior Detective Sloan, it appears the defence is asserting that the murderer was a man. Hence, Mr Johnstone's evidence is primarily relevant as rebuttal evidence. Rebuttal evidence by its very nature, does not have to be supplied to the defence before trial."

Robin rose again to speak.

"Your Honour, evidence that the murderer was a woman is more than just rebuttal evidence. As the accused is a woman, it is evidence that goes directly to the fact that she, as a woman, killed the deceased.

"The prosecution just cannot be allowed to present surprise witnesses; no matter how relevant their evidence is or whatever the reason for the witness coming forward at a late stage. It is just not fair to the accused," Robin pleaded.

Her Honour looked composed and appeared to come to her decision reasonably quickly.

"I note the late arrival of Mr Johnstone as a witness has been satisfactorily explained and his evidence is particularly significant as a rebuttal witness. Really the Crown could not have known the defence assertions until the trial started, that a man rather than a woman was the likely murderer of the deceased. I believe justice is best served in this case, if Mr Johnstone is allowed to testify and be cross-examined. The jury may now be recalled."

The jury quickly filed back into the courtroom. After they were seated, Tom Johnstone made his way through the heavy courtroom doors and up to the witness box. The first thing Dan noticed about Tom Johnstone was that he was a very short man, no more than 168 centimetres.

Tom Johnstone was middle aged, quite thin and he was almost bald except for some tufts of speckled grey hair on both sides of his head near his ears. Dan knew that Robin would not miss the fact that Tom Johnstone was wearing glasses.

After Tom Johnstone was sworn in and had squirmed in his seat for several moments until he was comfortable, he was ready to give his evidence.

"Witness can you tell the Court your full name?" asked Chad Gabriel.

"Thomas Mark Johnstone."

"Your occupation?"

"I am a dental surgeon. I have been practising as a dental physician for over 30 years."

"What can you tell me about the events of 25 July this year?"

"I used to live in Spring Hill, Brisbane, but on the 26th of July this year I moved to Townsville to live and work. On the 25th I was involved in packing all my personal belongings in readiness for the removalists who came to move me early on the 26th of July.

"At around 5:00pm on the 25th I went for a jog. I know it was around this time as I had just finished packing and I glanced at the clock. I couldn't believe how quickly the time had passed while I had been packing.

"I came out of my house and ran down my street. I then turned left into Vivienne Parade. After a couple of minutes I noticed a woman coming out of Mia Wong's house. I had known Mia as we lived near each other and we both liked to jog. Also, I had given her a lift to work a few times when I had seen her waiting at the bus stop.

"Anyway, I slowed down to have a quick chat to Mia when I noticed that the person was not Mia. This person was also a woman but she was larger than Mia. I noticed that she moved very quickly, like she was in a hurry and she was coming towards me.

"I said something like *g'day*, but the woman did not respond. I kept looking to see if I knew the woman. I thought it might be one of the other neighbours. Everyone in our area was quite friendly. However, this woman was wearing a baseball cap and she bent the cap down over her face as she strode past me.

"What caught my attention were red spots and red blobs on her jacket and jeans. I jogged on for a few minutes wondering what the red spots and blobs were, as there were quite a few. Then it hit me, they were blood. I stopped cold on the pavement and turned around to see the woman. I thought she may have injured herself and been rushing off to seek medical attention. Perhaps, I could help her. In any event when I looked back she was no longer there."

"Mr Johnstone, are you sure you saw a woman coming out of Mia Wong's house with what appeared to be blood splattered on her clothing around 5:00pm on the 25th of July this year?"

"Yes, I am quite sure."

"When did you first give the police this information?"

"On the weekend. You see I moved to Townsville the next day, the 26th of July. I didn't even know Mia had been murdered until I read about this trial in the weekend newspapers."

"No further questions your Honour."

"Cross-examination, Mr Banks?"

"Yes, Your Honour."

"Mr Johnstone, Townsville has television, the internet as well as newspapers. How is it that you didn't hear about Mia Wong's death until a couple of days ago?"

"Over the last ten years I have felt the need to help those people less fortunate than myself. Financially I really only need to work for nine months a year; I spend the remaining three months traveling to remote indigenous communities with my nurse, volunteering my dental skills. Many indigenous people do not have access to highly skilled dental care and I see it as my responsibility, no my privilege, to help these disadvantaged people as much as I can.

"The whole reason I moved my practice to Townsville was so I could be closer to the indigenous people of far North Queensland and the Northern Territory.

"For the last three months, basically from August until October, I have been traveling around remote indigenous communities in northern Australia helping them with their dental issues. I must say, news, any form of news, is hard to come by in those remote communities."

Well that was an answer Dan was not expecting. He, like the jury were spellbound as Tom Johnstone recounted his good works in the remote indigenous communities of Australia.

Good luck trying to attack this man's credibility but that's exactly what Robin's job was.

"Mr Johnstone, you have testified that the person you saw leaving Mia Wong's home on the day in question at around 5:00pm was a woman. I am just wondering if you can be absolutely certain of that? I mean no doubt at all?"

Dan was glad to see Tom Johnstone hesitate at answering this question, perhaps there was some doubt about that.

"On what do you base your opinion that the person was a woman?" Robin said clarifying his question.

Robin was skillfully turning Mr Johnstone's evidence about seeing a woman coming out of Mia's house, from fact to one man's opinion.

"She was dressed like a woman in jeans and a jacket. She had longish hair but I can't remember the colour. She just moved like a woman."

"What colour was her jacket?"

"I am not sure now, dark I think. I really can't remember."

"Are you sure the person was wearing a jacket? Could the person have been wearing a pullover say, or a cardigan, or track suit top?"

Mr Johnston again hesitated before answering the question.

"Look, to be honest with you I saw her for only a few seconds, nearly four months ago now. I have had many other things on my mind since then. I thought she was wearing a jacket and jeans but in all honesty, I can't be sure now exactly what particular type of clothing she was wearing."

"Mr Johnstone, I note that you are wearing glasses today. Did you have your glasses on when you went jogging this day?"

"No, I don't wear my glasses when I go jogging."

"Is your eyesight impaired if you don't wear glasses?"

"Yes, I am short sighted."

Robin stopped his questioning and took a moment to compose himself. Dan sensed Robin was about to go in for the kill.

"Mr Johnstone, it was winter, so it would have been getting dark around 5:00pm?"

"Yes."

"The person you saw was fully dressed but you can't remember now exactly what they were wearing?"

"Yes."

"The person wore a cap and tipped their head when you came past them. So you didn't see their face is that correct?"

"Yes."

"You have testified that the person had longish hair but you cannot even remember the colour of their hair, is that correct?"

"Yes."

And during the time while you were jogging past this person, you didn't have your glasses on, did you?

"No, I didn't."

"So you couldn't see absolutely clearly, could you?"

"No, I can't see things really well without my glasses."

"I assume that there were other people on the footpath, light poles and other objects around, such that you had to watch the path in front of you. Hence, you did not concentrate on the person or have the person in your full view the entire time from when they hurriedly came out of Mia Wong's door to when you passed them."

"Yes, that is true, I still had to look where I was going."

"Isn't it true, there were at most only a few of seconds from when you first noticed the person leaving Mia Wong's house to when you jogged past the person?"

"Yes, that's true."

"And during those few seconds your attention and concentration was drawn away from this person to other people and objects around you, so you didn't hit anybody else or trip over anything else."

"Yes, I suppose so, if you put it that way."

"Well then, Mr Johnstone, how can you possibly say that the person you saw leaving Mia Wong's house was a woman? In fact, it could just as easily have been a man, or a man dressed up to look like a woman. I mean it was getting dark, you didn't see the person's face, you weren't wearing your glasses and you saw this person for only a few precious seconds while distracted by other things going on around you."

Mr Johnstone did not answer the question.

"You're under oath, Mr Johnstone. Surely it could have been a man, you just don't know for sure do you, whether it was a woman or a man?"

Dan watched Tom Johnstone intently. He seemed to be rattled by the question. He just sat there and stared out towards the public gallery.

"Mr Johnstone, you have to answer the question," Robin insisted.

No sooner had Robin completed saying these words when Tom Johnstone said in a raised voice, "That's it."

The courtroom was again deathly quiet.

"I knew it was a woman, but you had me doubting myself. Thinking about it again now, you have unlocked something in my memory; it has just come to me. It was definitely a woman as when I went past her and she bowed her head, her left hand went up to hold onto the tip of her baseball cap.

"I remember now, yes she had a woman's hand, she had dark coloured nail polish and she had several large rings on her fingers, including a wedding ring. Yes, thinking about it again I am sure now that she was a woman. Why would a man go to all that trouble of putting on nail polish and rings? It was a delicate hand it was a woman's hand, I am sure of it."

Robin was stunned. He could not say anything, let alone ask any more questions. He just slumped into his seat.

Her Honour was first to speak. "I assume Mr Banks has finished with this witness. Any re-examination, Mr Gabriel?"

Chad Gabriel was grinning like the proverbial Cheshire cat, when he said, "No, Your Honour, this witness has said it all."

"In that case we will adjourn for lunch. See you all back here by 2:00pm."

As Tom Johnstone happily made his way out of the courtroom, he appeared blissfully unaware of the carnage he had caused to the defence case.

Dan and Robin did not speak. Dan turned and offered a fake smile to Elise as she was being led out of the courtroom. Perhaps Elise had not understood the full effect of Tom Johnstone's testimony, if she did, she would be in shock just like he and Robin.

His thoughts turned to advocacy training and the old chestnut of knowing when to stop asking questions; of mistakenly asking one question too many. He was reminded of the case where a man was accused of biting another man's ear off in a fight. There was only one eye witness and the defence lawyer had established that this witness was some 20 metres away when he saw the fight, that it was a moonless, dark night with little street lighting and that there were many trees between the witness and the fight obstructing his vision.

Had the defence lawyer left it at that for the jury to consider the evidence they had before them, he may have been successful. But no, the defence lawyer had to ask one final question. He had to ram it home to the witness and the jury.

How then in all the circumstances could the witness be so sure that the accused had bitten the ear off the victim? Answer, because the witness had run over to the fight and when he got there, he saw the accused spit out the victim's ear.

It was the classic case of asking one question too many. As in this case, Robin had asked one question too many. If only he had left the jury with doubts rather than asking that final question to Mr Johnstone, they would have been in a far stronger position.

Well no point crying over spilt milk. He and Robin had a job to do.

Somebody murdered Mia and it certainly wasn't Elise. It wasn't Elise, was it?

He stopped in his tracks. Could Elise, the person he had been living with for the last six years, be a murderer? No, that went against every bone in his body. That just could not be right, could it? Why was he having doubts about her innocence? She had this temper.

He literally had to shake himself out of that line of thinking. If he was thinking it could be Elise, surely the jury were also thinking seriously about her being right for the murder. He had to do something. He had to help her but what could he do?

All afternoon Dan was thinking what he could do, but his mind was numb; he couldn't come up with anything.

During the rest of the day prosecution witnesses came and went and Robin was unable or incapable of scoring points against any of them. Things were indeed looking grim for the defence team.

CHAPTER FORTY THREE

The next morning Dan arrived early again and went to meet Elise in the holding cells.

Elise didn't look well. The strain appeared to be getting to her.

"You look like death warmed up, didn't you sleep last night?" Elise asked.

It had never occurred to Dan that the strain of it all was getting to him as well.

"Don't worry about me, I am fine. How are you doing?" Dan asked in true Joey Tribbiani style from *Friends*.

"I've been better. I can't stop thinking about what happened yesterday?"

"Unfortunately, that surprise witness Tom Johnstone tore some holes in our defence. He conveyed pretty convincingly that a woman was responsible for Mia's murder."

"I was thinking about that. You know, maybe, he did see me."

"What are you saying?" Dan asked cautiously. He was not quite sure where Elise was going with this.

"Perhaps he saw me coming out of the house, certainly I was in a hurry to get out of there."

"What about the blood splattered on your clothes?"

"Well I bent down and turned the body over. I washed my clothes because they had blood stains on them."

"Did you have dark coloured nail polish on?"

"I can't remember for sure, but sometimes I do wear dark coloured nail polish. I remember wearing my wedding ring, engagement ring and my black pearl ring. You know I wear them most of the time."

"Yes, that could be it," Dan replied, trying to put it all together.

"But Tom Johnstone said the woman wore a baseball cap and she used the cap to hide her face. You hate baseball caps, in fact, I don't think I have ever seen you wear a cap or any hat for that matter."

"That's true I hate hats, particularly baseball caps but they don't know that, do they?"

"What are you saying?"

"I was at the house around 5:00pm but I found her body, I didn't kill her. If it was me that Tom Johnstone saw leaving the house at this time, well his evidence just supports my story, it doesn't detract from it or hurt it in any way.

"The only problem is the blood splattered clothes. But that can be explained away by my touching the body, getting blood on my hands and then touching my clothes."

"But it wasn't you that Tom Johnstone saw leaving the house because you weren't covered in blood and you don't even own a baseball cap, let alone would wear one."

"Yes, that's true, I was not wearing a baseball cap and I was not covered in blood, so it could not have been me that he saw leaving the house. But if we say Tom Johnstone saw me, that keeps open our defence that it was Brock Shepard or Samuel Sanderson who committed the murder. Otherwise, there is no one else to point to other than me. We only have male suspects; we don't have any female suspects."

"You really have spent some time thinking about this, haven't you?" Dan said.

"If we say it wasn't me that Tom Johnstone saw, then who do we say it was?" Elise asked.

"It probably was Samuel Sanderson in disguise. He would have needed a disguise to get into Mia's house anyway."

"Do you honestly believe the jury will think Tom Johnstone made a mistake and it was Samuel Sanderson in drag who committed the murder? Or that Mia would not have recognised Samuel Sanderson dressed in drag?"

"But, Elise, we can't lie to the court. We can't say it was you who Tom Johnstone saw, just to keep open our defence that Brock or Samuel committed the murder."

"Why the hell not!" Elise said with some feeling. "You believe I am innocent don't you?"

"Of course," Dan said instantly.

"Then telling a white lie isn't much in the whole scheme of things. One lie versus the rest of my life in prison. I think the answer is pretty clear, don't you?"

"I realize that Tom Johnstone's testimony has made it much harder for us to convince the jury that Samuel or Brock murdered Mia, and of course we don't have any female suspects to put before the jury; but we can't, I can't, Robin can't, just lie to the Court. That would be completely unethical."

"Unethical. I can't believe I am hearing this, from you of all people."

He looked away from Elise. He probably deserved the barb but that fact didn't prevent it from really stinging him.

"You're going to be disbarred anyway aren't you, once you testify?"

"There is a very distinct possibility I will be disbarred, but I am not sure about lying to the court in this way."

Elise opened her arms and said, "Dan you just wrote me a lovely poem which I will treasure for the rest of my life. In it you say that I will not fight alone, that you will always fight with me. That I will never stand alone, you will always stand with me. Yet here and now when I ask you to fight with me, to stand with me, you want to run away and desert me."

He was hesitating. What she wanted him to do went against everything he had stood for as a lawyer. Lying to the police was bad enough, but lying to the court? Anyway he had moved on from lying, hadn't he?

"Is your life just words? Do you ever take action? Do you ever do what you say you will do?" Elise demanded.

He was surprised how quickly Elise had turned on him.

"I am not sure."

"You won't do this for me!"

Elise was raising her voice and he was conscious that they were being watched by the correction officers on the holding cells monitor. Dan raised his hands and said "Shhhh."

"Don't tell me to, shhh! You have no idea what it's like to have your whole life just pulled from underneath you!"

Elise turned away from him and lowered her head. Dan reached over to put his arms around her, to comfort her, but she pulled away from him.

Elise was pleading with him now. "You know I didn't do this thing. Doesn't the end justify the means? One white lie and our case is back on track. I need you to go along with me on this. Please help me get out of here!"

He was always more responsive to a plea for help than criticism or intimidation. He reached over again to hug Elise and this time she did not pull away.

"Give me some time to think about it. I can't tell Robin or he will be faced with the same ethical dilemma I am faced with. I suppose the prosecution believe you were the one Tom Johnstone saw coming from the house anyway, so we would just be going along with what they believe happened."

"Thanks, Dan. I just need to get out of here. I don't think I can last another week inside these walls, let alone 20 more years."

"I will sort something out, leave it with me."

Dan was not sure what he should do. He didn't want to lie anymore but he could see how one small lie could really help their case. Surely Elise's freedom was paramount.

*

"The Crown calls Samuel Sanderson," Chad Gabriel announced to the court.

With that Dan turned around and noticed Samuel's wife sitting in the back of the courtroom by herself. He wondered if she had been there on any of the other days of the trial.

Then the doors of the courtroom were flung open and in walked Samuel Sanderson. Samuel looked handsome as ever. He confidently walked to the witness box, sat down and stared straight ahead.

Dan watched intently as Samuel answered Chad Gabriel's questions. He noted that Samuel was very calm, eerily calm. Nothing seemed to faze him and he behaved like the perfect witness.

In fact, that's what he first noticed about Samuel when he interviewed him over Mia's sexual assault allegations. He was very cool and calm, nothing seemed to really upset him. Even when Samuel became upset at some of Dan's questions; on reflection, he felt Samuel's upset demeanor was more of an act than actual emotion.

"Would you like to cross-examine this witness, Mr Banks?"

"Yes, I would Your Honour."

"Mr Sanderson, let's get straight to it shall we. Is your evidence that you did not sexually assault Mia Wong?"

"Yes, that's right."

"Mr Sanderson, have you seen Mr Grover's report, where after interviewing yourself and many other witnesses, he found that you did sexually assault Mia Wong?"

"Yes, I have seen it and it's rubbish. I mean how can anyone rely upon a report compiled by an investigator who was sleeping with the woman who complained about me?"

"We will hear from Mr Grover later in these proceedings and he will tell the court that he was not sleeping with Ms Wong. In any event do you deny and dispute the compelling evidence contained in that report, which points to the fact that you sexually assaulted Mia Wong?"

Chad Gabriel was instantly on his feet. "Objection, the witness has already answered this question."

"Mr Sanderson, let me put it to you simply, are you or are you not, someone who sexually harasses young women in the workplace?"

"I most certainly am not."

Robin looked longingly at the jury when Samuel made this denial.

Robin didn't need Samuel to admit he was a serial sexual harasser of young women to convince the jury of this. Indeed, Samuel's denial or untruthfulness on this point was worth far more to Robin as it would form the basis of his attack on Samuel's credibility in his summation.

"Witness, are you saying that Mia Wong lied about you sexually assaulting her?"

"Yes."

"Are you saying that Kathleen Brown is lying when she says that you sexually assaulted her?"

"Kathleen Brown, where did you dig her up from?"

"Witness your role is to answer questions, not ask them?" Robin said sharply.

"Yes, she is lying. Her complaint was never fully investigated because she disappeared before the complaint could be determined."

"Perhaps you threatened her, Mr Sanderson. Perhaps that is why she disappeared and couldn't pursue her complaint against you?"

"No, I did not threaten Kathleen Brown or Mia Wong, for that matter."

"What about Amanda Peterson? Before she disappeared permanently, she complained to her employer and to the police that you sexually assaulted her."

"I was found not to have sexually assaulted Amanda Peterson by the company we both worked for. It was all consensual. Also the police talked to me and then nothing happened, no charges."

"It was convenient for you though, that both Amanda Peterson and Kathleen Brown disappeared."

"It was most inconvenient that they left town, as I could not sue them for defamation. Therefore, people like you keep assuming I am guilty when I have done nothing wrong."

"You really think you have done nothing wrong, Mr Sanderson?"

"I have done nothing wrong. I don't know how many times I have to say it for you to accept it."

"Mr Sanderson, if you have done nothing wrong, why then have all these three young women either been in hiding, disappeared or ended up dead."

"Their disappearance has got nothing to do with me, and for your information I did not murder Mia Wong."

Samuel was as cool as a cucumber when he was being cross-examined. Nothing seemed to really faze him. Why was that? How could he just sit there and calmly deny sexually harassing these three young women when the evidence against him was so compelling?

Just then Dan had a thought. Samuel had been expecting this line of questioning and was just calmly sticking to his prepared answers. What if Robin could get him out of his comfort zone, maybe then we might see some of Samuel's true character. At the moment, he looked more a Zen Master than a serial sexual harasser scared of his secrets being discovered.

Dan wrote a few words on a piece of paper and slid them to Robin.

"Mr Sanderson what did your wife think of your sexual liaison with Amanda Peterson?"

"My wife, what's my wife got to do with all this? Keep her out of it!"

The question hit the mark. Samuel looked slightly rattled. He had not been expecting that question. Nor did it appear he appreciated questions about his wife.

"In your response to the Amanda Peterson complaint, you said that the sexual interaction was all consensual. I was just asking what you wife thought of it all."

Samuel looked at Chad Gabriel conveying a clear expression that he did not want to answer this question.

Eventually Chad Gabriel got the hint, but it was obvious to Dan that Chad Gabriel did not want to waste too much of his time helping out the likes of Samuel Sanderson.

"Your Honour, must we hear about what Mr Sanderson's wife thinks about her husband's behaviour. Is that really relevant to who killed the deceased?"

"Your Honour, we believe Mr Sanderson's predatory sexual behaviour is very relevant to this murder trial. Mr Sanderson has testified he has done nothing wrong. I am merely exploring the answer he has already given."

"I will allow the question, Mr Banks, but you are sailing close to the wind, be careful."

"What did your wife think of your admitted dalliance with Amanda Peterson?" Robin asked.

"My wife has nothing to do with this."

"Mr Sanderson you are a witness in these proceedings and, as such, you have to answer my questions."

"My wife knows nothing about all this. Any idiot can see that."

"Are you calling me an idiot, Mr Sanderson?"

Samuel lifted his head and in a raised voice proclaimed, "This is ridiculous!"

Samuel was losing it. For the first time the jury was seeing more than just his calm exterior, they were witnessing a glimpse into the inner turmoil that was his troubled soul.

"Do you prefer I call your wife to the witness box and ask her?"

"No!"

Samuel ran his hand through his hair and appeared to regain control of his emotions once more.

"Listen, my wife was upset but she forgave me because she realised that I was lured into the liaison by Amanda Peterson."

"You mean a young girl like Amanda Peterson seduced you?"

"Yes, that's exactly what I am saying."

Robin looked fervently at the jury, shaking his head.

"So in summary, Mr Sanderson, your sworn evidence is that these three young women who didn't know each other; they all just invented their sexual harassment allegations against you?"

"Yes."

"It has all just been a big coincidence, that you were accused of sexually harassing each one of them."

"Yes."

"And you had absolutely nothing to do with Mia Wong and Kathleen Brown being threatened?"

"That's right."

"And its all just coincidence that each one of these three young women have either disappeared, hurriedly left town, or been murdered?"

"Yes, that's right, it just coincidence."

Robin looked at the jury, then slowly and deliberately pronounced, "Coincidences are funny things, Mr Sanderson. The more they happen, the more likely it is that they are *not* coincidences."

Robin waited a few seconds for the jury to take in what he had just said. He then sat down and said, "I have no more questions for this witness, Your Honour."

"Any re-examination Mr Gabriel?"

"No, Your Honour."

Dan was in no doubt that the jury and even Chad Gabriel himself, believed that Samuel Sanderson had in all likelihood sexually assaulted all these three young women. But the question was, would the jury stretch the sexually assault theory to murder.

He watched Samuel leave the stand. As Samuel walked past, he flashed Dan a menacing stare. Dan had been on the receiving end of some dirty looks before but this one was different. This stare was seriously scary. It literally sent chills up his spine. He was glad the stare was given in the confines and protectiveness of the court and not in some dimly lit alley.

*

"Your Honour, I call Mr Brock Shepard to the stand," Chad Gabriel announced.

Dan looked at Brock Shepard for the first time as he entered the courtroom. Brock was a rugged looking, muscular young man. He was dressed in casual slacks and a short sleeve shirt with a tie. Brock had longish, dark-brown hair and a small tattoo on the right side of his neck.

He listened as Brock Shepard outlined how he had loved Mia and how he had been heartbroken to hear of her death.

In cross-examination about the DVO, Brock did not admit hitting Mia or holding her against the wall by the throat. Brock admitted only to pushing Mia against the wall after they had argued over his drinking.

Brock said that, since Mia's death, he had realised that alcohol was the problem in his relationship with her. He had now done something about that.

Robin put to Brock that his purchasing the concert tickets and making the airline booking prior to Mia's death was just a ruse, to hide his trail after murdering Mia. Brock broke down and couldn't speak at the suggestion he had pre-meditated Mia's murder.

Robin also put to Brock that he went to Mia's house on the day in question and when she rejected his overtures to get back with her; he flew into an alcohol fuelled rage and killed her.

Brock's response was to deny the allegation, though he did admit he could not remember much of what happened that day.

Brock's previous criminal convictions were put to him and he admitted that he was capable of violence, quite disturbing violence, if fuelled by alcohol.

Dan did not believe Brock planned to kill Mia but he certainly was capable of killing her. It was highly possible that Brock could have snapped and murdered Mia on the day in question, but now he was repressing that memory. Certainly Brock's admission that he was capable of doing anything in an alcohol fuelled rage was helpful to them.

Credit where it is due; Chad Gabriel's re-examination of Brock was quite brilliant. Chad Gabriel did not ask Brock a single question in re-examination but merely asked him to hold his hands out to the jury.

It was patently obvious that Brock's large and calloused hands were those of a brick layer, not a woman.

CHAPTER FORTY FOUR

"How are you feeling?" Dan asked. "By the way, this is great!"

Dan was at Claye's place, tucking into one of Dan's favourite dishes; *Lamb Shanks in the Pot.*

Dan reached the end of his first lamb shank, when as his ritual, he tenderly picked the bone up in his hands and slowly but surely ate every last morsel of the tender meat right off the bone. When he ate lamb shanks, there was never any meat left anywhere on the bone.

"Mate, I am glad you like it. And by the way, I am feeling fine, except I have no energy. I just seem to sleep all day. In fact, this is the first meal I have spent anytime cooking since I came home from hospital."

"But that's expected, right? You were always going to feel tired for months after the transplant," Dan said as he eagerly anticipated starting on his second lamb shank.

"Yeah, they told me the first few months would be the worst and it could take a year for my body to fully recover from the transplant."

"You still taking medication?" Dan asked as he began to devour his second lamb shank.

"I have this infection that just won't go away, so I am taking some heavy duty antibiotics to try and get rid of it once and for all. I am still taking medication to stop your stem cells from attacking me."

"You look pretty thin."

"Yes, and this lamb shank meal will be good for me. I need protein to build up my red blood cell count. So it was good of you to invite yourself over to my place for dinner and allow me to cook your favourite meal for you. I really appreciate it," Claye said with a smile.

"It was the least I could do," Dan said chuckling. "You know I am always thinking of you."

"Yeah, right."

At that comment they both laughed.

"So to what do I owe the pleasure of your company? I thought with the trial you would be too busy for social gatherings with your big brother."

"Actually, Claye, I have come for some personal advice."

"Wait, did I hear you right? You have actually sought me out for advice on a personal matter. After all those years of ignoring what I say, you have now come to me asking for advice."

"Yeah, don't rub it in. I need your help. See I said it."

Over the years Dan had rarely ever asked Claye for help. Dan had always been the popular successful brother while Claye had tended to live in his shadow, even though Claye was the elder brother.

"What can I do for you *grasshopper*?" Claye asked expectantly.

Grasshopper was a reference to Claye's favourite TV show as a child, *Kung Fu.* In this show a young boy was instructed in the ways of life by his master, who always referred to the boy as *grasshopper*.

Dan quickly brought Claye up to speed with what was happening at the trial.

"That Samuel Sanderson guy sounds very creepy and very dangerous. I think he is your man. Though why weren't his finger prints found on the murder weapon?"

"We have a finger print expert who will testify that given the amount of blood found on the vase, the police were lucky to find even one set of finger prints intact. Therefore the finger print evidence does not mean conclusively that Samuel Sanderson did not touch the glass vase.

"But here is the rub. We have Tom Johnstone whose credibility is beyond reproach, saying that he saw a woman leave the house at the time of the murder and she was covered in blood."

"Surely, Tom Johnstone was wrong about seeing a woman. I bet Samuel Sanderson dressed up as a woman."

"Tom Johnstone has to be wrong, but it will be hard to convince a jury of that."

"He ran past her didn't he? How could he tell a woman's hands from a man's hands in a fraction of a second?"

"His evidence was pretty compelling. It will be hard for us to convince a jury that he was mistaken and he actually saw a man dressed as a woman; not an actual woman.

"I mean he didn't have his glasses on, he was looking at other things beside this person and it all happened pretty quickly late in the afternoon, some four months ago; but his evidence of seeing a woman's hand with nail polish, a wedding ring and other rings was pretty convincing."

"But that's all you can do isn't it? Explain to the jury that Tom Johnstone is a nice guy but he is simply mistaken."

"There is another scenario we could explore. If Tom Johnstone actually saw Elise leave the building, then that would leave it open for us to put to the jury that Tom Johnstone was correct in seeing a woman, but that a male either Samuel Sanderson or Brock Shepard had killed Mia before Elise arrived."

"Mate, you've lost me. Was it Elise that Tom Johnstone saw leaving the building?"

Dan hesitated, not quite sure what he should tell Claye. In the end he figured he was here for Claye's advice, he had to tell him everything.

"Yes and no."

"What do you mean, yes and no? He either saw Elise or he didn't."

Dan breathed in heavily and sighed.

"Tom Johnstone didn't see Elise. She has never worn a baseball cap in her life and she told me on this day she was not wearing a baseball cap, so it could not have been her.

"However, if we let the court and the prosecution believe that Tom Johnstone did see Elise and she explains that she moved the body and then rubbed her bloodied hands on her clothes, then we are in a much stronger position. You see our whole case is dependent on the fact that Samuel Sanderson or Brock Shepard could have killed Mia; and by saying that Tom Johnstone actually saw Elise, we are maintaining our defence.

"If we say Tom Johnstone didn't see Elise, we severely weaken our case because we are then forced to say that some unknown woman killed Mia. Or that Samuel or Brock killed Mia and that they then fooled Tom Johnstone into believing that they were female by dressing as a woman; nail polish, rings and all."

"But in truth Dan, Tom Johnstone must have been mistaken. Don't you believe that?" Claye asked.

"Yes, I believe Samuel Sanderson or Brock Shepard murdered Mia and hence Tom Johnstone must have been mistaken about seeing a woman."

"So why don't you go with the truth?"

"Because Elise could spend the rest of her life in jail if we go with the truth. I mean it's not a huge lie. It's a very small lie. Heck the prosecution already believe that Tom Johnstone saw Elise coming out of the building, so they won't be proposing anything different. We just have to explain the blood splattered on her clothes."

"I can't believe I am hearing this. It's a small lie, not a big lie, therefore its ok. What are you, 12 years old? Any lie to the court is perjury, isn't it?"

"Nothing has happened yet. I really don't know what to do. Elise wants to do it. I am not so sure, so I wanted to run it by you, to see what you think."

"I think you should always tell the truth, regardless of the consequences."

"That's easy to say and hard to do, especially when Elise could spend the rest of her life in prison."

"Ok, my advice is to pray about it. I mean really pray about it."

"Be serious. You know I am not into praying. I'm still not sure God actually exists. Anyway, God doesn't just answer you."

"God says in the Bible, *if you seek me with all your heart, I will be found by you.*

"Fast for a day, then get on the floor, and seek God with all your heart. Not some two minute noodle job, but really clear your mind of everything else and seek him, really seek him and he will find you."

"How can you be so sure?"

"With faith all things are possible."

"But I don't really have any faith."

"Your need is strong. When you call out to him in that desperation, in that need, God will find you and tell you what to do. I will pray for you."

"That's all your advice, your words of wisdom."

"That's it. It has worked for me, it will work for you. You just have to step out and try it."

"Ok. I will think about it. What have I got to lose?"

"That's the spirit."

*

On the way home from Claye's place Dan prayed but he heard nothing from God. On the way to the trial the next morning Dan prayed but he got no response. He wondered what he was doing. Perhaps he was losing the plot.

Dan did not go and see Elise in the holding cells before the trial this morning. He caught up with Elise in the courtroom when she was brought into the dock to begin the day's hearing.

"How are you this morning?" Dan asked.

"So what's happening about my little suggestion?" Elise said totally ignoring the question Dan had just asked her.

"I don't know yet, I am still working on it."

"When am I giving evidence?"

"The prosecution evidence should wind up before lunchtime. Robin is going to put me on the stand later this afternoon. I will probably be cross-examined for some time by our smiling assassin, Chad Gabriel. You won't have to testify until tomorrow. I will talk to you tomorrow morning about what we should do."

Just then Dan heard the words, "All rise," followed by the noise of chairs being moved, people standing and Her Honour Justice Mary Hooper making her grand entrance into the courtroom.

He could see that Elise was not happy that he had not already decided to support her lie initiative, but he could do little about that.

Various prosecution witnesses gave evidence during the morning and the Crown rested its case. The defence called their first witnesses shortly before lunchtime.

He knew he was in for a tough time in the witness box and that his own testimony would probably lead to the sinking of his reputation, the obliteration of his legal practice and the end of his legal career. But all he could think about was should he, or should he not allow Elise to lie to the court?

CHAPTER FORTY FIVE

"I have no further questions Your Honour," Dan heard Robin say as he completed his evidence-in-chief.

He had told the court the whole story. He even admitted kissing Mia and then completing his investigation report over the next couple of days. Dan held nothing back. He felt quite strongly that he should tell the truth regardless of the consequences.

"Cross-examination, Mr Gabriel?" Her Honour asked.

"Yes, Maam, I have quite a few questions for this witness," Chad Gabriel replied.

"Now, Mr Grover, you have testified that you shared an intimate moment with the deceased, is that right?"

"We kissed and hugged for a short time, that was all."

"Well then, how do you explain the deceased's own words where she writes:

We really went for it last night, it was amazing. I literally
could not breathe. After all the jerks I have been with, could Dan
be the one? Dan said he might leave his wife and come to Sydney
to be with me. That would be awesome!!

"Seems to me like more than a kiss and a cuddle?"

"Believe me, that's all that happened between us."

"Believe you, I think that's unlikely, but we will get to more of that later."

"Objection, Mr Gabriel is abusing the witness," Robin interjected.

"Sustained. Mr Gabriel in my court everybody will be treated with respect."

Chad Gabriel nodded gracefully, flashed one of his charismatic smiles at Her Honour and then continued.

"Mr Grover, do you seriously intend to sit there and maintain that nothing more than a kiss and a cuddle took place between you and the deceased, when she is saying that you could be the one for her and that you are talking about leaving your wife for her?"

"I do intend to sit here and say that because it is the truth."

"The truth, well that's a concept I don't think you are acquainted with at all, but again more of that later."

"Your Honour!" Robin vigorously shouted.

"I am sorry, Your Honour, I will control myself, it won't happen again," Chad Gabriel said before Her Honour could say anything to him.

"Come on, Mr Grover, the evidence of the relationship between you and the deceased is in black and white, do you still maintain it was nothing more than a kiss and cuddle?"

"Just because Mia's evidence is in writing, doesn't make it any more convincing or likely to be true, than my verbal testimony.

"Mia got ahead of herself with me. I didn't know she felt so strongly towards me. I succumbed to a moment of passion with her but at the end of the day I chose to work things out with my wife. As I said in my earlier testimony, I spent the night on the couch."

Dan thought he had made a good point but Chad Gabriel just shook his head in the direction of the jury, indicating to them quite clearly that he thought Dan was making it up as he went along. Being in the witness box for the first time, he could feel the power and authority exuding from Chad Gabriel his questioner, while he as the answerer was virtually powerless, like a deer stuck in the headlights.

"Mr Grover, as a solicitor you are bound by a standard of ethics, a professional code of practice so to speak, aren't you?"

"Yes."

"In your opinion did you not breach those ethics by sleeping with the deceased before you had completed your investigation of her complaint against Mr Samuel Sanderson?"

"I did not sleep with Mia."

"Well let's call it a romantic tryst then."

"I imagine that I could be in breach by kissing and hugging Mia; although I had finished the investigation phase of the report by this time."

"It was unprofessional of you to engage in a romantic tryst with someone who was the complainant in an independent investigation you were conducting?"

"Yes, it was unprofessional of me."

"Mr Grover, when questioned by Senior Detective Sloan as to whether you had a romantic tryst with the deceased, what did you tell him?"

"I told him that nothing of a romantic nature had happened between us."

"You didn't think kissing and cuddling was activity of a romantic nature?"

Dan did not answer the question.

"In effect you lied to Senior Detective Sloan while he was conducting a murder investigation. Is that correct?"

"Yes, but at the time I had no reason to suspect that this information was relevant to the investigation."

"At this time you had inspected the crime scene, you had spoken to the deceased's neighbours and friends, you had reviewed the forensic evidence and the pathology report, is that correct Mr Grover?"

"No."

"So what information did you have about the murder?"

"I knew Mia had been bashed to death."

"So you were able to determine what was relevant information and what was irrelevant information, without knowing anything about the circumstances of this murder, other than that the victim had been bashed to death. Is that correct, Mr Grover?"

Dan did not respond to this question, there was nothing he could say.

"In fact, Mr Grover, you lied to the police about not having a romantic tryst with the deceased because you didn't want to implicate your wife in the murder investigation?"

"No, that is not true," Dan said with conviction.

"Mr Grover, let's talk about untruths, you know lies.

"Is it the case that you lied to your wife, or at least hid the truth from her, about having a romantic tryst with the deceased? At least at the beginning of when all this happened?"

"Yes."

"Is it the case that you lied to the police about not engaging in a romantic tryst with the deceased?"

"Yes."

"Is it the case that you lied or at least hid the truth from the company who employed you to conduct the investigation, that you had a romantic tryst with the deceased?"

"Yes."

"Is it the case that you just lied to this court, by saying that you did not tell the police about your romantic tryst with the deceased because it was not relevant to their investigation; when the real reason was that you wanted to protect your wife?"

"No."

"Mr Grover, how can we believe anything you have to say when you lie so much? You are so loose with the truth, you give even lawyers a bad name."

"Objection."

"I will withdraw that last comment."

Dan sighed and looked past Chad Gabriel out to the public gallery. He noticed Samuel Sanderson sitting in the second or third row. He was sniggering appearing to be enjoying Dan's discomfort. Samuel's wife though was not even looking at Dan. She was looking at Samuel and playing intently with his hair.

"Mr Grover, would you agree with me when I say sometimes it's hard to tell who is lying and who isn't lying."

Dan was abruptly shaken from his thoughts about the power Samuel Sanderson must have over his wife.

"I'm sorry, could you repeat the question?"

"Mr Grover, would you agree with me when I say sometimes it's hard to tell who is lying and who isn't lying?"

Dan was wary of this question, but he had no option but to answer it. He had no idea where Chad Gabriel was going with this.

"Yes, it can sometimes be hard to tell who is lying and who is telling the truth."

"Could it not be that the deceased was lying to you all along about seeing the intruder? Could the deceased not have switched her own power off?"

"I doubt that very much. She was very scared. I also saw with my own eyes the threatening note she received."

"Yes, but she could have compiled the note herself in an attempt to lure you to her house for a spot of romance. I mean, she could have even set the whole thing up, the threatening note, the intruder, the romance, in an attempt to get you to find for her in the investigation?"

"It's possible but extremely unlikely."

"Why do you say that? Do you believe you're the only male in the world who cannot be taken in by a woman's charms?"

"No, I say that because I saw the fear in Mia's eyes, it was very real. I also say that because Kathleen Brown received a similar threatening note and she took it so seriously she moved interstate and kept her whereabouts a secret. I say that because Amanda Peterson is missing, presumed dead."

For the first time in the whole trial, Chad Gabriel had the wind taken out of his sails.

"Your Honour, the Crown believes nothing can be gained by continuing the examination of this witness who is a self-confessed liar," Chad Gabriel said in an attempt to recover lost ground.

"No re-examination, Your Honour."

"You may step down from the witness box, Mr Grover. Thank you for your testimony."

Dan was feeling low until he heard Her Honour publicly thank him for his testimony. That was a good sign. She must have appreciated his honesty and preparedness to admit mistakes, even if they were going to cost him big time. What did that mean for his decision as to whether he allowed Elise to lie tomorrow?

"It's late. We will adjourn until tomorrow morning at 10:00am."

Dan whispered to Robin, "How did I go?"

"As expected you took plenty of hits early, but that was a good comeback at the end. I think we are still in this thing but only just. Samuel Sanderson looks likely and Brock Sanderson is still a possibility. If only Tom Johnstone had seen a man leave the building and not a woman."

Dan turned to Elise and said, "You're up tomorrow to give evidence. We will discuss it all tomorrow morning."

Elise looked weak and tense as she was led away by the corrections officer.

Dan walked out of the courtroom glad that he had finished his testimony and that he had told the truth regardless of the consequences.

But what about Elise? He had to have an answer by tomorrow morning as to whether she should lie to the court.

As he drove home he wondered how or if God was going to give him an answer to his question. Really he wanted to believe God would help him, but he just felt empty.

CHAPTER FORTY SIX

It was about 6:30pm when Dan heard his mobile phone go off. It was calling out to him again, demanding to be answered.

When he was younger, Dan believed mobile phones were one of man's great inventions. Now he just wanted a simpler life, of not being contactable at all times. He imagined tropical beaches, palm trees, beautiful lagoons and serenity.

"Hi, it's Sarah. How are you going?"

Dan was pleased to get a call from Sarah.

"Well we are not going too badly. I am confident the jury will find the truth."

"Are you confident like the Sharks are going to win the premiership next year, or confident like you actually believe it's going to happen?"

"Yeah, thanks Sarah. It's been a week since the trial started, and in that time no one has had a go at me about the Sharks."

"Well somebody has to do it. You'd miss it wouldn't you, if no one mentioned the woeful Sharks to you in a whole week?"

"Just you wait, Sarah Crabtree-Little, or whatever your name is. Just you and the rest of Australia wait. The Sharks will win the premiership one day and then the laughs will be on you."

"The laughs won't be on me, Dan Grover, because I'll have died of old age many years before then."

They both laughed.

There was a lull in their conversation before Sarah spoke.

"I saw you give evidence today, it was pretty rough for you."

"It was rough, but all I can do is answer the questions put to me."

"But aren't there going to be some repercussions for you? I mean by testifying at all, you opened yourself up to be disbarred by the Legal Services

Commission and to be charged with hindering a police investigation."

"Thanks for reminding me, Sarah."

"But I mean, was it all worth it?"

"We had to get the evidence in about Mia being stalked and threatened. Mia wasn't able to do it. So I had to be the one to get it in, even though I might become a target for some unsavoury consequences."

"So you always tell the truth now, regardless of the consequences?"

Wow, that was the exact question he was wrestling with. How did Sarah know to ask such as question?

"I have lied in the past and it hasn't got me anywhere. In fact, lying has only made things much worse."

Dan thought for a minute and then added, "The consequences of lying are always worse than the consequences of telling the truth."

"That's quite an impressive quote for a lawyer. Where did you get that one from?" Sarah asked.

"From a long lost brother of mine. But take it from me, I won't lose him again. We will be close from now on."

"You know, Dan Grover, you are a pretty impressive guy."

He was a little uncomfortable with Sarah's praise of him and tried to downplay it. "Well, I don't know if Mr Chad Gabriel would agree with you. I think he said at one point that I was so untrustworthy that I gave even lawyers a bad name."

"I think lawyers had a bad name long before you came along."

There was more silence on the line before Sarah spoke again.

"Dan, I have heard that the trial will be wrapped up soon. I was wondering if you would like to go out for a drink with me, when it's all over?"

There was more silence on the line before Dan eventually spoke.

"Sarah, look, I like you a lot. I really think you are terrific. But I have set my course, cast my die, my colours have been nailed to the mast."

"Geez, I didn't know you were into all those sailing metaphors. What do they actually mean?"

"They mean I am with Elise for better or for worse. There is no turning back in my mind. She needs me and as long as she needs me, I will be there for her."

There was more silence on the line, this time uncomfortable silence.

"You realise don't you, that everybody believes she did it? The evidence clearly points to the fact that Elise murdered Mia Wong."

"I know the evidence against her is strong but that does not mean she did it. You don't know her as I do. She didn't kill anyone."

"You have already thrown away your reputation on your belief she is innocent, are you really prepared to throw away the rest of your life if she is found guilty?"

There was more silence as Dan thought about this pivotal moment in his life.

"If she is found guilty, or not guilty, it doesn't matter. I am committed to her and hopefully she is committed to me."

There was another lengthy silence in this phone conversation.

"Dan Grover, all I can say about that statement is that your wife is one lucky woman. I envy her, even though she possibly stands only a few days away from spending the rest of her life in jail, I envy her."

Sarah sounded quite emotional when she said this.

"You're not going to cry on me now, are you Detective? I thought they made you crime fighting guys from stronger stuff," Dan said as he tried to lighten the mood of their conversation.

"No, I am not going to cry, well I am not going to cry now, maybe later."

"All the best, Sarah, and I mean that sincerely. You have been a great help to me over these last few months. I couldn't have done it all without you," Dan said being serious again.

At that Sarah terminated their phone conversation.

Dan liked Sarah, he really did. But it was all about Elise now. He had learnt his lesson about playing around with someone else. Playing around with someone else, even for a few minutes, could have terrible and far reaching consequences and he was not travelling down that road ever again.

*

Dan sat on the couch and stared at the ceiling.

He still was not sure whether he should let Elise lie to the court. Instinctively he felt the need to pray.

He did not know how to pray but he felt he should try. Elise's freedom, their marriage, his career, they all could disappear if he didn't get this question right.

Oh God, tell me what to do. Should we lie to the court?

Dan got no response.

He thought it would be best to outline the pros and cons and hopefully God would be able to show him which path to take.

Dan started with the pros.

Elise could be convicted, spend the rest of her life behind bars. They needed the jury to believe that a male, either Samuel or Brock, murdered Mia.

It was only a little white lie. It was unlikely they would ever be found out in the lie as the Crown wanted to believe Tom Johnstone saw Elise coming out of Mia's apartment.

It was highly likely he was going to be disbarred anyway, so what did it matter?

Elise wanted to lie, it was her idea. How would he ever be able to face her if he told her not to lie and she was convicted? She would never forgive him, and forever blame him for spending the rest of her life in jail.

Dan stopped and thought the pros were pretty powerful. Perhaps that was God's way of showing him what he should do?

Dan then outlined the cons.

He had had enough of lying. His lying had already led to terrible consequences. If he had been truthful with Elise about going to see Mia that night, Elise would never have followed him.

Elise would have some difficulty explaining away the blood splatter Tom Johnstone saw on her as just blood she picked up by checking the body and wiping her hands on her clothes.

As a solicitor Dan was an officer of the court. It went against his grain to lie to the court, to deliberately mislead the court.

Dan pondered the pros and cons for some time, the answer seemed clear to him. He had to support Elise lying to the court. That was the smart and rational thing to do in this situation.

But it still irked him that he had not heard from God about that. He wanted above all else, to do what was right.

He dropped to his knees and closed his eyes.

How had it come to this?

It had started with a kiss.

No it had started with a lie, only a small one at first.

It was just a little white lie, just an insignificant white lie.

....

"Oh God! Oh God!" he cried out.

"It's all my fault."

His knees hurt as they cut into the timber floor, his back ached, his head was pounding, but he was not getting up, he was not giving up.

Oh God please, please hear me. I don't want to stuff things up again. Please tell me, I need to hear from you, should we lie to the court?

Dan was thinking yes, it had to be yes for Elise's sake. Really it had to be yes, but it was *no*.

He didn't hear an audible voice but it was a clear answer which was unmistakably not from him. It was not his thought. It was a thought that came into his head, somehow from outside his brain.

That can't be right! She is going to be convicted if we don't lie?

Dan cried out to God as though his life depended on the answer to this question.

He then had another clear thought. It came as a picture in his mind. It was not what he had been thinking at all. He was unsure where this second thought came from because the picture was so bizarre. But he sensed this picture did not come from him.

He could scarcely believe what had just happened. He had been given the strangest answer to his plea – a picture of a wedding ring.

*

Dan could hear Claye's home phone ringing but there was no answer. What is he doing, where is he? Is he still sick? He can't be out on the town, surely.

"Hello," Dan suddenly heard Claye's voice, it was unsteady, raspy and quiet.

"Don't tell me I woke you up," Dan shouted into the phone. "It's only 7:30."

"I haven't been feeling too well, so I went to bed early," Claye said softly.

"You're not going to believe what I am about to tell you," Dan said excitedly.

"Ok, try me."

"I think God may have actually spoken to me. Guess what he said?"

"Mate, can you just tell me, I don't really feel like guessing at the moment."

"He told me quite clearly, not to let Elise lie to the court."

"That's great."

"But wait there's more. I think he has led me to who killed Mia Wong."

"What's that?"

"It was more what I should be concentrating on. I believe I know who the killer is. Now I have to work out how to prove it."

"What did God tell you?"

"Before we go there, can you answer one question for me?"

"Sure mate, anything."

"How do I know God has just spoken to me. When you say it out loud, it actually sounds kind of crazy. I mean I think it was God, but how do I know it wasn't just my own imagination playing tricks on me?

"Ask God to confirm it. Whatever he said to you, if it really was from God, he will confirm it through someone else."

"Ok, how does that work?"

"If you ask God to confirm it, he will. Somehow you will receive information from someone that the word you received is from God. It really could take any form."

"It could take any form?"

"Listen, mate, I am happy for you and you will have to tell me the whole story, but right now I have to go and throw up."

At that Claye terminated the call.

*

Dan asked God to confirm his word to him.

Within an hour of his call to Claye he received a telephone call from Rose Peterson. There was no doubt in Dan's mind that this call was his confirmation.

He stood there in his living room for a few minutes trying to take in what had just happened.

Did the God of the entire universe just speak to him? Not only that, but did God just confirm what he had said to him?

He began to dance around the room. Dan did not normally dance, that was something he did not do and could not do. Yet he was so elated he could not have stopped himself dancing, even if he wanted to.

He danced and punched the air. He danced and praised God. He danced and pointed to the ceiling. He danced and practiced Kung Fu moves he had seen on TV. Dan danced and felt on top of the world.

CHAPTER FORTY SEVEN

Dan spent the night researching and then going over and over his plan in minute detail. His lack of sleep didn't worry him one little bit. Today was the day when the truth would finally be revealed.

After running a few errands and making a few calls Dan arrived at the holding cells well before the trial was set to begin.

Elise was looking much calmer than he had expected her to look. He was unsure how he would approach Elise this morning. How could he convince her not to lie to the court? How could he tell her what happened last night without her thinking he was a complete idiot?

"What's happening?" Dan asked casually.

"Not much, how about you?"

Well that was good. Elise could have landed a blow in response to the *what's happening* remark but she took it in the good humour it was delivered.

"I have something for you."

Elise took the striped pink and white dress from Dan. Inside the clothes she found a small gift wrapped parcel.

"What's this?"

"It's something I hope you will like."

Elise slowly unwrapped the gift, a silver bracelet.

"I bought it for you this morning."

"I like it," Elise said as she put it on.

"Read the inscription."

Elise took the bracelet off, looked inside and found the inscription.

With Faith Anything Is Possible

"I like those words. The bracelet is beautiful."

He was pleased to hear Elise say that she liked his inspirational gift. Her reaction gave him the confidence to just tell her plain and simple what he believed God had shown him last night.

"Elise, I prayed last night and I believe God told me not to let you lie to the court today, about being seen by Tom Johnstone."

There it was, he had said it. He was not lying anymore, regardless of the consequences.

Elise displayed little reaction, other than to study her bracelet. He was worried that she would look at him as though he had two heads.

"The consequences of lying are always worse than the consequences of telling the truth."

Still no response from Elise.

"I should have told you the truth that night that I went over to help Mia. I am sorry for that lie. If I had told you the truth, we would not be standing here today.

"Elise, Claye believes *with faith anything is possible*. I am coming around to that belief myself.

"I need you to have some faith in me at the moment because I believe I know what to do."

Dan studied Elise's face not knowing what to expect from her. He really had no idea how she was going to react. He had to admit he sounded more than a little crazy.

Elise turned her attention from the bracelet and looked straight at him.

"I shouldn't, I know I shouldn't; you have let me down so many times. But for some strange reason, I still believe in you. I still want to be with you. I still love you. Whatever you want to do, I am with you."

With that they hugged each other tightly and kissed. It wasn't as passionate an embrace and kiss as they used to have when they were first married, but it was a more solid, committed and faithful embrace this time. It was as though all the garbage of blame and mistrust had finally been thrown out of their relationship and they were starting afresh.

"You will be fine, Elise, just tell them your story."

"I am scared. I could be locked up tonight for a crime I didn't commit."

"With faith anything is possible. Tell them the truth, they will believe you."

Dan took Elise's hand in his, finger against finger. He then kissed Elise's hand and gently let it go.

"I have to go now. I will see you in there. Remember, I have a plan. You are not alone and regardless of what happens today, you will never be alone again."

Elise looked close to tears as Dan tore himself away from her. He had to tear himself away from her as he had something very important that he needed to discuss with Robin.

*

Dan sat in the crowded courtroom waiting for Robin to arrive. Robin didn't arrive until right on 10:00am when they were supposed to start hearing evidence.

"You're late," Dan quipped as Robin hurriedly unpacked his papers and threw them across the desk.

"Sorry about that. Traffic jam, they just appear out of nowhere sometimes."

Dan could relate to traffic jams just appearing out of nowhere and he could relate to the fact Robin had arrived late. But the fact he could relate to why Robin was late, did not help him discuss his plan with Robin, before the trial began for the day.

"Is Elise ready to go this morning?"

"Yes, I have talked with her and she is right to go. I think she will be very good in the witness box today."

"I certainly hope so, or else we are dead in the water."

Dan was surprised by Robin's pessimism.

Just then everybody stood while Her Honour walked in and sat down.

"You said yesterday we were still in this trial?" Dan whispered as they sat down together.

"I was trying to keep your spirits up. Last night when I was preparing my closing address, it really hit me, we are in deep shit!"

"Mr Banks, we do not use that type of language in a court of law. I expect my barristers and solicitors to set an example to the rest of the community of appropriate behaviour in the courtroom."

"Sorry, Your Honour, I was just having a private conversation with my instructing solicitor."

"Next time do so in a more temperate language."

Dan smiled as Her Honour sprung Robin for using inappropriate language.

"Mr Banks, any more witnesses for the defence?"

"Yes, Your Honour we have one final witness. I call Elise Grover to the stand."

There was a stir in the court as Dan watched Elise rise from the dock and slowly make her way to the witness box.

"Just before we start with the examination-in-chief of this witness, please note that we need to finish this trial today or tomorrow at the very latest, as I have an medical appointment tomorrow afternoon that I can not miss," Her Honour informed the assembled gathering at the court.

During examination-in-chief with Robin asking Elise questions, she seemed quite calm and at peace with herself. Certainly Dan noticed many jury members listening intently to every word and watching every movement Elise made.

Elise told the jury she was wearing a dark brown jacket and jeans the day of the murder but that she most definitely was not wearing a baseball cap.

Elise ended her testimony by saying she was just a victim of circumstance, being in the wrong place at the wrong time.

So far so good. But the moment of truth had arrived. It was now or never. Elise was to be cross-examined by that super cool cat, Chad Gabriel.

"Mrs Grover, can you explain exactly what you saw your husband and the deceased doing on the night you followed him to her house."

"I saw them embrace."

"That's all?"

"That's all."

"Did you see them kissing?"

"Yes."

"That's more than an embrace, isn't it?"

"Kissing was part of the embrace."

"I see. Did they appear to you like they were kissing passionately?"

"I couldn't tell they were too far away."

"Could they have been embracing and kissing like old friends?"

"I suppose, I don't know, I only saw them for a few minutes."

"So are you telling this court you went to see the deceased the next day, to discuss what could have been a platonic embrace?"

"I didn't know for sure what happened."

"Exactly, Mrs Grover, you didn't know for sure what happened between the deceased and your husband that night, did you? Really they could have engaged in sexual activity all night. For all you knew they could have been at it like rabbits."

Elise did not respond to the question.

Chad Gabriel took the lack of response as a yes and looked to the jury to ensure they took it as a yes as well. Some of the jurors looked confused.

"Mrs Grover, the court needs an answer."

Eventually and reluctantly Elise nodded.

"Mrs Grover, we need an audible answer for the recording?"

"Yes, I don't know exactly what happened that night between my husband and the deceased," snapped Elise.

"Mrs Grover, what did you think happened between your husband and the deceased that night?"

"I have already told you, I don't know what happened."

"That's not what I am asking. I am not asking what happened; I am asking what you thought happened?"

"I believe my husband when he says nothing really happened, except some hugging and kissing for a couple of minutes."

"No, Mrs Grover, perhaps I am not making myself clear enough for you to understand. At the time you saw your husband and the deceased that night, at that time, what did you think they were getting up to?"

"Be honest now, Mrs Grover, you have sworn an oath today to tell the truth."

Elise looked over at Dan who nodded in her direction. He wanted her to tell the truth.

"I thought, I thought that they were having sex."

"How did that make you feel, Mrs Grover, knowing that your husband was having sex with another woman?"

"Objection, Your Honour. Mrs Grover has already testified she did not *know* that her husband was having sex with another woman."

"Your Honour, I will gladly rephrase the question for the benefit of my learned friend."

"How did that make you feel, Mrs Grover, sitting there alone in your car that night, thinking that your husband was in the house across the street having sex with another woman?"

Elise looked at Dan again with a concerned expression.

"Mrs Grover, if I could have your attention. You need to answer my questions truthfully and honestly without looking at your husband to get his approval for your answers."

Elise returned her gaze to Chad Gabriel. "Honestly, I felt betrayed, I felt angry. I was in shock."

"You were angry when you went to confront the deceased the next day weren't you?"

"I was angry the first time I went to see her, yes, I admit that."

"Why were you angry with her?"

"Because she had slept with my husband. I mean that's what I thought at the time."

"That anger you took with you to see the deceased led you to having an argument with her, didn't it?"

"Yes, we argued. I don't know if my anger led to the argument. It could have."

"You were angry with the deceased after you argued with her, were you not?"

"I don't know if I was overly angry with her then."

"You had an argument, a shouting match I believe, with someone who you believed had just slept with your husband and you are telling this court you were no longer angry with her. I would have thought you would have been more angry with her after the argument."

"I was still angry with her, I suppose."

"Why were you still angry with her?"

"Because she just would not tell me what had happened that night and she would not promise to stay away from my husband."

"You are still angry when you go back and see the deceased a second time."

"No, my anger had subsided by that time. The second time I just wanted to talk to her, without anger."

"Mrs Grover, are you expecting this court to accept that what, in an hour or two, the anger you felt towards the deceased just vanished into thin air?"

"That's right."

"Come now, Mrs Grover, we all live in the real world here. You were angry at the deceased for sleeping with your husband, you were angry at the deceased for arguing with you, you were angry at the deceased for not telling you what had happened between her and your husband, you were angry at the deceased for not giving you an assurance that she would stay away from your husband. In fact, Mrs Grover, I put it to you, you were so angry with the deceased an hour later that you went back over to her house with the intention of murdering her."

"No, that's not right," Elise said faintly.

"I put it to you Mrs Grover that you made nice to the deceased so she would let you into her house. Once inside the house, you took advantage of your situation and you struck the victim from behind with her own glass vase. Then you angrily, callously, repeatedly struck her around the head despite the fact that she had been killed from the first few blows."

"No, I didn't do that."

Dan could barely hear Elise and he was not sure the jury could hear her either. It was obvious to everybody that Elise was near tears.

Dan elbowed Robin in the ribs. "Make an objection, he is harassing her."

"He is just putting the Crown case to her, that is his job," Robin replied.

"I put it to you, Mrs Grover, that you were angry enough to confront the deceased, that you were angry enough to argue with the deceased and that you were angry enough to kill the deceased," Chad Gabriel said with vigour throwing his arms into the air and then looking at the jury.

Elise did not respond.

"I put it to you, Mrs Grover, that the evidence establishes that the murderer killed the deceased in a rage of passion, of intense anger and you are the only one we have heard from in these court proceedings, Mrs Grover, that fits this profile; an intensely angry killer who engaged in a crime of passion."

Tears began to roll softly down Elise's cheek. She could no longer contain her emotions.

"I object, Your Honour!" Dan shouted as he jumped to his feet. "He is harassing the witness. I thought everybody was supposed to be treated with respect in this courtroom."

Chad Gabriel sat down and let Her Honour deal with Dan's objection.

"Mr Grover, I have allowed you in good faith to act as instructing solicitor in this trial, even though you are the husband of the accused. If there is a legitimate objection to be made regarding Mr Gabriel's questioning of the accused, then I expect that objection to come from your Counsel, Mr Banks.

"I do not expect objections to come from someone who is related to the accused, especially when they have their own Counsel present to make such objections. Otherwise it appears that those objections are based on emotion rather than legal principle. I can't and won't tolerate emotional objections in my court, Mr Grover. Do you understand where I am coming from?"

"Yes, Your Honour."

"Mr Grover, I sympathise with your position but I just can't let you make objections. Can I trust you to remain at the Bar table or should you remove yourself if you are finding it difficult to control yourself?"

"Your Honour, I need to remain at the Bar table, I will control myself, I promise."

"Alright I will let you stay, but anymore outbursts and you will have to leave the Bar table."

Dan nodded and looked around the court room as he sat down. He noticed Samuel Sanderson and his wife sitting at the back of the courtroom. Samuel was grinning. It was a silly grin. Samuel seemed to be enjoying Elise's discomfort at the hands of Chad Gabriel.

Samuel's wife appeared to be more interested in Samuel and his hands, than what was going on in Court. Dan wondered what Samuel's hands actually looked like. From what he could see in the witness box Samuel had quite small hands but they had deliberately not asked Samuel to show his hands to the jury in cross-examination; just in case Samuel had calluses or some other distinguishing mark on his hands which would have made it impossible for his hands to have been recognized by Tom Johnstone.

"Mrs Grover, are you right to continue? As I said at the outset of proceedings this morning, we need to wrap this trial up today if possible, but if you still need a couple of minutes to compose yourself that would be fine."

"No, I am fine, Your Honour. Does that mean the jury will have to deliver their verdict today?"

"No, once the jury has been tasked to determine their verdict, we will vacate this courtroom. When the jury has reached a verdict, we can resume to hear their verdict. There is no set time for the jury to reach a decision. Mr Gabriel, are you nearly finished with this witness?"

"Thank you, Your Honour. I still have a few more questions.

"Mrs Grover, why did you lie to Senior Detective Sloan about handling the glass vase, the murder weapon?"

"I didn't lie to him. It was all such a shock for me. I was just trying to forget what happened. When he asked me out of the blue about a glass vase, I had just forgotten that I had touched it. To me the glass vase was an insignificant part of the whole picture.

"After my interview with Detective Sloan, it all came back to me. I remember that I moved the glass vase out of the way when I turned the poor girl's body over to see if she was still alive."

"That's very convenient, how you could remember touching the glass vase some time after you were told your fingerprints were on it," Chad Gabriel said looking intently at the jury while rubbing his hand slowly through his quite considerable head of black hair.

"Well I have been thinking about that, Mr Gabriel, and all I can say is it is similar to your witness Tom Johnstone."

"How so, Mrs Grover?"

"Mr Johnstone initially did not mention seeing the person's hands, their rings and nail polish in his evidence; he only remembered this in cross-examination when he was questioned about why he was so sure he had seen a woman leave the deceased's house. Then, it all came back to him.

"Similarly with me. After thinking about it, it has all came back to me."

Good point, Mrs Grover, Dan thought as he flashed her an encouraging smile.

Chad Gabriel did not like witnesses scoring points on him. It was fine for him to show them up, but he distinctly did not like being shown up by witnesses.

"You are quite clever, Mrs Grover, aren't you? Perhaps you can tell me how the murder weapon, the glass vase with your fingerprints on it, came to be found hidden under a sofa some four metres away from where the victim's body was found?"

"I have thought and thought about that, Mr Gabriel, and all I can tell you is that I honestly don't know how it got there. It was not found until some two weeks after the murder. Maybe, one of the other cleaners pushed it under there."

"Is that your evidence, Mrs Grover, that one of the cleaners pushed the glass vase under the sofa?"

"My evidence, Mr Gabriel, is that I don't know how the vase got under the sofa. I moved the vase out of the way but I can't explain how it got under the sofa across the room."

"Mrs Grover, you can do better than that. Think for a moment you will come up with an answer to fit the facts, I am sure of it."

"I am sure of this fact, Mr Gabriel, I would not like to be married to you; if you treat your wife with that same smarmy, disrespectful attitude you have shown me."

"You would much rather be married to your husband, Mrs Grover. Someone who is prone to extra-marital dalliances, who engages in unethical and unprofessional conduct, who lies to the police and who in all likelihood is going to be disbarred."

"Yes, Mr Gabriel, I would much rather be married to my husband than you, of that fact I am certain."

There was the spirited Elise, Dan had come to know and love.

"Your Honour, this is not cross-examination, it's a debate."

"Say no more, Mr Banks. Mr Gabriel, have you got any further useful and relevant questions for this witness?"

Chad Gabriel flicked his slick black hair one more time and said, "Yes, Your Honour."

"Mrs Grover, you have told this court that you found the deceased lying face down on the floor and you moved the glass vase out of the way as you reached down and turned the deceased over. You turned her over to see how she was. To determine the extent of her injuries. Is that correct?"

"Yes," Elise said tentatively.

"Well, I put it to you that you are lying."

"I am not lying at all. That's exactly what happened. It's not a story I just made up, Mr Gabriel."

"Well, Mrs Grover, perhaps you can help me out then with a problem I have with your story. The evidence from the pathologist which, by the way was not disputed by your learned Counsel, is that the deceased was first struck from behind and then later she was repeatedly struck to the side and front of her head. How then did the deceased come to be lying face down when you found her, when all the blows except the first one, came to front and side of her head, not the back of her head?"

Elise shot a worried look at Dan. He didn't have an answer for her. It was a good question. How did the body come to be lying face down, rather than face up? Dan didn't know the answer, nor did Elise.

"Mrs Grover, I am waiting for an answer to my question?"

"I don't know, I can't explain it," Elise mumbled somehow hoping the jury would not hear her answer.

"You can't explain it. You can't explain how you found the deceased lying face down. Well I can explain it and I will be explaining it to the jury in my closing address. I will be pointing out to them that your husband is not the only one in your family prone to making up stories." Chad Gabriel said these words loudly enough for not only the jury to hear them but everybody in the courtroom as well.

"Your Honour, is Mr Gabriel's performance really necessary. Could he just ask questions without the theatrics?" interjected Robin.

"Mr Gabriel, I am keen to move along with this trial. Do you have any further questions for this witness?"

"Yes, Your Honour, just a couple more questions."

"Proceed."

"Witness can you tell me why you repeatedly bleached the clothes you wore on the night Ms Wong was killed?"

"I am sorry, I don't understand the question."

"Alright, I will explain the question for you. The forensic report tendered to this court indicates that, despite you repeatedly bleaching your clothes and scrubbing your shoes, some minute particles of the deceased's blood were found on them. Why did you work so hard trying to clean your clothes and your shoes?"

"I wanted to get the blood off them."

"Ah ha, at last an honest answer, Mrs Grover."

Chad Gabriel turned to face the jury and said, "You admit to repeatedly bleaching your clothes and scrubbing your shoes because you wanted to get the victim's blood off them."

Chad Gabriel let his words just hang there for what seemed like a full minute. He obviously wanted the jury to remember them.

"Your clothes and shoes had a lot of blood on them, didn't they Mrs Grover? They must have or you wouldn't have worked so hard to clean them?"

"They had some blood on them but I wouldn't say they had a lot of blood on them."

"You repeatedly bleached your clothes and scrubbed your shoes but they didn't have a lot of blood on them?"

"Yes."

Chad Gabriel just smiled at the jury after Elise answered this question.

"Mrs Grover, is it your evidence that you were not the woman Tom Johnstone saw leaving the victim's house?"

"Yes, that's right."

"But you were wearing similar clothes to the woman he described, you had blood stained clothing and, from your own admission, left the victim's house around the time he came by. I am puzzled then as to who this other mystery woman could be?"

"I don't know who it might be. It could be that Tom Johnstone was mistaken and he saw a man who dressed to look like a woman."

"Come on, Mrs Grover, do you really expect us to believe that self-serving conjecture?"

"It could not have been me as I don't wear baseball caps. I never have. They give me headaches. I mean, the neighbour did not see me wearing a baseball cap when I entered the house did she?"

"No, she didn't, Mrs Grover, you are right, you are too clever for me. Perhaps you thought you were too clever for everybody. Perhaps you kept the baseball cap hidden under your jacket when you arrived and then put it on to hide your face after you had done the fateful deed of taking an innocent young woman's life. A young woman who was obviously no match for your intellectual abilities.

"I mean hitting her from behind like that, after she had let you in and turned her back on you. I mean that was pure genius."

"I didn't kill her!" Elise pleaded as she raised her distressed voice and banged a clenched fist down on the wooden rail beside her.

"Are you getting angry over there, Mrs Grover, do you feel like hitting me? Perhaps if I turn around you might want to hit me from behind?"

"Your Honour, is this a relevant line of questioning or is Mr Gabriel regressing back to his High School musical days of Gilbert and Sullivan?" Robin interjected.

"I will move on, Your Honour, only a few questions left.

"Mrs Grover, do you consider yourself to be a gentle, non-violent person?"

"I try to be."

"You try to be but sometimes your emotions get the better of you and you lash out at people who you believe have hurt you."

"If you are referring to the incident with my ex-boyfriend, that was a long time ago and I was very young and naïve at the time."

"Mrs Grover, you attacked your boyfriend and a female friend of his with a tyre lever."

"I did not attack them. I attacked his car."

"My information is that you were so angry you attacked your boyfriend's car while he and the young lady were still inside the car and at some point, you threatened to kill them both."

Elise did not respond but looked at the ground.

"Why were you so angry? What could possibly have led you to such violent behavior?"

Elise again did not respond. Her gaze remained fixed to the ground.

"Mrs Grover, there is no need for you to answer this question. If you like I can answer it for you and tell the jury."

Elise appeared to be in a trance like state and she did not move a muscle.

"Alright, I will answer the question for you and you let me know if I am wrong.

"You took a tyre lever to your boyfriend's car and threatened to bash him and his female friend because he was cheating on you. His infidelity caused your blood to boil with such anger that you became violent and aggressive towards him and his female friend.

"Isn't that right Mrs Grover? Tell the jury I am wrong."

Elise did not speak but continued to look down.

Chad Gabriel sighed, shook his head several times and looked to the jury.

"In fact, Mrs Grover, you were convicted of several criminal offences as a result of this frightening and frenzied attack.

Elise put her hand over her face and wiped away a solitary tear.

After a few seconds Chad Gabriel finally said, "I have no further questions for this witness, Your Honour. I have obtained all the information the Crown needs in this case."

"Any re-examination, Mr Banks?"

"Yes, Your Honour, one question.

"Mrs Grover, why did you want to wash the blood off your clothes and shoes?"

Elise did not respond.

"Mrs Grover, you should answer the question your Counsel has asked you," Her Honour said gently.

Elise still did not respond but continued staring at her feet.

"I will rephrase the question, Your Honour.

"Were you trying to avoid detection by cleaning your clothes and shoes?"

"No, I had done nothing other than discover a body. Why would I be trying to avoid detection if I had done nothing wrong? I just didn't want the poor young woman's blood on my clothes and shoes."

"No, further questions Your Honour."

"Well then it's time for closing submissions. Mr Banks, we will hear from you first."

Robin began to stand when Dan realised what was happening and he pulled Robin back down.

"We have another witness to examine, we are not finished yet," Dan whispered to Robin.

"Yes we are, we have called all the witnesses we planned to. Stroke of genius you were able to get Kathleen Brown to testify via video link. There are no other witnesses. Now it's time for closing submissions."

"No, there is still someone else to call."

"Mr Banks, time is marching on, can you begin your closing submissions now?"

Dan pulled at Robin's arm as he began to stand again. "Robin, no, I have to talk to you about something. Ask for a ten minute recess."

"Why, I am ready to present our closing submissions?"

"Mr Banks, please, you are holding me up."

"Look Dan, I don't want to upset the judge," Robin whispered.

"Your Honour the defence requests a ten minute recess. There is a possibility that one further witness may be called," Dan said, much to everyone's astonishment, not the least being Robin.

"Is this right, Mr Banks?" Her Honour said rather annoyed. "Are you running the defendant's case or is your instructing solicitor running the case for the defence? You know I would like to wrap this trial up today. "

Robin looked at Dan and then back at Her Honour.

"Your Honour, something has just come to my attention. I need to discuss it with Mr Grover. We will only need ten minutes."

Robin ignored Her Honour's question about whether he or Dan was in charge of the defence case.

"I will give you five minutes and I won't be happy if you intend to drag this case out. Court is adjourned."

CHAPTER FORTY EIGHT

Dan led Robin into a nearby interview room.

"What's going on?" Robin demanded before he had even sat down.

"We need to examine one last witness," Dan said.

"No we don't, we have heard from everybody. What's all this about?"

"I have been trying to speak to you about this. God spoke to me last night and from what he showed me I believe we need to examine…"

Dan stopped in his tracks. He had barely got the words out when he realised what he had said. To tell anyone, let alone an intelligent guy like Robin, that he had heard from God was like a putting a sign on his forehead saying:

I am crazy. Please take me to the insane asylum immediately.

"Let me rephrase that, I had a revelation last night. Our case has always been that Samuel Sanderson killed Mia. Brock Shepard could have killed her but it's more likely that Samuel killed her, agreed."

Robin nodded his head cautiously.

"We need to come at this from a different angle. We have sought to attack Tom Johnstone's memory. I mean, how can he be so sure he saw a woman not a man? But he was very convincing in the witness box.

"What came to me was that it may be smarter to come at this from a completely different angle. What we need to do is cross-examine Samuel Sanderson's wife.

"We know Samuel Sanderson is a serial sex offender, so surely she must know he is a serial sex offender. What has it been like for her to live with a serial sex offender, isn't she worried about her own children, why is she still living with a serial sex offender, why did she provide an alibi to a serial sex offender? Did she know about the threatening note? Can we shake her alibi evidence? If we can, then its game, set and match for us."

"I don't know, Dan, she seems pretty fixated with him when I have seen them together in court. I seriously doubt she is going to say anything against him."

"I think it is worth a try, you said yourself we are in trouble."

"Even if we can convince the judge to declare her a hostile witness, she will probably just clam up and give us yes or no answers. The judge wants to finish the trial today. I think it is better not to risk questioning the wife and keep the judge onside."

Robin stood up to leave.

"Robin, not only am I convinced that we need to examine Samuel Sanderson's wife, I need to personally undertake her examination. I have thought of a few questions which may fly close to the wind of appropriate questioning and it is better if you are not involved."

"What do you mean, not involved, I am Elise's barrister!"

"If someone is to get in trouble for the questioning that takes place then it should be me, not you. I am already likely to be disbarred."

"No, this is silly talk. I am not going to let you drag down Elise's case by hijacking her defence to ask some convoluted questions to Sanderson's wife. I just don't see the point in this whole exercise."

"I would love to have you with me on this. But if you don't agree to call Sanderson's wife, then Elise will sack you as Counsel and I will take over."

Robin sat back down.

"But I have got all my closing arguments prepared, why would you risk all that now?"

"I don't want to lose you. All I want is for you to agree to let me question Samuel Sanderson's wife, that's all."

"I don't know why I agreed to take this case on in first place. I must be stark raving mad."

Just then Her Honour's Associate knocked on their door, partly opened it and told them Justice Hooper was asking for them.

"Are you coming?" Dan asked expectantly.

"This has to do with you hearing voices, supposedly talking with God, doesn't it?"

"Yes," Dan said looking Robin squarely in the eye.

"You haven't told me the whole story of what's going on here, have you?"

"No, we haven't got time."

"Look, I have a reputation to uphold. I can't get involved in crazy stuff like this," Robin said as he remained firmly seated.

"Ok, Robin, thanks for all your help, I really appreciate it."

Dan walked backed into the courtroom alone.

"Where is Mr Banks? We need to move on with this trial," Her Honour was the first to speak.

Dan stood and said, "Your Honour, Mr Banks, is no longer representing the accused I am."

"Is that correct, Mrs Grover?"

Elise looked at Dan. He nodded and mouthed the words, *have faith.*

"Yes, Your Honour I want my husband to represent me."

"Well this is most extraordinary."

"Your Honour I would like to call just one more witness before the defence closes its case."

"Who is that, Mr Grover, and why do we need to hear from this particular witness now the trial is virtually finished?"

"Your Honour, the defence calls Mrs Grace Sanderson to the witness box."

"Your Honour, I object." Chad Gabriel was quickly on his feet but he hesitated slightly before speaking so that the members of the public who were talking feverishly would stop talking and listen to him.

"Your Honour, a check of the Court Registry this morning by my clerk indicated that the defence has filed no subpoenas. Are we to wait for the defence to prepare, file and then serve a subpoena on Mrs Sanderson?"

Chad Gabriel continued, "In light of Her Honour's expressed desire to finish this trial today, this is nothing more than a stunt, an outrage, a misguided attempt by the defence to delay this matter for some reason."

"Mr Grover, I agree with Mr Gabriel. You should have filed a subpoena if you wanted to compel Mrs Sanderson to give evidence. The fact you have lost your opportunity to examine her lies with you, not with me."

Dan didn't know what to say. It had slipped his mind that he needed a subpoena to examine Samuel's wife, in fact he only worked out his proposed examination of her last night. But why would God give him the picture from which he formulated his plan, if he couldn't examine her?

"I am sorry Mr Grover, but I can't allow you to delay this trial by issuing a subpoena to Mrs Sanderson. I therefore rule that her testimony not be ....."

"Your Honour, Mrs Sanderson can be examined without the issuing of a subpoena."

Dan looked around and there was Robin. He was talking as he was walking into the courtroom.

"I am sorry, Mr Banks, but I thought you were no longer representing the accused and Mr Grover was now representing her. I am confused. Can someone please tell me what is going on?"

"Yes, Your Honour, I apologise for the confusion. Quite simply, Mr Grover and I had a minor disagreement but that has now been resolved. I am still representing the accused, though my client's instructions are quite specific in that she wants Mr Grover to examine Mrs Sanderson, I will follow with closing submissions.

"As for the examination of Mrs Sanderson, she is present in the courtroom. I believe she is sitting over there."

Robin pointed to Samuel and his wife sitting at the rear of the court.

"As Mrs Sanderson is actually in the precincts of the court she can be compelled to take the stand regardless of whether or not a subpoena has been issued requiring her attendance."

Dan smiled and gave Robin the thumbs up.

"Mr Banks, I was not aware that Mrs Sanderson was actually in court. From what Mr Gabriel said I was led to believe that a subpoena would have been necessary to require her attendance before the court."

"That's understandable, Your Honour. Mr Gabriel can at times be quite persuasive, despite the fact that he is incorrect." Robin said turning to look at Chad Gabriel who was ever so slowly inching further into his chair.

"We are ready to go, Your Honour. The defence calls Mrs Sanderson" declared Robin.

"Your Honour, the defence has not outlined the relevance of this witness. Surely they cannot just pick names out of a hat," Chad Gabriel interjected back on his feet.

"Mr Banks, the relevance of this witness?"

"I can answer that question, Your Honour," Dan said. "This witness provided the only alibi for Mr Sanderson. It is the defence submission that other people, such as Mr Sanderson, should be considered by the jury as more likely to have committed this murder than the accused. Therefore, it is entirely appropriate and reasonable to test that alibi evidence in court."

"Your Honour the defence has continued to put Mr Sanderson on trial here, seemingly oblivious to the fact that he is not on trial here. Please invoke the mercy rule and put them out of their misery before it's too late," Chad

Gabriel said with some authority and posturing.

After some moments Her Honour spoke. "I will allow Mrs Sanderson to be examined. But Mr Grover please be careful in your questioning of her. I do not want this to be a fishing expedition. Ask only relevant questions and then stop. Do you understand me?"

"Yes ,Your Honour, I understand," Dan said.

"Alright, I understand Mrs Sanderson is in the court. Please stand up. I am sorry, but I can't see you," Her Honour said.

Just then a man shouted angrily at the judge, "You can't do this. This is bullshit!"

"Who are you?" asked Her Honour in amazement.

The man stood up and pointed at Her Honour. "I am Samuel Sanderson and this is a *mickey mouse* court. It's all bullshit. My wife is not testifying until I call my lawyer, Connor Mead."

"Mr Sanderson this is not your court, this is not *mickey mouse's* court, this is my court! Believe me when I tell you that you and your lawyer, no matter who he is, do what I tell you to do. I do not do what you tell me to do!

"Now is that your wife sitting next to you?"

Dan answered Her Honour's question, "Yes, that's Mrs Sanderson."

"Bailiff, please escort Mrs Sanderson to the witness box and please escort Mr Sanderson out of this courtroom. He can come back in once he has calmed down and found his lawyer. I will not stand for him or anyone else in my courtroom treating it like a circus. Do you hear me?"

The bailiff duly escorted Mrs Sanderson to the witness box. Samuel Sanderson shouted out to his wife, "Don't you tell them anything. Wait for me to get back!"

The bailiff then turned to escort Samuel Sanderson out of the courtroom but he had fled the courtroom well and truly before the bailiff could get hold of him.

CHAPTER FORTY NINE

Dan studied Grace Sanderson as she took the oath. She was an overweight, largely unattractive, middle aged woman with long, untidy brown hair. She was wearing a creased floral dress that barely covered her. Dan was no fashionista but surely floral dresses like that went out of fashion many years ago.

Before Dan began his examination of Mrs Sanderson he took a long look around the courtroom. He saw Chad Gabriel and then further behind him sitting in the middle of the courtroom he identified Sloan and Sarah. His extended view of the courtroom was cut short as Her Honour began speaking to the witness.

"Mrs Sanderson regardless of what your husband has said to you, this is a court of law and you must answer truthfully all the questions put to you. The only exception is that you do not have to answer a question on the ground that to do so, to answer that question, may incriminate you as regards to a criminal offence. Do you understand?" asked Her Honour.

Mrs Sanderson nodded her head but Dan felt she did not understand.

"Let the recording show that Mrs Sanderson nodded that she did understand. Mrs Sanderson you have been called to provide evidence in this trial by the defence. That means Mr Grover will ask you some questions and then Mr Gabriel, the prosecutor, will ask you some questions. It is very important having regard to the oath you just took, to answer each question truthfully and honestly to best of your knowledge. Do you understand?"

Mrs Sanderson nodded her head again but Dan was still not sure she really understood what was happening to her.

"Let the recording show that Mrs Sanderson again nodded that she did understand what was happening here. Mrs Sanderson we are electronically recording what is being said in this trial so you will need to answer questions verbally, you can't just nod your head. Do you understand?" asked Her Honour.

Mrs Sanderson nodded her head again.

For all intents and purposes Grace Sanderson appeared to be like a deer stuck in the headlights. She certainly did not appear to be overly bright.

Her Honour shook her head and gave up speaking to Mrs Sanderson.

"Your witness, Mr Grover."

"Witness can you tell the court your full name?"

"Grace Emily Sanderson," came the cautious reply.

"Are you married?"

"Sort of."

"What do you mean sort of? Are you legally married or not?"

"No, I am not married."

"Do you live with someone?"

Grace Sanderson hesitated before answering, "Yes."

"Who do you live with and how long have you lived with this person?"

"That's my business. It's got nothing to do with you."

"Your Honour, can the witness be directed to answer the question?"

"Mrs Sanderson, as I told you when you took the stand. Regardless of what your husband, or partner, or whoever that unruly man is to you, you are in a court of law now and must answer the questions put to you."

"Mrs Sanderson, who do you live with and how long have you lived with this person?" Dan asked again.

"I live with Samuel Sanderson and we have been living together for 13 years."

"Is your last name really Sanderson?"

"Yes."

"How can that be if you are not legally married to Mr Sanderson?"

"I changed my last name to Sanderson about ten years ago."

"Did you change your name legally, through the Department of Births Deaths and Marriages?"

"I don't know."

"Why did you change your name?"

"That's private between me and Samuel."

"Your Honour?"

"Mrs Sanderson you have to answer the question. Unless an answer to a question may incriminate you, you have no other option but to answer every question put to you."

"Why did you change your last name to Sanderson?" Dan repeated.

Grace Sanderson did not reply.

Dan looked at Her Honour.

"Mrs Sanderson this is becoming tiresome and time consuming. You have to answer the questions put to you or I will hold you in contempt of court. That means you could be sent to jail for not answering Mr Grover's questions. Do you understand?"

Grace Sanderson confirmed her understanding of contempt by answering Dan's question.

"Samuel and I are together forever, we are never going to separate. I wanted to show him I don't care that he doesn't want to get married. I mean it's just a piece of paper. I love him, he is everything to me."

"You wanted to show Samuel you were committed to him, is that right?"

"Objection, Your Honour, Mr Grover is leading the witness," Chad Gabriel said with authority.

"Your Honour, if I could have some latitude with this witness. She is the defacto wife of someone who the defence believes may have committed this murder. Perhaps if she could be declared a hostile witness?"

"Mr Gabriel, what do you think?" asked Her Honour.

"The witness has not said anything overtly hostile to the defence at this point, Your Honour."

"Given the circumstances surrounding how the witness came to be called to give evidence today, given the importance of the alibi evidence to be provided by this witness, given the witness has already exhibited an attitude of non-cooperation towards Mr Grover's questioning of her; I will allow Mr Grover's request for this witness to be declared a hostile witness."

"Thank you, Your Honour."

Dan looked at Grace Sanderson, she obviously had no idea what had just transpired. By being declared a hostile witness Dan could effectively cross-examine Grace Sanderson like she was a witness for the prosecution, even though he was the one who had called her to give evidence.

Under the rules of evidence, leading questions were only allowed to be asked in cross-examination, when you were examining the other side's witnesses. However if you were successful in having a witness you called declared *hostile*, you could effectively cross-examine them like they were the other side's witness. Hence you could ask them leading questions.

"By changing your surname to his, you wanted to show your partner that you were committed to him, isn't that the case?"

"Yes. Samuel is my soul mate and I am his, we will always be together."

"What is Samuel like?"

"Please, Your Honour, what is this, an episode of Oprah?" Chad Gabriel was again on his feet.

"Your Honour, if I might be allowed to ask my questions without interruption I will be finished with this witness much sooner and the trial will be over much quicker," Dan responded.

"Mr Gabriel, I don't know how someone as obviously as intelligent and as sure of himself as you, can't read the signals I am sending out. I allowed you to present evidence from a surprise witness. I allowed the defence to call a last minute witness. I allowed Mr Grover in these special circumstances to cross-examine his own witness. Can't you see that I have been extremely lenient in allowing both sides to present their evidence in this case.

"Now let Mr Grover finish his cross-examination of this witness unhindered, without wasting precious time on petty objections. If you have a legitimate objection to make then please do so. Otherwise sit tight and like the rest of us listen to what this witness has to say."

"You may press on Mr Grover but please make your questions relevant and to the point."

"Thank you, Your Honour.

"Mrs Sanderson, I am just trying to find out why you would want to change your name to Sanderson? Why you would want to be with someone who isn't prepared to marry you?"

"I love him."

"But what is he like, why do you love him?"

"He is very handsome. He looks after me."

"What else?" Dan asked.

"He is nice to me. He does special things for me."

"Has he ever hit you?"

"No!"

Grace Sanderson immediately looked at Dan in an aggressive fashion. Previous to this question Grace had been looking all around the courtroom but never straight at Dan. Now her piercing blue eyes looked straight into his eyes and he was a little taken aback with the intensity of that look. It alarmed him.

"Has he ever sexually assaulted you?"

"Of course not."

"Has he ever sexually assaulted anybody else?"

"What are you talking about? My Samuel would never do anything like that."

"Mrs Sanderson, I am talking about three young women, Mia Wong, Kathleen Brown and Amanda Peterson all of whom complained that your husband, Samuel Sanderson, sexually assaulted them."

"They all lied, I don't believe them."

"But why would they all lie, why would all three of these young women who didn't even know each other, all say the same thing about your husband? Why would they all say he is a sexual predator?"

"Because they are all prostitutes and tramps, that's why!" Grace Sanderson shouted.

Dan slowly moved his head from looking at the jury and locked his eyes on Grace Sanderson's haunting blue eyes. It was as if he had just had another revelation.

"It's funny you should use the word *tramp*, to describe these women. That is exactly the word that was used to describe them on a threatening note they each received before they were killed or disappeared."

"Why *tramp* that's a common word, plenty of people use it."

"But it was used on all three notes. The exact word you used to describe these three young women was used on all three threatening notes. That's pretty telling don't you think?"

"No, that's not right."

"That is right, Mrs Sanderson. You are wrong. I saw one of the notes."

"No, that's not right. You're wrong mr big shot lawyer. They weren't called tramps."

"I beg your pardon?"

"The word was *trollop*, not tramp. So you are wrong. Dead set wrong about everything. You have no idea what's been going on."

Dan leaned over the lectern on the bar table. He was almost hyperventilating. He was that nervous with the next question he was about to ask, he was breaking out in goose bumps.

"Tell me, Grace, set the record straight once and for all, what has been going on?"

Dan had just finished asking this question, when he heard noises behind him like chairs being flung across the room. He was much too focused on Grace Sanderson's answer to his question than to bother turning around and see what was happening.

Dan did hear the words, *You're dead*! shouted by someone near him, just before he was king hit. He crumpled to the side of the bar table and felt excruciating pain to his head and his ribs as the assailant then jumped on top of him.

At that point he recognized Samuel Sanderson kneeling on him and punching him in the face. He raised his arms and defended his face from the blows but he could not stop all the punches. It was like Samuel Sanderson was a mad man who was obsessed with punching him, inflicting pain on him, killing him.

Dan's vision became blurry. He wondered why the court bailiff and Elise's corrections officer were not helping him. Just then he noticed that there was someone on top of Samuel, gouging his eyes. It was a woman. It was Elise. She must have jumped from the dock and been the only one brave enough to help him.

Samuel stopped punching Dan and tried to fight off his attacker but Elise was not letting go, despite being hit several times by Samuel. Samuel threw Elise over the bar table.

Samuel was then swamped by at least four other people. He thought he recognized the court bailiff, Elise's corrections officer, Sloan and another man in a long black robe who must have been Robin. It had taken four men to knock Samuel to the floor and to physically restrain him.

Dan sat up in time to see Grace Sanderson leap from the witness box and jump on Elise who was lying on the floor in some pain. Grace took Elise by surprise. Grace punched Elise to the face and threw her against the Bar table.

Dan quickly looked around, though it hurt to move his head. No one seemed to be helping Elise. Everyone was working to restrain Samuel and no one else seemed to be able to help Elise.

He was still very groggy but Dan thought he could see blood coming from Elise's mouth.

He hurt all over, particularly his head which ached and was throbbing, but he was not going to let anything stop him from getting to Elise.

He jumped over the bar table, he didn't have the time to go around it. He landed on his shoulder and it hurt, probably dislocated he thought. Not to worry it was only pain and there were more important matters at hand.

He somehow got up and then threw himself on top of Grace Sanderson. She was a big woman and much stronger than Dan had anticipated. He effectively tackled Grace by pinning her arms and wrapping himself around her body. The force of his tackle rolled Grace away from where Elise lay motionless.

Grace managed to push free of Dan's grip and to his surprise, Grace ignored him and went straight over to where Elise was lying on the floor. Dan was horrified to see Grace begin to kick Elise in the head.

All pain was gone now, all reason was gone now, all self preservation was gone now. Dan knew in that moment what he had to do, there was no debate, it was now or never.

Dan launched himself at Elise. Dan's dive took him on top of Elise. He stretched out his body to protect her from Grace's kicks.

Everything was happening so quickly but Dan had thought help would have been on hand sooner. Perhaps in the panic no one had pressed the alarm button in the court, or perhaps the court security staff were all out to lunch. He didn't know and didn't care, all he knew was that he was being kicked and he wanted it to stop.

He felt several kicks to his head. Dan couldn't use his hands to protect his head very well because he was concentrating on protecting Elise's head.

He didn't know who or how Grace was subdued because he temporarily lost consciousness, but when he awoke he saw Sarah Little smiling down at him.

"Geez you sure know how to pick your girlfriends," Sarah said to Dan with a smile.

"Girlfriend," Dan said and then wheezed in pain. "She is no girlfriend of mine."

"Come on slugger just lie there don't move. That girl has beaten you up pretty bad. An ambulance is on the way."

"How's Elise?"

"She is unconscious but still breathing."

"Tell the paramedics to take her first, they can come back for me."

"Yeah, they are here now."

Dan was feeling pain like he had never felt before. It was all over his body, particularly his ribs, his left shoulder and his head. It hurt to breathe, it was unbearable to talk and unthinkable to laugh.

"I am impressed. I suppose you learnt that lead with your head trick from the Sharks. You know it's not a recommended technique for fighting, don't you?"

Dan winced in unfathomable pain as he fought to hold back a chuckle.

"For the first time, I have really got you where I want you, Dan Grover. I have complete power over you," Sarah said smiling.

Sarah turned around and shouted, "Over here, this guy needs medical attention now!"

Dan winced in pain.

"Don't worry about those two lovebirds, get over here," Sarah demanded.

"Elise," Dan struggled to say the word.

"Don't worry, Dan, two paramedic teams have arrived. The first team is attending to Elise and now this team is seeing you. Can you believe they wanted to treat the Sandersons first?"

Dan saw Sarah talking with the paramedics. He then remembered one of the paramedics bending over him but that was his last memory of that fateful day.

CHAPTER FIFTY

Dan woke up in a hospital bed the next day.

The first thing he saw was Gloria's smiling face.

"You've been out of it for a long time. How you are you feeling?"

Dan had all sorts of IV drips, tubes and bandages inserted in and over his body, but to tell the truth, he didn't feel that bad until he attempted to move.

"Owwww," Dan said sharply.

"Hey, take it easy, Danny; just rest. There is no need to move."

"How is Elise?"

"You had better ask the doctors."

"Gloria, if you know anything please tell me."

Gloria lightly touched Dan's arm. "The word is that she is touch and go. She is in the intensive care unit. Apparently she suffered bleeding on the brain and is in an induced coma. All the medical information at this point is that it's too early to tell whether she will make a full recovery."

Gloria and Dan didn't talk for a couple of minutes as he took in the distressing news.

"Don't you want to hear what's wrong with you?"

"Only if it's good news."

"You have two cracked ribs, a dislocated shoulder, a fractured jaw, a bad concussion and an egg on the side of your head the size of a tennis ball.

"The prognosis is good for you. Apparently every part of your body that is injured will heal itself. You just need to rest and not to do too much too early."

Yeah right, Dan thought. His plan had been thrown off course, so he had to right the ship quickly. There was no time for rest now. Hopefully that would come later.

"I have collected all the information you asked me to get yesterday morning. It's all here in the file."

"Thanks, Gloria, I appreciate your help."

"I had better be getting back to my kids. They have been left alone for about three hours, so by my reckoning they will be at each other's throats by now. Look after yourself Danny and don't try and do too much. I can look after the office for you."

Dan nodded slowly. It hurt even to speak.

"I really hope and pray Elise pulls through. I really want you two to get back together."

"I know you do, Gloria. I know you do."

"If there is anything else I can do for you, let me know."

At that Gloria turned to leave.

"Gloria, there is one more thing you can do for me."

"What's that?"

"Show me your hands?"

"Why do you want to see my hands?"

"Just humour me."

Bewildered as to what was going on, Gloria stretched out her hands and showed them to Dan as though she was a hand model.

"Thanks for that Gloria," Dan said.

Gloria, still bemused by Dan's weird request, turned on her heels and muttered about the stupid things lawyers make people do.

"Tell me about it," Senior Detective Sloan said as he shot Gloria a glance and entered Dan's room.

*

Later that evening Dan had another visitor.

"Well, slugger, what can I say, you've looked better."

"Thanks for coming to the hospital to see me," Dan responded.

"How could I refuse your charming text invitation? Hey do you still support the Sharks?"

"Of course, why do you ask?"

"I was just wondering if those kicks to your head had knocked some sense into you."

Dan winced in pain. It was much too painful to laugh.

Sarah seemed to enjoy his discomfort.

"Can you tell me what happened at the trial?"

"Let me tell you what I know. I will start from the beginning.

"Yesterday around lunch time Senior Detective Sloan and I were sitting in the back of the court when all hell broke loose. Don't you remember?"

"Can you break it down for me?"

"You were questioning Grace Sanderson when her husband jumped you from behind.

"Everybody was in shock. I mean, you don't see members of the public king hit lawyers every day in court.

"You took a couple of hits before your wife, of all people, came to your rescue first; she started eye gouging him. He fought her off and threw her over the bar table. Then the court bailiff, your wife's corrections officer and eventually Sloan and I restrained Sanderson. Actually, I think your barrister was in there too.

"He has a funny name, your barrister, hasn't he?"

"Yeah, Robin Banks. He is a bit funny, if you know what I mean," answered Dan.

Sarah smiled.

"Anyway, as Sanderson was being restrained, Grace Sanderson leapt out of the witness box and started hitting and kicking your wife. You jumped into the fray to protect her. Grace knocked you around a bit before Sloan and I could restrain her."

"How are the Sandersons?" Dan asked.

"From what I could tell they didn't need much, if any, medical attention. Although, I think Mrs Sanderson has a sprained ankle. You must have one hard head, though I suppose I knew that already."

Dan struggled to suppress a painful chuckle.

"I must say, you are an effective, if somewhat unorthodox, litigator. You really turned the tables on the Sandersons. They have not admitted anything yet, other than of course stalking and writing threatening notes to Mia Wong and the other women. It is only a matter of time though, before they confess to killing Mia Wong and that other woman you mentioned at the trial. I think Amanda Peterson is her name."

Dan sat up in his hospital bed and looked directly at Sarah.

"The Sandersons didn't kill Mia or Amanda Peterson."

"What are you talking about?" Sarah asked.

Dan turned away from her and bit down on his lip. He took a few deep breaths preparing himself and then turned back to face Sarah.

"Sarah, why did you hide the threatening note Mia received from the

Sandersons?"

"I don't know what you are talking about. Those kicks to your head must have really affected you."

"Sarah, the consequences of lying are always worse than the consequences of telling the truth."

"I don't know what drugs they have put you on, but you are not making any sense right now. In fact, you are starting to really worry me."

Dan delicately pulled out a piece of paper from a file that had been resting on his bedside table.

"Sarah, this is the threatening note Mia Wong received from the Sandersons. This note was found in your apartment."

"What do you mean, found in my apartment? You have never been to my apartment."

"While you were at the trial yesterday, I had a couple of bikie friends of mine break into your apartment looking for this note and they found it."

Sarah squinted her eyes. Her pained and perplexed expression at Dan's line of questioning was now quite evident.

"You wouldn't even know any bikies, let alone be friends with any."

"As a matter of fact I do know some bikies from the *Vandals*, though their description as friends is a little strong. But they helped me out once before when I needed a hand to correct an injustice and they were only too happy to help me out again."

"I don't believe you. Let me have a look at that note," Sarah demanded.

Sarah grabbed the note from Dan's hand.

"How do you know this is the actual note that the Sandersons sent Mia Wong?"

"Mia showed the note to me at the beginning of all this. Hence I can verify it as the real note. So my question to you is, what was this note doing in your apartment?"

Sarah did not respond immediately to the question but spent some seconds reviewing the note in detail, before crumpling it up and throwing it onto Dan's bed.

"You are crazy. First of all, I don't believe you can tell four months after seeing the note that this is the same note. Secondly, I don't know where you got that note from but you certainly didn't get it from my apartment. Thirdly, if you did organise for someone to break into my apartment yesterday, why did I see no evidence of that when I went home last night? Fourthly, you could be looking at jail time for this break and enter offence and your earlier offence of hindering police in the course of an investigation.”

Dan decided to change tack. “Sarah, you told me that you divorced your husband because he cheated on you, yet you still wear a wedding ring. Why?”

“That’s none of your business!”

“I would have thought that if you divorce someone, particularly if they have been unfaithful to you, you would not continue to wear their wedding ring. I know my secretary’s husband cheated on her and she no longer wears her wedding ring.”

“Dan, listen to yourself. I am your friend. I have always been your friend. I have always been devoted to you. Why are you attacking me like this?”

“Sarah, I did some checking on your background. I could not find any record of a Hamilton Clyde-Little in Sydney, let alone any record of an art dealer by that name.

“I did though find information concerning a Clyde Hamilton who was a psychiatrist in one of Sydney’s leading mental institutions. He was cited to appear in a professional disciplinary hearing in Sydney for carrying on sexual relationships with several of his patients. Apparently he died in a suspicious house fire before the disciplinary hearing could take place.

“You were one of his patients, weren’t you, Sarah?”

Before Sarah could answer Dan pulled a bundle of official looking papers from his file and offered them to Sarah.

Sarah ignored the papers offered to her.

“You obviously have the file there. I don’t know how you could get that information. It’s supposed to be confidential.”

Dan put the papers down on top of the file.

“He was a letch. He preyed on unsuspecting and defenseless women. He was supposed to be helping me, but all he did was help himself to me and other women.”

“But if you were never married, why wear a wedding ring?”

“For an intelligent bloke you are so stupid. It’s for you! It’s always been you, ever since we first went out together. Then Tarnook Crescent just burned you into my brain. It’s the only time anybody has ever done anything like that for me.”

Sarah moved a step closer to Dan and spoke softly to him.

“I love you. Don’t you love me? You must love me, after what you did for me at Tarnook Crescent.”

Dan did not respond.

"Dan, we could still go away together. It's not too late."

He decided it was time to change tack again.

"Sarah, you have been following me around for awhile now, haven't you?"

Sarah did not answer the question but jerked her face away from Dan towards the window in his room.

"You were in the white Commodore watching my house weren't you? The reason I felt like I was being watched wasn't because of the bikies, it was you, wasn't it?"

Sarah continued to ignore him.

"How did you know I like lemon coconut slices? I have never eaten them in front of you or told you I like them; yet you ordered one for me when we met in the coffee shop.

"How did you know I drive around looking for street parking, rather than paying to park at a private parking station? I have never told you that."

Sarah stopped looking out the window and turned her gaze towards Dan.

"You are never going to leave your wife for me are you? I mean, if you weren't going to leave her when it appeared to the whole world she was a murderer and would spend the rest of her life in jail, why would you leave her now?"

"I called Joseph Wong. He told me that he did not tell Sloan I had visited him. How did you know I went to Sydney to see Joseph Wong?"

"I don't want to answer any more of your stupid questions. You have no proof that I have done anything wrong. For goodness sake, the Sandersons have just beaten you up. Why are you accusing me of being the bad guy?"

"Because you were hiding the threatening note Mia received from the Sandersons. You did that to avoid suspicion for Mia's murder being placed anywhere other than on Elise."

"I did not hide the note. That is a lie. Your bikie friends, or acquaintances, or whatever the hell they are, are having a lend of you. They did not find that note in my apartment."

"How else could I have come into possession of the note, if not from your apartment?"

"Look it's not even the note."

"It is the note, I recognise it."

"It isn't the note."

"It is the note. I have seen it before."

"It can't be the note."

"Why can't it be the note?"

"Because I destroyed it."

Dan took a deep breath. He was not enjoying his interrogation of Sarah but it had to be done.

"Sarah, why did you destroy the note?"

Sarah offered no reply.

"Sarah, you killed Mia, didn't you?"

Again Sarah did not reply. It was as though she was weighing up what to do now that she had made the admission she had destroyed the note.

"Sarah, we are alone here. You can talk to me."

"Alright, I will tell you what happened if you promise me that you will come away with me?"

"What are you saying?"

"You always are saying that you don't lie. You tell the truth regardless of the consequences. Well tell me the truth now! If I tell you what really happened, will you come away with me?"

"Sarah, I can't answer a question like that."

"Tell me now and I want one of those yes or no answers you lawyers are so keen about in court. Will you or will you not run away with me, if I tell you what really happened?"

He was unsure what to do. He had made a commitment to always tell the truth regardless of the consequences. Yet here and now he had to hear from Sarah what happened with Mia. He owed that to Mia, her father and of course Elise.

He had no proof that Sarah had done anything wrong. There had been no break in at Sarah's apartment. The note that he had shown her was a fake. He had put it together to resemble the one Mia had shown him. The medical file he had offered to Sarah was one made up by Gloria from a similar file they held for another client of his.

He had just lied to Sarah about the burglary, the medical file and the note to induce her to confess her crime. So there appeared to be a legitimate exception to the always telling the truth rule and that was *to catch a thief*?

"Sarah, honestly, I would like to lie to you but I can't. There is nothing you can say or do that would ever convince me to go away with you."

In the end he figured you must live and die by your principles. To lie on this occasion would be to fly in the face of everything he had learnt since this whole sorry episode started.

Dan looked for Sarah's response. Her face had turned from the friendly version he had known to one of superiority and arrogance he had not seen before.

"Well, I have good news and bad news for you, Dan Grover. The good news is that you passed the test. You didn't lie to me.

"I knew you would never go away with me. I was just testing you to see if you would compromise your principles and lie. Because you passed the test, I will tell you what happened. I want to tell you."

Dan moved forward in his bed anxious not to miss a word of what Sarah was about to tell him.

"I went to Sydney to get over you. I got sick. Somehow I ended up in a psychiatric institution with crazy people. This psychiatrist said that if I slept with him, he would get me out of there. I did, he didn't. He was just using me and others. I eventually escaped but I couldn't let him get away with what he did to me. He deserved to die.

"I changed my name and my appearance and came back to Queensland. I got a job with the police. I found I was quite good at police work and eventually I was made a detective. After awhile I started watching you. Waiting for the opportunity to save you as you had saved me. All the time believing that you loved me, you bastard!

"It was me you saw in the white Commodore. I had been careless that day. I followed you around after that in another car. I was much more careful.

"Then one night I followed you to Spring Hill and I saw you kissing this woman. I wondered what that was all about. I knew you were married.

"As I was watching this woman's house the next day, wondering what was going on between you and her, your wife shows up and starts arguing with her on the verandah.

"I thought about it for awhile. Then it all became clear. I could save you from your wife and your mistress and all the mess that comes with them knowing one another. Also that would leave you free to be with me. It was a perfect plan."

Dan's throat felt like sand paper as he tried to swallow. He decided not to reach for a glass of water, lest he somehow interrupt and prevent Sarah from completing her story.

"Mia let me into her home after I showed her my police ID. Before I could even say anything she showed me the threatening note. She thought I had come to see her about that. The note did concern me as my plan was to kill Mia and have your wife blamed. I didn't want any other suspects.

"I killed Mia and made it look like a crime of passion. I turned her face down. I didn't want to look at that slut's face while I was tidying up the crime scene."

Dan was amazed at how calm Sarah was in telling her story.

"Then all of a sudden your wife comes to the door. I couldn't believe it. Her timing was perfect for me. I hid in a bedroom. I saw her roll the body over and move the glass vase out of the way.

"After she called triple zero, I didn't have time to check if her fingerprints and not mine were on the glass vase, so I had to take the vase with me. I hid the vase down the back of my shirt and got out of there quickly before the police arrived. It was me that Tom Johnstone saw."

Sarah took a deep breath. It appeared that she was enjoying, even relishing, that she could relive this moment of her life.

"Afterwards I took the glass vase to our laboratory and worked on it myself. I had to ensure that your wife's fingerprints and DNA were found on it, not mine.

"It was easy for me, as a detective, to return the glass vase to the crime scene, though I had to be careful to hide it in a place that may have been missed by the original investigators. I knew that the crime scene cleaners would find it eventually."

Dan was speechless. He still couldn't believe the Sarah he knew was this psychopath.

"Dan, don't you want to hear the bad news?"

"Not particularly. But I am sure you are going to tell me."

"The good news is that you got to hear my story, of what really happened that day. The bad news is that I can't let you live. I know now we can't be together. I was so stupid. I don't even know now why I loved you so much, for so long. So now it is you or me. And I choose me."

Dan was in no shape for a fight. He could not protect himself.

"Sarah, there is no need for that. Turn yourself in and I will speak up for you."

"Turn myself in. I am a cop. I know it would be pointless admitting my crimes and then spending the rest of my life in jail. No, it has to be you or me and as I said before, I choose me."

"You won't get away with it. We are in a public hospital."

"Did you really think you could outsmart me, Dan? That I would just happily admit my crimes and turn myself in?"

"What are you going to do just shoot me?"

"That's exactly what I am going to do. I came to see you. You were unhinged because of the knock on your head. You took my gun out of my holster and when I went to grab it off you, it unloaded straight into your skull."

"They will never believe that."

"Maybe so. But in the end, the only version they will hear will be mine; a serving police officer. You won't be around to tell them anything different."

"Sarah, don't do it. Please, don't do it."

"I am sorry, Dan, I really am."

"Sarah, remember Tarnook Crescent," Dan pleaded.

Sarah slowly pulled out her service revolver and pointed it at Dan.

"Sarah, there is one last thing you can do for me."

"What is it?"

"I want you to smile when you kill me."

"What are you talking about?"

"I want you to look at my TV and smile, because that's where the hidden camera and microphone are. If you are going to kill me, at least get the video showing a smile on your dial."

Bang!

A single gunshot was fired by Sarah. It found its mark. The TV was no more.

As soon as the gunshot was fired, several detectives including Senior Detective Sloan rushed into Dan's room from his bathroom and overpowered Sarah without any difficulty. She was so shocked at seeing them she dropped her weapon and surrendered without a whimper.

"Nice work, Grover," Sloan said as he handcuffed Sarah.

"Pity the recording device in the TV has been destroyed. In the bathroom we couldn't hear everything that was said."

"Not to worry Detective Sloan, I have a back up digital recording device right here in my file. You always have to have a back up," Dan said as he opened the file and handed Sloan the tiny digital recorder.

"That's *Senior* Detective. Oh why bother?" Sloan said as he led Sarah out of Dan's hospital room.

Just then Robin appeared from the bathroom and rushed straight over to Dan.

"What do you mean I am a bit funny?" Robin asked.

Dan laughed and winced in pain. He was so hyped up about what had just happened he couldn't help but release his emotions with repressed laughter, despite the fact that it was still extremely painful for him to laugh.

*

"So tell me, how did you get onto Sarah Little? I don't get it," Robin asked.

"It all comes back to what God told me."

Robin shook his head.

"I mean my divine inspiration."

Robin appeared to respond better to Dan receiving divine inspiration, than God actually speaking to him.

"Tom Johnston remembered seeing the wedding ring of the woman who left Mia's house at the time of the murder. It wasn't Elise because she does not wear caps or hats. So it must have been another woman.

"Then it came to me. I had seen Sarah with a wedding ring. I do not normally pay much attention to what women are wearing on their hands but the other night I got this vision of her hand. I mean a picture of her hand came into my head. On her hand she was wearing several rings, including a wedding ring."

"Go on," suggested Robin, who was eager to hear all the details.

"I thought, why is she wearing a wedding ring?

"Sarah had told me she divorced her husband after he had cheated on her. In fact, he was living with another woman she said.

"So I did some research into her background on the net, made a few calls in the morning before court started and discovered that she had been in a mental institution and had slept with her psychiatrist."

"You discovered Sarah had some psychiatric concerns, but how did you know Sarah was the murderer and not the Sandersons?" Robin asked.

"God confirmed that fact for me."

Robin stared blankly at Dan.

"Rose Peterson called me not an hour after I received my divine inspiration about Sarah.

"Rose told me that Amanda had just made contact with her."

"What do you mean made contact with her? I thought she was dead. Rose Peterson is not into this voodoo too, is she?"

"No, no, no, no. Don't get my divine inspiration messed up with voodoo. Amanda is alive. Apparently she had a nervous breakdown after the Samuel Sanderson incident and she went to live in a hippie commune in northern New South Wales. After 12 months or so, she got her act together and, with the help of a fake ID, she went to live and work on the Gold Coast.

"As time passed she became too embarrassed to notify her mother and friends that she was actually still alive. She just couldn't face her mother and explain why she hadn't contacted her after all these years.

"Anyway, Amanda saw the news of the trial, that she was missing and presumed dead. This finally convinced her that she needed to let her mother know where she was. Hence her call to her mother who gratefully and happily told me that her daughter was still alive. She was lost but now she's found."

"But what was the examination of Grace Sanderson all about?" Robin asked.

"I had a very strong feeling Sarah was the murderer but how was I going to prove it. The only way to do that was through Mia's threatening note. Mia would not have destroyed the note. It was evidence she would have needed. So Sarah must have the note or have destroyed it.

"However I needed to establish that the note actually existed. I had seen the note but for various reasons my testimony lacked credibility.

"I suspected the Sanderson's had sent the note. Kathleen Brown had received a similar note, so it had to be the Sandersons.

"So my purpose in cross-examining Grace Sanderson was to confirm she and or Samuel had sent Mia the threatening note. I created a similar threatening note as the original sent to Mia and I had planned to confront Sarah with it after my cross-examination.

"Unfortunately, the Sandersons went berserk and put Elise and I in hospital."

"You took a real risk confronting Sarah. I mean she is crazy and she had a gun."

"Sloan and his men were in the bathroom."

"How did you get Sloan on board?" Robin asked.

"That was easier than I had expected. He had been having nightmares about the glass vase not being found by his team when they first searched the crime scene. He could not believe something like that could happen. I gave him an explanation as to how that might have happened and some information about Sarah's psychiatric background. That combined with everything else that happened at court yesterday was enough to bring him around and let me be used as bait. What did he have to lose?"

"Still you took a big risk. She could have easily just shot you."

"All's well that ends well," Dan said.

"It didn't end well for your TV. Who is going to pay for that?" Robin asked.

"I don't really care to tell you the truth. I don't intend on watching too much TV while I am in here anyway."

"You're not watching sport on TV? I will believe that when I see it."

"Actually, I am planning to take my IV and go over and spend tonight, and for as long as they will let me, sitting in Elise's room."

"How is she?" Robin asked.

"They tell me she is still touch and go."

Both men fell silent for a short time.

"Well I have been touched and I certainly have to go. It's been a rollercoaster of a ride working with you on this case. Any idea when I might get paid?"

"We are all banged up at the moment. But I am sure it won't be too long."

"No divine inspiration as to exactly when?"

"Not at this stage, but I will be sure to let you know if God talks to me about it."

At that comment both men smiled.

"Thanks, Robin, I mean it. Thanks for everything, especially coming through for me at the end."

"Don't mention it. All the best for you and Elise," Robin said as he turned to leave.

As Robin was walking through the doorway, he stopped and turned back towards Dan and said, "I am thinking about praying for Elise; you never know, I might just do that."

CHAPTER FIFTY ONE

As Dan stood up to deliver the Eulogy he was surprised by the number of people there. Everybody has friends but when it came to a funeral, Dan was always pleasantly surprised by the number of people who usually attended, and this funeral service was no different. People he had never seen before, let alone heard of, seemed to be hanging from the rooftops.

He was not an overly emotional kind of guy but perhaps this death of someone close to him, perhaps his injuries, perhaps his new found faith in God had affected him. Whatever the reason, he found he was much more of an emotional person these days.

As he stood at the lectern, his heart was racing but his mind was stuck in quicksand. He fought hard to keep it all together.

"Friends and family, what can I say, where can I go, what can I do, to convey to you how important this person was in my life.

"Love is a word that is bandied about nearly as much as that other four letter word beginning with *f*, that is the opposite of love, the antithesis of love.

"Love is a word that should not be used lightly, it should not be used as a figure of speech, it should not be used as a turn of phrase. It should only be used if you really, really mean it. That you feel love emanating from every fibre of your body, that it must get out of you or you will burst because it is real and alive.

"My love was real, it is still alive."

Dan struggled to control his emotions. It had been three months since his hospitalization and he had fully recovered, but he felt a sudden stabbing pain in his throat as he fought to hold back his tears.

"My brother, Claye, was only 40 years old when he died from complications following a stem cell transplant to treat leukemia. Claye's death has wrought a terrible sorrow in me as I loved him dearly. I will miss him dearly.

"But today we don't mourn him. We celebrate his life. He was, as we all know, a man of God. He found God and, by his faith, led me to God.

"You may say why did God allow his life to be taken by this disease? I say God allowed him to have 40 great years on earth and now it's time for Claye to have an even greater life in heaven."

"Claye never gave up his faith in God, no matter what. So in remembrance of him, I ask you to never give up on your faith no matter what. *For with faith anything is possible*!"

Dan looked over at Elise as he said these words. Elise was smiling and nodded approvingly at him. Elise clutched the bracelet that she never took off and mouthed the words, "With faith anything is possible."

Dan continued, "Mate, I will miss you, all of us here will miss you. But you will not be forgotten, mate, that's just not going to happen."

He struggled again to contain his emotions as he returned to his seat next to Elise. She put her arm around him tenderly and comforted him. Dan couldn't believe it but he was crying, a little at first and then uncontrollably he sobbed as a river of emotion gushed out of him. Elise hugged him and cried with him.

Perhaps real men cry after all.

CHAPTER FIFTY TWO

It was a cool, overcast morning with a westerly wind beginning to howl down the street, as Dan stood outside his office. It had been eight months since the trial and five months since Claye's death.

Dan reflected at how his legal practice had really taken off in that time. He and Gloria were so busy he was even thinking about taking on a law clerk to help them. Apparently he now had a reputation as an *honest lawyer*, and that was really attracting the clients.

The police had not proceeded with the hindering an investigation charge and the Legal Services Commission had considered a warning a sufficient penalty for his unprofessional conduct.

Dan should have been concentrating on the case he was conducting in court today but all he could think about, all his mind would let him think about, was the altercation he had had with Elise last night. His mind was forcing him to rehash that altercation, no matter how hard he tried to concentrate on his work.

He had taken Elise out to dinner and they had had a pleasant evening celebrating their wedding anniversary. On returning home, Elise had asked Dan to turn the light on as she walked up the stairs from the hallway to the living room. He did not turn the light on and fiery Elise came marching down the stairs to complain.

Dan then turned the light on but as Elise got half way up the stairs, he turned the light out again. Elise yelled something to him about being a man and not able to understand even the simplest instruction.

He recounted with delight at the thought of Elise arriving in darkness at the top of the stairs and then being hit with a sudden and loud burst of light and noise.

Happy Anniversary was the resounding call from the forty or so family and friends who had hidden in the darkness of their living room waiting for him and Elise to come home.

Dan walked up to Elise and she was beaming. Shocked but beaming.

"I thought we had celebrated the anniversary by going out to dinner."

"That was not enough. I want the whole world to celebrate my anniversary with you. It's the most important night of the year for me."

At that Elise moved in, and although she usually shied away from showing affection in public, she planted a sweet kiss on Dan that he could still remember; it brought an almighty cheer from the assembled gathering.

"Hey, I thought State of Origin night was the most important night of the year for you," quipped Robbo.

"That was the old days, Robbo, them were the old days. Now I want to spend as much time as I can with my beautiful wife, and of course my new digital TV recorder," Dan said winking his left eye.

Elise punched Dan affectionately and said, "You, you are incorrigible."

Dan fondly remembered how he and Elise had walked happily together arm-in-arm as they mingled with their friends and family for hours.

THE END